"You don't have to be alone."

"I don't need help." She panicked as she imagined him being at the house with her every day, watching her.

As he walked away, he said over his shoulder, "I hope one day you stop seeing me as the enemy and let me be your friend."

"I can't," she said, tears burning her eyes. He was a minister. "I can't be your friend, Rory."

"Or you can't let *me* be your friend?" Before she could answer, he turned back. "I came here today because I saw someone in need. Not as a minister but as a person."

And then he was gone.

Vanessa wanted to run after him. But she had to be strong and fight the temptation. She'd taken care of herself for a long time now. Why should she believe a sweet-talking preacher who made her feel safe?

Her confusing thoughts about Rory had to stop. Because growing close to him would be a bad idea.

So why did she want to believe him?

With sixty books published and millions in print, **Lenora Worth** writes award-winning romance and romantic suspense. Three of her books finaled in the ACFW Carol Awards, and her Love Inspired Suspense novel *Body of Evidence* became a *New York Times* bestseller. Her novella in *Mistletoe Kisses* made her a *USA TODAY* bestselling author. Lenora goes on adventures with her retired husband, Don, and enjoys reading, baking and shopping… especially shoe shopping.

Visit the Author Profile page at Harlequin.com for more titles.

Lakeside Sweetheart

Lenora Worth

Recycling programs
for this product may
not exist in your area.

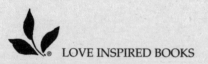 LOVE INSPIRED BOOKS

ISBN-13: 978-0-373-81914-0

Lakeside Sweetheart

Copyright © 2016 by Lenora H. Nazworth

All rights reserved. Except for use in any review, the reproduction or utilization of this work in whole or in part in any form by any electronic, mechanical or other means, now known or hereinafter invented, including xerography, photocopying and recording, or in any information storage or retrieval system, is forbidden without the written permission of the editorial office, Love Inspired Books, 195 Broadway, New York, NY 10007 U.S.A.

This is a work of fiction. Names, characters, places and incidents are either the product of the author's imagination or are used fictitiously, and any resemblance to actual persons, living or dead, business establishments, events or locales is entirely coincidental.

This edition published by arrangement with Love Inspired Books.

® and TM are trademarks of Love Inspired Books, used under license. Trademarks indicated with ® are registered in the United States Patent and Trademark Office, the Canadian Intellectual Property Office and in other countries.

www.Harlequin.com

Printed in U.S.A.

Jesus said to her, Everyone who drinks of this water will be thirsty again, but those who drink of the water that I will give them will never be thirsty. The water that I will give will become in them a spring of water gushing up to eternal life.
—*John* 4:13–14

To my cousin Nancy Anderson.
So glad you are back in our lives!

Chapter One

He always noticed new faces at church.

As minister of the Millbrook Lake Church, Rory Sanderson had a bird's-eye view of the entire congregation, including everyone from Mrs. Fanny Fitzpatrick in her fake-fruit covered straw hat to Alec Caldwell's aunt Hattie in her pearls and baby-blue pillbox.

But one person stood out today more than all the others.

Maybe because her discomfort could have shattered the rows of stained glass windows lining each side of the tiny chapel. The doubtful expression made her look a little lost, but her light brown hair shimmered with a luster that reminded him of sea oats at sunrise. He couldn't tell much about her eyes. She wore dark shades.

But he felt pretty sure those hidden eyes were staring straight at him. She must be one of those.

Someone had obviously invited her to the service today. And she so did not want to be here.

Rory took that as a challenge. He accepted the woman's distrust with a smile and a prayer. That was his job, after all. To turn that frown upside down. To bring the lost home. To make the backsliders and unbelievers faithful. Especially on such a beautiful spring day. A day full of rebirth and renewal. The best kind of day.

Easter Sunday.

The whole flock, maybe the whole town, had turned out in their Easter finery. And they all had smiles on their faces.

Except for that one, of course. The one in the pretty yellow dress that reminded him of picnics and wildflowers, wearing those dark Wayfarers and that shell-shocked expression. And Rory had to wonder. What had made this woman so reluctant to be here today?

"You could try smiling," Marla Caldwell said into Vanessa Donovan's ear. "It won't break your face."

"I told you I don't do church," Vanessa replied, uneasiness making her fidget. Tugging her turquoise floral wrap over her bare arms, she glanced around. "I only came because you invited me. And because I want some of that good food your mother and Aunt Hattie bribed us with—I mean—promised to us—for Sunday dinner."

"They are not above bribery," Marla said with a grin, her red-gold ponytail bouncing. "But church will do you good, you'll see. It sure can't hurt you."

Marla could afford to tease. She was still a newlywed. Happy and settled and very much in love with a former marine who lived in a big Victorian house not far from Vanessa's smaller Craftsman-style cottage. After a Christmas wedding, Marla and her cute preschooler, Gabby, now lived in that rambling house with handsome Alec Caldwell and his adorable aunt Hattie and two dogs. One big, happy family.

Something Vanessa would never have. But she didn't care about all of that anyway, she reminded herself.

Glad for her friend, Vanessa remembered she didn't believe in that sort of thing. She was a realist who'd decided long ago that marriage and family weren't for her. Marla teased her about being too pessimistic and cynical, but Vanessa was practical and resolved. Resolved to a life that didn't include a long-term relationship or attending church or bouncing a baby on her lap.

"I'm not quite ready to dive right in," Vanessa said, her eyes on the cute guy up front greeting everyone as if he owned the place. "What's the story with Surfer Dude?"

Marla giggled. "You mean Preacher? His name is Rory Sanderson. He does look like a surfer with that dark-blond hair, and he's pretty good at surfing and a lot of other things, now that I think about it. But his real passion is right here inside this church. He's our minister and he's good at his job. Amazing, considering he's all alone. No wife or children. Every matron in this congregation has tried to fix him up, but I think he's holding out for someone special."

Vanessa shook her head, shocked that someone so young and, well, hip, could be a preacher. "Right. Or he's so caught up in himself that he doesn't really see the audience."

"Not an audience. A congregation," Marla replied. "And you're wrong about Rory. He doesn't have an ego." She waved to a couple who sat down behind them and then pointed them out to Vanessa. "That's Alec's best friend, Blain Kent—he's also a former marine and is now a detective with the Millbrook Police—and his fiancée, Rikki Alvanetti. She's an interior designer. They're getting married in a few weeks."

Vanessa nodded and smiled at the couple. They'd make pretty babies since they both had dark hair and expressive eyes—hers almost black and his deep blue—and looked exotic and buff. And happy.

Everyone in this place seemed happy.

Chiding herself for being in such a snarky mood, she turned back to the front again. That minister seemed to be watching her. This hour couldn't get over with fast enough.

Then because she did feel guilty even thinking that, Vanessa lifted her eyes to one of the beautiful stained glass windows and asked God to give her a better perspective.

When she lowered her gaze, the cute preacher with the boyish grin and the dark-blond wind-tossed hair looked right at her and smiled. And then he did something even more daring. He came down from the front of the church and headed straight to the pew where Vanessa sat.

"Is he going to—"

"Yes, he is," Marla said with a grin. When he stopped near them, she said, "Preacher Rory, this is my friend Vanessa Donovan. She moved back to town a couple of weeks ago."

"Not moved back," Vanessa corrected. "I came back to take care of some things."

The preacher took Vanessa's hand, shaking it lightly before he stood back and smiled, his baby blue eyes centered on Vanessa as if she were the only person in this place. "It's nice to meet you, Vanessa. Welcome to Millbrook Lake Church."

"Uh…thanks," Vanessa said, a white heat of embarrassment moving up her spine. "It's nice to meet you, too."

He spoke to a few more people and then turned back to Vanessa. "Happy Easter."

She watched as he headed toward the back and greeted almost everyone else who entered the open double doors. "He's so friendly," she whispered to Marla. "I'm not sure how to take that."

Marla glanced back and then turned to Vanessa. "You know, you need to let go of that cynical attitude. Preacher is solid. He's a good man. He was a chaplain in the army."

"What?" Vanessa looked over her shoulder. "That sunny, happy, goofy man served in the military?"

"He sure did," Marla replied. "And…he wasn't always so sunny and happy and goofy."

Faith is the substance of things hoped for…

Vanessa thought about that verse of scripture on the short ride back to Alec and Marla's house. Why did that particular verse seem to move through her like the blue waters of the big oval lake centered in the middle of town?

Maybe it wasn't the verse so much as the preacher who'd read it. Rory Sanderson didn't preach. He talked. In a quiet, friendly tone that made you think he really was talking to you and only you. Which irritated Vanessa. She didn't want to like the man, but some of what he'd said made sense.

She had listened, too. He'd pointed out how Jesus liked to hang out with the misfits and the outsiders. How a lot of those kinds of people were there during His Crucifixion.

But she had to wonder if the misfits and losers had been allowed in the church today. Everyone at the service had seemed so fresh faced and full of joy. Were they all that happy, or had they been hiding their pain behind a pretty façade?

Vanessa didn't know and it really didn't matter. She probably wouldn't go back to Millbrook Lake Church. She hadn't been to church in a long, long time. And she didn't plan on staying in Millbrook for too long either.

Clean out the house. Sell the house. Pocket the cash. Get on with her life. Whatever that life might be. Right now, she had a solid team looking out for her interests, and she had a boutique and online business waiting for her back in New Orleans. So she took a deep breath and decided she'd try to be grateful for being invited to share a nice meal with Marla's family. She could deal with other people's families, but she did not need one of her own.

Pulling her small car up to the side drive next to Caldwell House, Vanessa got out and took in the scents of jasmine and wisteria, thankful that she didn't have to spend this gorgeous day alone.

But when she looked up and saw a man strolling up the sidewalk, she silently groaned.

The preacher headed toward her. And she had the sinking feeling he would be at Sunday dinner, too.

Rory waved to the woman who emerged from the cute little blue vintage roadster. Vanessa Donovan, still wearing those shades. She'd taken them off during the service, but he had yet to see her eyes up close. He'd been too busy preaching it to a full house. Now he might be able to have some one-on-one time with the interesting woman who stood staring at him as if she wanted to get back in the car and haul herself far away from here.

"How are you?" he asked, determined to make her take off those ridiculously big shades. He was pretty sure they were missing from the 1960s, too. And maybe even the dress.

But she made all of these old-fashioned things fresh and new.

"I'm good." She held a straw purse embellished with a big white daisy that Mrs. Fitzpatrick would surely love and met him at the intricate gate to the back garden. "I...I enjoyed your sermon."

Polite but cool. "Thank you. I'm glad you made it to the service today. How do you know Marla?"

She looked relieved to move away from the topic of church. "We were friends in high school briefly and then we ran into each other in Tallahassee before I moved to New Orleans. I'm so glad she's found someone. She deserves to be happy." Then she winced. "Oh, wow. That sounded so cliché."

Rory laughed and walked with her up the steps onto the back porch. Aunt Hattie and Marla had the porch decorated with white lace tablecloths and all kinds of fresh flowers. "But it's true. Marla and Alec are meant for each other. They had their wedding reception right here in the garden, in December."

"So I heard. Sounds beautiful."

"And romantic," he said with a grin. "One of the many perks of my job. I presided over their vows. Chilly weather but warm atmosphere."

She finally took off her shades and gave him a doubting stare with big hazel eyes that went from brown to green in a beautiful flash. But before Rory could counter her skeptical expression with something positive, the back door opened and little Gabby came running out, followed by two dogs.

"Hello, Uncle Rory," Gabby said, squealing in delight as both animals ran circles around Rory and Vanessa. "Angus, stop. Roxie, quit being so silly."

Rory squatted down and smiled at Gabby, careful not to get too close. The four-year-old had the little poodle Roxie for a reason, and Roxie sometimes wore a service vest for a reason. The tiny dog was trained to keep Gabby calm whenever she felt threatened or afraid. Which happened less and less these days, thankfully. The little girl had gone through a lot of trauma after being involved in a robbery that took her daddy's life.

"Hello, Gabby," he said. "This is my new friend, Vanessa. Don't you love her pretty dress?"

Gabby grabbed Roxie and stood back to stare up at Vanessa with big brown eyes. Bobbing her head in agreement with Rory's question, she asked, "Are you eating dinner with us?"

"I am," Vanessa said, clearly uncomfortable with the whole Sunday-dinner thing. Or maybe the child made her uncomfortable. "Is that okay?"

Gabby showed a snaggletoothed grin. "Yes, ma'am. Are you hungry? We have ham and mashed potatoes and asp-per-gus. I don't like that, though."

"I don't either," Rory said, grinning. "But I love me some mashed potatoes."

"And I like ham and asparagus," Vanessa said. "I hear your mother made cupcakes and pies, too."

Gabby did a little back and forth sway, her print dress swishing. "Uh-huh. She made Easter cupcakes with bunnies and flowers and grass. I'm gonna eat two."

"And I'll eat three at least," Rory said, glad that Vanessa was warming up to the little girl. Gabby would sense it if Vanessa wasn't comfortable.

"Hello there." Aunt Hattie came strolling out, her arms wide open and her cheeky smile warm. "Welcome, welcome. I'm so glad you're both here and that you found each other out there."

"We did," Rory said, shooting Vanessa an encouraging glance. "Ran into each other by the gate."

"Did that hurt?" Gabby asked, her eyes wide again.

Aunt Hattie hooted with laughter. "Out of the mouths of babes."

"I don't know yet," Rory said, his gaze still

on Vanessa. "It wasn't too painful to me. How about you, Vanessa?"

She smiled and shook her head. "We're fine, Gabby."

Then she walked with Aunt Hattie into the house, leaving Rory to wonder if *he'd* ever be fine again.

Of all the people he'd seen in church this morning, why did this woman have to be the one who'd come to dinner at the Caldwells'? And why did she have to be the one who'd left him wondering and wanting to help her when he didn't even know what she needed?

Why not?

God always put people in certain places for a reason. Vanessa was here for a reason. Rory should know better than anyone that humans didn't make their own paths.

Sometimes God put a woman in a bright yellow dress right smack-dab in the middle of the road so she could be found.

And sometimes He stopped a hopeful preacher cold in his tracks just to keep him on his toes. For a brief moment guilt gnawed at his conscience, but Rory took in the scent of flowers all around him and nodded. No matter what happened, this spring was glorious.

Chapter Two

Vanessa strolled around the big rambling back-yard at Caldwell House, her mind on everything she had to get done during the next few weeks.

"Tea?"

Rory handed her a refill while they watched Gabby, with Roxie right on her heels, searching for Easter eggs in the many dish gardens and potted palms displayed all around the colorful yard.

"Thank you." Vanessa took the goblet of dark tea flavored with lemon. Not knowing what else to say, she smiled. "What a meal."

She'd enjoyed listening to the easy banter, the tiny bits of good-natured gossip and the news of the week. Millbrook Lake was growing now that the local economy had finally improved. She knew Alec had a lot to do with that since he'd returned home. She hadn't kept up much with Millbrook Lake. Mainly because she'd never planned to return here.

"I'll say." Rory rubbed his flat stomach. "I shouldn't have had pie and cupcakes, but the cooking around here is so good I always double up when I get invited for Sunday dinner."

She had to laugh. Watching him eat had been an event in itself. "Do you get invited to lunch and dinner a lot?"

"Sure. And breakfast, too. A perk of the job. People love to feed the preacher. Especially since this preacher lives alone."

She glanced over at him and saw a darkness moving through his eyes like a cloud over a clear sky. She wanted to ask him about that, but he looked straight ahead and watched Gabby with a quiet intensity that belied his cheerful nature.

"The meal was amazing," she said, suddenly unsure around him. Suddenly remembering that she had not wanted to be around him. And yet, here she stood. But she also thought about Marla's words to her earlier about him not always being so sunny, happy and goofy.

She could handle cheerful and friendly. Those were easy emotions. But imagining Rory Sanderson sad made her concerned and curious. Though wary around men of the cloth, she didn't want to think of this man as anything

other than what he seemed. His carefree nature
didn't appear at all threatening.

But then, she shouldn't be thinking of him
anyway. He was the preacher. A man of God.
Certainly not her type. Not that she was looking.
She'd sworn off any long-term relationships, and
she certainly wasn't ready for anything else.
She thought of the tiny church up the road and
willed herself to push away the memories of another church that had been located on the out-
skirts of town. Gone now. Torn down for new
commercial real estate.

"I don't normally eat so much," she continued
in the small-talk vein. "But Aunt Hattie is famous for her meals, and Marla is amazing with
sugar and flour and butter."

"A dynamic duo," he said, the smile bright
on his face again. "I need a long Sunday-after-
noon nap."

She could picture him kicked back in a re-
cliner, snoring softly. That did make her smile.

"I'd think you don't get to rest much," she
blurted to get rid of that warm, fuzzy feeling.
"I mean, being a minister."

"I get eight hours of sleep most nights, but
things happen. A death, a birth, a trip to the
ER, a hospital visit now and then." He gave her
a quick but concise glance. "Sometimes people
need to talk, even in the middle of the night."

Vanessa got that image in her head, too. Her reaching for the phone, calling him. Telling him her worst fears.

She tried again with the small talk. "And you have to be there for all of those things."

"Spoken like someone who might know."

"I don't know much," she said, her tone sharp in her own ears. She didn't like the direction this conversation seemed to be heading—toward her. "But it's obvious enough."

"I guess it is," he said, his words somber now. "My reputation precedes me."

He'd misunderstood. Most people did whenever she made disparaging remarks regarding church. But she never explained her reasons for staying away from organized religion.

She wanted to say it wasn't *his* reputation she based her assumption on, but those of other people. Only, she wasn't ready to get that personal with him. She didn't plan on being around this man after today anyway. She had plenty to keep her busy.

"You seem to be popular with your people," she said.

"*God's* people," he corrected with a smile. "I try to help them along."

They came to a big swing centered underneath an arbor covered with jasmine. The fragrant scent of the tiny yellow-and-white flowers and the droning hum of bees made Vanessa wish for something she couldn't even define.

"Want to sit and watch the egg hunt?" he asked.

She glanced at the swing and then back at him. "I don't know. I mean, I should be going. I have a lot to do tomorrow." Needing to explain, she added, "I'm here to clean out my mother's house. She died a few weeks ago."

His expression turned compassionate. "I'm sorry. Did she live here?"

"She used to. She moved to a retirement and nursing facility in Alabama. She hadn't lived here in years."

He nodded, his expressive face couched in a calm that made him change from boyish to good-looking. "I get a day off tomorrow. If you need any help."

"I don't think so. This is one of your busy weekends. You need to rest after your big day."

"Yes. But then, I consider every Sunday a big day."

Vanessa gave him a hesitant smile. "I think I'll go and tell the others I'm leaving. It was nice to meet you—"

"Rory," he said. "Call me Rory."

She nodded and headed back to where Marla and her parents were helping Gabby find the colorful eggs. The little girl giggled and showed off her treasures while Roxie squeaked out excited barks and ran circles around the adults.

Angus watched the whole show from a warm spot on the brick terrace near the porch. The older Border collie didn't have a care in the world.

Aunt Hattie met her near the house. "We're so glad you came today, Vanessa. I hope you'll visit again."

"Thank you for inviting me," Vanessa said. "The food was so good, Aunt Hattie."

"Nothing like a home-cooked meal to nourish us, even if it does require a few extra calories."

Vanessa hadn't had many home-cooked meals growing up. "I can't argue with that." She hugged Aunt Hattie, the scent of sweet almond surrounding her. "I have to go, but I wanted to thank you again. Let me tell Marla I'm leaving."

"Oh, she wrapped you a plate," Aunt Hattie said. "I'll go fetch it."

Vanessa didn't need a plate full of leftovers, but she wouldn't be impolite by turning it down. She wasn't used to this kind of attention, and she wasn't sure how to respond. Somewhere in the back of her mind, she wished she'd had this kind of family growing up. But in that other place, the dark spot that colored her world in grays and browns, she figured she didn't deserve this kind of family.

She wished someone had trained her in proper manners or on how to actually conduct small talk. She wished she'd been happy in any of the many places her mother had dragged her. She wished she'd had nice clothes and pretty things.

And she really wished she'd had someone to truly love her.

But she couldn't change any of that now. Vanessa had learned about all of these things mostly on her own by studying people and reading books and watching television and movies. She'd learned how to dress by working in retail and devouring fashion magazines and with the help of her mother's last husband, Richard Tucker, who'd taken them on shopping trips. And she'd learned how to stay on her budget by shopping vintage and reworking second-hand clothes.

She still had to learn the truly-loving-her part. She didn't always love herself very much.

She sent Rory a brief glance and then dropped her gaze to her sandals.

"Hey, I'll come by next week and help you out with getting ready for the estate sale," Marla said as she hurried up to Vanessa. "I'll even find some able-bodied helpers to do the heavy lifting." She cast a glance toward Rory. "An estate sale is a big job."

A job Vanessa dreaded. "Yes. But…it has to be done."

"Are you gonna be okay, doing this?" Marla asked, her green eyes full of understanding and sympathy.

"I'll be fine." Vanessa glanced over to where Alec sat at a round wrought iron table with Rory. Were they actually having more cupcakes? "I have to get the house ready to sell, and I can't do that until I empty it out."

"Your mother was a pack rat from what I hear," Marla said with a smile. "I know this has been hard, Vanessa."

Vanessa nodded. "Yep. Especially since she and I never got along." She stared at the swing, where she could be sitting right now with Rory. "I guess I'll get to know her a little more now that she's dead, at least. I never could figure her out when she was alive."

"You did your best."

"I left."

It was that simple. She'd left after one divorce too many and after one particular stepfather's bad behavior. It didn't matter that her mother had tried to make amends to Vanessa after Cora had married Richard, her final husband. At least Richard had been kind to Vanessa during the short time she'd lived here with her mother and him. A good man, a very wealthy man, he'd paid off her mother's house and shown both mother and daughter a world they'd only dreamed about. He'd died five years after marrying her mother.

None of it mattered now. She couldn't live in her mother's house.

She heard the preacher's hearty laughter and stole another glance at him. "What's with him, Marla? I asked you about his story, and I'd like to know more."

Marla followed her gaze. "What makes you think he has a story?"

"We all do. You said he wasn't always this happy."

Marla shrugged. "I don't know much other than he joined the army after attending seminary, served as a chaplain and then came home to become a minister. And I don't ask beyond that. I'm not even sure Alec knows, but they have this buddy system that holds them all together and they don't press each other about what they went through while serving. I can allow that, given how I held everything inside when Alec and I started seeing each other."

"And now?"

Marla's smile was serene and sure. "And now I tell Alec everything and he shares a lot with me. We're good."

"But he doesn't talk about the preacher's past?"

"Nope. It's not his to talk about. But then, they were all over there serving our country in one capacity or another. It's a bond they share."

A bond that might not be broken, Vanessa decided. "I have to get going," she said. "I had a great time."

"I'm glad you came," Marla said. She hugged Vanessa close.

"And if you ever need to talk—"

"I'll call you," Vanessa replied. She didn't want to get emotional in front of everyone.

"Of course," Marla said. Then she inclined her chin toward Rory. "But you should call him, too. No matter what you've been through, he's the best person to listen and help you."

"I'll keep that in mind," Vanessa replied, remembering how he'd mentioned late-night calls from his congregation members. But she said it with a smile…and a shred of hope.

A few days later, Rory worked his way around the church yard, clearing away broken limbs and picking up palm fronds. A storm had moved over the area the night before, leaving debris in its wake. He didn't mind the busywork, though. Not on a nice morning with a cool breeze pushing over the nearby waters of the lake. A few seagulls cawed at him as they came in for a low flight, probably hoping to find some morsels for breakfast.

After dropping some twigs and leaves into a nearby trash can, he stopped to look over the grounds. The little clapboard chapel had survived worse storms than this one. It was over a century old and not much bigger than a shotgun house, but the people of Millbrook Lake loved their church.

He loved it, too. Once he would have gone on by this place, but that Rory was long gone. *This* Rory loved *this* place. He stared out over the moss-draped live oaks that edged the old cemetery behind the church and prayed that he'd never have to be anywhere else.

Purple wisteria blossoms rained down each time the wind blew through the trees, their old vines wrapped like necklaces around the billowing oaks. The sound of the palms swaying in the breeze sang a comforting, serene tune. Blue jays and cardinals fussed at each other near the bird feeders one of the church members had built and hung near the pergola where people liked to hold picnics. And the ever-present, pesky squirrels chased each other through the trees with all the precision of drag-racing champions.

What a view.

"You're not working."

He whirled to find Mrs. Fitzgerald standing with her flower-encased walker near the sidewalk, her hat today black straw with red cherries around the rim.

"I'm taking a thankful break," he explained with a grin.

"Can I come and take it with you?" she asked. "I'm thankful and I have corn fritters."

Rory brushed his hands against his old jeans. "Bring yourself on over to this picnic table," he said. "How did you know I had a hankering for corn fritters this morning?"

She gave him a mock scowl, her wrinkles folding against each other, her gray hair as straw-like as her hat. "Since when have you *not* been hankering for something to eat? I declare, I don't know how you stay so fit."

"I pick up limbs and trash all the time," he said with a deadpan expression.

"Yes, you do. And you ride that bicycle and carry that board thing out to the water." She moseyed over to the table and fluffed her yellow muumuu. "You swim and fish and surf and jog all over the place. When do you rest, Preacher?"

"I'll rest when I die."

She shook her head. "Oh, I doubt that. The Lord will put you straight to work when you reach the Pearly Gates."

They both laughed at that notion. Then she

pulled out the still-warm corn fritters that were her specialty. Part hush puppy and part corn bread, the fat mushy balls were filled with real corn nuggets and tasted like nectar to Rory.

"So good," he said. "I think I'll be able to finish this mess before lunch, thanks to you."

Mrs. Fitzgerald chewed on her food and studied the water. "Nice sermon yesterday. I think you impressed that newcomer."

Miss Fanny, as she liked to be called, took impish pleasure in stirring the pot.

Rory played coy. "We had a newcomer?"

The older woman playfully slapped his arm. "I saw you looking at her. And I'm pretty sure she was looking back."

"Don't you have cataracts?"

"Not since that fancy eye doctor up on 98 did some sort of surgery on me. I can see a feather caught in a limb up in that tree yonder."

He glanced at the tree and squinted. "Feathers are a bit different from watching me and making assumptions."

"I know what I see," she replied on a prim note. "It's springtime. Love is in the air."

"Well, aren't you the poet."

"I used to be, you know."

"You? A poet?" Miss Fanny was full of surprises.

"Me." She pointed to the houses lining the

lake. "See that Craftsman cottage with the blue shutters?"

He nodded and grabbed another fritter. "The one near your house that's in need of serious repair?"

She lived in a small Cape Cod style two-storied house across from the church.

"That's the one. I used to run around with the woman who lived there. We were artists. She dabbled in mixed media and men. I dabbled in poetry and one long and loving marriage."

"You don't say?" He'd heard about how much Miss Fanny loved her husband, but she was already a widow when he met her. "So what happened to your friend? That house has been vacant since I've been here."

"That was her home at one time, but after she remarried, it became a vacation home. The last man she married also had a home in Birmingham, Alabama, and they used to travel back and forth. But…she died recently." Fanny took off her hat and gave him a direct stare. "That woman you're pretending you didn't notice in church yesterday, that's her daughter. She's come back here to fix up and sell the house." Putting her hat back on, she added, "Vanessa hated her mother. And I might as well tell you she's not too fond of preachers either."

Chapter Three

Rory stood up to stare over at the rambling one-story house with the blue shutters. Well, the shutters used to be blue. Now they were a peeling, weathered blue-gray mess. The whole place wore a facade of neglect even though the neighbors kept the yard mowed and the flower beds pruned and trimmed, as a courtesy and in keeping with the pretty factor that Millbrook Lake prided itself on.

So that was the house Vanessa had mentioned the other day. And Miss Fanny had been a friend to her deceased mother.

"I've often thought someone needed to buy that place and fix it up," he said. "So that's where Vanessa Donovan used to live?"

And now she was back.

"Her mother lived there for years, but Vanessa only lived there for a couple of years after Cora and Richard got married and moved here. She finished high school and then she left. To my knowledge, this is the first time she's been back."

Rory thought about how long the house had sat vacant. "But somebody kept up with the place. I mean, it's still full of furniture and belongings."

Miss Fanny sat staring across at the house. "Cora, Vanessa's mother, went to a nursing home in Alabama near where her last husband had property, right before you came to town. After Vanessa graduated high school, Richard and Cora split their time between Birmingham and here. Then after he died, Cora came back here. But she got sick and that ended, so she moved to a retirement home that had around-the-clock nursing. We all tried to keep the house ready for her to come back, but she never recovered from her first stroke. She had another massive one about a month ago and died. Buried in Alabama beside the one man she truly loved." Miss Fanny's shrug was eloquent. "Maybe because he left her a ton of money. She never talked much about the men in her life, but Richard was very special to her."

Suddenly, Rory understood a lot of things. "So Vanessa came back to…settle things?"

"That's an understatement," Miss Fanny replied. "The girl inherited the house and probably some money and other property, too. But I'm thinking she won't want to live here. She'll probably sell out and leave again." Miss Fanny leaned close. "Vanessa loved her mother's last husband, Richard Tucker. He was like a true father to her after so many other men, but Vanessa and Cora did not see eye-to-eye about anything. Too many bad memories."

Rory thought about the woman he'd first noticed in church last Sunday. Afraid and unsure and wound as tight as fishing line on a reel. Yeah, he could see a lot of *settling things* needed to occur.

And he had to ask. "Why does Vanessa dislike preachers, Miss Fanny?"

Miss Fanny got up and adjusted her hat. "I'll give you one guess."

Rory closed his eyes and lowered his head. "Which husband was it?"

"Number three," Miss Fanny said without missing a beat. "Vanessa was around thirteen or fourteen, I think, when her mother married a minister from Atlanta. They moved here since she already had this house. He served a church out on the highway for a couple of years. Neither his assignment nor the marriage lasted. But while he was here, he tried to *reform* Vanessa but in the worst sort of way."

Giving Rory a pointed glance, she started pushing her walker toward the street, Rory following while he kept his gaze on the house. "Her mother sided with the preacher, of course."

The rich fritters Rory had woofed down now felt like lead inside his stomach. He had to wonder what Vanessa had been through, how much she'd suffered. He didn't ask. Miss Fanny probably knew, but he wouldn't ask her to tell him.

Vanessa would have to be the one to do that.

If she ever trusted him enough to tell him anything.

"Let me walk you to your door," he told Miss Fanny. He needed to think this through. He checked the driveway next door to see if Vanessa's little blue car was parked there.

"She's not there," Miss Fanny said, already reading his mind. "I think she went to the lawyer's office to take care of some business. Probably the reading of the will." The older woman turned when they reached her front porch steps. "But she's planning a big estate sale sometime soon. She'll need help…sorting through all that clutter." She shrugged. "And since you're also planning a rummage sale at the church…"

Rory nodded. "I'll be glad to help."

Miss Fanny nodded, her work here done.

"Thank you for the corn fritters," Rory said

after he'd made sure she was safe back inside her house. "Go take your afternoon nap."

Miss Fanny waved him away and shut the door.

Rory hurried back down the steps, but he stopped on the sidewalk and glanced over at the long, sprawling house to the left of Miss Fanny's place.

He hadn't said this to Miss Fanny, but Rory had often thought he'd like to buy the old Craftsman cottage and fix it up.

But now, he also had the added challenge of trying to help repair the woman who'd come to town to sell this house. He'd have to pray hard on how to manage that without scaring Vanessa away for good. And he'd have to pray hard for her to forgive the minister who'd obviously damaged her for life.

"What did you say?"

Vanessa stared at the studious gray-haired lawyer sitting across from her in the elegant conference room situated in an old Georgian-style building across town.

Charles Barton leaned up and studied Vanessa's face, his bifocal glasses low on his hawk-like nose. "I said you have inherited the bulk of Richard Tucker's estate. Mind you, after your mother's care and expenses over the last few years, a fourth of it is gone. But you have the Millbrook Lake cottage and you have the holdings in Alabama, namely a house in Birmingham and several commercial rental properties in that area."

Vanessa sat staring at the man across from her, unable to comprehend what he was telling her. Finally, she swallowed and spoke. "I knew Richard left my mother comfortable, and I was grateful that she had constant, around-the-clock care at the nursing facility, but I had no idea about something such as this happening."

When Mr. Barton had stated the exact amount of the inheritance, Vanessa had almost fallen out of her chair. Growing up, she'd often dreamed of that kind of money. Now, she was content with her shop in New Orleans and the online boutique full of eclectic clothes and artisan wares from hundreds of vendors. She wasn't rich by any means, but she made a good living, selling quirky items to quirky people. Vanessa's Vintage had taken off in the last year or so. The boutique in New Orleans had become popular with both locals and tourists, and the online store kept up a steady business.

"You are now a wealthy young woman," the lawyer stated. "Of course, we'll deal with probate and a few other minor details, but all in all, since Richard had no other close relatives, this should be an easy transition."

"I'd planned to clean up the cottage and sell it," Vanessa admitted, still numb. "I thought that was the only thing I needed to worry about."

"You can decide what to sell off and what to keep once this sets in," Mr. Barton said. "After a death, I always tell my clients who are left to take over estates not to make any rash decisions. Give it some time. You're still working through a lot of emotions."

The older man's soft-spoken advice calmed Vanessa. "You're right. I have a lot to do back at the cottage. Getting the place cleaned up and renovated to sell will give me time to decide where I go from here."

"Do you think you'll want to keep the mansion in Birmingham?" he asked.

Vanessa thought about the stately Tudor-style house sitting up on a remote bluff. "It's a beautiful house, but I never actually lived there. I visited a few times, but I can't see me living in that big, old house."

Mr. Barton's assistant began gathering files and folders. He stood, too, and waited for Vanessa to do the same. "Take your time. The money and holdings won't be going anywhere and there are trustworthy people in place to take care of things."

Vanessa thanked the lawyer and left, thinking she wouldn't be going anywhere for a while either. She now had a lot more to take care of than she'd ever imagined.

But for now, she'd focus on the cottage.

She drove around the lake and circled back toward Lake Street, where all the quaint Victorian houses sat next to the few Cape Cod homes and the other one-story Craftsman cottages that were scattered throughout. The view across the water was breathtaking and beautiful.

Until she spotted her house.

The cottage looked sad and lonely, neglected.

That mirrored how she'd felt most of her life. This house held a strong pull over her, one that she needed to resist and one she'd managed to avoid up until now.

Ironic that now she had the security and wealth she'd always craved but she didn't have anyone to share it with.

Her mother had finally found her fairy tale with Richard Tucker, but it hadn't lasted. He'd died a year after Vanessa left to go to college.

Vanessa had never wanted a fairy tale. She'd only wanted a family. They'd had that with Richard. He'd been kind and gracious and so patient with her mother's temperamental mood swings and crazy impulsive nature. He'd also taken time with Vanessa, showing her proper decorum and giving her instructions on manners and how to win over even her worst critics. But he'd done it all in a caring, loving way that made Vanessa feel treasured and special.

Not ashamed and embarrassed.

Still in shock from the lawyer's news, she drove on around the lake and pulled up into the driveway of her house. When she got out of the car, she glanced toward the church and wondered what Rory was doing. Marla had told Vanessa that he lived in a small garage apartment behind the church. Maybe he *would* be a good person to talk to in confidence about her situation.

But then again, maybe not. She was leery of showing him any signs of weakness even if he didn't seem the type to take advantage of her.

She wouldn't be pulled into something she'd regret. She couldn't be fooled into getting too close to organized religion again. She believed in God, but she was afraid of putting too much trust in people. The pain of her last encounter with a man of God still gave her nightmares.

She couldn't go through that again.

No matter how much she needed a friend.

Rory went on with his day. It was nearly sundown now, so he finished up the yard work behind the church, careful to stay out of sight of the house across the street. But it hadn't been easy to stay away after the heavy hints Miss Fanny had dropped regarding Vanessa's past.

Usually when a visitor came to church, some of the welcome committee members would take over a basket full of books, cookies, gift certificates to local establishments and ground coffee from Marla's place with a cute Millbrook Lake Church mug sporting a pelican sitting on a pew with the caption *Don't fly by. Come on in.*

Sometimes, he'd tag along on these welcome visits.

Not this time.

It wasn't that he didn't want to reach out to Vanessa. But he'd counseled enough members of the military to know that when someone didn't want to listen, it was hard to talk to them. Rory had his ways of helping people to find their faith, and those ways didn't involve being pushy and too in-your-face. He'd have to bide his time with Vanessa Donovan. He'd seen people hurt by those who used their own agenda in the name of the Lord.

It was never pretty.

So now, he raked and prayed and raked some more and tried to think about what he could have for dinner. Maybe he'd go to the Back Bay Pizza House and order a takeout meatball sub. Or maybe he'd swing by the Courthouse

Café and get a big hamburger and fries before they shut down for the day. Or he could pull out his bike and ride around the lake and stop at the Fish Barrel, the new alfresco dining truck that offered up some really good grouper sandwiches, shrimp baskets and other local fare.

He was leaning toward the bike ride and the grouper sandwich when he heard a low, feminine groan echoing out over the street. Then he heard a thump and a crash, followed by another groan and the word "Ouch."

Dropping his rake, Rory peeped around the corner of the storage shed behind the church and saw Vanessa standing in the front yard by an old wheelbarrow full of trash. He watched as she tried to move the wheelbarrow, but one of the wheels had obviously gone flat. The weight of the trash wasn't helping matters.

That old thing wasn't going to go anywhere except—

Onto its side.

It toppled over with a shudder of regret, causing another loud crash to reverberate up and down the street. Old glassware, plates, cups and other knickknacks spilled all over the driveway and sidewalk. And another groan of frustration followed.

Okay, now he had to walk over there because he had to be gallant and helpful, didn't he?

"Need some help?" he called, to show he was only trying to be a gentleman.

She glanced around, surprise brightening her shimmering eyes. Surprise, followed by what might be dread. "I'm beyond help."

"I wouldn't say that," he told her, his hands on his hips. "But…this wheelbarrow is beyond anything. I hope these dishes weren't important."

She stared at the shattered mess lying at her feet. "No, not really." But she picked up what looked like a children's cup that had colorful princess characters on it. "Just stuff my mom had shoved into the garage out back. She was a bit of a hoarder."

Rory heard the pain behind that comment. And saw that pain reflected in Vanessa's eyes while she moved her fingers over the faded little plastic cup. "Was that yours?" he asked as an opening.

She nodded. "Once, long ago."

"Where were you taking these things?"

"Out to the curb." She tossed the cup back onto the pile. "I thought someone might come by and take them."

He gave her time to get past what she had to be thinking. It must be hard to let go of so many memories. "Let me help you get this cleaned up."

She waved him away. "You don't have to do that."

"I have nothing else to do," he said. "I've been doing yard work, and I was about to quit for the day."

She glanced at the church and then back at him, the struggle in her mind evident in her brooding expression.

"I guess I could use some help," she said. "I have to clean this place up, and that shed is just the beginning. I want to put a lot of the items from the estate sale out there, on display."

"Are you hiring an estate-sale manager?"

Her dark eyebrows shot up. "I hadn't planned on that since this is what I do for a living." She stopped and stared at the little cup.

"You work as an estate-sale manager?"

"No, but I run a vintage shop in New Orleans and an online shopping site. Vanessa's Vintage."

"Then you do know what you're doing. We're planning a rummage sale at the church in a few weeks, and one of our members used to be an estate-sale manager. She offered her services free to us. But we could coordinate things with your sale. Maybe hold them on the same day since we're neighbors." He stopped, waited a couple of beats. When she didn't scowl at him, he added, "That is, if you're okay with that idea."

She glanced at the church, and then she

looked down at the old wheelbarrow. "I don't know. I hope I'll be gone in a few weeks."

"Forget I suggested it," Rory said. "You have too much on your mind to add a church rummage sale to the mix."

"It's okay," she replied, pushing at her shoulder-length wavy bob. "I don't know what I'm doing, really. I mean, I know vintage and collectibles, but I've never done this before. But I always managed to figure things out on my own."

He picked up the princess cup. "Well, now you're not on your own. You have help. Starting with me."

She stared over at him, her gaze moving from his face to the pile of broken dishes. "And what's in it for you, Preacher?"

Chapter Four

"What do you mean?"

Rory tried the tactic he used whenever someone asked him a disconcerting question. And prayed it would work on Vanessa.

She gave him a surprised glance, her brow furrowing. "It's a simple question. You're offering to help me. You must have a reason."

"Wow. Does there have to be a reason?" Not sure how to handle this kind of skepticism, he leaned his head down and gave her a smile. "Part of my job is to help others. Part of my nature is to be sincere about it."

She actually blushed. "I'm sorry. I shouldn't have said that. I've had a trying day and I have trust issues."

He widened the smile. "You think?"

She shook her head and shot him a wry grin. "I guess I should loosen up, right?"

"No. Don't do anything on my account. This ain't my first rodeo."

She laughed at that. "You look too young and carefree to be a preacher."

He thought of the man who'd obviously hurt her. "Ministers come in all shapes and sizes. And personalities."

"Yeah, you can say that again."

He stuffed the cup inside one of the deep pockets of his baggy work shorts and started picking up the broken dishes in an effort to distract her. "Hey, if you find me a broom and a dustpan, I can get this done a lot quicker. And then I'll be happy to buy you a cup of coffee or a cold drink."

"So you can work me over?"

That skeptical imp again, hiding serious pain. "Work you over?"

She started walking backward toward the big shed beyond the open gate to the backyard. "You know, telling me that God loves me and that He can make things better for me?"

"Of course," Rory said, stooping to pick up the bigger pieces of shattered porcelain. "That's part of my job, too."

She turned and hurried. "At least you're not trying to slip it under the radar."

"Nope. I'm not that kind of guy," he called after her. When she kept walking, he called louder. "What you see is what you get with me. It's pretty much the same with God, too."

He glanced up to find an older couple across the street with their dog watching him with a curious regard.

"Oh, hi," Rory called. "Nice day, don't you think?"

They nodded, waved and hurried away. The little dog, however, woofed a quick reply.

No wonder they'd moved on. He seemed to be talking to himself.

Worried that Vanessa had run off in the other direction, he stood and checked the open gate. Maybe she'd gone inside the house to find the broom and dustpan.

Rory cleaned up a bit more and then decided to check on Vanessa. He strolled through the open wrought iron gate and searched the big backyard. Lots of vintage patio furniture and nice palm trees and old oaks, but no Vanessa.

Turning toward the big shed she'd talked about, Rory went to the open French doors. "Hey, Vanessa, you in here?"

He found her standing at a table, her hand on an open book. A photo album from what he could tell.

When he moved toward her, she whirled, her gaze locking with his. "I'm sorry. I…I can't find the dustpan."

Rory walked over to where she stood. "Do you want me to leave?"

She nodded and then she shook her head no. "I…I don't want you to leave but…I can't…I'm not ready for this."

"Not ready for me and my poor attempts to comfort you? Or not ready to clean out this house?"

"Not ready for…accepting that my mother is gone," she said. Then she sniffed and wiped at her eyes. "I'll clean up the mess out front later. You…you don't have to hang around."

Rory wasn't going to leave her like this. "Nonsense. You go in the house and have a good cry or make yourself a cup of tea or eat ice cream. I see the broom over there, and I can use the lid off this old box as a dustpan. I'll clean up the broken things out front."

She gave him a confused stare, her eyes misty with a raw-edged pain. "You don't have to clean up my mess."

Rory wondered how many times she'd said that to other people. "I don't mind."

She nodded, grabbed the photo album and pushed past him for the door. But she turned once she was outside. "Thank you, Rory."

He nodded and smiled at her. "Hey, listen. Grief is a sneaky thing. One minute you're doing fine and the next, you want to punch something. Or…break dishes."

She smiled through her tears. "I guess I've done that already today."

She turned and ran toward the house, her flip-flops hitting against the steps up to the back porch. He watched her until he heard the door slam.

Rory tore off the box top and took it and the broom back up to the sidewalk and began to clear away the debris. But in his heart, he wanted to go inside that house and help clear up the debris of Vanessa's broken heart. Because he didn't have enough prayers to give her the kind of comfort she craved and needed.

And yet, he knew the comfort of God's love.

So he prayed anyway, until he had the yard clean again.

He'd have to keep working on the woman sitting inside, crying over an old photo album. And he'd have to do it in a gentle way that would help her to heal.

Vanessa wished she hadn't fallen apart in front of the preacher. Now he'd really want to talk to her. She only wanted to sit here and stare into space. But she had so much to take care of before she could go back to New Orleans.

Her fingers touched on an old photograph of

her mother with Vanessa on a beach blanket, forcing her to remember the good times. They'd been few and far between, but she had brief flashes of laughter and sunshine and a warm feeling.

A feeling of being loved. Had she forgotten the good and focused too much on the bad? The pictures in this album only showed smiling faces and what looked like good times.

Why were there never any pictures of the bad times? Never any proof of how she remembered things? No, those things had been hidden away, swept underneath the heavy carpet in a facade that was hard to pull away.

A soft knock at the back door brought her head up. Vanessa wiped at her eyes and shut the old photo album. Then she rushed to the door and opened it to find Rory standing there with two ice cream cones.

"The truck came by," he said, smiling. "I like chocolate and I got you caramel-vanilla. But if you don't want it—"

She grabbed the waffle cone and took a small nip. "Oh."

"I take that as a yes." He ate some of his and glanced around. "Nice house."

"Come in," she said, her mind still on the caramel-vanilla.

He stepped inside, and Vanessa realized no

one had been invited inside this house in a long time. Shame and embarrassment hit at her with the same freezing intensity as the ice cream sliding down her throat. The built-in cabinets on each side of the enormous fireplace were true to the Craftsman style of the house. But the shelves were practically groaning with old books and side-by-side knickknacks. Not to mention stacks of newspapers and scraps of all kinds of fabric remnants lying here and there in front of the shelves.

"It's a mess," she said, lifting her free hand in the air. "One room at a time. I keep telling myself that's how I'll get it done."

Rory glanced around, his gaze settling on the folded blanket and bed pillow she'd left on the couch. She didn't want to explain that she'd slept in here last night.

But Rory didn't mention what had to be obvious. Instead, he said, "So...are you going to sell off everything in here?"

"Not everything all at once," she said. "I have my online vintage store, so I'll place some of the items there." She ate more ice cream, the cold sweetness making her feel better. "And if you're serious about me having the estate sale when you have the church rummage sale, then I'll probably get rid of a lot of the bigger pieces there, since shipping them is kind of costly."

"Of course I'm serious. If you don't mind staying a week or so longer than you planned. We hope to hold it sometime in May, but I'll pin the committee people down on an exact date."

"That would help," she replied. "A deadline will force me to stop procrastinating and get this over with."

And what could a few more weeks hurt? She could handle this. She had to get this house on the market, and she couldn't do that until she had it cleaned up and spruced up.

"Then it's settled. We can go over the details in the next week or so," he said. "The church members will appreciate having the draw of an estate sale next door." He walked around, studying the house. "This place has good bones, you know."

And a few good memories. She needed to focus on those, instead of the bad ones she'd experienced here as a teenager.

"It is a classic house," she admitted. "It needs someone to love it enough to save it."

"I think you're right," Rory said, his warm, sunny gaze moving over her face.

Vanessa tried to ignore how his nearness made her feel kind of gooey inside, so she forced herself to see it from someone else's perspective. Her mother had been an artist, dabbling in collages and mixed media. Cora Donovan

Tucker never threw anything away. So every nook and cranny, every shelf and table, held what her mother had considered treasures. A feather here, an old button there. Tarnished jewelry with missing rhinestones, old purses with worn handles, books of every shape and size, yellowed with age. Clothes, dishes, trinkets. Cora had collected husbands in much the same way. Tarnished, washed up, broken people. Losers, except for Richard. He'd been a true Godsend.

Her mother had always been a work in progress. But even ravished by two strokes and unable to speak, Cora had died with a peaceful look on her face. Thankful that she'd made it to the nursing home in time to be with her mother at the end, Vanessa wondered what she'd left unsaid.

Rory picked up an object here and studied a piece of art there. "Interesting collection."

"A lot of stuff, huh?" she said, wondering what Rory really thought. Wondering why she'd let him in. *Really* let him in.

"Yes." He munched on his waffle cone. "But that's not your fault. And you don't have to go through it alone."

"Do you mean clearing away this clutter or grieving?"

He gave her that blue-eyed stare that left her feeling light and heavy at the same time. "Yes."

"I don't need a lot of help," she replied, panicking. The cold ice cream burned at her stomach. She imagined him being here every day, watching her, checking on her, asking her pointed, preacher-type questions. "I can handle this, Preacher."

He didn't speak. He kept munching on his cone. Finally, he finished chewing and nodded. "I don't doubt that, but why should you have to do this alone?"

"Why are you so determined to make sure I get help?"

He seemed to accept that she was turning ugly again, and Vanessa felt ashamed at herself. "I'm sorry. I guess I need some more time to process this."

"Okay." He finished his ice cream and went to the kitchen sink to wash his hands. "And I should leave you alone to do this in your own way."

If he noticed the dishes everywhere or the half-eaten sandwich she'd left on the counter, he didn't blink. Instead, he dried his hands on a butterfly-embossed dish towel and walked over to where she stood holding a melting ice cream cone.

"Appetite gone?" he asked, taking the cone from her.

"Yes."

He took her ice cream and went back to the sink and dropped the dripping cone inside and washed his hands again. Then he came back to stand near her. "You do what you need to do. We're all here, though. Remember that. Miss Fanny next door—she knew your mom. She's willing to help, and she's willing to listen."

"I don't need anyone to listen to me," Vanessa retorted, needing him to leave. Needing to be away from his soft, sweet gaze. "I… I'll figure this out."

"I believe you will."

"But you'd like it better if I opened up and told you all my troubles and my fears?"

He started backing toward the door. "No, I wouldn't like that better. I wouldn't like that at all. But what I would like is for you to stop seeing me as the enemy and let me be your friend."

"I can't do that," she said, tears burning at her eyes. "I don't think you're the enemy, but I can't be your friend, Rory."

He held a hand on the doorknob. "Or you can't let *me* be your friend? Because I'm what you consider a pushy minister?"

"That's part of it. That especially, and you being so nice and *not* being a pushy minister in the way that I know, is really messing with my head."

"I wish you'd reconsider things," he said, "but

I understand. I'll see you soon, I guess. You know where to find me if you need me." He opened the door, but turned back. "But *you* need to understand, I didn't come over here today to badger you. I came because I saw someone in need. That's my nature as a human being, not only as a minister. Sometimes, people tend to overlook that I'm as human as they are."

And then he was gone, just like that.

For a split second, Vanessa wanted to run after him and tell him all of her troubles. But she had to be strong. She had to fight that notion with all her being. She'd told a minister her innermost secrets before, and that man had used her fears and her insecurities against her. Never again.

She'd been taking care of herself for a long time now. Why should that change? Why should she believe a sweet-talking preacher who brought her ice cream and made her feel safe?

She rushed to the sink and turned on the hot water and watched as the caramel-vanilla ice cream melted into nothing. Her confusing thoughts about Rory had to melt into nothing, too. Because growing close to him would be a bad idea all the way around.

Why should she believe him? Why did she *want* to believe him?

Because Rory was different. She could tell

that. He'd never been through the type of horrible, mortifying things she'd endured. He was happy and settled and well-rounded and content.

He didn't know the kind of pain she knew.

Did he?

Chapter Five

Rory sat behind his desk, a spot he tried not to occupy very often. He much preferred being up and about, talking to people one-on-one. Paperwork always made him antsy and tired, but today was Monday.

Paperwork day.

He signed a few more checks and went over some notes for the committee meeting he had to attend later in the week. Then he checked his watch. Blain and Rikki were coming in today to go over the last-minute details of their upcoming wedding.

Thankful that they'd managed to get past her family's alleged criminal activities and that Blain had saved her from some nasty people, Rory was glad that Blain, a detective, had fallen for Rikki, the daughter of a reputed Mafia boss. Rikki had made peace with her family since she'd found out her powerful father had truly mended his ways long ago, and Blain had made peace with his father, a retired sheriff who'd helped him crack the case.

Rory's heart warmed at the harmony all around him. Another win for the good guys.

Now he was in charge of yet another wedding. He'd married off Alec Caldwell and Marla Hamilton right before Christmas of last year. They were thriving.

He wanted that for Blain and Rikki, too.

He might even want that again for himself one day. But he tried not to think about the past or his own heartache too much. Rory didn't talk about that time in his life. He'd been so happy, so ready to start his career as a minister. But then, his life had changed in one quick heartbeat.

People would be surprised to know he'd had to crawl out of his own dark place.

He stopped reading over the budget report and glanced out the office window, across the street to the Craftsman cottage. And wondered for the hundredth time how Vanessa was doing. She hadn't come back to church yet. But it had been only a week. He'd hoped she'd come yesterday, but he hadn't seen her in the congregation. He hadn't talked to her since the day he'd helped her with the pile of broken dishes. But he kept that little kiddie cup she'd almost tossed right here in his desk drawer so he could return it to her one day.

When she was ready.

He had a good vantage point to keep an eye on her. He'd seen her coming and going, taking boxes to the trash, loading her tiny car with bags of stuff. She was busy. She was avoiding him. Maybe she was avoiding the whole world.

He'd also seen her staring off into space, sometimes up at the house, sometimes out toward the lake. And a couple of times, over toward the church.

He prayed she'd walk over and see him one day soon.

In God's own time.

Some people believed you had to rush right in and grab people by the lapels to convince them that God loved them. Rory preferred to let people come to that notion on their own.

So he prayed them into taking the next step. And he'd been doing a lot of praying for Vanessa lately. She was going through a deep pain, no doubt. No one here really knew he'd been through that kind of pain. Not even his best friends.

Rory wanted to keep it that way. He couldn't let people see beyond his good-natured, friendly attitude. He'd hidden that side of himself away for so long, it didn't match anymore.

He'd scare people and confuse them if he told them about the man he used to be. Not that he'd ever been scary. But he didn't want to go back to that dark spot in his soul. Ever. He'd come a long way to get to this place, and he liked his work and his life. No way did he want to go back.

And yet, when he saw his friends finding true love, he wanted to go back. He wanted to fall in love again. But at times, the bitterness reared its ugly head, and he felt envy and anger pushing at his hard-fought-for peace.

So he understood what Vanessa was fighting.

A knock at his partially open office door brought Rory out of his musings. His secretary, Barbara Rowan, peeped inside. "Hey, you awake in here?"

Rory grinned. "Barely. It's too pretty outside to be in here pushing a pencil."

Barbara, petite, with a brown bob and a blunt attitude, put her hands on her hips and gave him a mock stare, her flamingo lapel pin blinking at him in shades of pink bling. "Well, I feel so bad for you, stuck in this stuffy old office. But you have company. Blain and Rikki are here."

"Oh, right." Rory glanced at the clock again. "Send them in. This will make my day better."

Barbara nodded and opened the door wide. "Here they are."

Rory grinned at seeing Blain and Rikki holding hands, smiles on their faces. "Hello, you two."

Blain shook his hand and Rikki hugged him. "We're here for the premarital counseling you suggested," Rikki said.

"Did I suggest that?" He chuckled and motioned to the floral chairs across from his desk. "So a few more weeks, huh?"

Blain nodded, his dark blue eyes moving over his bride. "Yes. Wedding here in the church and reception out at the Alvanetti estate."

"Got it marked in red," Rory said. "Any questions?"

Rikki gave Blain a sweet smile. "How do we get past everything we went through? I mean, I've forgiven my family but…how do Blain and I keep my family issues out of our marriage?"

Blain squeezed her hand and glanced at Rory. "We want to make this work. We love each other but sometimes the world can get in the way."

Rory loved his friend Blain and he liked Rikki, too. So he leveled with them. "It's not easy. But loving each other is the first line of defense. Loving the Lord helps. Your faith is important, and that shows with you two. Be open and honest with each other, of course. Seek help when you need to. I'm always here for either of you, and I won't repeat anything said in this room. But you need to talk to your families, too. And other friends you can trust."

He glanced out the window and saw Vanessa getting into her car. She was wearing a colorful patterned sundress and tall, strappy sandals. When he glanced back at Blain and Rikki, Blain was giving him a one-eyebrow-lifted knowing stare.

Rory tried to cover. "And…uh…you should be honest with your families, too. Don't hold grudges. Talk things out. Remember the good times and try to get past the bad."

He groaned inwardly. He was talking in clichés today.

After a few more questions, he went over the wedding arrangements with them and gave them some pamphlets and books to read. They both asked more questions, and Rory said a prayer with them. "I think you two will be fine."

Blain glanced at Rikki. "Can you visit with Barbara for a minute? I need to ask Rory something."

"Sure." She gave him a brown-eyed smile, her long dark hair flowing around her shoulders. "Already keeping secrets."

"It's more guy stuff," Blain said. "Regarding my bachelor party."

"Oh, right." She grinned at Rory and went into the reception area.

"What's up?" Rory asked, his mind still on Vanessa. "You know we're having a low-key party out at the camp house, right?"

Blain laughed. "Yes, I know all about that, surprises not withstanding."

"Okay, did you need something else?"

"Are you scouting the house across the street for a reason?"

Blain was on to him. "I might be since it's going up for sale soon. I've always liked that house, and it's near the church." He shrugged. "I'm outgrowing my tiny one-bedroom apartment."

"Right." Blain rolled his eyes. "I was referring to the woman living there, not the house. Preacher, do you have your eye on Vanessa Donovan?"

Rory didn't want to squirm underneath the scrutiny of Blain's eagle-eyed gaze. "She's in a bad way, so I've tried to befriend her. Offer her my help and advice."

Blain nodded. "It's amazing. All these years, I've never seen you go beyond being friends with a woman. You don't even date. But since Vanessa rolled into town, you've seemed distracted."

"How do you know that?" Rory asked, affronted. "You haven't been around me that much when women are nearby."

"Relax," Blain said. "I saw you on Easter Sunday, and Alec told me you and Vanessa seemed chummy at Easter dinner at his house."

Rory laughed. "What you and Alec call chummy, I call being friendly."

"Oh, okay. We'll go with that then," Blain said. "It's nice to know you're human after all. You could do worse. She's cute, and Rikki says she's nice, too."

Rory rubbed a hand over his choppy hair. "Really? I hadn't noticed."

Blain shook his head. "Right. I'll shut up now. Are we still on for pizza Thursday night?"

"As always."

"And we are gathering at the camp house for my bachelor party in two weeks?"

"You better believe it. And I *do* have surprises lined up for you."

"What? Choir rehearsal and memorizing Bible verses?"

"After we play a serious game of tic-tac-toe, yes."

"Wild night. Love it." Blain shook Rory's hand and headed to the door. "Hey, Alec and I, we've been there. We should be the ones giving *you* advice these days."

Rory finally caved. "I might take you up on

that offer. I like her. A lot. But…she's not returning that feeling."

"Give her some time," Blain suggested. "Like you said, she's been through a lot. One thing I've learned, dealing with Rikki and her family, strong women don't like to be messed with until they're ready to be messed with."

"Got it," Rory said, grinning at Blain's down-to-earth assessment. "I'm learning that, my friend."

After Blain and Rikki left, he turned to Barbara. "Please tell me it's quitting time."

"It's quitting time," she said. "You know you officially have Mondays off, so why are you still here?"

He shrugged. "Habit." Then he went back in his office and tidied up. "I think I've signed all the proper checks and documents so yes, I'm taking off early. I might take a run around the lake or maybe go kayaking."

"Great idea," his secretary called back. "Me, I'm going to go home and piddle in my garden."

"Okay. See you tomorrow."

Barbara left by the side door.

Rory locked up and was about to head to the garage underneath his apartment to get his kayak out when he saw Vanessa's car moving up Lake Drive.

She was home.

* * *

He was standing by his garage apartment.

Glad she was wearing her shades, Vanessa noticed Rory out of the corner of her eye. She'd tried not to think about him, but he seemed to be front and center in her mind. Reminding herself that he did live and work right across the street, she chalked up this preoccupation with the cute preacher to being in such close proximity to him. Hard not to think about him when the pretty white church stood as a reminder every time she looked out the window.

So she pulled her car into the drive and geared up for a warm, soothing bath and a bowl of ice cream. Yes, she'd been craving ice cream all week. His fault, too. But she'd had a long day of talking to lawyers and discussing things on the phone with Realtors both here in Millbrook and at the various properties she now owned in Alabama.

Overwhelmed, she glanced back toward the church.

And saw Rory heading straight for her.

She almost ran into the house, but her heart stopped her. She couldn't be rude to the man. He'd been nothing but kind to her. The least she could do was say hello to him.

Hello. And then on to ice cream.

"Hi," he called when she turned and waved. Then he walked over. Did he seem relieved?

"Hello," she replied, smiling. "How are you?"

"Good. I'm calling it a day," he said. His dark blond hair was in a perpetual state of shagginess, but it suited him. "I'm going kayaking. Wanna come?"

Kayaking? The thought of putting on shorts and a sleeveless top made her cringe. The sun had not touched her legs all winter. Did she have the nerve to actually relax and go for a ride on the lake? With him?

He must have sensed her hesitation. "I'm sorry. You're probably really busy."

She glanced at the glistening water and then gazed at him. "I've been going nonstop all day dealing with my inheritance, but that water looks so tempting."

And so did he. Not what you'd expect. Better than ice cream even.

"I have an extra kayak. It's actually Alec's, but he won't mind if you want to use it. He stores it over here so some of the kids I mentor can borrow it."

"You mentor kids?"

He nodded and looked sheepish. "Yes. Mostly teens. We have a get-together here at the church once a week. Anyone is invited, but some of the kids are in foster homes."

"Wow." She only wished she'd had a safe place to go when she was a teen. "That's a good idea."

He smiled at her comment. "They need someone to talk to at times. They come with their guardians or foster parents, but we team each kid up with a mentor. Supervised, of course."

"That's good. That they're able to talk to someone and that it's supervised."

He went quiet for a couple of moments. "Listen, if you don't want to go—"

He was talking about kayaking, but he must have seen the darkness in her eyes. Pushing aside the flare of distant painful memories, she gave him a weak smile.

"Let me get inside and change," she said, making a snap decision she hoped she wouldn't regret. "I haven't been kayaking in a while so I might slow you down, but yes, I'd like to take a ride around the lake."

"Good. I'll go get the kayaks ready. You can meet me at the boat landing."

"Okay." Vanessa hurried into the house, her mind buzzing with good and bad thoughts. She didn't want to group Rory in the same category as her mother's ex-husband, but how could she not think about it? She'd been a troubled teen, and her so-called stepfather had pretended to be her mentor.

And yet he'd betrayed her in the worst way. Would Rory do that?

No. Because for one thing, Vanessa was a grown woman now. Stronger and more assertive. No longer afraid to stand up to people.

Rory Sanderson wasn't anything like Gregory Pardue. Not at all. Thank goodness.

And yet when she came back outside, Vanessa felt a shiver moving down her spine. Was she making a mistake, getting to know the preacher?

She looked up at the sky and for the first time in years, she asked God to protect her heart. Because she didn't want to be wrong about Rory.

Chapter Six

She'd found a pair of old cutoff jeans and rolled them up over her knees. A sleeveless cotton blouse covered the shorts. Swallowing her trepidations, Vanessa walked the short distance to the lake's boat landing near the marina and boardwalk. The sun felt good on her skin, and the sound of seagulls flying overhead reminded her that summer was coming.

She saw Rory waiting with the two kayaks. He waved and she waved back. He had on shorts and an old T-shirt. He was much darker than her, which showed he got outside more than she did.

Not the pasty-skinned pallor she considered more minister type. But then, Rory shattered all of her notions regarding preachers. He looked as if he belonged on a California beach instead of here, standing by two kayaks and waiting on her.

"You ready for this?" he asked, sincerity in his blue eyes.

"Yes. I'll probably regret it tomorrow—sore muscles—but I need to get out and get some exercise. Moving boxes and going through closets and cabinets doesn't count as a fun way to get in shape."

He gave her a quick once-over. "You know how to kayak, right?"

She thought she remembered. "Yes. Love it."

He motioned her to where he had the kayaks pulled up in the shallow water by the concrete landing. "We can do this at the dock or I'll hold yours while you get in."

"I can get in here," she said, glancing around to make sure no one would see her if she fell headfirst into the shallow water. "Or at least I'm going to try."

Rory took her hand while he held the bright blue kayak steady with his foot. "Okay, sit and turn."

Vanessa tried to ignore the warmth of his fingers holding hers. He had a strong, secure grip. "Like a lady getting into a car," she said on a nervous laugh.

"Sorta." He grinned and held on to her while

she plopped down into the low, narrow water-craft. "See, you're in."

"Yes, now I have to get my legs in, too." She turned forward, her water shoes intact.

Once she was settled, he handed her the paddle. Vanessa wondered how he'd manage getting inside his red kayak, but he slid in with the ease of someone who was a born athlete. She noticed his muscular arms and broad shoulders. What else would she notice about this man?

Too many things, she decided.

As they glided out onto the lake, Vanessa worked to keep up with Rory, having no doubt that he was purposely going slow to stay with her. But they laughed and talked as they paddled around the big oval body of water. The ducks and geese squawked and fussed as they glided by. People waved from the shore, some of them calling out to Rory.

Spring was in full bloom, showing off in the dappled sunlight. Azaleas lush with pink-and-white flowers clustered underneath the tall pines and old oaks. Crape myrtles along the streets were bursting with tiny blossoms that were beginning to bud in hot pink and deep purple. The old magnolias hung heavy with huge white petals. The green fronds on tall palms danced in the wind, the sound of their frenzy sending out a steady swish, swish. The whole lake smelled like a fragrant, earthy garden.

With the wind in her face and the sun warm on her skin, Vanessa relaxed and remembered the short time she'd spent here in Millbrook Lake so many years ago. Her last couple of years of high school had been spent here. Marla had been one of her friends back then.

Marla was trying to be a friend to her now.

And so was Rory.

"How you doing?" he asked as he paddled close.

"Fine." She held her oar still and smiled over at him. "This is really nice."

Nice. That small word, usually so boring, was fast becoming her favorite expression.

"Anytime you want to go for a spin, let me know," he said, his eyes bright with expectation.

Vanessa nodded and wished she could feel that same hope. But she'd given up on hoping or expecting a long time ago. The best she could manage was a day-to-day positive feeling that involved her work. She'd learned to take care of herself since she'd left Millbrook Lake, and that accomplishment kept her going. Her life involved salvaging vintage clothes and items and reselling them to like-minded people. Which was odd, considering how long she'd been running from her past.

Or maybe she clung to old things so she could hang on to the little bit of good in her past. No matter. She knew what would be in her future. She'd be alone. By choice. She couldn't risk messing things up with someone the way her mother had. Over and over.

Clearing those cobwebs out of her head, she gave Rory a quick nod. "Thanks. I won't have much time, but I need to remember what a special place this is. The lake and the town—it's all like a picture book."

He drifted closer. "Oh, it looks pretty but we're all living our lives, day by day. Reality can set in at any time. But I can't complain."

"Are you trying to burst my bubble?" she asked, surprised that he'd made such a pointed observation. Where had Mr. Feel Good gone?

He gave her a perplexed glance. "No, not at all. But you know how it goes. This is a great place to live, no doubt about that. But it's our state of mind that adds those little nuances and warm, fuzzy feelings to our lives."

"Oh, so we're discussing that now, are we?" She started paddling again. "My state of mind is in a constant state of turmoil."

"I didn't mean to imply that," he said, pulling up beside her again. "I was trying to say it had more to do with me than you. I didn't mean for it to sound so corny."

She doubted that. He was usually so happy-go-lucky, even the ducks liked him. "And what could you possibly have to be negative about, Preacher?"

He didn't answer right away. Which made her only want to know everything about him. Finally, he said, "More than you'd realize. But you're right. I know better than to preach to someone who's been through enough already. I'm sorry."

Since she'd never heard a negative tone in his voice before, she glanced over to check on him. He looked dejected and brooding. Different. Definitely human.

"No, I'm sorry," she said. "I'm a little prickly these days. I know you mean well, and I should appreciate how you aren't trying to gloss over things. This isn't Disneyland, after all. I mean, look what Marla went through after her first husband died. And Alec, coming home with wounds that almost turned him into a recluse. Blain and Rikki were almost killed a few months ago. I really don't have it that bad, after all."

"Neither do I," he said. "Look, I want to get to know you, all preacher talk aside. I don't want to preach to you. I want to…talk to you."

"I like talking," she admitted. "Even when I'm down and grumpy."

"You're grieving. Sometimes being still and listening is the best thing for that."

"Now that is good advice," she said with a wry smile. "Truce?"

"Truce," he said. "I need to listen to my own advice."

"Race you to the other side of the lake," she said, taking off in a whirl of paddles and water. Trying to get away from the intimacy of their conversation, too.

Soon they were laughing and calling out to each other. Relieved that they'd gotten past that sticky moment, Vanessa still wondered when this sweet man had been through any kind of turmoil.

They turned back toward the landing just as the sun began to set behind the tree line. Rory hopped out first and tried to help her, but she was up and dragging her kayak close to the shore before he could make a move. When she slipped and almost went down in the muddy shallows, he took her by both hands and lifted her up, his hands moving to her elbows to steady her.

Their eyes met as she came face-to-face with him.

"Thanks," Vanessa said, her breath leaving her body. It had been a long time since she'd felt such a buzz of awareness with a man. And their conversation out there on the lake had only added to that feeling. Something about that little dent in his armor had endeared Rory to her.

"You're welcome." His eyes went a deep sky blue, showing her his awareness of the ripple moving over them like a current. "As I said, anytime."

"I...I'd better get home," she said, pulling away to steady herself. "I've still got lots to do."

Rory tugged the kayaks away from the landing. "Okay."

"Do you need help? I can carry one of these."

"No. I can't make you carry these heavy things."

"I don't mind." She flexed her arms. "I'm not helpless, you know."

He swept her with an appreciative look. "Yes, I've noticed that, but I've got it." Then, he grinned. "I enjoyed having someone to tour the lake with. And to talk to."

"Me, too." She turned to go, feeling as if she'd done something wrong. Her abrupt nature could scare anyone away.

"Hey?"

She whirled. "Yes?"

"You're welcome to come to Youth Night if you'd like. I can always use volunteers, especially female volunteers. We get a lot of girls in, and they don't want to open up to a male minister." He shrugged. "It's a tough gig, but we're always looking for mentors."

Vanessa's heart started racing. She felt even more winded than she had after kayaking around the lake. "I…I'll have to think about that and let you know. I'm not sure I'll be here long enough to get involved."

"Okay. But even attending a few meetings can make a world of difference for someone." He gave her one of his dazzling grins. "We order pizza and sometimes watch movies."

"Sounds like fun." Or something she couldn't deal with.

After thanking him again, she escaped to the darkness of the house, shutting the door and leaning back against it. Closing her eyes, Vanessa wished she'd had a better answer than a stumbling, halting maybe. Could she be any more obvious?

But being around troubled teens? Did she want to live through that kind of turmoil again? Even if she wasn't the one going through it?

She'd have to really think hard on how to handle that request. With each invitation, Rory was also drawing her in more and more.

In spite of that, she liked him. A lot. But she did not like the idea of getting involved in church. At all.

"What should I do?" she asked the darkness. "What should I do?" she asked God.

She remembered when she'd been alone and frightened, with no one to talk to because she was so afraid no one would believe her. Her own mother hadn't believed her, so why would anyone else?

What if one girl out there needed a friend, someone she could trust?

It doesn't have to be me.

But why shouldn't it be you?

Going to the refrigerator, she found a bottle of water and opened it and took a long drink. Why not her? What else did she have to do besides go through this sad, cluttered house and then leave town once it was sold?

No commitment. Just a helping hand.

She could do this. She needed to do this.

Even if she'd vowed never to have children of her own, she might be able to help a teenager at least. Now she'd have to find the courage to take those few steps to the church doors.

Rory checked the snack table. Mr. and Mrs. Peppermon had outdone themselves tonight. The couple fostered two of the teens who attended Youth Night, and they always insisted on helping with the food, too. In spite of their tight budget and dealing with their grandchildren's busy schedules, they loved helping out at the church. Devoted. They were devoted.

Rory thanked the Lord for that.

"Hello."

He turned to find Miss Fanny ambling into the small gathering room at the back of the church. "Hey, there. What are you doing here?"

"I was in the neighborhood," she said, coy. "I made some oatmeal cookies, and I can't possibly eat all of them. Thought the kids might enjoy them."

Rory gave her a hug. "Of course they'll love your cookies. And you can visit with them and have dinner with us since you *live* in the neighborhood."

"I'd like that." She grinned and glanced around. "Is your new friend coming tonight?"

"My new friend?"

"Vanessa. I've tried to catch her coming and going to introduce myself, but she's too quick for me."

"She is a slippery little thing," Rory retorted. "And I did invite her to come. But…she's still a bit gun-shy."

"We can fix that by making her feel better about things."

"Right." Rory thought about how he'd botched that idea out on the lake the other day. He hadn't talked to Vanessa since. For oh so many reasons. "I think we should let her hang out and see how it goes."

"Okay, I'll mind my own business," Miss Fanny said, her pink hat full of real flowers and plastic Easter eggs. "She won't even know I'm here."

Rory grinned and offered Miss Fanny a chair. "The kids should be arriving soon."

Wanda Peppermon came out of the small church kitchen, carrying a huge casserole dish of lasagna, the spicy scent wafting straight toward Rory's hungry nose.

"Let me help with that," he said, grabbing the pot holders and the dish from her. "You didn't have to cook, you know. We have a hefty pizza budget."

"I know," Wanda said, her salt-and-pepper hair curling against the collar of her blousy shirt. "But Kandi loves homemade lasagna, so I thought this might cheer her up. She's been in a mood all week."

Rory searched the room. "Where is Kandi?"

"Outside, sitting on a bench. She didn't want to come tonight. I think it's got something to do with her mother's birthday. It's this week."

Rory's heart went out to the pretty teen. Her mother died when she was ten and she never knew her daddy, so she'd been forced into the foster program. She'd resented the world for a long time now.

"Should I go and talk to her?" Rory asked Wanda.

"Let her sit a while," Wanda said. "She'll be in when the others start coming. She has her eye on a boy she met in school, and I'm not so sure that's a good idea. He's not exactly a good influence, so we've been keeping an eye on that situation."

Rory nodded. "Okay. We'll give her some space. I'll go help Carl with the cups and ice."

Wanda chuckled. "Check on my husband's choice of drinks, too. He got sugary soda when I told him to get lemonade."

"We can have both," Rory said. "I have big cans of powdered lemonade."

Rory glanced around one more time when he heard the door to the sunny gathering hall opening. Would Vanessa show up?

Chapter Seven

Vanessa stood on the front steps of her house, casting covert glances over at the church. She'd been standing there at least ten minutes, watching as a few adults and several teenagers trickled into the church gathering room.

She should go on over there and get it over with. She'd gone by Marla's Marvelous Desserts and bought two dozen cupcakes, and she sure couldn't eat them all by herself.

Well, actually she could do that. But she shouldn't. She wouldn't. Unless tonight went badly, and then she'd bring them back home and eat at least three. But she'd promised Marla she would make an effort.

"Oh, please do," Marla had said, all cheery and smiling. "Rory tries so hard, and a lot of these kids need the affirmation of good adult friends. You'll be perfect, Vanessa."

Not so perfect but she was interested.

Steeling herself, she grabbed the cupcake boxes and checked her black jersey flared skirt and floral T-shirt. She'd pass muster since most of the teens were wearing shorts and T-shirts anyway.

Halfway there, she noticed a young girl sitting on the top of an old picnic table near the curb. The girl looked so dejected and alone, Vanessa's heart went out to her. Maybe she'd come inside and Vanessa could meet her. But what would they talk about? The weather? The latest movies?

Vanessa felt out of her element. How could she even think she might be able to be some sort of mentor to a troubled teen? She'd be leaving soon and besides, she avoided children like the plague.

As she neared the church, the girl glanced up and right into Vanessa's eyes with a daring stare full of attitude. She had short brown spiked hair and wore a torn bright blue T-shirt over baggy black pants, the dark kohl around her eyes matching her even blacker lace-up boots. Bangles and string bracelets of every shape and color folded against each other like an accordion up and down both her wrists. And a big clunky necklace full of various charms weighed down her neck like an albatross.

Immediately intrigued, Vanessa smiled. "Hi," she said as she neared the girl.

The girl kept staring but didn't say anything.

Vanessa tried again. "I...uh...I love your jewelry. Eclectic."

A distrustful stare followed by surprise and a mumbled, "Thanks."

"Are you going inside?"

"I'm waiting for someone."

"I'm new here," Vanessa said, her heart hurting for this girl. She looked forlorn and lost, and her attitude was too familiar. "I kind of dread going in there."

The girl gave her another bored glance. "Why?"

"I don't like being part of organized religion."

A snort followed by another baffled stare. "Then why are you here?"

Vanessa moved a couple of feet closer. "I don't know, really. It's just that—"

A tall, lanky boy with jet-black hair walked up behind the girl and put his arms around her waist. Giving Vanessa a sullen glance, he said, "Hey, baby," into the girl's triple-pierced ear.

"Rocky," the girl said with a real smile that made her beautiful. "I thought you'd ditched me."

"Never. But you could ditch this stupid place and come with me."

The girl shot Vanessa a glance—part tell-me-stay and part don't-you-dare-stop-me.

Vanessa saw trouble all over this. "Hey, let's get inside before all the food is gone."

The girl glanced back at Romeo-Dracula and then gave Vanessa a strange glaring look. "I have to go inside, Rocky. My foster mom won't let me leave with you. So if you don't want to stay, I guess we can't do anything together after all."

Rocky shot Vanessa an accusing stare full of blame. "So, don't ask her. This nice lady won't tell, will you?"

Vanessa stepped closer. "I don't want to sound bossy, but you really should come inside with me. You're right. Your foster mother will be worried."

"Hey, lady, back off," Tall, Dark and Pale said, his winged eyebrows reminding Vanessa of a skinny bat.

The girl whirled on him. "She's trying to be nice."

"Nice?" The boy stepped away as if he'd been burned. "Nice? Is that seriously a word?"

"It is if you know how to use your manners," the girl said. "Which you obviously don't."

"Whatever!"

The boy gave Vanessa a rage-filled glare and turned to stalk away. The girl hopped off the bench and almost went after him. But she pivoted instead, her face full of a jagged resolve. "Well, that didn't last very long."

"I'm sorry," Vanessa said. "I shouldn't have interfered."

But she was glad she had.

The girl brushed past her with more than a dollop of swagger. "I was gonna break up with him anyway."

Vanessa wanted to say something else when she looked up to find Rory standing outside the gathering hall doors, a surprised grin on his handsome face.

"How much of that did you hear?" Vanessa asked Rory after Kandi whirled past him with her gaze on her boots.

"Enough," he said, wondering why Vanessa and Kandi had been talking in the first place. "Did she say something smart-alecky to you?"

"No. We were beginning to have a conversation when some sort of Goth James Dean tried to entice her to go away with him."

Rory took in Vanessa's pretty outfit and the white boxes marked with Marla's trademark dessert label. "So…you stopped Kandi from making a really bad mistake?"

"I suggested we should go inside, yes."

"Good move. Wanda, her foster mother, told

me Kandi has been hanging out with a boy who might not be suitable. So where is Mr. Wonderful?"

"He got mad and swooped away after Kandi basically told him to get some manners."

"Good for her." Rory took the pastry boxes. "You brought goodies."

"I wasn't sure what to bring," Vanessa said, looking as if she'd like to run back home. "I wasn't sure if I'd even come."

"I know." He leaned close. "You can leave at any time. We have several exit doors."

She gave him one of her half smiles. "Thanks." Then she glanced toward the door to the building. "So that girl, Kandi, is in the foster program?"

"Yes. She just turned sixteen. Lost her mother when she was ten and never knew her father. The Peppermons have had her for about six months now. She's a handful but she's been through a lot. She's been better lately, but her mom's birthday is this week. She would have been thirty-two if she'd lived."

Shock registered on Vanessa's face. "She died?"

"In a car wreck. She was drinking and driving. She had Kandi when she was sixteen, so I'm sure the whole thing is weighing on the girl."

The shock changed to understanding. "Oh. That's horrible."

Rory wondered if Vanessa was thinking of her own mother. "Yep. Kandi's acting out because she misses her mother. She has no grandparents who live near. Her mother's parents live in California and don't really want anything to do with her since she gave them so much trouble when they did try to raise her."

They strolled into the long building behind the church. "I can't imagine that," Vanessa said. "Even on our worst days, my mother and I still tried to communicate. Obviously, we never succeeded but still…"

"Maybe you two were closer than you realized."

She glanced around the room full of teens of various sizes and ages. "Maybe so. I guess we'll never know now, will we?"

Then she took the pastry boxes from him and marched toward the food table.

Rory decided Kandi wasn't the only female around here with attitude. But Vanessa had pushed aside her issues to come tonight. It was a start. He followed her and began introducing her to various people.

"I think you met Kandi Jordan outside," he said to Vanessa when they walked by the girl. "Kandi, this is my friend Vanessa Donovan.

She lives across the street, but she's only here for a few weeks. She came back to clean out her house and sell it."

Kandi shot Vanessa a sullen glance. "Why are you selling your house?"

Vanessa's eyes grew wide with concern. "My mother died a few weeks ago. I don't want to live here so I have to sell it."

Rory filled in the blanks to keep the awkwardness at bay. "Vanessa loves vintage stuff, and she's agreed to hold her estate sale in conjunction with our rummage sale here at the church. If you volunteer to help out, I'm sure you might find some cool items."

"I don't need anything," Kandi said before turning away to talk to another girl.

But Rory saw the way she sent a kohl-eyed glance back at Vanessa. "I think she's warming up to you," he whispered to Vanessa.

"Right." Vanessa shook her head. "Reminds me of myself at that age."

"I imagine you were cute at that age."

"I was a real pill," she replied. "All gangly legs and messy hair. And braces."

"I wore braces," he said. When he spotted Miss Fanny, he nudged Vanessa toward where the older woman sat holding court. "I want you to meet someone."

Miss Fanny looked up at Rory with a wide

smile, and then her gaze moved to Vanessa, her hands going to her mouth.

"Miss Fanny, this is Vanessa. Your neighbor."

"Hello," Vanessa said, her eyes moving from the woman in the chair to Rory, a questioning look in her eyes. "It's nice to meet you."

"You look like your mama," Miss Fanny said. "She was a pretty woman."

"You knew my mother?" Vanessa asked, her words caught on a breath of surprise. She sent Rory another glance, this one with a tad of accusation coloring it. He didn't remind her that he'd mentioned this to her.

"I sure did," Miss Fanny said before Vanessa could argue the point. "We were good friends back in the day. Artists, you know. Sensitive and so sure we could save the world with words and colors. I live right next to your house. I wish I could talk to her over the fence one more time."

Vanessa's eyes went misty. "Me, too." Then she gave Rory an expression full of pain. "It's good to see you. I…I think I need to find the ladies' room."

"Down the hallway," Miss Fanny said, pointing. After Vanessa hurried away, she lifted her eyes to Rory. "I didn't mean to upset her."

"She's still grieving," Rory explained. "In more ways than one."

"Grief never really goes away," Miss Fanny said, eyeing the hallway. "I could go and check on her."

"I think she'd rather be alone right now," Rory said. "I'll send someone in if she's not out soon." He checked his watch. "I need to bless the food so we can get started."

But he took one more glance toward the ladies' room. Would Vanessa come out, or would she sneak out the back door and go home?

She should go home.

Vanessa blew her nose and stared at herself in the mirror, her gaze moving over the fresh flowers on the vanity and the picture of a mother and child walking along the lake centered on the wall over an inviting wooden bench. When she heard someone coming in, she threw the tissue in the trash and pushed at her hair.

Kandi stood behind her with big eyes wide with questions. "So…your mother died?"

Vanessa put on a brave face. "Yes. She'd been sick for a while."

"My mom died in a bad wreck. Her birthday is Friday."

Vanessa turned to face the girl and noticed her vivid green eyes. "I'm so sorry to hear that."

"I was young," Kandi said. She shrugged and leaned over the counter, her black polished nails raking through the tufts of spiky hair around her face. "I don't really remember much about her."

Right. A ten-year-old would remember a lot of things.

Vanessa figured Kandi remembered way more than she needed to. "Do you have pictures of her? Things that might help you remember?"

Another shrug and then a swipe at dark red lips. "I have two pictures. I'm in one. And I have some clothes and stuff. I move around a lot, so I don't have much of anything."

"The Peppermons seem nice," Vanessa said, not wanting to upset the girl.

"Nice." Kandi actually cracked a smile. "There's that word again."

"Yep." Vanessa smiled right back, remembering how that seemed to be her new word. "Let's change it to special, understanding, sweet, tolerant—"

"Fun, playful, determined, demanding, fair," Kandi finished. "I like them. I didn't like some of the others."

A dark shadow passed over the girl's eyes. A shadow that Vanessa recognized immediately. But before she could ask Kandi if anything had happened to her in one of the other homes, a woman poked her head inside the door.

"Preacher wanted me to check on you two and tell you supper is served."

"We'll be right out," Vanessa said. "Ready, Kandi?"

The girl nodded and brushed past the woman at the door. "As ready as I'll ever be."

Vanessa and the woman exchanged knowing glances. "I know that feeling," she said with a smile.

The woman grinned. "Me, too." Then she gave Vanessa a big smile. "I'm Barbara, by the way. I'm the church secretary."

"Nice to meet you," Vanessa said. She cringed inwardly. That word *nice* was being overused today.

When Vanessa came back up the hall, she saw Rory and waved. He walked over to her. "Want to sit with Miss Fanny and me? Or do you want me to walk you home with a to-go plate?"

"I'm staying," she said, her tone firm. "I'm hungry."

"That's a good sign," he said.

But Vanessa wasn't staying for the food. She wanted to get to know Kandi a little better. Because she needed to know if that young girl had suffered the same humiliation that she had.

And if so, she intended to do something about it.

Chapter Eight

Vanessa listened while Rory did his thing. He read a short devotional about accepting God's love and allowing the Lord to love us.

"Sometimes, we think we're not worthy of God's love," he explained. "But if we think that, we're doing the Lord a disservice. He died for our sins. That makes us worthy. We need to honor His sacrifice by accepting His love into our hearts."

And that was it. No shout-outs about sinners. No condemnations about not sitting in church every Sunday. After the devotional, Rory asked some questions and got the kids to talking. He glanced at her a couple of times, his smile so sure and full of life that Vanessa had to swallow back the pain that seemed to clog her throat.

Why couldn't she feel that kind of peace and joy?

Was she worthy?

Or was she being too cynical for her own good?

"What if we don't deserve God's love?"

She glanced around to find a young boy sitting toward the back. Rory nodded at the boy, too.

"Hi, Mark," Rory said. "That's a good question. And the answer is even better. We *don't* really deserve God's love, but we are worthy. That probably doesn't make a lot of sense, but we're worthy only because we are alive and because God's love is unconditional. So that makes all of us worthy in His eyes even if we don't feel worthy."

"I don't get it," Mark said with a shrug. "Why would God want to fool with someone like me?"

"You don't have to actually get it all the time," Rory said. "But stay open to the possibilities. A lot can happen when you're open to love. Good things can happen—to you, to me, to anyone who wants the Lord in their life."

"Not always. Bad things can happen, too."

Kandi.

Vanessa's gaze slammed into Rory's, and she saw the understanding and compassion in his eyes. "You got me there, Kandi," he said. "I've had some bad things happen in my life and… it's not easy. I turned on God, ranted at Him.

And then I made some bad choices to prove my point."

"How'd you become a preacher then?" someone else asked.

Rory's gaze locked on Vanessa. "I kind of went into a bad spot, and then I went to war."

Vanessa tried to remain passive. Marla had mentioned Rory had served as an army chaplain, but it sounded as if he'd gone to war to fight. Or maybe to escape?

Kandi lifted her gaze to Vanessa. "Have you had anything bad happen to you, besides your mother dying?"

Still reeling from Rory's candid admission, Vanessa nodded. "Yes. I've been hurt by people. At times I feel as if God has abandoned me." Because she didn't like being pinned to the spot, she shrugged. "But I've managed to take care of myself for a very long time."

"Don't we need God in our lives?" another teen asked, his eyes wide with hope. "To help us through the tough times?"

"Yes," Rory said. "Yes, we do. But it's hard sometimes to see that. Christ offers us comfort when we feel alone and abandoned, even if we can't understand how it all works."

"I pray," someone else said. "I pray and hope...and I wait."

A petite blonde bobbed her head. "Me, too."

Kandi rolled her eyes and sliced her fingers through her hair, her gaze still on Vanessa. "I'm tired of waiting."

Vanessa certainly knew that feeling. But maybe waiting was all part of the process. Maybe she needed to be still and listen. And wait.

"You went to war," Vanessa whispered to Rory a while later, her gaze full of questions. "Marla mentioned you were a chaplain, but I didn't think of that as being dangerous. I mean, it is dangerous but I didn't understand why you joined up. It sounded as if you were pretty angry about a lot of things."

Rory wasn't ready to talk about this. He rarely talked about his past to anyone. But this was Vanessa. It wouldn't be fair to her that he'd tried so hard to draw her into his world without telling her a little about himself.

"I should have explained it to you."

And he should have explained things when that kid had asked, but he'd managed to get by with a vague response about joining the army and really seeing what life and death were all about. It wasn't enough and it didn't give anyone any answers. Rory didn't have all the answers. Who did?

He needed to tell Vanessa the truth, at least.

But not yet. "I had some issues," he said, hoping to leave it at that.

"So you were mad at God?"

"Yep. I was so mad at the world and at God that I up and joined the army. I'd finished seminary, and I thought I was ready to find my first church home and I did. But I kind of messed up things from the get-go."

"Why were you so angry?" she asked, surprise in every word.

Rory guided her toward her house. Everyone else had left, including Miss Fanny. He'd offered to walk Vanessa home and she'd accepted, but only because she obviously wanted him to finish his story.

"That's for another night," he said, not ready to bare his soul. He glanced back toward the church. "I hear you and Kandi plan to meet up at Wanda's house once you're all cleared to become a mentor."

"Yes." She looked uncertain and maybe a little disappointed that he wasn't telling all. "I'm nervous."

"Listening is key when you're a mentor to a troubled teen."

"I don't know if I can do that. What if I mess up?"

"You can't mess up. Wanda will monitor you two and help you out." He shifted on his dock shoes. "But we made progress tonight, don't you think?"

She stopped at the steps to her house. "Oh, you mean, you got me across the street? So now, you'll keep stringing me along with little tidbits of your story so I'll keep coming back?"

"I'm not stringing you along," he said, wondering if she had him pegged. "I have a past, too, Vanessa. And I don't always like to talk about it."

"You?" Her eyes glistened in the moonlight. "You have a past?"

"It happens," he said on a defensive note. "It happens to most people, you know. We all make mistakes or have bad times."

"But you, not you." She sat down on the porch steps. "You're so...well...nice." She groaned. "I've used that word way too much tonight, but it fits with you."

"Sometimes nice guys make bad mistakes," he said. "Nice can cover a multitude of sins."

She looked surprised. "Can you tell me a little about what happened and why?"

Rory took that as an invitation and sat down next to her. "Why me?" He gazed out at the moonlight hitting the lake in a gray-white shimmer. "I can tell you this much. I...was an orphan."

"What?" She twisted to stare over at him. "You were a foster kid?"

"Yes." He gave her one quick glance and then turned back toward the night. "I bounced around a lot but when I was twelve years old I came here to live with a wonderful couple who decided to adopt me. We moved to Crestview when I was a teenager. But I didn't stay there, obviously. I left right after I graduated high school."

"Where did you go after that?"

"I got a job and paid my way through college." He stopped and took a breath. "I went to seminary and set out to be a minister but...I had a few setbacks. I was angry and confused, so I wound up joining the army."

He hadn't talked about that part of his life in a long time. His buddies knew he was adopted and that he'd served as a chaplain, but they didn't even know all of the details about his adult life and they didn't ask. They knew Rory would talk about it when he was ready.

But could he ever be ready?

Vanessa sat staring at him. "You decided to join the army because you were angry? Were you angry because you were a foster kid?"

"Yes," he said. It had started there. He still didn't know who his real parents were. "I guess I was angry for most of my life, even after I was placed with good parents. I was abandoned as a baby. And my adopted father died when I was a teenager. My mother is still alive, thankfully. She still lives in Crestview."

Vanessa didn't speak for a couple of moments. "Wow."

"Yep, wow."

"I'm sorry. I mean, that's tough."

"Tough comes in all kinds of ways, to all kinds of people."

"But that really *is* tough."

"I got over it."

"You are full of revelations, Preacher."

"Yep. We all are." He wanted to hear her revelations.

"So is that why you started this youth program?"

"One of the reasons. I want to help them, give them hope before they do something stupid. I understand how they feel."

"I do, too," she said, her tone quiet. "I'd like to get to know Kandi a little more. What should I do besides visit with her and Wanda?"

Happy that she'd decided that, Rory turned to Vanessa. "I'm sure Wanda told you there are rules, of course, to protect the children. You'd be vetted and you can't be alone with her, so that's why you have to meet her with Wanda nearby, probably at their house and at the church, of course. We get together each week, and each mentor sits with their teen. Let her talk without judging her and respond as a friend, as someone who cares."

"Okay. I…I'm not good with children. I don't know if I'll ever have any of my own."

Rory muzzled his surprise with a laugh. "I don't think anyone feels they're good with children until they actually have children."

"And sometimes, they're not good then either," she said on a quiet whisper.

Before he could respond, she pushed to stand. "I should get inside."

Rory stood, too, and placed his hand on her elbow to steady her. "And I should get back to the church. I have to check everything and lock up."

Their eyes met, the moonlight playing over them like a diffused spotlight. Rory saw so much in her gaze, but he also saw the hidden things. "I'm glad you came," he said, his throat going raw with a huskiness that seemed too intimate.

"Me, too." She didn't move to go inside. She kept her eyes on him. "I hope Kandi will let me get to know her."

"We'll try it," he said, stepping back. "I'll help you with her. She's a special girl, and she could use a friend."

Vanessa nodded and looked out at the lake. "I guess we could all use a friend at times." Then she smiled at him. "I hope one day, you'll tell me the rest of your story, Rory."

Rory wanted to hug her close. This was crazy. Feelings he'd long buried swirled and resurfaced in a different current, in a new pattern. But this time, with a different woman. A woman who didn't want children. A woman who might not want anyone.

But she needed someone. And she needed to believe in herself, too.

Suddenly, Rory couldn't breathe, couldn't decide whether to run away or move closer. He'd vowed never to fall in love again. It hurt too much.

He'd only planned to minister to this woman.

Now he also wanted to kiss this woman.

"Vanessa," he said, about to explain why he couldn't do this, why he wasn't ready for this.

"I have to go," she said, moving up the steps.

"Me, too." He stepped down to the walkway. "I'll see you…later."

She turned at the door. "Yes, later."

And then she was inside. Out of his reach.

Rory took his time getting back to the church. He had some serious praying to do. But he wasn't sure how to pray. Did he ask God to bring him closer to Vanessa? Did he ask in a spiritual way? Or did he plain out ask God to help him in a romantic way?

Was he finally ready to love again?

* * *

The next day, Vanessa stared at her mother's cluttered bedroom. In the early-morning light, it looked even worse. Gaudy and tarnished, dusty and dirty. Sad. When had Cora gone from being an artist to becoming a hoarder?

Maybe after you left?

But her mother had been happy with Richard. That marriage had worked out for the better. Richard Tucker was a decent, loving man. He'd spent his time divided between this home and the big house in Birmingham, and her mother had traveled with him. But he'd also been a busy man who owned several vast properties and businesses. Had Cora felt lonely and neglected? She must have been lonely after Richard died.

Vanessa remembered arguing with her mother, trying to make her see that Gregory Pardue had been a bad man. Cora wouldn't hear any of it.

"I don't believe you. You're angry that we moved here. You ran him off, you know. Your lies forced Gregory to leave me."

"I'm getting away from here," Vanessa had screamed. "As soon as I can."

A few weeks later, her mother was back out there, trolling for another husband. And she'd found Richard Tucker. Richard had calmed both of them.

Vanessa had attended his funeral in Birmingham, but she hadn't stayed around to help her mother with anything. Selfish? Or part of Vanessa's need for self-preservation?

She should have stayed a few days longer, but Cora had a way of starting in on people that soon turned to playing a blame game. Vanessa blamed herself enough without having to hear it from someone else.

Her mother had always been needy.

And Vanessa had fought hard never to need anyone.

"Time to get this over with," she said to the dust balls floating all around her. And to the guilt hovering on her shoulders. She'd avoided this room. Keeping the door to the other bedroom closed had been easy. That room had been Vanessa's. She didn't sleep there. She'd been sleeping on the couch in the den and sometimes on the rattan sofa out in the enclosed sunroom on the far side of the house.

But she couldn't put this off any longer. She'd have to clean all of the bedrooms, starting with her mother's and working her way through the small room her mother had used mostly for storage and more collectibles. And then, what had once been Vanessa's room.

Deciding to start with one corner of the big master bedroom, she planned to work her way around the perimeter. The dresser begged to be rescued from the weight of too many paperbacks and old newspapers. No telling what she'd find, but it would be good to have one clean surface.

After dragging a trash can over by the window, Vanessa opened the drapes wide and then pried the window up to let in some fresh air. Then she leaned against the windowsill and thought about Rory.

Why did he tug at her heartstrings so much?

Vanessa went over her usual checklist for men.

Kind. Cute. Steady income. Respectful to women and children. Good with animals. Hardworking and compassionate.

Rory fit the bill more than anyone else she'd ever come close to dating.

But he couldn't. He shouldn't. He was a preacher. So not her type at all. Plus, she hadn't come here to date anyone. She couldn't consider Rory as anything but a friend.

And what do you have to base that on besides an older man who had his own agenda?

Rory had secrets. Now that he'd admitted that to her, Vanessa had one very good reason to avoid him. She didn't like secrets. She'd carried hers long enough to know how they could fester and destroy anything good.

But he's different. Rory is a good person.

Vanessa turned away from the window and the view of the quaint church across the street. She'd never even noticed that church when she'd lived here. Nor did she remember Miss Fanny from next door. Probably because she had been so self-absorbed and so intent on making her mother miserable that she didn't have room in her heart for anything else.

"I'm paying for that now," she said into the morning breeze. "And I'm praying about it, too. In case anyone is listening up there."

Determination made her start digging through the rubble of this room. After about an hour of tossing magazines and sorting through clippings of projects her mother had never started, her hand hit on a leather-bound book. Dusty and worn, it looked like a notebook.

She turned it over and saw a lock on it.

A journal?

Her mother's journal?

She held it close, wondering if she should throw it away without trying to read it or if she should tear it open and find a quiet spot to pore over the whole thing.

When she heard a knock at the door, she jumped and tossed the journal onto the old faded-blue chenille bedspread. Thinking she should ignore the knock, Vanessa checked her hair in case it was Rory.

She looked like she'd just woken up, all smudged and unkempt. Well, he'd get to see the real Vanessa.

But it wasn't Rory standing at her door.

The older woman she'd met last night stood there, leaning on a cane, her big floppy straw hat covered with tiny plastic daisies. "Hello, Vanessa. Remember me? I live next door."

"Miss Fanny, right?" Vanessa asked, surprised to see the woman. "How are you?"

"I'm good, darlin'. I baked you some braided bread. It's mighty good with butter and jam for breakfast."

"Oh, how nice." Vanessa took the foil-wrapped bread. It was still warm, the scent tickling at her nose. "It sure smells good."

"I can assure you, it is good. I've been baking that bread for over forty years. My husband, Herbert, liked it with lasagna."

Vanessa's stomach growled in glee. "I haven't had breakfast. Maybe I'll just have a nibble." She gave Miss Fanny a smile and waited for the woman to leave.

Which she didn't.

"Do you have any tea?" Miss Fanny asked. "I have a hankering to sit out in the garden and drink some hot tea. You could join me, and we could slice up that bread."

Vanessa couldn't say no. Miss Fanny had brought her food…and this woman had known her mother. Maybe they could compare notes. "You know, I've been going through my mother's bedroom, clearing out the junk, and I need a break. We could sit out in the sunporch. I have the windows open, and it's nice and shady. If you'd like to come inside, I'll make the tea and slice the bread."

"I'd love that," Miss Fanny said. "I know my way to the porch, suga'. Your mother and I used to sit out there a lot."

Vanessa held the door while Miss Fanny took her time moving inside. Then she led the way to the back of the house. The French doors to the sunporch were open. "I did clean the porch the other day. I like it out here."

"I'll find a chair and wait for you," Miss Fanny said, her gaze settling on the pillow and blanket on the sofa. "We have a lot to talk about."

Vanessa glanced toward the bedroom where the journal lay on the big bed. She itched to read that journal. But maybe she did need to wait a while.

She had little time to spare, but talking to someone who might actually shed some light on her mother's strange but colorful life could be a step toward forgiveness and understanding. And besides, Miss Fanny was safe and comfortable and easy to talk to.

Not like the preacher across the street. He was easy to talk to, of course. Too easy. Too tempting. But he deserved someone special in his life. A woman who'd be willing to help him serve the people he loved.

Vanessa needed to get to know a few more people while she was here. Just for variety. And for her sanity.

Because having bread and tea with a lonely but considerate old woman had to be safer than standing in the moonlight with Rory Sanderson.

Chapter Nine

The weekend stretched out before Vanessa like a welcoming beach blanket. The sun was shining and the humidity was low for a change. Spring popped out on every corner and in every color, bringing the fragrances of a thousand blossoms wafting out over the warm breeze.

Standing at one of the open windows, Vanessa inhaled the scents of jasmine, honeysuckle and gardenias. Her mother had always loved gardenias. When Richard had heard Cora talking about the sweet-smelling plants, he'd ordered several from the local nursery and had them planted by both the front and back doors.

"When you sit on either of the porches, darlin'," he'd told Cora in his cultured Alabama voice, "you'll be able to enjoy your gardenias."

Why couldn't Richard have come into their lives earlier? Vanessa thought how different things might have been. Stability, love, hope, contentment, joy. All of those things could have been theirs. But instead, Vanessa had been pulled from pillar to post, and Cora had been used and abused by men who didn't care about or respect women.

Not even when one of those men had been a so-called minister.

Turning from the window, Vanessa stared at the racks full of clothes and the card tables covered with knickknacks she planned to display at the estate sale.

Making a mental note to check one last time with the newspaper about the ad, Vanessa walked through the house again. So much left to throw out, give away or sell. But she had found some gems.

Gorgeous retro dresses from the sixties and seventies and beautiful pieces of costume jewelry, several shelves of books and cabinets full of old china and valuable ceramics.

Her mother had collected odds and ends for her art, but she'd also collected designer shoes and handbags and exquisite Hull vases and Roseville pottery. Each husband or boyfriend had bought Cora things, hoping to make her love them.

Cora had loved Richard. But Vanessa had to wonder if he hadn't died a few years after they'd gotten married, would Cora have turned on him, too?

This house was a gold mine.

But Vanessa figured the real jewel would be her mother's journal. She'd only found the one. Could there be more, hidden somewhere else? Would she find out anything about her absent father in there?

I'm too afraid to read it.

She shook her head, hoping to get back on track. She'd learned not to ask Cora about her father, so why start wondering now? She had too much to do.

Vanessa would keep some of the items and sell the rest on Vanessa's Vintage. She'd already taken photos and cataloged those and put them up on the site. Those items would be shipped to buyers or to the small warehouse she rented in New Orleans. She could sell the jewelry and clothes in her boutique, but she'd wait until after the estate sale to see how much was left.

She'd read that journal when she was done here. Somehow, she couldn't bring herself to do so until she'd cleared up this house. But with each room, a new revelation came. She'd found some of her mother's artwork tucked away in a big closet.

Cora had been a talented artist. Her mother had created whimsical pieces out of mixed media. Big metal flowers stuffed with bits of fabric and button faces. Pretty picture frames made from old jewelry and exotic materials. Purses and hats covered with feathers and flowers. She'd have to save a couple of those for Miss Fanny. Their talk yesterday had helped put some of the pieces together.

"Your mother was a good person, honey. She stumbled a bit."

Vanessa could certainly vouch for that. "I wish I could have really known her," she told Miss Fanny. "The way you did. I watched her work, of course, but she didn't share her artistic side with me very much."

"She didn't share that with anyone," Miss Fanny said. "I had to force her to share with me. She was afraid someone would steal her ideas."

"She always was possessive." Of her art and her men. But not her only child. Cora would shut herself away in the old garage out back—her studio. Even now, Vanessa expected her mother to bark, "Go away, I'm working," when she entered the doors.

Miss Fanny took a sip of tea. "She had a jealous streak."

Miss Fanny told Vanessa stories of their time together, which happened mostly during the hours when Vanessa was at school. Sweet stories that showed a side of Cora that Vanessa had never noticed. They went to the beach together and shopped and ate meals together. Miss Fanny's husband tolerated these outings since he was a professor and was always buried in a textbook. And Miss Fanny tolerated Cora's mood swings and constant self-doubts.

"We were back and forth across the yards. We'd go to art fairs and sit all day, hoping to sell one or two pieces. It wasn't a profitable life, but it was a good life. Your mother gained some notoriety as a local artist. After she married Richard, she was happy here until—"

"Until I left and then Richard died."

"Yes. She missed both of you terribly."

They'd talked a bit more before Miss Fanny went back home. But so much had been left unsaid. Vanessa wondered if her neighbor knew the truth, knew everything. Didn't good friends share such things? Had Cora walked across to the little white chapel and asked God to forgive her?

The phone rang, jarring Vanessa away from the dark memories.

"Hi, it's Marla. How's the sorting going?"

"Slow," Vanessa said. "How are you?"

"Busy," Marla replied. "A lot of birthday parties and anniversaries. Everyone wants cupcakes or a big cake. And graduations and Mother's Day are coming up. Busy blessed."

"You are blessed," Vanessa replied. "I'm preparing for the big sale and shipping things out for my online site."

"Need any help?"

"No. It's easier to take my time and do it by myself."

"Well, you also need a break. We're having a cookout Saturday. Want to come over?"

Vanessa glanced at the things still left undone. "That's tempting. A lot of people?"

"No. Just a few."

Would Rory be there?

She couldn't keep doing this. "I don't know—"

"Yes, Rory will be there," Marla said, her intuitive nature shining through. "Is that a deal breaker?"

"I'm not sure. I mean, he's nice and interesting and…kind."

"But?"

"But I…I want to get this over with and go back to my life."

And she needed to run away from Rory. She would only make him miserable.

"Is it that hard, going through her things?"

"Yes. And no. It's soothing in one way but horrible in another. I found her journal."

"Wow. Did you read it?"

"Not yet. I'm too chicken."

"It's yours now, Vanessa. And it might give you some answers."

"Or it could make things worse."

"You need to hear the good and the bad," Marla said. "Or you'll always wonder."

"I think you're right. I'll read it once I have things in order here."

They talked a few more minutes and then Marla asked, "So, do you want to come over for burgers or not?"

"I'll think about it and let you know. Thanks for inviting me."

She'd put down her phone when the doorbell rang.

Thinking she might not ever get back to work, Vanessa hurried to the door.

And opened it to find Rory standing there.

"Hi," she said, feeling like a guilty kid for having just talked about him. He wore casual clothes, as usual. A button-up shirt and jeans, dock shoes, no socks.

Again, so different from the image of a minister she held in her memories.

"Hi." He gave her that dazzling smile. "Uh… I was supposed to tell you that we're having a meeting about the rummage sale tonight. Barbara, my adorable and organized barracuda of a secretary, said you need to be there since you'll be having your estate sale at the same time.

We'll do flyers to advertise both so people will expect to find both, if you agree. She likes everything neat and tidy with no surprises."

Vanessa had to smile at that. "And you kind of go with the flow, right?"

"Right." He gave her a hopeful stare. "Can you come?"

He looked like a little boy, all grins and excitement.

Contagious.

He was contagious. And she was catching it bad.

"I guess that might be wise. I'll share the cost of the ads. I don't mind paying as a contribution."

"No, oh, no. We take care of such things with an army of stoic volunteers who take their jobs very seriously. Ad cost has been donated already. We might get a healthy competition going between us, though. So be warned."

"You're on," she replied with a smile. She'd give part of her final tally to the church. "What time is the meeting?"

"Six tonight." He glanced behind her. "Hey, you've made progress."

"Yes." She lifted a hand and ignored the warning bell inside her head. "Come in and take a glance."

"Are you sure?"

"Yes." She wasn't sure at all, but she liked being around him. "I've managed to get through a couple of rooms."

"I can't imagine having to do this. Each item must have a memory."

She nodded. "But they're more her memories than mine. Every now and then I find something that makes me remember more and more, though."

He trailed his fingers over an old leather jacket hanging on a rack. "Do you want to remember?"

"Not all of it, no. But it wasn't all bad. I can see that now."

"I've said it before but I'm offering again. I can help," he said, turning to her. "I want to help."

Vanessa wasn't sure. She couldn't let him in too close to her heart. "You mean, with my memories or this house?"

His eyes went a soft, gentle blue. "With whatever you need."

"Shouldn't you be out nurturing souls or comforting sick people?"

He actually snorted out a chuckle. "Yes, but wouldn't I be doing that by helping you?"

"Do you think I need nurturing or that I'm sick?"

He stepped closer, his blue eyes locking on

her. "I think you're grieving and dealing with a lot. You don't have to do it all alone."

"It's getting better," she said, wishing that were true. But pushing him away shielded her from breaking down completely.

He wasn't buying it, however. "Let me help, Vanessa."

Doubt clouded over her need to give in. Anger filtered through the tug and pull of his words. "Why do you want to help?"

"It's what I do. It's how I'm made." He shrugged. "And besides, I like being with you. Keeps Barbara from badgering me."

"Oh, so you came over here with an excuse about a meeting, but you really want to hide out from your secretary?"

"Yes, something like that."

She knew if she said yes to his offer, this would be a turning point between them. If she said no, he'd go on about his business but he'd keep trying. He *was* made that way.

"Okay," she said, the decision already set. Keeping her tone light, she added, "I do need a big strong man to do some heavy lifting."

"I don't see one of those," he quipped.

"I think you'll do just fine, Preacher."

He winked at her and flexed his muscles.

And Vanessa had to admit, he looked strong and healthy and...good. Too good. She willed herself to a calm she didn't feel. "Let's get started then."

"Lead the way," he said, right behind her.

Too close. But having him close was a new kind of sensation. A pleasant one.

Rory groaned and collapsed on the grass near the open doors of the garage. "Remind me to never, ever ask you if you need help again."

"You did keep after me."

He glanced up at the woman grinning down at him, her fawn-colored hair flowing like a mysterious waterfall around her face. "I did offer, yes."

And he would keep offering. This had gone from trying to get her back right with God to trying to find the courage to ask her out on a date. Could he witness to her over a candlelight dinner?

"I brought iced tea," she said, holding the big plastic cup out over him. Her moods were as swift and unpredictable as the waters out in the Gulf.

A cold drop of condensation hit Rory square on the forehead. "Hey!"

She laughed and backed away. "You might be more comfortable in a chair."

Rory got up and checked his watch. "Okay.

A quick drink and then I have to report back, or Barbara will send out a posse."

Vanessa gave him his tea and then took a sip of her own. "I didn't mean to keep you over here so long."

"It's fine. We don't have a lot going on." He shrugged. "Today is sermon day. I'm usually holed up in my office on Thursday afternoon, trying to decide what to say on any given Sunday."

"How *do* you decide what to say?" she asked, her ever-changing hazel eyes shining with questions.

Rory felt that rush of joy he always got whenever someone wanted to know about God. "I pray about it and I search the Scriptures and I follow the calendar—the seasons."

One of her eyebrows lifted while her eyes narrowed. "Ah, the seasons. You mean, like Christmas and Easter?"

"And a whole lot of other seasons," he replied. He could tell her all about that, but now that he'd moved from ministering to possibly making the moves on her, he had to tread very lightly. "Right now it's spring and the flowers are blooming and it's the season of rebirth and new beginnings. Spring always gives me hope."

"Hope?" She looked hopeful. She looked beautiful with the afternoon sun chasing at her.

"Yes, hope. We have to have hope, don't we?"

"I don't know," she said, her smile dimming. "I've forgotten what that's like."

"Well, then, we'll have to remedy that." He stood and drained the sweet, icy tea. "I will see you tonight for the meeting. That's the first order of business."

She followed him to the side gate. "And what's your next order of business after that, Preacher?"

Okay, she was flirting with him.

Now *he* was hopeful. He turned and lifted a finger to her wispy bangs. "That you'll have dinner with me one night soon."

She looked surprised, and then she looked confused. "Are you going to Marla's cookout this weekend?"

"Yes," he said, the one word hinging on so much. "Are you?"

"Yes." She didn't move. "We can let that be a test date."

"A test date? Is there such a thing?"

She turned and tossed a grin over her shoulder. "There is if you're asking *me*."

"Okay," he said, calling after her. "The cookout it is. I love cookouts." And he'd pass the test. He hoped.

"So do I," she shouted back. "I'll see you across the way, Preacher."

"Yes, ma'am."

Rory grinned all the way back to the church.

When he got to the office, he found Barbara standing there, staring up at him with a soft smile. "I think you got lost over there."

"You could say that," he replied. Then he went into his office and closed the door.

Or maybe he got *found*.

Chapter Ten

Well, she'd been in this spot before. Caught between a rock and a hard place, as her mother used to say.

Rory was coming by to walk Vanessa to the cookout. Which was a surprise since he'd been all business at the rummage sale meeting the other night. Nice, polite, full of charm and wit, but he'd also been focused and full of suggestions. He'd glanced at her a couple of times, but always with a shy smile.

He stated their business at the meeting. "So the plan is to open our gathering hall up for the public to come and shop at the Annual Millbrook Lake Church Rummage Sale."

He said this in a booming, official voice, a bit of mirth in his vivid eyes.

"And we'll send our shoppers over to Vanessa's estate sale and encourage them to find some good bargains there, too. Right, Vanessa?"

"Yes. I'll have it all organized and tagged so they can move from room to room. I'm willing to negotiate, too. I have to empty my house and put it up for sale."

Rory had nodded and moved on to other business, but she'd noticed that bit of regret in his gaze when he'd smiled at her.

Maybe he was being careful since several church members had attended the meeting, too. Not that it mattered. Nothing was going on between them.

But he'd called her early this morning. "Hey, want me to pick you up for the cookout?"

"Uh…it's a block down the street. I thought I'd walk."

"Yes, and I'm coming by to walk with you. I mean, if that's okay."

She almost giggled at the trepidation in his words. Was *that* okay? She'd see him there anyway. "I'd like that. Thanks."

So here she stood, staring in the mirror, wondering if she looked all right. She'd gone way casual, maybe to make a point. A white T-shirt, long jean shorts with rolled cuffs and a colorful scarf draped around her neck. Flip-flops and her hair down around her face. She didn't shout *needy*, but she didn't say *don't look at me* either.

The scarf was her mother's. One she'd found trailing on a closet hook like a clinging vine.

A knock at the door startled Vanessa away from the memories in the mirror. Grabbing the avocado dip she'd made and her phone, she tucked the phone in her pocket and started for the door.

"Hello," she said after opening the door.

The scent of fresh rain greeted her, but it hadn't rained today. Rory had obviously taken a shower since his hair was still damp and curling around his face, and he smelled so clean and outdoorsy she wanted to touch his forehead and play with that sun-streaked hair.

But she'd drop the bowl of dip if she did that.

"Hi," he replied with a smile. "You look great."

Pleased, and annoyed at herself for feeling pleased, she followed him out the door and made sure it was locked. "Thanks. I worked all day, loaded some pictures on to my site and made calls to some of my vendors, checked on my boutique in New Orleans—"

"Stop! You're making me tired."

She laughed at his mock look of fright. "So what did you do today?"

He glanced out at the lake. A sailboat drifted by like a white bird. "I got up early and went fishing with my friends, and then I came back and went over my sermon for tomorrow and did a little praying and then I took a nap and…now I'm here walking along a beautiful street with a pretty woman. Life is good."

His positive attitude amazed her. She wanted to know more about his life. He must have gone through hard times as a foster child, but now he was so full of life and hope. Contagious, but it was scary. Her heart bumped little beats of warnings coupled with little leaps of joy.

"What's in the bowl?" he asked, taking it from her.

"Hey!"

"I'm trying to be a gentleman. I'll carry it for you."

"It's guacamole dip. I don't cook a lot, but I do make a mean guacamole."

"Sounds good. I'm starving."

"Didn't you eat lunch?"

"Hours ago."

"Poor baby."

He rubbed his flat stomach. "Are we ever gonna get there?"

Vanessa breathed in the scent of jasmine and watched a flock of pelicans flying in a symmetrical line above them. "This is a nice town. I'd forgotten how idyllic it is here."

He let out a contented sigh. "Today is one of those good days where the humidity got zipped up in a big cloud somewhere on the other side of the world and the sun is clear and the air is crisp." He gave her a sideways glance. "And I'm escorting the prettiest girl on the lake to a picnic. Perfection."

"Do you flirt with all the single ladies in your flock?"

"My flock? What am I, a shepherd?"

"You're with a black sheep."

He looked surprised, his mouth opening to respond. But they had arrived at the open side gate to Alec and Marla's house. "I don't think of you that way," he blurted.

She couldn't help but tease. "You mean, in a flirting way? Or in a black sheep way?"

"Hello!"

Marla's greeting stopped him from replying, but he shot Vanessa a helpless look and gave her a shrug. When she smiled at him, he relaxed a little and followed her into the big backyard.

Marla had gone all out with checked tablecloths and Mason jars full of fresh flowers on each table. An old barrel held iced soft drinks and bottles of water. Up on the deep porch, a long table covered with the same checkered cloths held the side dishes and desserts.

Alec was holding court by a large grill full of burgers, chicken and ribs. He waved. "Hi. Glad you came."

Marla grabbed Vanessa by the arm while

Rory went off to talk to Alec. Vanessa noticed a dark-haired man with shaggy hair sitting off to the side, a canned soft drink in front of him on the table. And Gabby's poodle Roxie in his lap. "Who's that?"

"Hunter Lawson," Marla replied. "He's one of the four who own the camp house. But he comes and goes. He got back a few days ago. He's a private investigator now."

"And why is he holding Roxie when he doesn't look like the poodle-dog type?"

"Roxie used to be his—or she belonged to someone he cared about and he inherited her. For a long time, Roxie rode around with him on his motorcycle, but last year he gave her to Gabby. To help Gabby get over her anxieties around strangers. If we go anywhere in a crowd of people, Roxie wears her official service-dog vest."

Vanessa glanced back at the rugged-looking man staring off into space. "He gave Gabby the dog?"

Marla looked over at Vanessa, tears in her eyes. "It was one of the kindest gestures I've ever seen in my life, and I'll be forever thankful to him."

Vanessa didn't know what to say. You never knew about people. What had it cost Hunter to give up the little dog he so obviously loved?

What had it cost Rory to serve his country, trying to give people peace in a war-torn world?

Marla checked the food table and turned back toward the kitchen. "I'm going to see about Gabby. She should be waking from her nap soon. Oh, and Blain and Rikki are on their way. Will you watch for them?"

"Sure." Vanessa gained a new respect for the brooding man sitting in the corner. Which only reminded her that she should let go of some of her preconceived notions about people in general. Mainly, preachers in general.

She glanced at Rory and he winked at her.

"He's so cute."

"Yes, he is."

She whirled to find Aunt Hattie standing there with her. "Oh, did I say that out loud?"

Aunt Hattie's smile was serene and sure. "You were mumbling, but I have excellent hearing aids."

"I see." Vanessa busied herself with straightening the perfectly straight napkins. "I should go and see if Marla needs anything."

"She's fine," Aunt Hattie said. "I tend to leave her to it whenever she's getting together her presentation. After all, she knows what she's doing."

"But you're an amazing cook, too," Vanessa pointed out. "I ate here at Easter, remember?"

"Yes, and Marla and I share the kitchen without any animosity whatsoever," Aunt Hattie replied, a twinkle in her eyes. "But in case you haven't noticed, I'm old and I've done my turn. I don't mind pitching in when needed, but I'm so glad Alec found someone he loves. I couldn't have picked a better person myself. Plus, I love Gabby to pieces. She and I have grand adventures. So I get to kick back and enjoy the happiness around here and help where I'm needed."

"That's not a bad gig." Vanessa loved Aunt Hattie. She was like everyone's fairy godmother.

"And she's needed a lot around here, especially for hugs," Marla said from behind them, pulling Aunt Hattie close.

Gabby giggled and ran past them, her long brown hair flowing around her purple-flowered dress. "Look, Mommy. Uncle Hunter's holding Roxie."

"I see that," Marla called. Then she shook her head and glanced at Vanessa. "She's wide-awake now!" Laughing, she said, "Let's go check on the men."

Vanessa felt a tug of envy and regret as she followed the other women out into the yard. Each time she came here to this old Victorian home, she felt transported to a place she'd never known. A place that shouted home and family. And love. This house looked like a wedding cake and the garden smelled like a perfumery. She thought she could stay in this yard forever.

She glanced at Hunter Lawson. He nodded and went back to staring at nothing, but he did smile when Gabby ran to greet him. Then she remembered that not everyone had such happy endings as this one.

The rest of the afternoon went by quickly. Good food, a lot of small talk, good conversation and a sense of belonging.

Vanessa had enjoyed herself, but her heart ached for something she couldn't seem to see or feel.

"You're deep in thought," Rory said as he slipped up beside her. "Everything okay? We're about to have dessert."

Vanessa couldn't speak. She shouldn't have come here. Now that she'd had a glimpse of this type of happiness, she wanted things she could never have. "I don't know," she said. "I…I think I'm ready to go home."

If she stayed, she'd blurt out her feelings and humiliate herself. Was she being petty and selfish? No. She needed to remember that she had decided long ago to keep her guard up. She couldn't have this kind of life. She was afraid of this. So why was she subjecting herself to this, getting to know a man she couldn't possibly have a relationship with and becoming more and more involved in a world to which she didn't belong?

Rory's concern etched his face in shadows. "Vanessa?"

"I'm tired. I've had a long day, and I guess it finally caught up with me. Would you tell everyone thanks for me?"

She turned and hurried out of the garden.

And she didn't look back.

Rory almost kept walking, but he had to check on Vanessa. After she'd left the cookout, he wanted to go after her, but Marla and Aunt Hattie had cautioned against that.

"She's still dealing with a lot of things," Marla reminded him. "I think seeing all of us here, happy and together, only magnified her pain. I know how she feels. I was like that myself for a long time."

Aunt Hattie had encouraged him to stay for a while. "We'll send a dessert plate with you when you leave. You can check on her then."

So Rory had stayed, and even though the dessert had been as delicious as always, he didn't remember what he'd eaten. He'd counseled a lot of people, but he'd never before gotten so all tied up in wanting to help someone so badly.

Maybe that was part of the problem. He could be too emotionally tied up with Vanessa. He needed to keep a clear head and remember his duty as a minister.

Therefore, he should…walk on by.

But here he was, knocking at the front door.

After several knocks, he decided she didn't want company. Especially not his company. But just as he turned to leave, she opened the door.

"I almost kept going," he said, the foil-wrapped plate in front of him like a shield.

"I almost didn't open the door," she retorted. She had on the same outfit, but her eyes were red and her hair was everywhere.

"Do you want me to go?"

She stared at him, her expression edged with confusion and regret. "Yes. No. I don't know."

"That's not very reassuring, any way you look at it."

"Come in," she said. "I might need that dessert."

"Oh, so I'm just the delivery man?"

"Yes."

He smiled, thinking she was such a paradox. "I hope I get a tip."

She motioned him into the kitchen and pointed toward one of the old chairs tucked underneath a long, plank table. "The best tip I have for you, Preacher, *is* to keep walking."

"Too late for that," he replied. He removed the foil from the plate. "We have some Give

Me S'mores Brownies and a couple of cookies. White Chocoholic and Snickerdoodle Oodles, as Marla pointed out…"

She took the plate from him and started nibbling on the brownie, crumbs and marshmallow merging in giant chunks. Rory got up and found her a napkin.

She nodded between chews. "Thanks."

Soon, she was fully engaged with the sweet treats in front of her. "I tend to eat when I'm stressed."

"Don't we all?"

"Food was my comfort growing up," she explained. "When things would go bad, I'd find something to eat. Even though I got my weight under control, kinda, that habit hasn't stopped."

Rory enjoyed watching her, but he wanted to hear about more than her eating habits. "So… why did you bolt?"

She finished the brownie and wiped her hands and face. "Too much beauty," she said in a small voice.

"Excuse me?"

"It was all too much. Everyone so happy and healthy and the house is like the prettiest thing I've ever seen and the yard is this perfect secret garden and I looked at you and it suddenly became too much."

"Do you resent them? Or is this about me?"

"No, I'm happy for them. And yes, this is about you…and me. I've accepted that I'll never have that. I'd made a point of not allowing myself to even think about that type of life—the big house with a garden and kids and dogs running around. I can't see me ever being a mother."

Rory hated the defeat in her words. "Why can't you have all of that?" And what did she mean, telling him this was about him?

And her. Him and her together? Apart? Maybe? Maybe not?

He was beginning to like the *together* idea. Or the *near you* idea, at least.

The image of her sitting in a swing with a child in the backyard of the house she was about to sell hit him somewhere near his solar plexus. Too soon. Way too soon for that kind of daydream. No wonder she'd panicked. He was about to panic, too.

"I've set my standards very low, and I have to get past some issues before I even consider that kind of life."

She was certainly dropping enough hints to give him the picture. She wanted him to back off.

He tried speaking the truth. "Maybe it's too soon after everything you've been through. No one around here expects anything of you,

Vanessa. Take time to grieve and to figure out what you need to do for yourself. This isn't about you and me. We're good. We're friends. The rest is up to you."

"Yes, and I should be able to deal with it. I have some good memories, but I'm afraid I brought the bad ones with me because I never cleaned up that part of my life."

Rory could see it now. She'd packed away her emotions, but now that she was being forced to face her past, the clutter was coming out. The clutter and the baggage of a deep pain. "This is not an easy process."

She grabbed one of the cookies. "No. I thought it would be easy but it's hard, Rory. And I want to thank you for being so kind to me." She broke off a chunk of cookie. "I think this is something I have to do on my own. I know I keep telling you that, but it's the only way I can clear my head."

"Is that my cue to leave?"

"No. I need you to understand. You are an amazing man who cares about other human beings, but some things, some people, can't be fixed. And you might need to accept that I'm one of those."

Chapter Eleven

Rory stilled beside her. "You think I'm trying to fix you? Is that why you left today?"

She gave him an imploring stare. "Well, aren't you?"

Rory ran a hand over his hair and shook his head. Had he been that obvious or that arrogant? "No. This isn't about *fixing* a person, Vanessa. Me, reaching out to you, at first, it was all about the pain I saw in your eyes. I *did* want to fix that maybe. That's my calling. That's my job. My hope. I want you to feel God's love and know that you're not alone. I want you to be happy. But I understand that I can't *fix* you. Being a minister, a man of God, doesn't mean I have all the answers. There are no easy answers. But I can help people who are in pain. Because I know that kind of pain."

"Why?" she asked. "Why do you know that

kind of pain? Why can't you open up to me the way you expect me to open up to you?"

Rory sat in stunned silence. No one had ever turned the tables on him before. Most people were so glad to have someone to talk to in confidence that they never suspected their minister might have suffered at some point in his life. And Rory certainly never offered up his life story.

"You see," she said, nodding when he didn't answer her question. "How can you expect me to pour out my soul to you when you can't be honest with me? I've had too many people in my life who withheld things from me, Rory. I don't even know my father. Never even saw the man. And I really didn't know my mother. But I learned from her...and from the lifestyle she chose. I can't live like that. I'm afraid to hope because I'd probably be a horrible wife and a terrible mother. And I don't think God can help me change."

"But He can," Rory said, shocked that she'd become so bitter and jaded. "I never knew either of my biological parents," he said, giving in, crossing a line. "And I fell in love once before. But that didn't last either. So I decided to serve my country, but I joined the army for all the wrong reasons. Until God showed me the one right reason for being there. I could help people who thought they were beyond help."

Tears misted in her eyes. "I'm sorry. My problems are small, really, compared to all of that."

"No, Vanessa." He grabbed her hand. "To God, no one's problem is small. He can handle it. He can take the smallest problem or the biggest problem onto His shoulders." Staring over at her, he added, "It's not the size of the problem. It's the strength of our faith that matters. No matter the problem and no matter the outcome. Good or bad, God will see us through."

"But how will I know if He's willing to do that for me?" she asked, tears moving down her cheeks.

He touched a hand to her arm and then pointed to his heart. "That has to come from inside you. You have to allow Him into your heart. And when it happens, you won't have to do anything. You'll know. You'll feel it and your life will change."

"How do I reach that point?" she asked. "How do I become more like you? Truly happy and truly thankful?"

"You're doing it right now, here in this house. Step by step, day by day. You have to open yourself up to the possibilities. You have to accept that in God's eyes, you matter."

She looked so surprised he wanted to take

her in his arms and reassure her. "You'll get through this but it won't be easy. It might take a few days, or weeks or years, even. Grief is a never-ending process. You've lost your mother, but you've also lost a part of yourself. I think part of your grief stems from not knowing a lot of things, of what might have been, what could have been. You can't find peace or closure because you've never had those things in the past. You're left with a lot of questions."

Her eyes widened, as if a lightbulb had gone off. But then the light in her eyes dimmed again. "Will I ever have that feeling, Rory? That feeling of standing in a beautiful garden, in the sunshine, with love all around me?"

"I hope so," he said. Then he did reach for her. He took her into his arms and hugged her close. "I've never done this before. I'm trying so hard not to cross that line. I want you to trust me."

She pulled back and gave him a wobbly smile. "I do trust you, more than I've ever trusted anyone. But that scares me."

Rory's eyes met hers. "It doesn't have to be scary." He wanted to kiss her and tell her about how his feelings were changing each time he was around her. "I don't want to scare you. I want to make you feel better."

He couldn't stop the feelings coursing through him. He pulled her close and held her.

"I'm afraid, too, Vanessa. I'm afraid to share things with you. I'm afraid to give in to you. You'll leave and I'll be alone again."

She pulled back to stare up at him with misty eyes. "You were in love once?"

"Yes."

"And it ended badly?"

He closed his eyes to the scenes in his head. "Yes."

"You don't have to talk about it, Rory," she said. "I understand."

He pulled her back into his arms. "It was a long time ago."

They didn't speak for a while. He held her there and savored the quiet of having someone to hold. Even while the weight of his guilt tried to drag him back down.

Finally, she pulled away and wiped her eyes. "Thank you."

Rory touched a finger to her moist cheek. "You're going to pull through. You're safe now. We're all with you. We're all praying for you."

"I know," she said. "I can feel it." She touched a hand to her heart. "Here."

After telling her good-night, Rory stepped out into the moonlight and stared up at the heavens.

I'm in deep here, Lord. I could use some grace and guidance.

Because he didn't want to watch Vanessa walk away again.

She was in church the next day. And she waited to talk to him after the sermon. "I've decided I can't rush this. So I'm staying here a little longer than I'd planned." She pushed at her hair and looked out at the lake. "I'll be here for a few weeks at least."

He wanted to do a fist pump, but he refrained. "That's probably a good idea. The rummage and estate sales are at the end of next week, and that'll be exhausting. Give yourself time to get through that and then rest up for a while. This is a good place to heal, I promise."

"I'm beginning to see that," she said. "I'm sorry about how I left the cookout, but I appreciate you checking on me last night." She shrugged. "I've already talked to Marla about it, and she made me feel better about things. She went through a lot of grief when her husband was killed and Gabby had such an ordeal." Glancing around, she said, "Thank you for checking on me."

"Of course," he said. He wanted to add, "Anytime." But he was beginning to think in terms of "All the time."

Two little kids ran by, squealing and giggling. Vanessa whirled to stare at them. "So full of energy. That's another thing that scares me about ever having children. I'm not equipped to handle all the needs of a child. Maybe I shouldn't volunteer to be a mentor since I'm not practiced in that area."

"They can be intimidating," Rory said. But he didn't buy that she'd never want children or that she wouldn't be good with children. Kandi might help in that area—if she didn't mow down Vanessa before they ever got to know each other. They'd made progress the first time they'd met, but being a mentor to a troubled teen took staying power. If Vanessa got close to Kandi and then left out of fear, they'd both suffer for it. So he hoped she'd dive right in with the youth program. She'd have to explain to Kandi that it would only be for a few weeks, but they could be friends for life.

"I liked your sermon," Vanessa said, her eyes following the children as they chased each other around the church yard.

He'd talked about coming to God with the attitude of a little child—open and honest and inquisitive, full of possibility and hope. He wished for that kind of acceptance and grace in Vanessa's life.

"I'm glad you decided to come today," he said. "And that you liked the message."

She gave him a soft smile. "Well, I've got a busy afternoon. Tagging, bagging and dragging."

He laughed and almost offered to help her. But he was going to step back and let her decide how much she wanted from him. It was the only way. "Then I guess I'll see you Wednesday night. I have some shut-ins to visit today."

Rory waved to her once she was on the other side of the street and saw the light from the afternoon sun casting her in golden whitewashed rays. She looked beautiful, standing there.

She was staying a while longer. That gave him hope. Because he'd felt it again today, standing beside her on the church steps. The kind of love that felt so beautiful, it pierced through the hardest of hearts. The kind of love that faith brought to a relationship.

He'd almost forgotten how that could feel.

"I want that," he said into the sun. Then he closed his eyes and took a deep breath and allowed himself to hope again.

Because now, he was thinking he wanted that with her.

On Monday morning, Rory's office phone jingled. When he didn't hear Barbara picking up, he remembered she had a doctor's appointment this morning. So he grabbed for the phone on the third ring. "Hello?"

"Oh, hi. I was hoping to talk to Barbara."

Vanessa.

"Hi. She's out for an appointment. How are you?"

"I'm better," she said. "Got a lot done yesterday."

"That's good. We're bringing stuff out this week and next. We store donations in the back of Alec's big warehouse and move them over here for the sale in our gathering hall."

"I'm almost ready, too," she said. "But I'm calling about Kandi, and I thought Barbara might have an answer. Did I ever get cleared to be her mentor?"

Rory sat up straight. "I'm pretty sure you did. I'll call Wanda and find out for sure. Are you coming Wednesday night?"

"I thought I would. For a midweek break and because I've been where she is and I thought maybe I could at least listen to her and encourage her while I'm here."

"I think that's a great idea," he said, lifting his eyes heavenward in a thankful prayer. "At least she's not seeing that boy anymore, according to Wanda."

"I hope not. They could be sneaking around though."

"I know." He prayed not. "I'll call Wanda and get back to you, but I don't think it'll be a problem. Kandi needs positive adult role models."

"Not sure I'm that, but I'll try."

She sounded kind of down. He wished he could make her see her worth. "You're more than qualified."

"If you count the school of hard knocks."

"Been there, got the diploma," he retorted. "Believe me, that counts for a lot."

"One day you'll have to explain that to me but only when you're ready."

He laughed, thinking she might be dropping him a hint to give her time, too. "It's a long story." Then he hesitated and took a deep breath. "Are we okay, you and me?"

A pause. "Yes, why wouldn't we be?"

He let out a sigh. "I don't know. I mean, I hugged you the other night."

"Don't you hug a lot of your church members?"

"Yes, but they don't all feel as good in my arms as you do."

Her smile held a hint of mischief and a dollop of doubt. "Are we doing something forbidden, Rory?"

"Not that I know of. I might be a preacher, but I'm still a man and… I'm attracted to you."

When she didn't respond, he thought he'd lost

her again. But finally she said, "It felt good, being in your arms."

"So are you staying here a while longer because…in part because of that?"

"Maybe. That and Kandi and the house and a thousand different reasons."

"Well, I'm glad I might be one of them."

"I'll talk to you later."

He sure hoped so. "I'll see you later this week."

Vanessa checked the bag she'd bought this afternoon. She'd been approved to mentor Kandi, so she'd bought the teen all kinds of girlie stuff. Lotions and nail polish, earrings and a colorful necklace and a tie-dyed scarf. She'd even thrown in some books, young-adult type stories that the salesclerk had assured her would be suitable for a girl Kandi's age.

Time to go. Her nerves rattled a protest, which was silly. Just talk with Kandi and visit with everyone. It would do her good to get out of her gloom to try and help someone. Or so she told herself.

And she'd see Rory there, of course.

But she also reminded herself that she'd made a solemn vow never to have children. She didn't want to put a child through some of the things she'd endured. She was so afraid she'd turn out like her mother. Vanessa didn't think she had what it would take to raise a child.

She knew she needed to focus on something besides her own problems. And the preacher. She had to stop thinking about Rory. Something had happened between them the other night. Something that was soft and soothing but also exciting and intriguing. She'd never felt that way in a man's arms before.

Cherished.

Rory made her feel cherished. He was willing to fight for her, and Vanessa had never known that feeling before either.

But she couldn't stay here, waiting for what might or might not develop between them.

And yet there he was, front and center, when she entered the gathering hall. He looked so unpreacher-like in his faded khaki shorts and chambray button-up shirt. Now *he'd* make a great father. He loved this group.

Vanessa sent up a prayer for strength. She seemed to have a big crush on the preacher. But ministers did have a personal life, so she shouldn't feel so guilty.

Mainly, she needed him to tell her what had happened with his first love. And she had to explain to him that she might not be the marrying, settling-down kind. No matter how she felt in his arms.

She looked around and saw Kandi talking to some other teens. So she headed that way, giving Rory a wave as she went.

"Hi," she said when she neared Kandi.

The girl wore old overalls over a black T-shirt, her high-top sneakers scuffed and worn but ultra cool in pink-and-black checks. She had on huge pink Lucite earrings.

"Hey." Kandi tried to look nonchalant but gave up. "What's in the bag?"

Vanessa smiled. "It's for you. Rory—I mean Preacher—told me I've been cleared to be your official mentor. So I celebrated." She offered the bag to Kandi.

But the girl looked embarrassed. "I didn't ask for a mentor."

Vanessa could tell she'd moved in too quickly. "I know. I mean, I volunteered. I want to get to know you. I'll be leaving soon anyway, so you'll only have to put up with me for a few more weeks."

"Yeah, whatever." Kandi took the bag. "Thanks." Then she shrugged and walked off with the other girl who'd been fascinated by this whole exchange.

Vanessa turned, thinking she'd leave in humiliation.

"Don't go out that door."

Rory. Had he seen that whole exchange?

Chapter Twelve

"She's not interested. Did I do something wrong?"

"No, you did everything right. And she's interested. She's not used to people being kind to her."

"That's a horrible way to live."

He guided her toward the buffet line. "And yet, a lot of children learn to live that way. It's called survival mode."

"I guess I have a little of that in me," she admitted, thinking he'd probably learned his own survival test, too. And obviously neither of them wanted to delve too deeply into the past. "I hurt for her, Rory. How can I reach her?"

Rory watched the corner of the long room where the pack of teens had gathered. "By being here. Wanda told her you were her new mentor, but she's playing hard to get. That's what she does, and most people give up or ask for another kid to work with." He eyed Kandi. "It's hard to trust when you've been let down so much."

Again, Vanessa got the impression he'd been there himself. "I guess I have to *earn* her trust, right?"

"Yes, so don't take it personally. We all go through that, don't we?"

"Touché," Vanessa said. "But you're right. And I was thinking pretty much the same thing about myself. You and I—we're still in that stage, that learning-to-trust stage." She shrugged. "I was kind of snarky when I first met you."

He did an eyebrow quirk, his eyes full of mirth. "Really? I don't recall."

"Right." She couldn't stop the low laugh. "I was a real pill."

"Well, you're better now," he said. He gave her one of those blue-eyed hopeful glances. "And we're both getting there. Let's eat and laugh and have fun. She'll come around when she sees her tactics aren't working on you."

Vanessa wondered about that. Kandi had enough attitude to launch a ship. But Vanessa remembered her own hard times and how she'd acted out and rebelled. Big-time. She also wondered if she and Rory would ever be able to trust each other enough to truly open up about everything that had brought them to this point.

She had him figured out a little more now. He counseled and consoled others, but he didn't believe he was worthy of asking someone to listen to him. He was a good man. A kind and loving man, but she couldn't help but see that he didn't seem to expect those traits in return from others. Rory shielded his own hurts and pains behind that cheery, positive facade. He put others ahead of his own needs, an admirable trait. But it was also a front that protected him from the world. He needed to heed some of his own advice.

Because wasn't that a horrible way to live, too? Keeping your own hurts buried away while you counseled everyone else? Especially for a man of God?

Vanessa knew there was always a reason for such behavior. Her past was one of the main reasons she didn't want to risk settling down and having children of her own. What was Rory's reason for deflecting love from himself?

She thought about Kandi and decided for now she'd have to concentrate on that. "It takes one to know one," she said to Rory in a quiet whisper.

"Maybe," he replied. "And it might take one to win one over, too." He gave her a soft smile.

"One who understands and can be a positive role model in her life. One who has survived and thrived in spite of everything."

"You give me too much credit," she said. "I'm trying to get on with my life."

"I give you a *lot* of credit," he replied. "I admire you, and I'm proud that you're willing to put aside your discomfort and personal feelings to help a troubled young girl."

She was proud of him, too. But Vanessa also hurt for him. She suddenly wanted to know the real Rory Sanderson, flaws and all. "You got me into this," she said on a low, soft note. "I don't want to let you down."

His gaze washed over her with a tender longing. "That won't happen."

Vanessa followed him and filled her plate with spaghetti and French bread. "Maybe I just came for the food. This smells wonderful."

"Wanda's homemade spaghetti," he said, piling his plate full. "She cooks it for days. And if it got you here…"

Vanessa laughed at his lifted eyebrows. "Amazing."

He grinned like a school kid. "Marla sometimes provides food, too."

"I'll gain ten pounds, being here."

He laughed at that, but his gaze slid over her in a warm flow. "You'll be fine." Whirling, he called out. "Round up, people, so we can bless the food and then eat the food."

Relieved that they'd moved on to another subject, Vanessa found a round table where an older man sat with a teenaged boy. Rory grabbed a seat next to her. "Vanessa, this is Paul Middleton and Johnny Thomason."

"Hi." Vanessa managed a smile, her instincts still telling her to bolt.

The man spoke to her, but the boy nodded and went back to eating, a sullen expression on his face. So maybe she wasn't the only one experiencing difficulties with this.

"Mentor and mentee?" she whispered to Rory.

"Yep. And yours should be here any minute."

Vanessa glanced around. "What if she left?"

"She can't leave without her foster parents."

Vanessa tried to eat, but the bread stuck in her throat. Why did she have to go and get involved? She couldn't help anyone. She was too confused and messed up to know what kind of advice to give to a teen.

She'd have to tell Rory she'd changed her mind. And she'd have to learn to avoid him and those beseeching blue eyes, too.

But a swish of air and a plop next to her caused her to look around. Kandi made a lot of noise getting into her seat, but she had the bag of goodies in one hand and her plate of food in the other. Her frown dared anyone to question her.

Vanessa glanced at Rory. He gave her a quick smile and then turned to the young girl. "Hey, Kandi. What you got there?"

"As if you didn't know," Kandi retorted. Then she stared over at Johnny. "Did you get a bagful of fingernail polish?"

Johnny looked unsure about how to respond. He had fine blond hair with long bangs that hid his eyes. He shrugged. "I dunno."

"I brought Johnny some books," Mr. Middleton said. "I heard he likes to read."

Johnny looked mortified. He kept his eyes on his plate.

Kandi laughed. "I got some books, too. Can't wait to read them."

The sarcasm fairly dripped from her words.

Mr. Middleton tried again. "Books can change your world. The more you read, the more you can learn and grow. A good book can help solve a lot of the world's problems."

Johnny looked relieved but Kandi gave a little snort. Then she turned to Vanessa. "Hey, thanks for the bag. It's almost like Christmas around here."

Vanessa glanced at Rory. He nodded in encouragement, so she dived right in. "I'm glad my gift makes you feel like it's Christmas," she said to Kandi. "But I'm not here just to give you gifts. I'm here because I know how it feels to be all alone and scared and confused—"

"I'm not confused and I'm not scared," Kandi said. Then she got up and walked away, leaving her food and the bag behind.

"I'll walk you home."

"You don't have to do that," Vanessa said, wishing the last couple of hours could have gone a little better. "I'm going to help clean the kitchen and… I can find my way home."

"I'll meet you at the door when you're finished," he said, his tone determined.

Vanessa nodded, deciding she wouldn't argue with him right now. She hurried to the kitchen and soon had her hands immersed in soapy dishwater. The dishwasher was already full and running, so she was washing these few big pieces by hand.

Kandi walked up and picked up a dish cloth. "I'll dry," she said, her scowl belying the polite offer.

Vanessa didn't hide her surprise. "Now you decide to talk to me?"

"I'm drying dishes, not talking," Kandi said, still stubborn, still full of bite.

"Oh, okay." Vanessa scrubbed a baking sheet with renewed determination.

"I think it's clean," Kandi said with a smirk.

"I don't know." Vanessa wanted to show a bit of her own attitude. "I still see a few grease spots."

"Those have been there forever," Kandi retorted. "They won't come out, no matter how hard you scrub them." Then she whirled to stare at Vanessa. "I'm sorry I was rude to you. I like the stuff you gave me."

Vanessa tried not to show too much enthusiasm, but the comment about those dark spots on the baking sheet stayed with her. "Okay."

"Wanda told me I needed to say that."

"Of course."

The girl did a fabulous eye roll. "But…I'm sorry. Really. You put some pretty cool stuff in that bag." She wiped the baking sheet dry. "I might even read that book. Looks like it could be good."

"I'm glad to hear that," Vanessa said. "Wanda invited me to come by her house sometime. So you and I can have some quality time together."

"Yeah. Whatever." Kandi threw down the dish towel. "Later."

"Later," Vanessa called. Then she grinned. Big.

And looked up to find Rory grinning back at her.

* * *

Rory wanted Vanessa to trust him. *Him.* Not just the preacher in him, but the man he'd become. So when they reached her porch, he pointed to the big glider hidden behind some overgrown jasmine bushes. "Let's sit a minute, okay?"

She looked unsure. "What is it?"

"Nothing." He took her by her hand. "I think we need to talk."

"I did something wrong, didn't I?" She fell onto the old metal glider, causing it to squeak and groan in protest. "Did Kandi's foster mom tell you to never bring me back to the youth meetings?"

He smiled and shook his head. "No. In fact, she wants you to come to visit with Kandi next week. Maybe Tuesday night?"

Vanessa looked shocked and pleased, all at the same time. "I'll see if I can clear my schedule." When he squeezed in beside her, she asked, "Is that what you wanted to talk to me about?"

"No." He took in a deep breath, the scent of her floral perfume warring with the smell of jasmine and gardenia. "I wanted to tell you… about me."

She looked surprised again. "Really? I mean, everything?"

"Maybe," he said, dread in the one word. "I

need you to understand how I feel, how I can identify with you and Kandi and all of the other foster kids we try to help."

Vanessa took his hand, her fingers curling against his with a grip that felt sure and strong. "I want to hear all about you."

Rory nodded and stared out into the moonlight. He could hear the distant sound of the lake's gentle waves hitting the shore in a never-ending tug. "I told you I was a foster child. I never knew my real parents, and I wasn't adopted until I was older. I always thought something was wrong with me since no one wanted me. But when my parents brought me home, my mom told me that there was nothing wrong with me. She said God had been waiting to find the perfect family for me. And she told me how long she and my dad had waited to have a child."

"She sounds like a wonderful person," Vanessa said. "Did you...do you love them?"

"Yes." He could admit that easily. "They were older than most who adopt, but they gave me a good life. My father was retired military, gruff and demanding but fair and always willing to listen. When he died, I fell back into this kind of despair. But we got through it, Mom and me."

He wasn't sure he could do this. So he stopped and took another long breath.

"It's hard," Vanessa said. "Death is hard because it doesn't give you a second chance."

"Right." Rory certainly understood that concept, but he knew death was another phase. "It's final here on earth. But God promises us we will all be reunited in Heaven." He touched her hand. "That's our second chance. Seeing our loved ones again in eternity."

Vanessa looked down. "Do you think my mom is in Heaven, Rory?"

Rory heard this question a lot. "I didn't know your mother, but I'm hoping you will see her in Heaven, yes."

"But you can't promise me that?"

"I can't, no. But Christ promises those who follow Him eternal life."

Vanessa gulped a deep breath. "I wish I could have talked to her before she died. By the time I got there, she was already in a coma. I was so angry and bitter and awful."

Rory stopped talking and pulled her into his arms. She felt fragile and delicate, but he'd seen the steel she'd placed around her heart. "I don't have all the answers, but we can always hold out hope that everyone we love had a change of heart toward the end of life and will be there waiting for us. I hope your mother felt your presence there in her last hours."

Vanessa lifted her head and looked into his

eyes. Rory forgot the rest of his story. He wiped at her tears and then he leaned down and kissed her. Vanessa's lips were soft and silky. She pulled her hand through his hair and tugged him closer.

Rory became lost in the kiss, lost in her touch, lost in what this felt like, holding a woman in his arms.

And he knew without any doubt that Vanessa could be the one for him. But how in the world could he ever convince her of that?

But it wasn't about convincing Vanessa. He had to let go of all the things he'd been holding to so tightly, too. So he pulled back and touched a hand to her face. "I can't do this, Vanessa. Not yet. I'm not ready to let go of my secrets, because it'll be like saying goodbye to the woman I loved all over again."

He hated the hurt and fear in her eyes. "Rory...?"

"I'm sorry." He kissed her again, and then he got up and went back to his side of the street.

Chapter Thirteen

Friday morning. Vanessa yawned and glanced around the house. She still had a long way to go, but things were shaping up. She had another week until the church rummage sale and her estate sale. Then she'd be forced to fling the doors of this home open to the public.

And watch part of her life go out the door. But maybe that was for the best. Rory had kissed her Wednesday, and then he'd told her he was sorry, just up and walked away. She hadn't slept much in the last couple of nights.

So what did she do now? He'd made her care and now he couldn't deal? Or had he stopped things before they went any further because he didn't want to hurt her? Or watch her leave?

They'd hit a snag. And she thought she knew what that snag was all about. He was reliving his past, too. A past that involved loving and losing another woman. Vanessa figured that if she hadn't come along, he'd have stayed trapped behind that brilliant facade for the rest of his life.

"My turn to minister to you, Preacher."

But right now, she had to finish up things here. The busywork would help her sort through her feelings for Rory much in the same way she'd sorted through her own secrets for the last few weeks. In the meantime, she hoped he'd come back around.

"So not fair. So wrong." Vanessa shook her head, determined to stop mumbling and get on with things.

He'd been patient with her. She would do the same for him.

Staring at the big, cluttered kitchen, she wished she'd cleared out this room already. But when she'd started, she'd crashed and burned out on the sidewalk with Rory watching her. That day, she didn't know him well enough to tell him her fears and concerns or why she'd become so upset. She wasn't sure she could tell him anything more now either. But this kitchen represented so much of the struggle between Vanessa and her mother. The silent meals. The shouting matches. The clashing of dishes. The burned food. The lost hope. This would be another hurdle. One more thing to clean up and tuck away.

And then she'd have to tackle the last bedroom. Her old bedroom. She had a lot to overcome before she put this house on the market. Up until now, Vanessa had believed all of her nightmares were holding her back. But it was more than that now.

Vanessa thought about Rory and how he'd tried to open up to her the other night. And he'd kissed her. That first kiss had left a lasting impression on Vanessa, like an imprint that marked her as cherished and special. They'd kissed several times, there in the rickety old glider, until he'd bolted like a forest animal on the run. Rory brought her the kind of security and comfort she'd only hoped for in her dreams. Now, he needed to feel that same kind of security. Or did he already?

"What are *you* afraid of, Rory?"

How could she ever forget Rory and his kisses? Could she make him see that he needed her as much as she needed him?

Because daydreams had replaced a lot of her nightmares. Daydreams of being with Rory, which seemed impossible. So here she stood, wondering what to do next.

Maybe she should ask Rory how to handle all of these mixed-up, scary feelings. Marla had urged her to do that from the beginning. As a minister, he was bound to keep what she told him between them, and he'd listened to a lot of her rants already.

But as a friend, as a man she was attracted to, he should be the last person she needed to confide in. He had opened up to Vanessa about his past until the kissing had taken over and stopped the soul sharing. Then he'd practically run away screaming. But she needed to hear everything about him, good and bad. She needed to be honest with him, too.

Rory had become too important to her, even after she'd fought against her growing feelings for him.

Giving up, she called Marla. "Rory kissed me."

A soft squeal and then a giggle. "This is interesting."

"Yes, but he took himself back across the street after he kissed me. Couldn't get away fast enough."

"Did you two fight?"

"No. We kissed. A lot." Vanessa sipped on her bottle of water while she stood at the big window and stared over at the church. "I…I finally gave in to all these feelings and now…he's hiding out over there in his sanctuary."

She heard a cash register dinging. Marla was at work. Vanessa wished she had a cupcake.

"Have you talked to him since the kissing session?"

"No." Vanessa turned away from the window. "No. I'm giving him time to think about things." Then she took a deep breath. "So you don't know what happened? In his past?"

Marla didn't speak for a minute. Then Vanessa heard, "Thank you, Mr. Houston. Give Miss Becky a hug for me." A customer. Marla's Marvelous Desserts stayed busy.

"I should let you get back to work," Vanessa said, the image of white icing covering rich chocolate enticing her.

"No. I'm on my way back to the office," Marla replied. "Now, I can talk without my gossip-loving staff listening in."

Vanessa took in some air and then rushed on. "So you do know something?"

"No. I only know that he served at a small church near Crestview before he enlisted in the army and went through training to become a chaplain."

"Did he serve over there with any of his current buddies?"

"No," Marla said. "They all met here, remember. He was army and Alec and Blain were marines—even though I called Alec Soldier Boy when we first met, but now that's our special joke with each other. And Hunter, well, no one talks much about what Hunter did. Some kind of black ops, maybe."

Vanessa realized she had a lot to learn about Rory's friends. But she needed to learn more about him first. "He said he'd loved someone and it ended badly."

"Preacher?" Marla seemed as surprised as Vanessa had been. "He's never mentioned that around me. Are you sure?"

"I know—hard to believe. Yes, that's what he said. I think he's buried his feelings so deep, no one can find them. Not even him." Vanessa turned back to the window. "And now that I'm here and he kissed me…well, something is sure bubbling to the surface. But he's having a hard time. He pushed me to open up, and I'm getting better at talking about my life and now he's the one who's clamming up. Or shutting down. Or whatever you want to call it."

"I'm glad you're here," Marla said. "You sound stronger every day and, well, we've all been praying for Rory to find a soul mate, someone to love him. He has so much love to give. It sounds as if you and he have something, Vanessa. Don't give up on him. Don't give up on yourself either."

"I believe he cares," Vanessa said. "And I'm

beginning to care about him. More than I want to care. I don't know if I'm worthy of his love."

"You are," Marla said. "Rory needs you, and God wants you to feel worthy, too. You and Rory could be so wonderful together."

After they talked a few more minutes, Vanessa hung up, more confused than ever. But maybe Marla was right. If God had a plan for their lives, she prayed He'd reveal it soon. Because it would be so hard to fall for Rory and then have to leave him.

"What's up with you?"

Rory turned from the porch railing and the view of the full moon hanging over the bay to find Hunter Lawson propped up against a door frame at the AWOL camp house, his face in the shadows.

"I'm admiring the moon," Rory replied to Hunter's question. "What's up with you?" And did he really want to hear the answer to that question?

"I'm wondering why the man who planned this grand bachelor party is staring up at the moon. We've got pizza and wings, cold drinks and old movies. And you promised games."

Hunter rarely said more than one-word comments and now this. The third degree?

"It's all there," Rory said, turning to shove

past Hunter's stoic stare. "Hey, Blain, want us to help you make a wedding dress out of toilet paper?"

Blain Kent stayed on the couch but lifted one dark eyebrow. "I think I'll have to pass on that one, brother."

Rory grinned. "Barbara said that's what they do at girlie bridal showers. Just asking. We could make you a duct-tape tuxedo."

Alec got up to get another slice of pizza. "What are we supposed to do at bachelor parties, anyway?"

"Not what they do in Vegas," Rory said, nodding toward the movie they'd been watching. "This is a regular get-together before Blain here goes off the market. Same as we do every week but with more feeling."

Hunter grunted. "Two down and one to go." He pointed his can of soda toward Rory. "'Cause I'm thinking you've got it bad, man."

"You left yourself off that list," Rory retorted.

"I don't have any aspirations on that account," the Okie replied in a steady, sure voice.

Blain and Alec glanced at each other and then back to Rory.

"Do *you* have aspirations, Preacher?" Blain asked, his dark eyes now full of interest.

"I aspire to turn up the music on this party," Rory said. He'd been looking forward to this for a while now, and they'd planned it a week before the wedding since Blain had a lot going on next week. But his heart wasn't in it. And he could tell that his buddies could tell. He wanted this to be a festive, joyous night, since the wedding would be the Sunday after the rummage sale.

Next weekend. Vanessa might leave after that.

Or she'd probably go sooner, after the way he'd left things the other night. The way he'd left her.

"Let's go for a boat ride," Alec said, getting up to throw away his paper plate. "Full moon. Nice wind. Good for the soul."

Rory watched Alec. The limp he'd sustained due to being injured while he'd been deployed a couple of years ago was just about gone. Even the scar on Alec's face was less noticeable now. But Rory knew some scars never went away.

"Okay, a boat ride." He nodded. "That was next on the agenda anyway."

Blain got up and finished his drink and then poked Rory in the chest. "And while we're out there, maybe we'll hold you under until you tell us what's on your mind."

An hour later, they sat rocking in Alec's sleek boat, the moon laughing down on them while a balmy breeze moved over the blue-black, soothing waves. So far, so good. They hadn't dunked him yet.

Hunter sat off to the side with his legs propped up, looking back at the shore.

Blain and Rory sat opposite each other on the wraparound seats while Alec stayed at the helm.

"Are we having fun now?" Rory asked.

"Yep." Hunter didn't even turn around.

"More fun than a kangaroo on a trampoline," Blain replied.

Rory decided this was a good place to lay it on the line. "I kissed Vanessa the other night."

"An aspiration if ever I heard one," Alec said through a grin. He twisted around on his seat. "So why aren't we celebrating?"

Rory rubbed a hand down his face. "I enjoyed kissing her. Too much."

"Is there such a thing as too much kissing?" Blain asked. "I sure hope not."

Alec sat still. "Go on, Preacher."

"I think I'm falling for her, but we have a lot to work through."

Blain and Alec both lifted their drinks in a mock toast.

"Been there, got married," Alec said.

"Been there, about to get married," Blain added.

"Never been there. Ain't gonna happen," Hunter said into the wind.

Rory loved their dry wit. "I was married once."

The boat stopped rocking.

Hunter turned around.

The moon became a spotlight.

Alec twisted away from the wheel and came back to the stern. "Say that again."

Rory couldn't take back the confession, so he went on. "I was young. Just out of seminary. About to start my career at a small-town church. We were happy. And then I was alone and I struggled and then because I was so angry, I joined the army and thought I'd take out my frustrations. And we all know how that went. I found my calling again, but I'm still alone. And I feel guilty for kissing one woman when I can't let go of another one."

"What happened?" Blain asked. "I mean, to the first woman."

Even now, Rory couldn't say the words. "Life happened."

He left it at that, and his friends left him to his silence.

Finally, Hunter grunted. "It's always something, man." But he touched Rory on the arm before he turned his face back to the sea.

Alec moved back to the cockpit and cranked the boat, and they listened to her purr for a few seconds. "I suggest you take advantage of those kisses, my friend," he said over his shoulder to Rory. "Don't run away from a second chance. Turn back toward her and fight. You're a fighter,

Preacher. But you have a different weapon than most. You are more of a warrior than anyone I know."

They went silent again for a few minutes.

Blain nodded and let out a hoot. "Well, since I'm the one about to turn toward the woman that *I* love, how about we take this baby for a spin and see what she's got?"

Rory finally grinned, and strangely, he felt better. "Let's go."

Hunter grunted again. "Glad we had this chat."

And they were off into the night, laughing and talking about all the things they rarely talked about. Including women.

When they slowed at the marina, Alec cut the engine again.

And Rory finally told them the story of his young wife and her death.

Chapter Fourteen

He was giving her the space she needed, and now she missed having him around. Saturday and Sunday had come and gone. A long, silent weekend that Vanessa had tried to fill with work and cleaning up. She'd planned to attend church Sunday, hoping she'd hear some words of wisdom from the man she'd come to admire as a minister and as a friend. She felt so alone here in this big, rambling house. Instead, she'd gone for an early-morning walk around the lake, and then she'd come home and talked to her lawyer on the phone and processed more shipping instructions for some of the items she would be keeping.

Exhausted, she'd curled up on the big sofa early in the evening, hoping to get some sleep. But that hadn't worked. So she'd stayed up late last night working on the photos for her website. Now she was exhausted and cranky. Monday morning had never looked or felt so bad.

She glanced at her mother's journal lying on the big plank dining table. What if what she needed to hear was inside that journal? Why couldn't she open it?

Because the truth might be in there and Vanessa wasn't sure she was ready for the complete truth. It seemed too intimate and invasive to read her mother's journal and hear Cora's innermost thoughts. Her mother's accusations could be there, inked beside what they had for dinner and what she was wearing on her latest date. Vanessa couldn't bear to view the horror of her time in this house with Gregory Pardue, all spelled out in black and white. And yet, she needed to sit down and read the whole thing.

Didn't the Bible have a verse about the truth setting you free? Vanessa suddenly wanted to be free. She needed to be free if she wanted a chance with Rory, didn't she?

Touching a hand to the thick, worn journal, she shook her head. "Not yet."

She'd open it tomorrow after she got back from Kandi's house. Wanda had called her and set a time for her visit with Kandi. "And dinner," Wanda had added. "We'd love to have you stay and eat with us."

The last thing Vanessa wanted right now was

to sit down with a big, rowdy family and eat a meal. But saying no would be impolite. The Peppermons were a wonderful couple who truly sacrificed for the sake of helping children in need.

She reminded herself that if she'd had someone like that in her life growing up, she might be a different person today.

You do have someone like that now.

You have Marla and Alec and Aunt Hattie and Marla's parents. You have the Peppermons and Miss Fanny and you have Rory.

But she wouldn't have Rory or any of the other people who'd befriended her once she left here. She'd go back to New Orleans, and she'd be okay. She had friends there, and she had her work to keep her occupied.

But now that she'd experienced Millbrook Lake with different people, in a different time, she knew being okay—just okay—wouldn't ever be good enough again. Nor would working day and night. Nice, but not amazing.

That about summed it up. This place had turned into something amazing. She could almost be happy here. But she couldn't stay here, of course.

She'd miss the lake and kayaking, the ducks quacking and the seagulls cawing. She'd miss watching sailboats glide by or hearing speed boats charging along or children laughing in the park and dogs barking in return. Miss Fanny calling to her across the way, always with a smile and a kind word of encouragement and the beautiful music when the church choir was practicing. She'd miss the sweet smell of flowers and the earthy smell of the lake.

She'd miss that little white church across the street and the man who took care of everyone but himself.

I could be the one.

I could be the person who takes care of Rory.

No. Bad idea. Vanessa started digging through cabinets and dragging out old cookware and aged baking dishes. She'd never been one for settling down, married with children.

She wasn't maternal enough. She didn't want to turn out like her mother. She didn't want to bring a child into the world because she knew firsthand that little children weren't always protected in this world.

You'd never be like that. You'd be a good mother.

She could tell herself that all day long, but Vanessa would never believe it.

Gregory Pardue had told her something she'd never forgotten. "You're just like your mother. A big tease. A big dreamer. You aren't fit to be anyone's girlfriend or wife. You should plan on being alone all your life because no decent man will want you and you certainly won't be able to take care of any children."

He'd spouted all of those ugly things to her after he'd tried to molest her, in her room, here at this house.

A man of God, trying to molest his wife's only daughter.

Vanessa sat in the middle of the kitchen floor and stared at a scratch mark on the old cabinet door. And like all the pots and pans and old dish towels spilling out of the cabinets, her memories came tumbling out, cluttered and chaotic, cloying and stifling, much in the same way this house was beginning to stifle her with its secrets.

But she looked up and saw a brilliant ray of sunshine hitting on an old wall plaque that she'd never noticed before.

And her heart stopped and started beating in a fast-moving lift that echoed with each pulse inside her head.

"He heals the brokenhearted and bandages their wounds."

Psalm 147, Verse 3.

The tiny little square plaque had been varnished to a bright luster, but the black words were written in calligraphy on a stark white piece of canvas. Vanessa had no doubt that her mother had made this little sign and hung it there.

Her mother, who had never darkened the doors of a church. Even when she'd been married to a man who claimed to be a minister.

Vanessa got up and grabbed the plaque off the wall and held it close. Then she turned it over and saw the initials on the back.

CDT. Cora Donovan Tucker. Cora had created this after she'd married Richard Tucker.

Her mother had died alone and brokenhearted in a nursing home. But she'd been brokenhearted long before she became ill.

"Everyone left you," Vanessa said. "We all abandoned you."

Vanessa sat down and cried, the little plaque held tightly to her heart. Then she put the plaque back in its place and turned to find her mother's journal.

"I think it's time to clear away the real clutter, Mama."

The clutter that had to have been documented in this journal. Vanessa knew she needed to read this journal, good and bad, in order to heal her own broken heart.

She called Rory. "Will you come over? I…I need your help."

He immediately agreed. "Of course. Give me five minutes."

Rory was a decent man. He would help her deal with this. She needed to remember that. It could never work between them, no matter how much her heart ached with each day that passed. But he could help her right now, in this moment, when she needed him the most. And when it was time for her to go, she could go with his kindness and his kisses embedded in her memories.

Good memories replacing bad ones. She'd have that at least.

"I'm out for the day," Rory told Barbara as he hurried out of his office.

"Did someone die?"

He turned and shook his head. "No, but I think someone is having a crisis of faith. I have to go."

"I hope everything works out for her," Barbara said, guessing who that someone had to be. "Sending prayers to cover both of you."

"Thanks." He could use those prayers. He'd certainly been doing some serious soul searching himself. But right now, he hurried across the street to Vanessa's house and knocked on the door. After his full disclosure on the boat the other night, his friends had encouraged him to tell Vanessa everything.

Now Rory prayed for the courage to do that. She opened the door in a slow, cautious way, one hand hiding her face from the late morning sun. Rory took one look at her and pulled her into his arms. "What's wrong?"

She burst into sobs and pulled back, trying to wipe at her tears in a frantic way. "Everything. I...I...need to get out of this house."

"I know just the place," he said. "Do you trust me?"

She bobbed her head and took on a gritty, determined expression.

"I'll get my truck."

She nodded again. "I'll meet you out front."

Rory ran back across the street to the garage apartment and quickly cranked his old truck. Soon he was parked in the driveway of Vanessa's house. When Miss Fanny came out on her porch and waved to him, he waved back but didn't go over to talk to her.

Instead, he ran up the steps to Vanessa's house. She opened the door before he could knock again. "Are you ready?"

"Yes." She had a big tote bag with her, and she held something else in her hand, too.

Her mother's journal.

"Where are we going?" Vanessa asked Rory a few minutes later. She'd stopped crying, but her eyes were red rimmed and swollen.

"A special place," he explained. "It's private and secluded. No one will bother us there."

She nodded and watched the signs. "I haven't gone anywhere outside of the city limits since I got here. Sorry I fell apart, but I...I needed to get out of that house for a while."

He took one of her hands in his. "Understandable since you've been sorting and cleaning for three weeks now. And you haven't cried a lot in all of that time."

"Has it been three weeks?" Her surprise turned to resolve. "I have to get this done."

"Are you in such a hurry to leave?" he asked, wishing she wouldn't go at all. Wishing he hadn't left her sitting there the other night.

"Not so much now." She gave him a watery stare. "I need a couple of hours away from that place, and then I'll get back and finish up. I only have the kitchen and a couple of other rooms left."

But she'd need more than a couple of hours, Rory thought. He'd stall her all afternoon. She also needed rest, and she needed to let go and mourn.

When he pulled the truck up to the rustic square beach house that sat high up on pilings near the waters of the big bay, Vanessa glanced around and then back to him.

"What place is this, Rory?"

"We call it AWOL," he said. "This is the camp house I own with Alec, Blain and Hunter."

"I thought no women were allowed here. That's what Marla told me once."

"Darlin', we seem to be breaking that rule a lot lately. It's okay. We're only allowed to bring very special women out here. Alec brought Marla here and Blain brought Rikki here."

He almost added that they'd gone on to become couples and…they were making lives together now. But Rory didn't think Vanessa was ready for that. He wasn't sure right now if he was ready for that either. But he did owe her the truth, at least.

He got out and came around to open her door. She turned to stare up at him. But her question was somber. "Do you think I'm special?"

"Oh, you have no idea," he said. Then he kissed her on the forehead. "I think you're amazing."

She didn't move. She sat there staring up at him, her eyes clear now. "I'm not all that amazing."

Rory hugged her close. "Let's get you inside so I can feed you and pamper you and…listen to you."

Vanessa reached up a hand to touch his face. "You really are a true minister, Rory."

He nodded. "Thanks, and I'm thinking that today I'll certainly be earning that title, right?"

She dropped her hand away. "Yes. You're exactly what I need today." Then she took his hand and followed him up the path to the house.

Chapter Fifteen

Vanessa steeled herself against breaking down again. She wasn't a crier. Never had been. She held her emotions in check because she'd seen too much drama growing up. Her mother's theatrics had left her cold and wanting. And unable to love anyone.

She'd been trying to fill that void in her heart since the day she'd left Millbrook Lake. Now she could see that all of her excuses—wanting a peaceful life, not wanting children, needing her space and turning away from God—had been just that. Excuses.

And yet, her excuses held steady. She wasn't ready to relinquish control yet. She didn't want to lose control anymore today either. So she wiped at her tears and lifted her spine into a straight line. She had to hold it together, somehow.

Once they were upstairs on the deep plank

porch that faced the bay, she wiped her eyes and took in the view. "I can see why this place is so special to you and your friends."

Palm trees rustled in the breeze, a couple so close to the porch and so tall and gangly, she could reach out and touch their fronds. Hibiscus bushes and bougainvillea vines graced the yard, their colorful blossoms shining in the sun. The porch was long and deep, a good place to sit, no matter the weather.

Vanessa felt safe here, away from the lake and the town. Safe, hidden, covered. Had she become that kind of person? The kind who cowered behind closed doors and drawn-together curtains? The kind who ran away to a place like New Orleans, where everyone left you alone if that's what you wanted? Yes. She'd become a reclusive, shy, scared human being. She didn't have it all together at all. At some point, she'd given up on having grand adventures or finding someone special.

Special. A special place for special people. Rory had brought her here…and it felt right.

She stared out at the big bay waters and remembered how much she'd enjoyed kayaking around the lake with Rory. Rory was an adventure all wrapped up in a great package. And that was the main reason she kept resisting him.

"I take care of the yard," Rory said from behind her. "Blain is in charge of the security system. And Alec, well, he foots the renovations. Oh, and Hunter comes and goes, but he's good with mechanical things and he's a stickler for clean sheets and towels. So he's in charge of laundry. We all take care of maintenance. And we take turns cooking or ordering pizza."

"Sounds like you make a good team."

"We're tight," Rory said, coming to stand beside her. "We formed a bond that can't be broken. We help each other, guard each other and… we trust each other."

She pivoted to the big glass doors he'd flung open. The house looked clean and efficient but seriously lacking in anything remotely feminine. No floral throw pillows, no bright pretty dishes, no potted plants or whimsical pictures on the walls. Just a minimalist, manly interior with worn leather furniture, chunky wooden tables and bar stools for extra seating. And the biggest flat-screen television she'd ever seen.

"I've never had friends like that," she said, her tote bag and her mother's journal held close to her stomach. "We moved around so much when I was growing up, and by the time my mom settled here, I was in full-out rebellious mode and I only wanted to finish high school and get out on my own."

"Do you have friends now?" he asked. "For

when you get back to New Orleans? So I won't worry about you."

A twinge of regret hit her in her stomach. What would her life be like now? Without Rory in it?

"I have employees in the boutique. They're taking care of things while I'm here. I have people hired to help me run the online site, too. I don't know what I'd do without my team."

"A team," he said, taking her by the hand and pulling her inside the house. "I didn't ask about a team. I asked if you had friends."

Wow. He had a way of zooming right in on things.

"No." She dropped her bag and the journal onto the butcher-block counter and pretended to study the row of cabinets underneath the big side window. "I don't make friends."

"We all need friends."

"Do we?" She whirled to stare over at him, needing to put that shield back up between them. Now that she was here, alone with him, she wished she'd never called him for help. She didn't need rescuing. She didn't need him. "I've been self-sufficient since I was eighteen, even before that, really. I do okay on my own."

He didn't make a move. He stood there, his eyes holding hers. "How's that working for you right now?"

He had her there. She lowered her head and then glanced up at him. "Not so well."

Rory took another step, getting closer. "Why did you call me, Vanessa?"

She glanced at the journal. She should tell him to take her home, that this had been a mistake. That kissing him had been a mistake. But she needed someone to talk to, and Rory had tried to be her friend. He wanted to listen. He was good at listening even if he didn't want to kiss her again.

"I need to…" Her voice trailed off. "This isn't easy for me. I need to talk to someone I can trust."

"You know you can trust me."

"As a minister."

"As your friend, too."

She nodded. "Okay. I need to read my mother's journal. I want to see what she wrote about me, and what she wrote about the men she paraded in front of me, and about the one man who tried to ruin me forever."

Rory moved a little closer. "This one man— he was a minister?"

She lowered her head again, ashamed, embarrassed and mortified. Keeping her gaze downcast, she nodded.

Rory pulled her chin up, his face inches from

hers. "You do not need to hide in shame anymore, Vanessa. Not with me. Not with God."

Her skin flared hot as she sent him a burning stare. "Where was God the day that man walked into my bedroom and pushed me up against a wall and…put his hands all over me? Where was God that day, Rory?"

Rory's heart hurt with all the agony of arrows hitting him in the chest. How did he answer that question?

"He was there, Vanessa. God's love can overcome anything."

"But how could He have been there?" she asked, whirling around, her hands flailing out in front of her. "How?"

"What did this man do to you? How far did it go?"

She gave Rory a hard glare. "You don't want to answer my questions, do you?"

"I'm working on that, but right now I want to know what this man did to you."

"He tried to kiss me, but it didn't get very far. But him touching me went way too far for me," she said, putting a hand to her mouth. "He'd always flirted with me, but I ignored him. When he and my mom started dating, he'd hug me a lot and it felt so creepy. But after they got married, he kept insisting I come to church. He had this little start-up church west of town.

A storefront kind of thing because his credentials were almost nonexistent. I refused at first, but Mom talked me into it, telling me I'd make new friends. *He* tried to become my new friend, always hovering, always making sick jokes. He'd talk to me in soothing tones, telling me he knew what was best for me. I hated being around him."

She stopped and took a shuddering breath. "That day, he was angry with me for not showing up for some sort of youth rally. That's why he came into my room. Mom thought he was disciplining me for not attending his important get-together. But he wanted to make a point, I think. He wanted to prove that I was a bad person."

She looked up at Rory, as if half expecting him to question her, too. "I pushed at him and scratched his face. I told him to stop, and then I ran out of the room."

Rory schooled his expression while his insides boiled with rage. "And what happened next?"

"I went to my mom," Vanessa said, dropping both of her hands down to her side and turning to stare into the dark fireplace. "I told her what he'd tried to do and how he'd been flirting with me, but she didn't believe me. Then he came out of my room and called me all kinds of names.

He told me I'd never amount to anything because I was a liar and that no man would want me because I was unfit." She shook her head. "He implied I'd come on to him, of course."

Rory closed his eyes, his own questions ricocheting inside his brain with a pounding of despair. *Dear God, help me. Help me to say the right thing. Help her to heal, Lord. Show her Your grace and love.*

"And your mother didn't ask him about what he'd done? She never questioned that he was the one lying?"

Vanessa whirled around. "No. Instead, she asked me what *I'd* done to provoke him."

"What did you tell her?"

"I tried to tell her the truth. That'd he come into my room and shut the door and that he'd tried to kiss me and…that I had to push him away." Rory heard her gulping in a breath. "I kept trying to explain, but she looked so disappointed, so horrified. And he stood there, smug and sure. It was awful. Awful." Vanessa took in a heaving breath. "And the worst—she turned on me. I had to live in that house with both of them, condemning me, challenging me at every turn, isolating me to the point that I forgot how to make friends."

She stopped, her hand going to her mouth again. "I was so ashamed."

Rory saw her face go white, saw the panic in her eyes. He pointed. "Bathroom—down the hall to the right."

She took off running, already retching. He heard the door slam, heard her being sick. He wanted to go to her, hold her and tell her it would be all right. But he knew she didn't need to hear that right now. He understood why she'd turned away from him at first, why her attitude had been stilted and distant toward him. No wonder Vanessa hadn't trusted *his* motives. He'd tried to invite her in and had suggested she come to the youth meetings. His actions had been strictly on a friendly basis, a way to reach out to someone he sensed was hurting.

But to Vanessa, his actions had mirrored those of a man who'd abused her and scarred her.

Dear Lord, what can I do now? How do I reach her?

Rory waited in the silence of the quiet house, the sound of the bay's gentle waves hitting the shore echoing inside his head like a soothing lullaby while he prayed the prayer that would guide him past his own understanding. After a few minutes, he heard the faucet water running and then the door opened and she came out, still pale, her eyes red rimmed and swollen.

"I'm sorry," she said, pushing at her hair.

Rory moved across the room and took her into his arms. "Don't ever apologize for this, Vanessa. You did nothing wrong." He stepped back, his hands gentle on her wrists. "I'm the one who should be apologizing. I didn't understand what you'd been through when I first met you. I can see how my overtures to invite you to church must have frightened you."

"No," she said, shaking her head. "No. You're not him. You're not like him."

"You're right on that," Rory replied. "I'm not like him, but if I had him right here in front of me today, I'd become reduced to brawling like a street fighter. I'm pretty sure I'd pulverize him."

"You're not that kind of man," she said. "You went to war to help others, to serve others. You fight with a different kind of strength, Rory. You fight for the broken people of this world."

He thought of Alec's words to him. He didn't admit that up until the other night on that boat, he hadn't completely trusted anyone either. Some minister he was, holding back his own confessions and angst while he tried to take care of everybody else. His friends were the best. Understanding and undemanding. Now they knew all he had to share. He'd bared his soul there in the dark on that boat. But he was glad they all knew about his past. He wondered why he'd held back for so long.

Today, he was taking their advice. He was turning toward the woman he thought he could love for a long, long time. He would be a warrior for this woman.

Rory swallowed back the emotions brimming over in his mind. "I'm fighting for you right now. And I know God's fighting for you, too. He brought you back here for a reason. It might have taken a lifetime, but His timing is never wrong."

She looked up at Rory, her eyes overflowing with doubt and hurt and anger. "I'm afraid, Rory. Afraid to move on and find happiness. Afraid of my feelings for you. Afraid to read my mother's journal." She stalled out, her eyelids fluttering. "But mostly, I'm afraid to give myself over to God."

Rory tugged her toward the couch. "Sit. I'm going to make you something to eat, and then I'm going to tell you about how much God loves you and wants you in His arms."

"I don't think—"

"And something to drink. Hot tea or cold?"

"Water with lemon."

"We have lemons," he said, smiling at her. He got up and found bottled water and sliced a lemon and put ice in two plastic cups, his hands steady again now. Then he poured the water into both, grabbed some crackers and cheese and a bag of grapes and brought it all back to the coffee table.

"I can't eat," she said.

"It's okay. You'll eat when you're ready."

Then he sat down beside her and pulled her into his arms. "Cry on my shoulder, Vanessa. Scream at me, rant at me, do whatever you need to do, but know this. I am not going to judge you or condemn you. I care about you. And so does God."

Then he kissed the top of her head. "And about God's timing—He brought *you* into my life at just the *right* time. You've helped me see that I have some long-held issues that have been holding me back, too." Snuggling her close, he added, "And I think it's time that we both settle up."

Chapter Sixteen

Vanessa's heart stopped and then skidded into a fast beat. "Are you willing to lay it all out there between us, Rory?"

"Yes," he said. "I'm willing to tell you things I've never told anyone. Not even the friends I'd trust with my life. But those friends know everything now. And they encouraged me to talk to you. To be honest with you."

"And why me?" She had to know that this was real and that he wouldn't panic again. And she needed to know what was holding him back. "Do you think you can trust me?"

"Yes," he said again, his usually animated eyes turning solemn and somber. "I've needed someone like you in my life for a long time now. But like you, I was afraid to let go or to give in to God's plan for my life."

Surprised at this candid conversation and

touched that he felt this way about her, Vanessa smiled for the first time since she'd had her meltdown earlier. "How do you know if I'm in that plan? What if I mess things up for you the way my mother accused me of messing up things for her?"

"Didn't your mother, with all her flaws and problems, finally find a man who could love her and change her and make her see that she'd damaged you?"

Vanessa's mind reeled from the implications of that statement. "Marrying Richard did make it better for me, yes, but she never saw that her actions had damaged me, Rory. She might have found happiness and a husband who brought her the security she always craved, but she never once told me she was sorry for what she did to me. For what that man—the other husband— did to me. I can't forget that, and I sure don't have to forgive it."

"Forgiveness is the hardest part of following Christ," Rory said. "It never comes easy but you need to understand something about forgiveness, Vanessa. It's more about helping you to heal and grow through grace than it is about soothing the other person's feelings. Don't get me wrong. When you forgive someone it releases them from any guilt or debt. But it also releases you from bitterness and heartache and that yoke of despair."

Despair.

She'd felt a sense of desperation and despair for as long as she could remember. She'd become so cynical and jaded that she'd stopped making the effort to understand what being a Christian could mean. And she'd given up on one of the most important things in life.

Love.

She'd given up on love.

"Maybe it's time to make that next move," she said, getting up to reach for the journal she'd been avoiding for days.

Rory waited for her to sit back down. "Are you sure you want to do this with me here? I can take a walk along the bay, give you some time alone."

"No. If I'm supposed to forgive her, I'll need you with me to remind me of that."

"You know that, in your heart."

"But my head is a tad too stubborn to follow that notion."

"That's the thing about humans. We think we have all the answers."

She swallowed the rising fear tearing through her throat. "Okay, I need to get this over and done so I can get on with my life."

Rory gave her a quick kiss. "You can do this, Vanessa. You're strong and you're a fighter."

Vanessa opened the worn journal and took a deep breath.

Soon, she was immersed in baby pictures of herself and several pictures of her mother with various men. Some that Vanessa remembered and others that she'd just as soon forget.

Each picture was dated and marked with captions.

Vanessa's first birthday! We survived even after her daddy walked away. He offered to help me make ends meet, but I told him to never come back if he couldn't come back to stay.

"I don't remember him," Vanessa said, shock jarring her memories into action. "I don't remember having a daddy."

Rory studied the photo. "You were young, a baby still. How could you remember?"

Vanessa went back to searching through the journal.

Vanessa's first day of kindergarten. I hope she'll be okay.

And then, two months later:

We had to move again. Got evicted from that cute little apartment on the beach. I have to find another job. I'm no good at cleaning condos.

"Do you remember any of that?" Rory asked after she'd read the captions out loud.

"Some of it," Vanessa admitted. "This is bringing it all back. I remember a man with dark hair coming to see us right after I started first grade in…what was that little town?" She stopped and stared at her smiling, snaggle-toothed image. "Somewhere in Alabama. I can't remember."

Rory encouraged her. "What happened? Do you remember anything the man did or said?"

"No. Not really." She closed her eyes, the image of her mother sitting out on a porch crying drifting through her memories. "She cried after he left."

Now Vanessa needed to see every page in the little scrapbook. She pored over each and every caption and touched her hand to some of the faded photographs. A few of her mother marrying again, always smiling that hopeful, determined smile. Always looking for love. Searching. Always searching.

In between husbands and a history of Vanessa's childhood, her mother talked about her artwork and how she needed to make a living at it. She wrote about art shows and selling her work to all kinds of customers, from rich, eccentric donors to poor but interested individuals.

Vanessa began to see a pattern here. Her mother had met three of her four husbands at these events. Vanessa couldn't remember how Cora had met Richard.

"A lot of this is about you," Rory said, drawing her back to the journal. "In spite of everything, she treasured these memories of you."

Vanessa pushed at her hair and took a calming breath. "I never knew she kept all of these photos and other things."

Her school pictures. New shoes. A good report card. Walking on the beach and finding seashells. Lying on the floor, on her stomach, reading a book. Her first teenaged dance. Wearing vintage clothes.

"I remember being bored at the art shows. I'd go shopping on my own. No wonder I love vintage things so much. I was raised in flea markets and art colonies."

Rory grinned and punched her on the arm. "Well, you always look pretty to me, and you have a good thing going with Vanessa's Vintage, so that's something."

"Yes, that's something."

And then:

I got married again today. He's a preacher! Can you imagine that? But he's so sweet and so kind to me and he buys me pretty things.

Vanessa stared at the photo of her mother with Gregory Pardue. Cora wore a cream-colored suit, and he wore a dark jacket and light-colored pants.

She put the journal down, her stomach churning. "I remember the wedding. I cried because I knew he wasn't a good man. I was afraid of him from the beginning."

"Your instincts were right," Rory said. "But you were too afraid to say anything to anyone."

"I wanted this one to work," she replied. "I so wanted to have a good father, someone who'd take care of us so we could live in a decent house and so I wouldn't have to buy second-hand clothes all the time. By the time they got married, she'd already bought this house, but it needed a lot of work. Later…when she married Richard, he had the whole house redone, and he paid off her mortgage."

"So Richard was the kind of father figure you always wanted."

"Yes." Vanessa held the journal close, her gaze stuck on her mother holding Gregory Pardue's hand. She couldn't stop the shivers moving down her backbone. "I don't remember why she and Gregory broke up. I saw her crying and him packing a suitcase and storming out the door."

"Is that his name? Gregory Pardue?"

"Yes. You don't know him, do you?"

"No. I needed to put a name with the face. In case I do ever run into him."

"I don't think you will. He left the state of Florida, last I heard."

She put the journal down. "I can't read any more right now. But I think I can finish it now. I've moved past the worst part."

"Does it help, knowing your mother did love you? Most of this journal revolves around you, Vanessa. That has to mean something to you."

"It does," she said. "It helps." She got up and moved around the room, that nervous feeling hitting her in the stomach. "I should go and get back to setting up for the estate sale."

Rory started gathering their dishes and the half-eaten food. "I need to get back, too." Drying his hands on a towel, he turned to her. "Are you okay? I mean, do you need me to stay with you at your house for the rest of the day?"

"No. I'm much better now. I don't know what I was so afraid of. I should have read this journal when I first found it."

"It could help you finish what you started," Rory said.

She helped him clean up, relief washing over her. "Remembering things wasn't so bad. Good in places. Sad in others."

But she had a feeling the end would be the

worst. Her mother being all alone for the first time in her life. She'd have to deal with that later.

They were headed out the door when she turned to Rory. "Hey, you aren't getting off so easily. You promised you'd share with me, Rory. Or are you stalling out on me again?"

He locked the door and turned to stare over at her. The morning had changed into afternoon. The sun glistened off the water in shades of aqua and sky blue. Birds were chirping in the nearby pines and oaks. Out in the shallows, a brown pelican perched on an old stump with an unmoving calm.

"I was married once," Rory said on a low, calm note.

She turned so quickly to stare over at him the pelican lifted its vast wings and took flight. "What?"

"It's true." He studied the water, his expression etched with sadness. "I knew early on that I wanted to be involved in the church in some sort of capacity. So I went to seminary and while I was there, I met a girl. And we fell in love and got married."

Shock rocketed through Vanessa, burning her with curiosity. "But…what happened?"

Did he get a divorce? Or worse? "Rory?"

"We'd been married for about six months when she got sick," he said. "It was sudden.

An aneurysm in her brain. She woke up with a headache one morning and she died that night, in the hospital. She was twenty-four."

Vanessa took in a breath and held both hands to her face so she could keep from sobbing again. "Rory…"

"I know. It's awful. It was awful. We lived in Texas, near the college campus. She was studying to be a nurse, and I was preparing to move us back here so I could begin my ministry. She was six weeks pregnant with our child."

Vanessa sank into the nearest chair. She couldn't speak, couldn't imagine what he'd been through. She reached out a hand to him, but he wasn't looking at her. He was there, back in the past, remembering, reliving.

"I buried her…them…and then I graduated and took on my first assignment, a small country church about fifty miles east of here. I had nowhere to go, but I wasn't really ready to be a minister. I couldn't preach. I wanted to be buried there with them safe in my arms."

Vanessa started crying again, but this time her tears were silent. She got up and went to him and took him in her arms.

Rory didn't say anything. He held her there for a long time, his arms tight around her, his breath moving over her hair and her skin.

"What can I say?" she asked, her fingers stroking his jawline. "What can I do?"

"There is nothing to say or do," he finally managed to say, his words husky and low. "I've heard it all. They're in a better place. It was their time to go. God needed some new angels in Heaven. God has a plan for you, Rory. There's a reason for everything." His eyes burned a deep blue. "I never could figure out the reason for their deaths, however."

Vanessa stood back, her hand stilling on his face, her eyes holding his. "How did you ever come back from that to become the man you are today?"

His eyes, so bright with memories and grief, held her. "I told you. I went to war."

She could understand him so much better now. He'd been angry, and with good reason. "You didn't go over there to fight, did you?"

He nodded his head. "Yes, I thought I'd fight or that maybe I'd get killed. But I was drifting. I'd been assigned to a small church here in Florida, but my heart wasn't in it. I talked to a counselor, a retired minister, and she actually suggested I consider serving as an army chaplain. She'd been through it." He gave Vanessa a weak smile. "So I read up on what it would take, and I did something very impulsive. I joined up and told the recruiters I wanted to go through the Chaplain Candidate Program."

"You became a soldier?"

"Yes, a soldier of sorts. I didn't carry a weapon, but I had a protection detail with me at all times. I went into it hoping to find my soul again. Instead, I found death and heartache and wounded, suffering people. The anger left me when I started talking to the men and women who were serving over there and when I truly started praying for guidance. I guess you could say I had an epiphany. Their pain gave me a reason to live, to help others who were suffering worse than I ever had."

His eyes met hers, holding the trace of darkness she'd sensed when they'd first met. "I realized I wanted to live. And I wanted to help others to live. Men and women who'd seen the worst and suffered the worst. I counseled them and prayed for them and found my calling again. One dark night after a horrible battle, after I'd held the hands of too many dying men, I promised God that if He'd give me the strength to help and serve others, I'd try to lead a happy, content life serving Him."

Vanessa lifted on her toes and kissed Rory, her heart opening and lifting in a way that reminded her of that pelican taking flight. And she finally accepted that she might be falling in love with a man of God.

Chapter Seventeen

The next night, Vanessa checked her reflection in the mirror by the front door, hoping her outfit was suitable for dinner at the Peppermons' house. She wore jeans and a white T-shirt with a bright green fringed scarf around her neck. Wanda had insisted she didn't have to bring anything food-wise. But she had brought a gift for Kandi—some black rose earrings and a long chain necklace. Goth looking but not too far out there.

Vanessa thought about Rory. They'd held each other and talked for a long time, there on the big porch of the camp house.

"I never dreamed you'd been through something so sad, so tragic," she told him. "You're a living example of God's love, Rory."

"It took me a long time to get here," he explained. "And even now, I still have bad days or moments where I sit down and cry. I'll always miss them. I'll always wonder what our child would have been like. But God has blessed me in so many ways. And He gave me the gifts of compassion and understanding."

"You understood me right away," she said. "You saw the pain in my soul."

And now that she could see his pain, she appreciated him even more. They'd made plans to have dinner together on Friday night, after the rummage and estate sales on Friday. Then Blain and Rikki's wedding on Sunday. Rory had asked her to come as his date.

"The minister gets to bring a date?"

"This one does, and he wants her to be you. Or you to be her. Just be there."

So she'd agreed.

They'd taken a new turn in their relationship.

But tonight, she'd made a commitment to be here with Kandi.

The Peppermons lived on the other side of the lake and down a side street that had a partial view of the water. Vanessa followed the directions Wanda had given her and soon saw the big, wood-framed house that Wanda had described.

The house was painted a deep blue, with white shutters and porch railings. Several white rocking chairs lined both sides of the wide front door. Hanging baskets with red geraniums and pink-and-white petunias swayed at each corner of the long porch. The yard was also full of flower beds, mulched and overflowing with blossoms and plants of every size and color.

Vanessa thought that if she lived here, she'd never want to leave. She walked up the steps to the big door and pressed the doorbell, nerves ringing in her head right along with the bell that loudly played Beethoven's "Ode to Joy."

Then she heard the pounding of several feet thundering throughout the house, followed by shouting.

The door tore open and a young boy with pecan-colored skin grinned up at her. "I got it," he called over his shoulder. "It's Kandi's friend, Van-Esther."

Vanessa smiled at the mispronunciation of her name. "Hi," she said, unsure what to do next. A full house scared her a lot more than an empty one.

"Hi," he said, tugging her inside the wide hallway of the house. "I'm Derek."

"Hello, Derek," Vanessa replied, the whirl of a ceiling fan cooling the cold sweat sticking to her backbone. Why was she so terrified of children? It wasn't that she was afraid of kids. She loved them. But she had a fear of doing or saying the wrong thing around them. What if she did that with Kandi?

A vision of Rory holding a baby planted itself inside her head and caused her to sweat even more.

"Hi, come on back," Wanda called, her head peeking out from what had to be the kitchen on one side of the long hallway.

Derek reached for Vanessa's hand. "We're having the best dinner. Taco salad."

"I love taco salad," Vanessa said, wondering how Wanda and Carl managed to feed so many mouths. She'd seen kids hanging out in rooms on both sides of the hallway, some reading and studying and others watching television. But she hadn't spotted Kandi yet.

Derek guided her to the right side of the house where a country kitchen ran into a big dining room, both rooms spacious and bright and spick-and-span clean.

"Welcome," Wanda said from her spot in front of the stove. She stirred a huge pot of taco meat with one hand while one of the younger children hung away from the stove's heat on her hip.

"Find a seat. It's about ready." She lifted her chin toward the stairs. "Kandi is cleaning her room. She'll be down soon."

"Okay."

Vanessa smiled at Wanda, noting her clipped salt-and-pepper hair and her chunky, solid frame. She wore old jeans and a faded yellow shirt underneath a white apron splotched with all colors of paint that said *We are all God's children*.

Vanessa decided she *would* stay here forever. Who would ever notice her anyway? She'd merge into the crowd of children of all ages and colors that moved at random through the many rooms of the house. The energy was magnetic and endearing.

Then the back door opened and Carl walked in, wearing work clothes. His shirt pocket was embroidered with the title of Millbrook Gardens Nursery and Landscaping.

That explained the lovely front yard and the many hanging baskets. She could imagine Wanda and Carl puttering around in the garden with a string of kids following them.

"Hi," he said, waving to Vanessa. Then he kissed Wanda and took the giggling toddler off her hip. "Hey, honey, you got room for one more tonight?"

Wanda laughed out loud. "Sure. We'll add another taco shell or two to the twenty-four we already have. Who'd you invite to dinner this time?"

Carl walked back to the door and motioned. "Oh, just the preacher. He was walking along the lake like he'd lost his best friend."

And in walked Rory, bearing a sheepish smile. When he looked up at Vanessa, he shrugged. "I told him I was fine, but he insisted I hop in and come home with him."

Remembering their intimate conversation yesterday, she felt as shy and unsteady as he looked. And yet she was so glad to see him. "Hi."

She wanted to run to him and hold him close, but she'd settle for having him nearby for now. When they'd parted late yesterday afternoon, Vanessa had accepted that she was in love with Rory. She wasn't sure what to do about that.

She felt a strong sense of relief at seeing him. He'd help guide her through this maze of children and keep her from saying or doing the wrong thing. Probably in the same way he'd helped her since the first time she'd laid eyes on him.

But Vanessa also now knew *he* wasn't always fine. He probably enjoyed these gatherings more than anyone because he loved people and he was so good with children. She smiled to reassure him, then got up and decided to get busy. "Wanda, what can I do to help?"

Wanda stirred meat and barked orders. "We all have jobs around here. If anything is left over after everyone does their assigned task, I guess you can get out that other box of taco shells and stick 'em in the oven."

Vanessa motioned to Rory. "Don't think you're gonna get away with doing nothing."

Rory appeared relieved and hurried toward Vanessa. Together they raided the big pantry that Wanda pointed to while she issued orders all around. Rory winked at Vanessa and whispered, "I didn't plan this, but I've wanted to see you all day long. How are you?"

"Good, now that you're here," she replied. "How about you?"

"I'm great. I feel lighthearted and…free."

Vanessa could relate to that feeling. "Me, too. I guess confession *is* good for the soul."

"You can say that again. You're good for my soul."

"I'm going to get cleaned up," Carl called over the chaos. "That way I get out of being bossed around."

"You have cleanup duty in here later, too," Wanda called.

Vanessa's heart filled with something so foreign and sweet, she had to stop and watch the confusion in order to figure it out.

Joy. She felt a great rush of joy.

No wonder Wanda wore that apron.

Rory saw her expression, his gaze holding hers. "They are amazing, aren't they?"

She nodded. "Yes, they are." Then she turned to him. "I'm glad you're here."

He took the bag of taco shells and grinned over at her. "I didn't want you to think I'd wormed my way in on this dinner so I could see you. But that is an added bonus."

She shrugged. "Carl invited you, so you had to accept."

"Yes, but I accepted two seconds quicker when I remembered you'd be here."

"I'm doubly glad now. I need you for moral support."

"You're scared?"

"Completely," she said. "I don't think I'd be a good mother. I wouldn't know how to handle any of this, let alone a crying baby or confused teen."

He passed her the tacos to put on a baking sheet. "You keep saying that, but I think you'd make a great mother."

Vanessa stared over at him, wishing she felt the same way. Then it occurred to her that Rory had almost been a father. He'd lost the baby his wife was carrying, along with her.

If he ever found the right woman, he'd want more children.

But as much as it hurt her even to think such a thing, Vanessa wasn't sure she was the motherly type. She hadn't had a very good role model.

And that meant she and Rory might not have a future together after all.

Rory enjoyed watching Vanessa as she got to know the kids. Kandi and Vanessa were in the kitchen, cutting and serving brownies and ice cream. They talked and laughed as if they were old friends. Kandi could either help Vanessa get over her fear of motherhood or cause her to stand firm on never having children.

He prayed both of them would find some sort of encouragement by being around each other. He thought of yesterday and how he and Vanessa had held each other and kissed after they'd both opened old wounds. His heart bumped faster each time he thought about their time together.

The old guilt pushed at him, making him wonder if he could take that final step toward finding his soul mate. Was Vanessa that woman, the one who could finally fill that hole that ran deep inside his heart? He believed it and he prayed about it.

He wanted her in his life.

"You look awfully pensive," Carl said as he handed Rory a bowl full of vanilla ice cream mixed with brownie chunks. "Troubles, Preacher?"

Rory grinned and shook his head. "No, not really. Trouble, but in a good way, I think."

"The way you keep staring at Vanessa, I think I know that kind of trouble, my friend. And I've been married to her for close to thirty years."

Rory took a bite of the vanilla ice cream and chased it with a chunk of moist brownie. The brain freeze almost jarred him out of his musings. "I think I might be ready for the challenge," he admitted, knowing Carl wouldn't repeat his words, except maybe to Wanda. "We'll have to see what happens."

"Do you want her in your life?" Carl asked on a low chuckle. "Are you ready for everything that involves?"

"I think so. The problem is convincing her that she's the one for me. Her confidence level needs boosting. She thinks she's not good wife-mother-marriage material."

Carl shook his head and laughed and then grabbed up a four-year-old little girl and gave her a big hug. The child smiled shyly at Rory and pointed a chubby finger. "Peacher."

"That is the peacher, Betsy," Carl said without correcting her. "He's a good guy."

"Good," Betsy said, smiling at Rory.

He grinned back and tickled at her shoulder. "Where's your ice cream?"

She wiggled out of Carl's embrace. "More," she said in a singsong voice as she headed back to the kitchen.

Kandi scooped her up and sat her on the counter. "Here's yours, Betsy-bell."

Rory imagined Vanessa with a child, his heart burning with an intense need. "Kandi seems happier than I've seen her in a while."

"She's doing better," Carl admitted. "Her grades have come up and she's helping out more around here. Wanda and she have lots of late-night talks."

"Vanessa really wants to be a good mentor to her," Rory said. "She's been through a lot herself."

Carl studied the action in the kitchen. "We've all got something, don't we?"

Rory nodded and finished his dessert. "Thanks for asking me over, Carl. And thanks for the pep talk. I'm a little rusty in the 'figuring out a woman' department."

Carl slapped a meaty hand across Rory's back. "I hate to break it to you, Preacher. But there ain't no such thing as figuring out a woman."

Rory laughed and lifted his spoon in the air. "I do believe you're correct on that matter."

When he glanced back to the kitchen, Vanessa smiled at him.

"And Kandi wants to go to college to study fashion design. She's an artist, too. She showed me some of her sketches. She has a lot of talent."

"So I take it tonight was a success?" Rory asked as they drove along Lake Street. She'd insisted on giving him a ride home, and he hadn't argued with that notion.

"Yes. She was like a different person. She laughed and talked and I felt as if we really connected—" She stopped and glanced over at him. "I sound so corny, don't I?"

"You sound happy," Rory said. "You sound as if you were born to be a positive role model."

"Not born to it," she quickly corrected. "But hopeful, Rory. I hope I'll make a difference in Kandi's life. She opened up a little about how her mother had died, and it broke my heart. I know she's been through all kinds of things, but she can't tell me everything." Vanessa pulled into the driveway of her house. "She goes to a therapist. She did tell me that much."

Rory turned so he could see Vanessa's face. "Did you ever go through therapy?"

"No. I buried it all deep inside. You're the first person I've ever told the whole truth."

Rory wondered how Miss Fanny had found out and decided maybe Vanessa's mother had confessed to her friend in a final attempt to find some peace before she died. Why hadn't she made an attempt to ask Vanessa to forgive her?

"I'm okay, Rory," she said. Then she shook her head. "I have issues. A lot of issues. But

I'm working through them with each room in this house."

"Do you sleep in that bedroom?" he asked.

She went still, her eyes on the house. "I sleep on the couch in the den most nights."

"All the time," he amended. Then he reached for her and tugged her close. "You're not alone, Vanessa. I want you to always remember that."

"I will," she said against his chest. Then she lifted away and opened the car door.

Rory got out and stood watching her.

She turned at the steps. "Want to come in for coffee or a soda?"

"I thought you'd never ask," he said.

He didn't want her to be alone tonight. At least this way, he could stay with her for a little while before he had to go home. But it also occurred to him that accepting her invitation to come in for coffee worked out for him, too.

Because he didn't want to be alone anymore either.

Chapter Eighteen

Wanda had sent brownies home with them, so Rory watched as Vanessa made coffee and got a plate.

"I shouldn't eat another one," she said, bringing the plate to the living room coffee table. "But they're so good."

"She makes them from scratch," Rory said. He helped pour the coffee and followed her into the living room. "We can walk this off or go kayaking again. But I think working the sales on Friday will take care of burning off a lot of calories."

Vanessa seemed pensive, her emotions close to the surface. "It's really going to happen, isn't it?"

"Are you ready for this?" he asked. "I did push you into holding your sale in conjunction with ours. Maybe I should have let you handle things on your own."

"No. I'm glad you forced the issue." She lifted her hand in the air. "I'd still be sitting in the middle of the floor trying to sort through all of this. I needed a firm deadline." Then she shrugged. "I need to get this part of my life over and done with."

Rory wondered what she would do with her life once this place was out of her system.

After they'd settled onto the old couch, he glanced around. "I like this house."

"It'll be for sale soon. Make me an offer."

He'd buy it in a heartbeat. But only if she'd come with it. "That's tempting. You're tempting."

She smiled at that. "Is this brownie tempting?"

"Yes." He grabbed the last one and held it away from her. Then he fed it to her, piece by piece, thinking he could get used to nights such as this. Nights with her.

"So where will that leave us?" he asked, hoping he wouldn't break the tender understanding they had between them now. "What happens after you sell this house?"

"I don't know." She put down her coffee and stared out onto the big sunporch. "I never planned to stay here."

"And I never planned to ask you to stay here."

Her eyes glistened with hope and confusion. "Are you? Asking me to stay?"

"I can't make you stay but…I want you to stay."

She gave him a sweet smile, but her eyes still held that trace of hesitancy and doubt. "I have my boutique and my website to consider."

"And I have no right to tell you what to do about either of those. You're a businesswoman. You have obligations."

Which didn't include him. So where did that leave them?

"I can visit—a lot."

"Not if you sell the house. You wouldn't have any reason to come back here."

"You'd be my reason, Rory. I mean, if you want to be my reason. If you want me to come back. And you can come and see me in New Orleans."

"So we'd have this back-and-forth, long-distance type relationship?"

"Yes. I could stay with Marla and Alec. Or in a hotel out on the bay."

He wanted more, but he couldn't ask for more. This was all so new and different. "We probably need to think about things and consider what we're saying here."

Vanessa nodded, but he saw a trace of disappointment in her eyes. "You know how hard I fought this. I'm not the typical starry-eyed woman looking for love."

He'd certainly seen that from the first. "You have a lot of love to give." He had to ask. "Don't take this the wrong way. We're still…getting to know each other, but these are things I have to ask. Is the having-a-family thing holding you back? You really don't want to have children? Or is it me? Maybe you like me but you don't want to have a relationship with a minister."

She stared over at him with those big eyes. "You have a right to know the answers to those questions. I just don't know the answers. I'm still afraid I'll mess it all up—marriage and a family. You. I'd rather keep you as a friend than lose you because I make the wrong move."

Rory pulled her close. "You will never lose me. Ever. No matter what."

And he prayed he wouldn't lose her.

Vanessa leaned over and kissed him. "I can't believe how I feel, Rory. It's so…rich. I feel full and rich, and my heart is doing a funny dance. I—"

Her cell rang. And then Rory's cell rang.

"It's Wanda," she said, glancing at Rory.

"And Carl," he said. "This can't be good."

He answered Carl's call while she did the same with Wanda.

"Kandi is missing," Carl said. "We went up for bed check, and she'd stuffed her mattress with pillows and clothes. But she's gone."

"I'll be right there," Rory said. Then he stood and watched Vanessa's face.

"We're on our way," she said. She ended the call and rushed into his arms. "They think she's with the Goth guy."

"Let's go," Rory said. He needed to call in reinforcements. Blain would help. "I'll call Blain on the way."

"We have to find her," Vanessa said. "She was so happy tonight. She seemed like a different person. We talked and laughed, and she was so pleasant."

"That's because she knew she would be leaving after dinner to meet up with him," Rory said. "They've probably been planning this for weeks."

"I should have paid more attention," Vanessa told him. "I worried that she'd been through a lot of what I went through."

"Not that I know of," Rory replied. "But she might have been pushed around by other boyfriends. She spent a lot of time out there on her own growing up."

They made it to the Peppermons' house in record time.

When they pulled up, all of the lights were

on and a patrol car was parked in the yard. So was Blain's pickup truck. Blain must have put the pedal to the metal, too.

Rory and Vanessa rushed toward the house, but he pulled her close before they got inside. "We have to stay cool and positive, for their sake, okay?"

Vanessa nodded. "Rory, should we pray?"

Touched that she wanted that, he nodded and pulled her into his arms. Then he whispered an urgent prayer as they held each other there. "Help us to find this confused young girl, Lord."

Vanessa held tight to him and then stood back. "I'm ready. Let's go inside."

"We're doing everything we can to find her," Blain told the Peppermons. "She can't get far since you discovered her missing a little while ago."

Vanessa sat holding one of the younger children who'd woken in the middle of all the chaos. Her heart hurt for this loving family and for Kandi. Maybe this boy was okay and truly cared about her, or maybe he only wanted to seduce her and hurt her.

I need You, Lord.

Vanessa kissed the little girl's reddish-blond hair. Emma. Little Emma. She now knew the names of all the children who lived in this house.

And she wasn't afraid of them anymore. Instead, she wanted to cuddle each of them and fight for them and protect them from that big, scary world out there. Why had she ever worried that her heart couldn't love? Right now, her heart ached with love.

Then realization filled her mind. It was the *love* she was so afraid of. This kind of love that took your breath away and held your soul in a tender capture. This fierce, protective love that made you want to harm anyone who dared hurt a child.

Had her mother felt that way at times?

She'd have to finish reading that journal.

She listened to Blain's soft, steady voice. He'd gone over every detail. Where did the boy— Jerome "Rocky" Asher—live? How old was he? How had they met? Did they hang out at school?

Jerome lived on the other side of town, and they'd met at an ice-cream stand out on the beach. He had dropped out of school and hung with an older crowd known for drug use and vagrancy.

The worst possible scenario. What if he'd taken her somewhere and enticed her to use drugs?

Wanda came over to Vanessa. "Do you need anything?"

"I should be asking you that," Vanessa said. "I wish I could do more."

"You're here and that counts." Wanda took

Emma. "I'm going to get her back to bed. You can man the drink counters. I have snacks in the pantry."

Vanessa gladly took over kitchen duty. She made coffee and sliced homemade banana bread. Soon, several people from the church and the foster-parent support group showed up. Vanessa listened and watched and got everyone something to eat or drink. It was going to be a long night.

She watched Rory. He made sure everyone got prayed over or prayed with or prayed for. She loved him. She knew that in her heart right now, and she also knew that she couldn't leave him.

But she'd have to make some tough decisions about staying here. In this town, married to a preacher.

What do you think about that, Mom?

"How you doing?" Rory asked, his fingers tangling with hers after he'd walked up close.

"I'm okay. It's hard to breathe, but I'm doing what you said. I have to be strong for them. I love this family."

"We all do."

He gave her a quick kiss. "You should rest."

"I can't. Do you want something to eat or drink?"

"I'm fine."

He stood with her in the kitchen, waiting. The agony of not knowing, of imagining the worst, or hoping for the best, made Vanessa want to throw something.

But Rory's hand in hers held her there, steadying her like an anchor holding a lost ship.

"Is this how it feels?" she asked him. "Is this how God holds us when we're scared and out of options? The same way you're holding me now?"

"Yes."

"I'm beginning to get it, Rory. I need Him in my life. I could never get through this night without Him. Or you."

"We're here, both of us," Rory said. "Hang tight."

Vanessa heard her phone ringing. Searching on the counter for her purse, she dug inside.

"It's Kandi," she told Rory.

Rory immediately called out to Blain and the Peppermons.

"Hello?" Vanessa said, trying to keep her voice calm.

"I need help."

"Where are you?"

"In the park by the bay, underneath the white gazebo. Vanessa, come alone, please."

"I'm on my way."

She ended the call and told Rory and the others what Kandi had said. "I'm going. I have to."

Blain nodded. "Okay, but you won't really be alone. I'm going to follow you and park my truck on the other end of the park. I'll walk it the rest of the way and stay in the trees."

"I'm going with you, Blain," Rory said.

Blain didn't argue. "Let's go then."

"We'll call you," Blain told Wanda. "Meantime, stay here and if she calls again, just assure her that Vanessa is on the way. Alone."

Vanessa grabbed her purse and went to her car, glad they'd brought her car to save time earlier.

"Be careful," Rory said. "It could be a setup."

"I'll be fine," Vanessa said. But she was glad to know Blain and Rory would be nearby.

And that the Lord would watch over Kandi and Vanessa, too.

Chapter Nineteen

The Bayside Park was dark and deserted this late at night. With one road forming a horseshoe that circled in and out, and dense shrubs and trees all around, it could be beautiful by day and dangerous by night.

Vanessa hadn't been here in over ten years. But she knew exactly why Kandi would come here with a boy. It was secluded and shadowy. Private. Too private.

Vanessa pulled her tiny car up into the gravel parking space and cut the engine. The white gazebo sat in the middle of the open area by the water, glowing eerily in the moonlight.

Taking a calming breath, she got out and started walking up the dirt lane to the water. "Kandi?"

"I'm here."

Vanessa followed the sound of the girl's shaky

voice. And then she saw a dark figure huddled on the round table inside the wide gazebo. Hurrying now, she rushed up to Kandi's side.

"Are you all right?"

Kandi looked up, and Vanessa saw the fear and shame on the girl's face. And the swollen right eye. "What happened?"

"He…he didn't like the word no," Kandi said through a sob.

Vanessa felt sick to her stomach. "Did he…?"

"No." Kandi shook her head and wiped at her eyes. "It got ugly but I'm okay."

"Where is he?" Vanessa asked, hoping Blain and Rory would take care of finding Jerome.

"He took off through the park after we fought. I told him I was going to call the police."

"Smart girl."

"Not so smart," Kandi retorted. "He had me fooled, you know. Said I was the one for him. That he could take away all my troubles." She gulped in a sob. "Then later he told me he'd come back and finish the job if I ratted him out."

"He won't," Vanessa said. "The police will find him."

"I should have known he was a loser," Kandi said. "But he treated me so good at first."

Terrible memories whispered around Vanessa, making her shiver in the warm wind. Gregory Pardue had been sweet and generous to her mother and to Vanessa, too, at first. Pushing the dark thoughts away, she asked, "Did he… try to give you drugs?"

"Of course," Kandi said. "And I almost let him." She wrapped her arms against her ribs. "He told me I'd feel good, that all of my troubles would disappear. But I thought of Miss Wanda and Mr. Carl and how much they'd done for me, even when I was so mean and ugly toward them. And I thought of my mom and how drugs and alcohol had killed her."

Vanessa kept her hand on Kandi's arm but didn't speak. Emotion clogged her throat, but she had to keep it together.

"It was almost as if my mom was standing here, telling me to stop. Telling me to run away. When I was little, she used to tell me that I was special. That I'd be okay, no matter what. I had this image of her in my head, and that's when I told him no."

"She's watching over you," Vanessa said in a quiet voice.

A tear moved down her right cheek, an image of her mother whispering sweet words in her ear. *You'll be okay, honey. One day, your daddy will come for us.*

How could she have forgotten that? And how could she love someone so much and still resent that same person for her past troubles? It all stemmed from needing to know the truth, from needing proof. But faith was the substance of things not seen…

Vanessa wished that day her mother had promised her had come, but she understood a lot now about what being a parent involved. Kandi and the Peppermons had taught her that. Rory had talked to her about family, too. Marla had shown her what a real family could be like. Miss Fanny had been family to Cora.

"Why did you call me?" she asked Kandi. "Why not Wanda or Carl?"

Kandi shrugged and sniffed, her cheeks shadowed with smeared mascara and eyeliner. "Because you're like me," she said. "You lost your mother, and you never mention having a daddy either. And you were afraid to go inside that church the first night we met."

"Yes, all of that is true," Vanessa said. "You've got me pegged."

Kandi looked out toward the woods. "I trust you."

Vanessa's heart fell open, but instead of hurting, the old wounds tingled with a new awareness, a sort of healing. "I'm glad you called me."

"I'm in a lot of trouble," Kandi said. "I don't know how to get out of this mess. This life."

"You will be okay," Vanessa said. "You used

your head, and you stopped this before it became too late."

"But what if it's too late for me anyway?" Kandi asked, tears streaming down her face.

"It's never too late for you to turn your life around," Vanessa replied, hearing the words herself. She needed to remember that. "You've got good people in your life, people who are willing to help you and love you. Let's get you home."

Kandi got up and pulled at her torn clothes. "Are they mad at me?"

"They're worried," Vanessa said. "But as soon as I call them, they'll be relieved, too."

After she'd phoned Wanda and told her she was bringing Kandi home, Vanessa called Rory. "We're on our way."

"I know," he said. "You were great with her."

Vanessa breathed a sigh of relief, knowing Rory and Blain had been there in the shadows. "She's the one who helped me, Rory."

"Blain has put out the word on Jerome Asher. He'll be brought in for questioning on several counts, and if we find drugs on him, he'll be in a lot of trouble. But it'll be up to the Peppermons and their caseworker on how to handle this situation. Or whether or not they'll press charges."

Vanessa glanced over at Kandi. The girl

leaned against the window, her eyes closed. "You know what I think should be done."

"I'm getting the picture, yes. And I tend to agree with you. Get her home and we'll talk."

At around two in the morning, Vanessa pulled up to the Peppermon house. Now that everyone knew Kandi was safe, most of the people who'd come to help had left. Probably best since the girl was exhausted, embarrassed and in no mood for prying eyes.

"Let's get you inside," Vanessa said.

She guided Kandi up the steps, but the front door burst open before they could reach it.

Wanda opened her arms, tears misting in her eyes.

Kandi ran to her and held her tight. "I'm sorry, Miss Wanda."

"Shhh," Wanda said. "It's okay. We'll talk tomorrow. Right now, let's get you a nice bath so you can sleep." She looked at Vanessa over the girl's head, her eyes wide with the one question.

Vanessa shook her head and mouthed, "She's okay."

The look of relief in Wanda's eyes mirrored the relief Vanessa felt in her soul. She'd avoided a similar incident when she'd been Kandi's age. Another shiver moved down her spine. She was so thankful the girl had managed to get herself out of a bad situation, too.

Thank You, God.

After Wanda gave Kandi some water and crackers and took her upstairs, Vanessa stood in the kitchen and stared out the window. The darkness swirled with memories and pain, a sort of frustration that she couldn't shake.

When she felt a hand on her shoulder, she turned to find Rory standing there. He took her into his arms and held her close, his lips touching her temple.

Vanessa took one long breath, and then she burst into tears.

An hour later, Rory and Vanessa made it back to her house.

"I'm exhausted," she said, her voice raspy. "I'm sure you are, too."

"Yep." He felt the weight of the night pushing against his shoulders. "I hope Blain hauls Jerome in and gives him a few good reasons to leave Kandi alone."

"I hope he sends him to jail," Vanessa said, a bitterness edging her words.

"This brought it all back, didn't it?"

He'd seen the way she kept staring out the window. How she held herself, her arms in a protective shield against her body.

"Yes." She turned to him, her expression grim. "Jerome is younger and more edgy, but it's the same. Gaining her trust, telling her what she wants to hear, promising her something better. I heard all of that from Gregory. My mom heard all of that, too. I never thought about it until tonight, but that man tricked both of us."

"He was evil, Vanessa. And he was working to put a wedge between you and your mother."

"Well, it worked," she said. "I let him do that to us. She let him do that to me."

"You can let go of all of that now."

"Can I?" she asked. "I thought I could. But tonight, it all came tumbling back."

Rory didn't know how to reach her, and he worried that she would slip away again. "You helped a young girl, Vanessa. You helped her *because* of what you've been through and in spite of it, too. Look at the blessing in that…and be thankful that you were able to get through to Kandi enough that she trusted you to call you."

Vanessa leaned against the kitchen counter and stared over at him. "It's late and we're both tired. We have a busy week, starting tomorrow."

"I guess that's my cue to go," Rory said, wishing he could stay. But they did have lots to do before the big event on Friday. And they still had work to do before they'd be free and clear of their past hang-ups.

He turned to leave, a heaviness centered in his heart.

"Rory?"

He whirled around. "Yes?"

"I'm sorry. You're right. I've still got a long way to go before I feel secure in this new skin. But I did turn to God tonight. I did pray for Him to help us. I need to accept that He's with me—all the time. Even at the worst of times."

"I'm glad about that," Rory said. "And I believe He hears our prayers even if He doesn't answer them in the way we think He should. But I also believe there can be a blessing in everything that happens to us, good or bad. Having faith is all about searching for the blessings. It's about the things we can't see."

"That verse—you talked about it on Easter Sunday. It stayed with me, Rory." She came to him and hugged him close. "I think faith is about the things we can't feel either. The things we long to feel, the things the Lord wants us to feel."

"You're so right on that," he said. Then he kissed her and headed back to his place, thankful that they'd managed to help Kandi and hopeful that the whole experience would help Vanessa, too.

"So I'll see you on Friday, too," Marla told Vanessa the next day. She'd come by to help Vanessa get the last of her items on display. They'd tagged some of the big items and put signs on all of the display tables and surfaces to show the price structure. "You've got some good stuff here, Vanessa. The place is looking good."

"Feel free to shop now," Vanessa told her. "Things might get busy Friday. I'll even throw in some freebies to pay you back all the cupcake donations and to thank you for offering to help me man the checkout table."

"I've only given you a couple of cupcakes," Marla said. But her eyes lit up at the prospect of shopping early. "And I won't be the only volunteer here helping out."

"You've given me more than just cupcakes," Vanessa said. "You're a good friend, Marla."

She'd told Marla about what had happened last night. But the Millbrook Lake grapevine had already taken on the story anyway. And Jerome Asher had been apprehended and brought in for questioning. If nothing else, at least maybe it would scare him into thinking about the consequences of his actions from now on. He was over twenty-one, and even though Kandi had gone with him of her own accord, she was still a minor.

"I'm so glad everything turned out okay with Kandi," Marla said now. "And I'm really glad that you and Rory have grown closer."

Vanessa couldn't deny her feelings for Rory.

"He's amazing. He's been patient with me. And he's helped me work through some of my angst."

"Rory is a good man," Marla said, her green eyes bright with hope. "He needs someone to love him."

"I think I do love him," Vanessa admitted. "But I'm afraid to tell him that. I have to be sure."

Marla tried on a straw sun hat. "What's holding you back?"

"I don't know," Vanessa said. "Well, I do know. I live and work in New Orleans. I want to sell this house and get on with my life. This house has become an albatross of sorts, and now that I've inherited all of Richard's holdings, too, I'm not sure what to do with myself."

Marla dropped the hat and picked up a floral cotton scarf. "You're blessed, Vanessa. You don't have to worry about money anymore. And believe me, I know that feeling. I married Alec because I love him so much, but the security of not having to worry about how to pay the bills is nice." She tossed the scarf around her neck and lifted her red-gold hair. "Alec and I don't take any of it for granted. We can help the community and the church, and Alec is happy with his Caldwell Canines training facility."

"You've both found your purpose," Vanessa said. "I'm still searching for mine."

Marla placed the pretty scarf in her growing pile of "to buy" things. "Well, now you can find a purpose. You have the ability to make a difference in the world."

Vanessa glanced over at her mother's journal and wondered if Cora would have been happy with more money and more status. Richard had tried to give her those things, and for the last few years of her life, she'd been content.

Wishing now she'd spent more time with her mother during those happy years, Vanessa told herself she had to get past all the mistakes and failures in her life and start living, really living. With Rory.

"You're right," she said to Marla. "I have an opportunity that few people get. I can do something good in this world. Now I have to figure out what that is."

A knock at the front door caused her to whirl around. "That might be Rory."

Marla grinned. "I need to get out of your hair and get back to the shop."

But when Vanessa opened the door, Kandi was standing there.

"Hi," she said, surprised that the girl was here. "Why aren't you in school?"

"Half day," Kandi said. "Miss Wanda is parking the car over at the church. She's coming over, too. To help you."

When she saw Marla, Kandi looked embarrassed. "I...I didn't know you had someone in here with you."

"You remember Marla, I'm sure," Vanessa said. "She's the cupcake lady. Marla's Marvelous Desserts."

"Right," Kandi said. "You brought cupcakes from her shop to the youth meeting that first night."

"I sure did," Vanessa said. "They were a hit."

"Good to see you again, Kandi," Marla said. "I've seen you in church a lot, of course."

Kandi nodded and pushed at her always-rumpled hair. "Want me to start in another room, Vanessa?"

"You can help me in here," Vanessa replied, deciding she should keep Kandi close just in case the teen needed to vent some more.

Marla gave Vanessa a questioning glance and then smiled at Kandi. "I'm so glad you're here. I'm always looking for summer help in the bakery, and I was wondering if you might be willing to work a few hours a week. I can only pay minimum wage and I know we'd have to clear things with your foster parents and your caseworker, but will you consider it?"

Kandi stared at Marla for a few seconds, her eyes wide and her expression unsure. Finally, she said, "I could use some spending money."

She gave Vanessa one of her kohl-rimmed stares. "I'd already thought about finding a summer job since I'm sixteen now."

"Great," Marla said as she breezed by. "I'll call Wanda and we'll set something up for you to come in and fill out an application."

After Marla headed out the back door, Kandi turned to Vanessa. "Do you think she'll let me work for her?"

"She wouldn't have asked you if she didn't mean it," Vanessa said. "You'd be great at the bakery."

Kandi lifted a red leather purse and toyed with the strap. "Your mom sure had a lot of stuff."

"Yes, she did," Vanessa said. Then she finished sorting through some T-shirts. "How are you?"

Kandi stared at a T-shirt with a dolphin motif on its front. "I'm okay. I stayed home from school yesterday, and then we had only a half day today. People were staring at me. I guess I'll have a reputation now. Even worse than before."

"People are curious," Vanessa replied. "And some of them will be cruel. But you hold your head up and ignore them. They don't know what you've been through, so they shouldn't make speculations. Don't let them get to you."

"Or what? You'll storm the school yard and scare them away?"

"If you need me to do that," Vanessa said. "But I'm thinking you're able to overcome that kind of stuff all on your own."

Kandi's smile wasn't so sure. "What do you need me to do?"

Vanessa dropped the subject and pointed to a box of old books and magazines. "We need to get these in some sort of order. I'll toss the ones that don't have any value and save some for the collectors who'll show up tomorrow. If you can sort them by magazine name, that would help. And put the books on that table over there with the rest of them. And if you find any documents or business papers, put those here on this old desk." She pointed to the old rolltop near the front window.

Kandi went to work with the various magazines, books and old folders. Soon Wanda came in with a platter of snack cake. "I think Rory smelled this spice cake. He might show up over here."

Vanessa nodded. She missed Rory. She hadn't seen much of him yesterday. And she wasn't sure about anything regarding their feelings for each other. "The more the merrier," she said. "I'm so ready to get this house in order."

Chapter Twenty

Rory never made it over on Thursday.

But Friday dawned bright and sunny, with the church parking lot full to capacity and the side streets along the lake lined with vehicles. The rummage sale at the church was in full swing, and Vanessa had a steady stream of people moving through her house.

Her house.

She had to grit her teeth and turn away because she wanted to shout to all of them to leave. She wasn't ready to give up her memories or her pain. Each item she sold tore at her hurting heart like a jagged knife. How could she let go of her mother's possessions by selling them to strangers?

But she would have to let them go. She would because Rory had shown her how Christ had been willing to die for her pain. To save her from any pain. To wash away her sins and make her whole again in a new life.

A new life.

She couldn't wait to see Rory and to tell him how she felt. The pain of letting go was slowly being replaced with the hope of living again. With Christ at the center of her life.

Two hours later, she took a breath and went to the rolltop to look for a notepad. Then she saw a note from Kandi lying there.

Found this in one of the books. I didn't open it.

It was a sealed envelope addressed to Vanessa.

From her mother. She recognized the elaborate handwriting, all scrolls and loops and curlicues. The same kind of handwriting as the verse she'd read on the little plaque she'd found in the kitchen.

"Vanessa, can you help me with this dresser?" one of the volunteers called. "We're haggling on the price," she whispered when Vanessa whirled around.

"I'll be right there," Vanessa said, her mind still on that sealed envelope. But it would have to wait. She had too many people in her house right now to open it anyway.

She'd need to open this in private. So she tucked the envelope into her mother's journal, which she'd placed on the desk before the sale.

Then she put the journal back into the cubbyhole inside the open rolltop and pulled the cover back down.

Rory looked around the church gathering room.

They'd had a very successful sale, which had netted a lot of money for the church. That money would go toward their mission work, which included helping the homeless, giving funds to the foster-parent organization and even donating always-needed funding to the new animal rescue shelter that had opened up in town. He glanced across the way, wondering how Vanessa had fared.

He'd gone over a couple times to help move heavy purchases, and they'd spoken briefly but she'd been busy, very busy.

They were supposed to go to dinner tonight. Then she'd be at Blain's wedding on Sunday afternoon, too. After that, he wasn't sure what would happen, but Rory knew the Lord would show him the way. Always.

"What about all of this?" Barbara asked, her short hair sticking up like tufts of grass while her gaze scanned the leftover items that hadn't sold.

"We'll clean up tomorrow and send a truck

full of stuff to the local thrift store," he said. "You go home and rest. You worked hard today."

"And don't my tired feet know it," Barbara retorted. "What about you? You got plans?"

"I do," Rory said. "I'm taking Vanessa out to dinner."

Barbara stared at his feet. "You aren't wearing those flip-flops, are you?"

Rory chuckled. "No. I'm wearing pants—which is good, I think—and a nice shirt. And real shoes."

"Whew, scared me there for a minute."

His secretary, ever the dramatic clown.

After Barbara and the other volunteers left, he glanced back across the street, his heart full and grateful.

He couldn't wait to have a real dinner with Vanessa.

Vanessa checked her reflection in the bedroom mirror. She'd found a gorgeous blue dress in the back of her mother's closet, and she'd had it cleaned for tonight. It had a white portrait collar and a full skirt that flared out around her legs. She wore white strappy sandals with it, and she'd put her hair up in a loose chignon.

She was nervous.

But ready. So ready to have a night with Rory where they didn't need to talk about the big sale or her problems or his administrative duties as a minister. Tonight, she wanted small talk, silly, quirky, fun talk. And maybe a nice walk along the lake, in the moonlight.

She moved through the house, amazed at how big and empty it felt now that so much of the furniture and clutter had been removed. This old place had good bones. It was spacious and rambling and sunny in places but nice and cool in other places.

She prayed someone would buy it and make it into a showcase again.

Then her gaze hit on the old desk by the window.

And the sealed envelope she'd stuck into one of the cubbyholes.

Checking her watch, she debated whether to open it before Rory came over to pick her up. She had to know in the same way she had to know the rest of the journal's content. She'd waited all day, and then she'd hurried to get a shower, followed by the frenzy of hair and makeup and what shoes to wear with this vivid blue dress.

Did she want to read the letter? Or was she putting that off right along with finishing the journal?

Why can't I finish what I started here? Why am I stalling?

But before she could lift the aged seal, she heard a knock at the front door. Rory. Always prompt. And yet he was early tonight. A good excuse to stall out again.

Should she ask him to sit with her while she read this?

No. Her mother had left it for her eyes only. It would have to wait a little bit longer.

Glancing longingly at the yellowed envelope, Vanessa took a deep breath and opened the front door. When she saw Rory, she had to take another breath.

Dressed in a crisp light blue shirt and pressed khakis along with polished brown loafers, he looked good. So good that Vanessa wanted to reach out and smooth his always this-side-of-disheveled, dark-blond bangs.

Instead, she enjoyed the way his eyes moved over her.

"You look like a movie star wrapped up in a summer package. A summer movie. A blockbuster."

She couldn't stop the giggle that bubbled up in her throat. "I've never had quite that kind of compliment before."

"And I rarely wear real shoes on a date," he said as he came inside and kicked the door shut. "We could be in a fifties sitcom."

"And yet here we stand in real life."

"I like real life better," he replied as he tugged her into his arms and danced her around. Then he leaned down and gave her a gentle kiss. "And we have plenty of room in here now."

"Yes." She pulled back and swung her arms wide. "We did it, Rory."

"You did it," he replied, pride in his eyes. "You did it and now, this place looks like a different house."

She smiled at that. "I tried to leave a few pieces to showcase the Craftsman features. And the spaciousness of this place. I'd forgotten how beautiful this house used to be."

Rory tucked a finger underneath her chin. "How ya doing?"

"I'm good. Okay. Sad but happy, too. I feel as if I've cleaned out a lot of the clutter in my mind, too." She almost told him about the envelope but held off.

He checked his watch. "We have a lot to talk about, don't we?"

"Yes. Let me grab my purse." She hurried to the desk and picked up the straw clutch she'd found to finish her outfit, her gaze drifting over the journal and the letter.

She wanted this special time with Rory. Later tonight, she'd finally sit down and take care of this one last task.

Reading the rest of the intimate details of her mother's strange, sometimes happy, sometimes sad, life.

The quaint French restaurant sat on the pass where the lake followed a tributary out into the big bay. Rory had asked for a table out on the patio, overlooking the water. A perfect spot for one of the Gulf's famous sunsets.

The night was perfect. A gentle tropical breeze teased at Vanessa's hair while he longed to take every pin and clip out of it and pull his fingers through it. Seagulls lifted out over the water, their soft caws as much a part of his life as praying. Candles and flowers adorned the white tablecloth, and an attentive waiter refilled their drinks and water without either of them having to lift a finger.

"This place is so beautiful, Rory," Vanessa said, her smile lighting up the gloaming. "I can't believe we're on a real date."

"Our first real date. My first date with anyone since…"

"Since you lost your wife," she finished. "Do you still miss her?"

"All the time," he admitted. "But I'm all about waiting on God's timing. Or at least I was until I met you."

Vanessa's eyes grew misty. "Are you sure?

I mean, you two were so in love. This has to be hard."

"Hey, I'm okay. I'll be all right." He reached for her hand. "I had this battle going on in my head. I couldn't let go, but I think Allison would approve of you."

"Good to know." She took a sip of her drink. "I've dated so many men but nothing special, obviously."

"Does that include me?"

She gave him an indulgent smile that made his throat go dry. "You know you're very special. You've been so much more to me than someone to date. You've counseled me, consoled me, taught me grace and forgiveness and…made me rethink my whole way of life, including my future."

His heart hammered like a swinging pendulum. "Hey, I'm good, what can I say?"

"You are good. A good man."

He reached for her hand. "And since I'm so good, are you considering a future closer to me? As in, across the street? Or even closer?"

Her eyes went dark. "I'm considering a lot of things. But I don't know if I can live in that house again."

"You know, fresh paint and new furniture can—"

"Cover a multitude of sins?"

"Can give you a new perspective," he said, wishing he could wipe away the stains that only she could see.

"I'll have to think about keeping the house," she said.

Rory wisely changed the subject. They talked about the weather, about Blain and Rikki's wedding on Sunday, about her business and how much she loved finding and reselling wonderful collectibles. He told her about some of the fishing trips he'd been on with his buddies and about some of his darkest days during his deployment.

By the time their entrées had come—chicken for her and seafood for him—they were laughing and enjoying each other. All of the issues holding them apart seemed to settle down with the setting sun.

He held her hand while they waited for dessert, and together, they watched the bright golden sun slipping behind the water, its light leaving the heavens and the water washed in muted pinks and bronzed yellows. Cameras snapped the moment all around them, but Rory and Vanessa sat silent and held this moment close. That intimacy lasted through the crème brûlée and coffee, too.

And Rory knew in his heart, this was the woman for him.

Then he prayed that somehow Vanessa felt the same.

He kissed her good-night. Over and over. While they stood on the porch.

Vanessa finally slapped at his shirt. "Miss Fanny will be scandalized if you don't stop."

"Miss Fanny is a forward-thinking romantic who will appreciate that I've finally found a woman who can meet my high standards and amazingly handsome looks."

"You are so cute."

"Yes, I am that, too, of course."

He kissed her before she could form a retort. Then he whispered, "But you are beautiful and talented and you smell like spring and you're way out of my range, darlin'. I'm amazed you even looked at me twice."

"I tried not to," she reminded him. "Now I can't stop looking at you."

"I like looking at you while you're looking at me."

Vanessa didn't want to move out of his arms, but she was tired. Happy but exhausted. "I have to go inside before dawn, Rory."

"Hmmmm. We could cuddle in the swing all night."

"The mosquitoes will like that."

"I'll nibble on your neck and keep them away."

"Scandalous."

And tempting.

She pushed away and grinned at him. "You have a busy day tomorrow, too. Cleaning up the church, then rehearsal dinner for Blain and Rikki and then your sermon Sunday and then the wedding."

"I'll see you at the wedding. And in church, too."

"I plan to be at both. And I can help with cleanup tomorrow. We want the church to look good for that wedding."

He finally let out a sigh and stepped backward. "If I don't leave now, I'll never want to leave." But he took her hand in his and held it, their arms stretched out like a connecting bridge. "I want you to think long and hard about this, Vanessa. About how much you'll miss me if you leave."

"I know I'll miss you."

"And you know I'll miss you, too, don't you?"

"I believe that, yes."

"Okay then. We've established a strong attraction and we have to figure out what to do about it. But later, darling."

"Later," she said. "I enjoyed dinner."

"Me, too." He waved good-night, and then she watched him, heard him whistling and smiled to herself.

She didn't want to leave him. She was in love with Rory.

Somehow, she'd figure out a way to tell him that…and deal with it.

Chapter Twenty-One

An hour later, Vanessa settled on the couch with her mother's journal and the envelope she'd been avoiding all day. She realized avoidance was her specialty. She'd avoided facing the truth in her life and she'd avoided any serious relationships. She'd avoided coming back to confront her mother about the things they'd left unsaid through the years. She'd avoided making sure the world knew about Gregory Pardue and what he'd done to her. And in a weird way, selling vintage clothes and collectibles had allowed her to avoid moving into the future.

She'd also avoided God and the kind of love that only having faith could bring into her life.

But she had to face facts now. No more excuses. She was done clinging to the past.

And because she wanted Rory in her life and

that might mean moving back to Millbrook, she knew it was now or never on getting through this journal.

But first, the envelope, please.

She opened it and found a one-page letter from her mother.

And a birth certificate.

By the time she'd finished reading the letter and glancing over the birth certificate, Vanessa's whole life had flashed through her mind with a glaring intensity that left her gasping for breath, her sobs caught in her throat.

She didn't have to read her mother's journal to realize her whole life had been based on a lie.

Rory shoved another box of clothing into the big rental truck they'd loaded with what was left from the rummage sale.

"This should be the last of it," Alec called out, sweat beading on his forehead as he shoved another box up the loading ramp.

Rory nodded and glanced across the street. Vanessa had never shown up to help, and her car had been gone when he'd gotten up. Early-morning errands?

He'd get a shower and go over once he'd checked on the gathering hall. But Wanda and a few other volunteers were giving it a once-over with the vacuum and brooms. The place would be spotless before Wanda released her crew.

Kandi lifted up a bag full of jewelry to him. "Have you seen Vanessa? She called Miss Wanda yesterday after we left the sale and said she had some things for me."

Rory shook his head. "No. I'll call her later. Her car's not in the driveway. Must have gone out early for something."

"I know where she is."

Both Rory and Kandi turned to find Miss Fanny standing there leaning on her walker, a gloomy expression on her face.

"Where?" Rory asked, concern mounting only because Miss Fanny had never looked so glum.

Miss Fanny waited until he finished with the truck and came down the ramp. "She's gone, Rory."

"Gone?" He checked the house again. "What do you mean?"

"I found this tucked into my screen door." Miss Fanny handed him a square blue envelope. "It has your name on it."

Kandi eyed the envelope and then shook her head. "She told me she might not be around for long. But I thought—"

"Me, too," Miss Fanny said. "I thought we'd won her over."

Kandi shot both of them a disgusted stare. "I should know not to count on anybody or anything."

"Hey, we haven't heard what happened," Rory warned, his heart sinking. "I'll read this, and then maybe I'll call her."

"Right." Kandi turned and stalked back into the church.

"I'll leave you to it," Miss Fanny said to Rory, her eyes full of sympathy. "I hope it's nothing bad."

Rory hoped the same. "I'll find out, good or bad."

After they'd finished and he'd closed up the church, he went up to the little porch of his garage apartment and sat down in the rickety old lawn chair. Then he opened the card.

Rory,
I have some urgent business in Alabama. I don't know when I'll be back. Thank you again for last night. And for everything.
Vanessa

That was it. No explanation, no reason for leaving in the middle of the night. Or at least before dawn, since he'd been up that long. Rory pulled out his phone. Not even a text or missed call. It was close to two in the afternoon. He had a few hours before the rehearsal dinner for the Kent-Alvanetti wedding.

Taking out his phone, he called Vanessa.

No answer. It went straight to voice mail.

Now he was really worried.

After finding the number on her website, he called Vanessa's Vintage boutique in New Orleans. But the sales associate who answered said they hadn't heard from Vanessa today.

"She told us she'd call when she was on her way back," the woman said. "But for now, that's probably going to be late next week since she's mostly finished with clearing out her mother's house."

Rory thanked the woman and ended the call. "Hey!"

He glanced down to find Alec standing by the steps up to his place. "Everything okay?"

Rory nodded and hurried down the steps. "Vanessa is gone. Left me a note saying she had to go to Alabama."

Alec rubbed the scar that slashed across one cheek. "Well, she does have property there now. Maybe something came up."

"Maybe," Rory said. "But she could have called. I'm worried. Leaving a note seems odd, considering."

Considering how they'd left things last night.

"How was she last time you saw her?"

"She was great. We had a good time. I thought things were looking up."

Alec slapped his hand against Rory's arm. "I'm sure she's still dealing with a lot, so try not to worry. Maybe she'll be back later today."

Rory hoped so, too. And he prayed all day long, about a lot of things. When he still hadn't heard from her later that night after the rehearsal dinner, he had to accept that she might have left because she was scared of what they felt for each other.

That meant he'd have to give her some time to decide what she really wanted to do. Or if she really wanted to be with him after all.

Vanessa stood looking up at the staircase of the Tudor-style house in Birmingham that had belonged to Richard Tucker.

Her house now. But not just because the man was generous.

She was his daughter.

A mirror centered on the wall in the entryway caught her eye. Vanessa studied herself, seeing it all so clearly now.

Richard Tucker was her father.

The dark-haired man who'd come to visit when she was young.

The man who'd bought the house in Millbrook Lake for her mother, even when he was married to another woman.

A woman who couldn't have children.

The man who'd made her mother cry over and over again.

His wife had died and Richard had come back to Cora at long last, after years of quick visits and whispered words. But neither of her parents had thought it important to explain this to Vanessa.

We felt it best to leave things as they were. We were happy and we tried to make you happy. It could have made things worse, telling you the truth since Richard had been absent from our lives for so long. I hope you will forgive us. We both loved you so much. I tried to tell you so many times.

Her mother's words in the letter.

She'd read the journal, too, even though it had made her sick to her stomach and boiling mad with anger.

But the last words of her mother's journal had finally saved Vanessa by showing her the final thread to the past.

One day, your father's legacy will become yours. He worked very hard to make sure you'd have a secure future. Vanessa, please don't waste this opportunity. Use this gift to move forward with your life. And learn from our mistakes.

Always be honest.

Always be kind.

Trust in God.

Fall in love.

Vanessa wondered why none of this had been mentioned in the will, but then Cora was ever the dramatic one. Her mother knew she'd find the journal. Knew she'd be curious.

So Cora had created one last piece of art. Pictures and words, pasted like a collage of Vanessa's life, against paper, with glue that would stick for a lifetime. Cora also knew that if anyone else found the journal or the letter, they'd make sure Vanessa got them. But mostly, her mother knew that Vanessa would come back to the house because Vanessa loved old things. Because Vanessa would want to know about the past.

So here she stood, in a house that could have been her home. Vanessa moved around the sprawling, elegant mansion, her mind thinking of so many scenarios. Should she sell this place?

Move here and try to recapture her youth?

Go home to Rory?

She voted for the last one.

Checking her watch, she saw the late hour. Then she pulled out her phone.

Rory picked up on the fourth ring. "Hello?" His voice slid over her in a husky whisper.

"It's me," she said, forcing the tears out of her words.

"Hi. Are you okay?"

"I am now. I wanted you to know...I'm coming home."

"Home? As in, to me?"

"Home to you, yes."

"When?"

"I don't know. Maybe soon. Maybe in a few days. Or weeks."

"Vanessa—"

"I'll explain everything when I get there."

"Are you sure you're all right?"

"Not yet. But I will be as soon as I see you again."

"Vanessa, I—"

"Don't. Not yet. I'll see you soon, Rory."

"Okay, but when you get here will you please stop interrupting me?"

"Probably not. I have to go."

She stood in the big, empty house and realized big houses didn't make homes and bad memories didn't have to ruin a house or a home. Or a future full of promise.

When her phone rang again, she shook her head. "Rory…"

But it wasn't Rory.

"Why did you leave? You know Rory loves you."

Kandi.

"It's hard to explain."

"Complicated? Right. Look, I know all about complicated. You're gonna have to do better than that."

"It's tough. I found out something that kind of rocked my world."

"In a good way?"

"Good and bad. I'm still in shock."

"Well, snap out of it. We…I mean… Rory needs you."

"I'm coming back," Vanessa said to reassure Kandi and herself. "And once I get back there, I don't think I'm ever going to leave again."

"That's more like it. Later."

"Later."

Vanessa put away her phone, her mind still on Kandi. She couldn't disappoint the girl. She didn't want to disappoint Rory either. Mostly, she didn't want to let go of the good parts of Millbrook Lake. The church and her friends and Rory.

I can't avoid this. I love him. I want to be with him.

Help me, Lord. Show me the courage to follow my heart instead of holding on to my pain.

She went from room to room in the big house, studied the huge, airy bedrooms and several roomy bathrooms, stood in the huge kitchen and imagined many happy times here, sat on a white wicker chair in the second-floor solarium and thought about reading books and drinking tea right here, and by the time she'd made it back downstairs, she knew what she wanted to do with this house.

And she knew she wasn't going to sell the Millbrook Lake house.

"I don't think she's coming back," Rory told Alec and Blain right before the wedding was about to begin. "Something caused her to run. Something about that house and her mother. Maybe she finally read the rest of that clunky journal she kept moving from room to room."

Blain quirked his detective eyebrows up in a question. "Do you think she found out something in the journal? Or that she's using any excuse to avoid commitment?"

"Sounds like the voice of experience," Alec said with a wink toward Blain.

"It is the voice of experience," Blain replied. "I wasn't one for committing to a relationship until I met Rikki."

"The least likely candidate," Alec said.

"Same with Vanessa," Rory said, nodding. "She made it clear she didn't want marriage and children. And she knows how I feel about that."

"Maybe she just wants a low-key relationship with no strings attached," Blain said.

Rory could hear the organ music starting up. People were piling into the church. The smell of fresh lilies and sprays of jasmine filled the air. He had to get it together for Blain's sake. And the fact that Rikki would throttle him if he didn't present a happy face while he read their vows to them.

"I could live with that," he told Blain. "For a while."

Alec adjusted his tie. "Yes, but you want more, right?"

Rory nodded. "I fought against wanting more for a long time. After I lost Allison—"

"You deserve more," Blain said. "And Preacher, you might take some of your own advice and trust in the man upstairs."

Rory couldn't argue with that. "You're right. And it's time to get you to the altar. Your bride will come looking if we're late."

Blain grinned, his dark eyes bright with love. "I can't believe I'm getting married today."

"We're both happy for you," Alec said. "I love being a married man."

Rory would love that, too. But while he was happy for his two lovestruck friends, he had to wonder if he'd ever have that dream of marriage and a family again.

Vanessa might talk herself right out of coming back to Millbrook Lake.

She stood in the back of the church until she saw an open spot in the very last pew. Vanessa slid in without being noticed and took in the scene.

White lilies and baby's breath, trailing sprays of jasmine mixed with tiny white and pink roses. Candlelight and soft music. Blain looked so happy, so expectant, waiting for his bride.

Rory stood staring up the aisle, his own expression expectant. Had he seen her come in? She'd driven across Alabama to get here, but it had taken her a lifetime to find him.

The music swelled and Rikki came into view, her proud father, Franco Alvanetti, walking her down the aisle. She looked beautiful in the slinky white dress that flowed out into a long train complete with a huge bow tied at the back.

Vanessa watched, her eyes tearing up, as Rikki and Blain said their vows. Rory officiated with pride and humor, making everyone laugh and cry.

"Cherish this moment," he told the couple.

"Cherish the people you love. And keep God in the center of your lives."

He said a prayer, and then he told Blain to kiss his bride.

After that, they turned around and he presented them to the guests as man and wife.

Man and wife.

Soon, everyone poured out of the church to head out to the swank Alvanetti estate. But Vanessa held back and walked up to the altar and closed her eyes. She needed a minute. Just a minute. To tell God that she was home now.

When she opened her eyes and turned to leave, she saw him.

Rory. Standing at the back of the church in a nice navy suit. He looked lovable and scruffy, like a lost puppy come home. Like a man who'd been searching for someone for a long time, his blue eyes bright with hope and surprise.

Vanessa hurried toward him. They met somewhere in the middle of the long aisle.

"You're here. Now." He looked completely surprised.

"I told you I'd be back."

"But—"

Panic rushed over her. "Are you glad I'm back?"

He reached out his hands to hers and laced

their fingers together. "I'm thrilled that you're back. I thought it might take you a while."

"I thought about taking a while," she admitted. "You know, avoiding what I could see so clearly."

He gave her one of his soft smiles. "And what do you see so clearly now?"

She didn't want to cry, but she couldn't stop the tears. "You. And that dream. Remember when I told you about standing in the garden at Caldwell House, how I wanted that one day—the garden, the house, the sound of children laughing."

His eyes got misty, too. "I remember."

"I think I've found it, Rory. And when I turned around just now and saw you, I felt it, too. That feeling you told me I'd feel one day. It's like a warmth flowing through me and over me, and my soul is full of lightness and joy."

"Yeah, that feeling," he said, pulling her close.

Vanessa held him there, silent tears moving down her face. "Richard Tucker was my real father."

Rory lifted away. "What?"

"She left me a letter and my birth certificate. He was married, but they fell in love and had an ongoing affair. He and his wife never had children and then his wife died. He bought my mother the house here. And of course, he came here and married her, but they both felt it would be too confusing to tell me the truth. So as a conciliation prize, he left everything to me. Everything, except the truth."

"Vanessa, I'm so sorry," Rory said on a shattered whisper. "I don't know what to say. Are you sure you can handle this?"

"I didn't think so at first. I got in the car last night and left, determined to go to Birmingham and walk through the other house. I think I was searching for something, a sign maybe."

"And what did you find?"

"A sad, empty house. But I also found closure because now I know the truth." She wiped her eyes and smiled up at him. "And I realized that instead of avoiding the truth, I wanted to be here with you—living our truth."

Rory couldn't believe what Vanessa had told him. "What will you do now?"

She took his hand, and they started toward the back of the church. "Well, our friends are about to celebrate their wedding day, so first, I want to have a big piece of wedding cake."

He grinned at that. "We can make that happen. They're probably wondering what happened to me after the photo session was done. I came back in to lock things up."

"Then we'd better hurry," she said. "We'll take my car."

When they reached her driveway, Rory stared over at the house. "Are you still going to sell this place?"

"No." She gave him a hopeful smile. "I'm going to renovate it. Sweep it clean of all the cobwebs and secrets. I want it light and bright and sunny and warm."

His heart did a little flip of joy. Before she could get in the car, he tugged her close. Her eyes were clear and sure, no cobwebs or secrets left there. She looked young and carefree and ... at peace. "It's a really big house, Vanessa. You don't need to be there all alone."

"I won't be alone." She reached up to kiss him. "You'll be nearby."

"No. I don't like that," he said. "I want to live there with you. I want to marry you."

"Yes," she said.

"Yes?" He laughed, glad she agreed. "Did you just interrupt me again?"

"I didn't interrupt you."

"Can I at least ask the question?"

"Yes. Yes."

"Okay." He wanted to laugh and cry, but he held his emotions back and took her hands in his. "Will you marry me, Vanessa?"

"Yes."

"Are you willing to have my children?"

"Yes."

"Are you mad that I don't have a ring for you yet?"

"No. But I can get you a good deal on one through Vanessa's Vintage."

"I love you," he said.

"I love you." She kissed him again, and then they got in the little car. When she put the top down, they laughed into the wind and made plans for the future.

"I'm going to turn the Birmingham house into a girls' home," she told him. "And I want to help Kandi with college and maybe give her a job."

"And I want to remodel the Craftsman and make it so beautiful, you'll only have happy memories there," he told her.

By the time they reached the reception, they'd made a lifetime of plans. A commitment to be together for a long, long time.

Rory got out and came around to open her door. "Let's go party."

Vanessa laughed as he lifted her up in his arms and swung her around. "I love you so much," he told her.

Then they heard a grunt off by the big garage. Hunter Lawson sat there on his motorcycle, watching them. "And another one bites the dust."

But he was smiling, a twist of bittersweet mixed with the happiness in his eyes.

"Thanks," Rory said. "You can be my best man."

"Ain't gonna happen," Hunter said. Then he cranked his bike and left.

"He never stays at parties for very long," Rory explained. "But I love me a good party."

They laughed and held hands as they headed through the house. They found everyone in the backyard by the pool, enjoying the beautiful view, where the lake and the big bay merged.

"There you are," Blain called out with a grin.

"Better late than never," Rory replied.

And he felt sure God thought that a lot, too.

* * * * *

Dear Reader,

I have to admit this story captured my heart. I fell for Rory the moment he came into my head. He had a good soul, and he cared about other people. He needed a special woman in his life after all the things he'd been through. In spite of his pain, he became a true man of God.

Vanessa was the opposite. Bitter and disillusioned, hurting and skeptical. What better person to show her that life can still be full of joy? Rory didn't even realize that he needed someone to take care of him, too. Sometimes, we work so hard to help others, we forget to take care of nurturing our own souls.

I hope you enjoyed Rory and Vanessa's story. Please visit me through my website at www.lenoraworth.com. And I hope you'll look for Hunter's story as my Men of Millbrook Lake series continues. I might not ever leave Millbrook Lake.

Until next time, may the angels watch over you. Always.

Lenora Worth

LARGER-PRINT BOOKS!

GET 2 FREE
LARGER-PRINT NOVELS
PLUS 2 FREE
MYSTERY GIFTS

Love Inspired®

SUSPENSE
RIVETING INSPIRATIONAL ROMANCE

Larger-print novels are now available...

REQUEST YOUR FREE BOOKS!
2 FREE WHOLESOME ROMANCE NOVELS IN LARGER PRINT
PLUS 2 FREE MYSTERY GIFTS

٭٭٭٭٭٭٭٭٭٭٭٭٭٭٭٭٭٭٭٭٭٭٭٭٭٭

HEARTWARMING™

٭٭٭٭٭٭٭٭٭٭٭٭٭٭٭٭٭٭٭٭٭٭٭٭٭٭

Wholesome, tender romances

YES! Please send me 2 FREE Harlequin® Heartwarming Larger-Print novels and my 2 FREE mystery gifts (gifts worth about $10). After receiving them, if I don't wish to receive any more books, I can return the shipping statement marked "cancel." If I don't cancel, I will receive 4 brand-new larger-print novels every month and be billed just $5.24 per book in the U.S. or $5.99 per book in Canada. That's a savings of at least 19% off the cover price. It's quite a bargain! Shipping and handling is just 50¢ per book in the U.S. and 75¢ per book in Canada.* I understand that accepting the 2 free books and gifts places me under no obligation to buy anything. I can always return a shipment and cancel at any time. Even if I never buy another book, the two free books and gifts are mine to keep forever.

161/361 IDN GHX2

Name _____ (PLEASE PRINT) _____

Address _____ Apt. # _____

City _____ State/Prov. _____ Zip/Postal Code _____

Signature (if under 18, a parent or guardian must sign)

Mail to the **Reader Service:**
IN U.S.A.: P.O. Box 1867, Buffalo, NY 14240-1867
IN CANADA: P.O. Box 609, Fort Erie, Ontario L2A 5X3

* Terms and prices subject to change without notice. Prices do not include applicable taxes. Sales tax applicable in N.Y. Canadian residents will be charged applicable taxes. Offer not valid in Quebec. This offer is limited to one order per household. Not valid for current subscribers to Harlequin Heartwarming larger-print books. All orders subject to credit approval. Credit or debit balances in a customer's account(s) may be offset by any other outstanding balance owed by or to the customer. Please allow 4 to 6 weeks for delivery. Offer available while quantities last.

Your Privacy—The Reader Service is committed to protecting your privacy. Our Privacy Policy is available online at www.ReaderService.com or upon request from the Reader Service.

We make a portion of our mailing list available to reputable third parties that offer products we believe may interest you. If you prefer that we not exchange your name with third parties, or if you wish to clarify or modify your communication preferences, please visit us at www.ReaderService.com/consumerchoice or write to us at Reader Service Preference Service, P.O. Box 9062, Buffalo, NY 14240-9062. Include your complete name and address.

HW15

READERSERVICE.COM

Manage your account online!

- Review your order history
- Manage your payments
- Update your address

> *We've designed the*
> *Reader Service website*
> *just for you.*

Enjoy all the features!

- Discover new series available to you, and read excerpts from any series.
- Respond to mailings and special monthly offers.
- Connect with favorite authors at the blog.
- Browse the Bonus Bucks catalog and online-only exculsives.
- Share your feedback.

Visit us at:
ReaderService.com

Bed-and-Breakfast Mysteries by
Mary Daheim

MARY
DAHEIM

This
OLD
SOUSE

A BED-AND-BREAKFAST MYSTERY

AVON BOOKS
An Imprint of HarperCollinsPublishers

AVON BOOKS
An Imprint of HarperCollins*Publishers*
10 East 53rd Street
New York, New York 10022-5299

First Avon Books paperback printing: August 2005
First William Morrow hardcover printing: August 2004

Avon Trademark Reg. U.S. Pat. Off. and in Other Countries, Marca Registrada, Hecho en U.S.A.
HarperCollins® is a trademark of HarperCollins Publishers Inc.

Printed in the U.S.A.

10 9 8 7 6 5 4 3 2 1

This OLD SOUSE

ONE

JUDITH MCMONIGLE FLYNN hurried to answer the front door, took one look at the hideous drooling green creature on the porch, and screamed. Panicking, she slammed the door and leaned against it. The thing was six feet tall, with gaping holes for eyes, viscous green scales, and sharp yellow fangs. Judith was so shaken that she couldn't move to call 911.

"Hey!" shouted a voice from outside. "Open up! It's me! Renie!"

Judith held a hand to her racing heart. Renie, along with other family members and friends, always used the back door. The front was reserved for guests at Hillside Manor. "Coz?" Judith croaked, and slowly turned to open the door just a crack. There, next to the gruesome green creature, stood Serena Jones, more familiarly known to her family as Renie.

"Did SuperGerm scare you?" Renie asked, brown eyes wide.

"Good grief." Judith wilted against the doorframe. "I thought I was going to have a heart attack. What is that awful thing?"

"I guess I shouldn't have stood behind it," Renie said, looking apologetic. "I would've gone to the back door, but this guy is kind of awkward to carry around." She gave the creature a pat on one of its long, scaly arms. "It's just a cutout. I created it for the county board of health's antigerm campaign. Garth Doyle made this model in his studio. The county will put posters of SuperGerm in all public restrooms to remind people to wash up."

"I'm about washed-up after that," Judith said, regaining some of her aplomb. "How about getting that thing off the front porch? It's not good advertising for a B&B."

"Hmm." Renie examined the cutout from stem to stern. "Probably not. But don't you think it's good advertising for hygiene?"

"Yes, fine, super," Judith retorted. "Now put it back in your car before you come inside."

Renie, who was on the small side, struggled a bit as she carted SuperGerm off to her car, which was parked in Hillside Manor's driveway. Waiting on the porch, Judith surveyed the cul-de-sac. Just three days away from the start of summer, the spring shrubs, trees, and bulbs had faded away. The grass was green, the leaves were glossy, and some of the roses were in full bloom. But the sky was overcast, the temperature lingered in the midfifties, and there was a 40 percent chance of rain. It was, Judith knew, a typical June day in the Pacific Northwest.

"All gone," Renie announced, bounding up the

steps. "I could use some strong drink. You got any Pepsi?"

Judith nodded. "I just got back from Falstaff's Grocery. I have a full house tonight, so I had to fill the larder. Now that school's out, the B&B reservations are pouring in. I'm pretty well booked up through early August."

"That's great," Renie said, sitting down at the kitchen table. "I'm not so busy. Summer's always a slow time in the graphic design business. Everybody goes on vacation. Good for you, bad for me."

Judith took a can of Pepsi and a diet 7UP out of the refrigerator. Even after more than a year, she was still delighted with the renovations—particularly in the kitchen—that had been made following a disastrous fire almost two years earlier.

"Say," Renie said as Judith joined her at the table, "have you got time to take a little ride with me?"

Judith frowned at her cousin. "And with SuperGerm?"

"Well . . ." Renie took a deep drink before finishing her reply. "Yes, actually. I have to drop him off at Garth's. He needs some fine-tuning. SuperGerm, I mean, not Garth."

Judith looked skeptical. "And why would I want to help chauffeur SuperGerm to Garth's studio?"

Renie reached into the sheep-shaped jar on the table and filched three oatmeal raisin cookies. "Booy-oommerthathouthnmoofle?" she inquired with her mouth full.

Judith was accustomed to her cousin's voracious appetite; she had also grown adept at translating Renie's food-marred speech. "The house on Moonfleet Street? Sort of. Why?"

"Ahmobthethd."

"Oh." Judith nodded. "You've always been obsessed with that place, ever since you were a kid. What about it?"

Renie finally swallowed. "Garth lives in my old neighborhood, about four blocks from that house. As you may recall, it's Spanish-style architecture, very unusual for this part of the world."

"I recall." Judith turned as her cleaning woman, Phyliss Rackley, stomped into the kitchen carrying two black plastic bags. Upon seeing Renie, she stopped and glared.

"You," Phyliss breathed. "Don't start in on me with your Romish ways."

"Bite me," Renie snapped.

Phyliss kneaded the plastic bags with her skinny fingers. "False gods. Painted idols. Craven images."

"Funny," Renie remarked, about to pop another cookie into her mouth. "I thought they were *graven* images."

"You're a blasphemer," Phyliss declared, pronouncing the word as if it were "blass-FEMUR." She turned to Judith and shook the black bags. "I don't like giving these to the St. Vincent de Paul. What's wrong with the Salvation Army?"

"Nothing," Judith replied, ignoring the long-standing religious animosity between Renie and Phyliss. "I'm the one who's giving that stuff away, and it'll go to whichever charity calls first. For now, I want those bags out on the back porch. They're cluttering up the second-floor hall."

With one last dark look for Renie, Phyliss proceeded down the narrow hallway to the porch.

"The pope has spies everywhere," Renie called after the cleaning woman. "Better check the recycling bin, Phyliss."

Judith shook her head. "I never bait Phyliss the way you do," she admonished Renie. "I don't rile her. She's too good at her job."

"I didn't start it this time," Renie responded.

"You didn't need to," Judith said. "You've done it often enough in the past. Which," she went on as Phyliss returned from the porch and headed down the basement stairs, "brings us back to the house on Moonfleet."

"Yes." Renie finished the third cookie before she resumed speaking. "All the years my folks and I lived in that neighborhood, I wondered about that place. When I was in junior high and high school, I'd walk by it sometimes. It's basically a beautiful house, in a beautiful setting, with the original evergreens surrounding it. But nothing about it ever changed. I never saw anybody inside or outside. Oh, once in a great while I'd see a tricycle in the yard or a fresh load of wood in the shed, but otherwise, it seemed deserted."

Judith's memory stirred. She had grown up on Heraldsgate Hill, in the same house that she'd turned into Hillside Manor after the death of her first husband, Dan McMonigle. Renie and her parents had lived across the canal, in the neighborhood known as Langford. Judith recalled Renie talking about the house and even driving her past it a couple of times.

"So what's your point?" Judith asked her cousin.

"Working with Garth Doyle has taken me by the property several times in the last two months," Renie explained. "Going on fifty years later, it hasn't changed a bit. The trees are bigger, the house's exterior is shabbier, but otherwise it's the same. I asked Garth about it. He knows the place, of course, but hadn't given it much thought. Garth agreed he'd never noticed anybody outside, but it wasn't falling down, and it's never been for sale or for rent in the twenty-odd years he's lived in the neighborhood."

Judith toyed with her soda can. "Stop. It's beginning to sink in. You smell a mystery. How come? It's not like you, coz."

Renie grinned a bit sheepishly. "I know. It's more like you. Maybe I've got too much time on my hands. What with business slowing down for a couple of months and the kids finally married and living away, I suppose I could be bored. Bill's so self-sufficient. He seems almost as busy now as he was before he retired. He's like Joe—our husbands still keep occupied."

Judith allowed that was so. Bill Jones retained a few patients from his psychology practice and occasionally consulted at the University where he'd taught for over thirty years. Joe Flynn had his own detective agency, taking on as many—or as few—clients as he wished. Neither man was the type to follow their wives around, pleading to be entertained.

"You're at loose ends," Judith murmured.

"Not entirely," Renie replied. "I do have one big project, but the deadline isn't until late August. I'm doing the artwork on a brochure for your old buddy Bart Bendarik. He wants line drawings of every style of architecture in the city. The Moonfleet house is perfect. None of the wear and tear would show in my illustration. But if I have to get permission, I'd like to scope out the place first."

Judith sighed. Bendarik Builders had done the B&B renovations. Bart had extended deadline after deadline and seemed to prefer embracing problems rather than solving them. In some cases, Judith believed he'd actually invented difficulties, not merely to make more money, but for the sheer joy of passing the bad news on to the Flynns. He had also had the nerve to ask Judith if he could oversee her plans to build an inn and guesthouses on the former site of the family's summer cabins, but she'd turned him down. The river property could wait. She had, as Joe kept reminding her, enough on her plate as it was.

"Okay," Judith said. "I'll ride over to Garth's with you. None of the guests are due until late this afternoon. I'll make Mother's lunch and then we'll go. It shouldn't take us long, right?"

Renie brightened. "Less than an hour."

Judith stood up. "Just this once, though. You may not be busy, but I am. If I go with you today, at least I'll know what you're talking about when you jaw my ear off about your new obsession."

Renie finished her Pepsi while Judith prepared Gertrude Grover's lunch: egg salad on white, with butter, mayo, and lettuce; a half-dozen fresh strawberries, liberally doused with sugar; a few potato chips—the plain, old-fashioned kind. Gertrude didn't like any ruffles, riffles, or additional flavors.

"What's that?" Gertrude demanded when her daughter arrived with the tray.

"Your lunch," Judith replied, juggling the tray. There

wasn't a bare spot available. As usual, clutter was everywhere—decks of cards, magazines, newspapers, TV schedules, mail advertising that had been opened but never discarded, and a box of Granny Goodness chocolates. Judith was forced to place the tray on top of some typed papers her mother had apparently been reading.

"Stop!" Gertrude cried, holding up her gnarled hands. "Move that thing! It's on my movie script!"

"Oh!" Swiftly, Judith obeyed. "Can you move the script to make room?"

Gertrude placed her hands on the script, as if she expected Judith to whisk away the pages. "No! I'm making changes. They've got my life story all wrong. That writer fella in Hollywood keeps getting things mixed up. When did I ever fight in the Spanish Civil War?" Gertrude's wrinkled face was suddenly puzzled. "Or did I?"

"No, Mother," Judith replied. "It was Uncle Corky who wanted to fight in Spain, but Grandpa and Grandma Grover wouldn't let him. That happened around the time you and my father got married."

Gertrude brightened. "We eloped." She tracked the script with an unsteady finger. "This says we met in a rebel camp on some river. E-B-R-O. Ebro. Never heard of it. Your father and I met at a pinochle party at Doc and June Workman's houseboat on the ship canal."

"I warned you," Judith said. "So did your agent and the screenwriter. If your life story as a member of the Greatest Generation was to be made into a movie, they'd change things, even basic facts."

"I don't like it," Gertrude declared, stabbing at a

sugar-covered strawberry. "They describe your father as having wavy hair. Even when we first met, he'd already waved most of his hair bye-bye."

"Do you want to wave your money bye-bye?"

A year ago, Gertrude had received fifteen thousand dollars for the rights to her life story. She'd put every cent into her regular savings account and hadn't made a single withdrawal. "I'm saving it for a rainy day," she'd declared when Judith had hinted that her mother might want to spend some of the money to help pay for improvements to her apartment in what had once been the toolshed. Judith and Joe had benefited from their homeowners' insurance as well as from a generous sum given them by the film company that had been involved in the fire. But the Flynns had gone well over the original estimates. Still, Gertrude wouldn't budge. "If you hadn't married Lunkhead in the first place," the old lady had asserted, "I wouldn't have to live in the toolshed." It had done Judith no good to argue that if Gertrude hadn't been so stubborn about not living under the same roof as Joe Flynn, the old lady would still be occupying the third-floor family quarters. So she remained in her apartment, which—as Joe perversely put it—at his mother-in-law's advanced age, they might as well call the "drool shed." It was no wonder that the two couldn't coexist in the same house.

"I don't like it," Gertrude repeated. "I'm going to have my say."

"Go for it." Judith smiled. Gertrude always "had to have her say," no matter what the consequences.

As Judith went out the door, Sweetums came in. The

big orange-and-white cat sneered, sneezed, and made a beeline for the divan. To avoid hearing the cat's scratching and clawing at the floral fabric, Judith quickly closed the door behind her. She was halfway to the back porch when Phyliss, on the run and screaming, suddenly appeared from around the corner of the house.

"Beelzebub! Satan! The Archfiend!" She threw her apron over her head and collapsed on the bottom porch step.

Startled, Judith approached Phyliss. "What's wrong?"

But Phyliss could only shriek and moan. Her thin body shuddered. The cleaning woman was clearly on the verge of hysteria.

"Phyliss!" Judith cried sharply. "Stop it!" She grasped Phyliss's heaving shoulders and gave her a hard shake.

Slowly, Phyliss began to regain control. Judith didn't let go until the other woman removed the apron. Her face was drained of color; her gray eyes were huge.

"It's *him!*" she whispered in a terrified voice. "See for yourself—if you dare."

Judith was losing patience. "See where?"

Phyliss pointed in the direction of the driveway. "Your cousin's car. I told you she was in league with the devil! *She brought him with her!*"

Judith slumped in relief. She should have known. "Phyliss," she said, putting a hand on the cleaning woman's shoulder, "that's a cardboard cutout. It represents a germ. My cousin is working on a project for the county to promote hygiene."

"No." Phyliss's jaw jutted. "It's the Evil One. I always knew he'd look like that."

"That's odd," Renie said from the back door. "I always thought he'd look like the head of the IRS."

Phyliss jumped and screamed. "Help! I'm surrounded! The fires of Gehenna are at hand!"

Judith shook Phyliss again, but this time more gently. "You're being fanciful. Please stop. Renie and I have to go now. We'll take . . . the germ cutout with us."

Phyliss narrowed her eyes at Judith. "You will?" She sounded suspicious.

"Yes. I'll be back in an hour or so." She patted the cleaning woman's shoulder. "Come on, let's go back inside."

Still wary, and darting Renie distrustful glances, Phyliss complied. Five minutes later, the cousins were driving off in the Joneses' Toyota Camry.

"She's getting nuttier by the day," Renie remarked as they reached the top of Heraldsgate Hill and proceeded through the business district.

"Maybe," Judith allowed, "but she's still a wonderful worker. I gave her a raise the first of the month."

"You're too good," Renie declared.

"No," Judith responded. "She deserves it. During all the months that the workmen were repairing and renovating the B&B, Phyliss had to put up with a lot. We all did. And after everything was finished, upkeep had to be relearned by both of us. Different upholstery, different drapes, different appliances—it's an adjustment when everything comes at once."

"That's true," Renie agreed as they turned off Heraldsgate Avenue to head for the bridge across the ship canal. "I'm still figuring out all the features of my new washer and dryer. It's like flying a jet. The control panels have me baffled. By the way, we're dropping off SuperGerm first."

"That's fine," Judith said. "Should I stay in the car?"

Renie shook her head as they waited for a lull in traffic to get onto the city's major north-south thoroughfare. "It won't take long, and I'd like to have you meet Garth. He's a good guy. Creative, too, though he doesn't possess much curiosity about everyday things."

"Such as your mystery house?"

"Such as," Renie said, stepping on the gas as the Camry approached the bridge. "Bill isn't interested in it, either. Of course, being from Wisconsin, he didn't grow up in the neighborhood. But Madge Navarre did," Renie continued, referring to her friend from junior-high-school days, "and I think she thinks I'm crazy."

"I get it," Judith said with a smirk. "I'm supposed to prove you're not nuts."

Renie had taken the first right-hand turn at the end of the bridge. "Well . . . maybe. But you're even more intrigued by mysterious people and things than I am. In fact, I'm the one who usually tries to talk you out of your frequent flights of fancy."

"Which," Judith said, looking grim, "too often turn out not to be fanciful."

"All too true," Renie remarked. "So humor me, okay?"

Judith held up her index finger. "Just this once. I told you, coz, I'm getting into the busiest part of the year. I honestly don't have time to devote to your little mystery."

"You wouldn't say that if a corpse turned up in your freezer," Renie retorted.

Judith shuddered. "Don't say that! I've had more than my share of bad luck. It's been over a year since I've run into . . . any problems. Let's keep it that way."

"Of course," Renie said, slowing down on a street of relatively modest homes. "I'm not wishing for trouble. If I alter a couple of features in my artwork, I won't need to get the owners' consent. But I'd really like to find out why that house looks so vacant when it isn't. Or so I figure."

On-street parking was at a minimum. Judith and Renie had to walk almost half a block to reach Garth Doyle's residence. A trio of children in a neatly kept yard stared as Renie carried SuperGerm past them.

Garth's studio was in the basement of his Tudor-style brick home. The cousins entered through the attached garage and knocked on a wood-frame door with a brass plaque that read DOYLE DESIGNS.

Garth answered promptly. "If it isn't Serena and her cousin. Which is which?" He looked from SuperGerm to Judith and back again.

"Very funny," Renie shot back, then made the introductions. "Garth's quite the kidder," she added for Judith's benefit.

Judith observed that Garth was indeed a jovial man with a hearty laugh. He was of average height, but substantial girth; his hair and beard were turning gray; he wore rimless half-glasses and a shabby brown sweater over a denim shirt and blue jeans. Upon entering the studio, however, Judith noticed that everything appeared to be state-of-the-art. Or as far as Judith could tell from her limited experience. Renie was terrified of anything more complicated than a computer with basic design software. It had taken her several years to make that jump, and she remained entrenched in outmoded technology.

As Renie and Garth discussed how to tweak SuperGerm, Judith admired several works in progress. While Garth might rely on technology, he was also a hands-on kind of guy. There were several small clay models of all sorts of things—trees, animals, buildings, people. Judith was studying three-inch figures of Snow White and the Seven Dwarfs when Renie called to her.

"Garth and I have finished," she said to Judith. "Come join us."

Garth's expression grew curious as Renie launched into her explanation about the nearby Spanish-style house. "Have you asked anybody about that place since I last mentioned it?"

"I did," Garth replied, looking amused. "I saw a man come out of the house across the street—the south side. He told me that it was occupied, though when I pressed him for details, he admitted he hadn't seen anybody that he could recall. But he'd noticed the mailman deliver there a few times, so he assumed the owners might be elderly and not likely to go out much."

"They'd have to be elderly," Renie said, "if they've been there for fifty years. But that doesn't account for them not ever leaving the house."

Garth chuckled in his rich, deep manner. "Now, Serena, how many times have you actually been by that place over the years?"

Renie made a face. "Okay, until lately I probably haven't gone by it more than half a dozen times since I moved away. But in the old days, I suppose I'd walk by it once a month, coming from junior high and high school."

"Always at the same time?" Garth inquired.

"Well . . . yes, around three in the afternoon," Renie said. "I forget what time school let out. In fact, at my age, I've practically forgotten going to school. But," she added in a stubborn voice, "I certainly remember the house. It's as if it were in a time warp."

Garth rubbed his bearded chin. "Langford is such an ordinary part of town. Most of the houses are strictly middle-class, mainly built after 1910. Oh, there are a few big, expensive homes—including your villa, if it were better maintained—but by and large, this is what we used to call a lunch-bucket neighborhood."

"I know." Renie smiled. "Our house had four rooms until Dad expanded the attic."

Garth waved a hand. "This one was six rooms—until I finished off the basement and put in the studio."

Judith listened with half an ear as Renie and Garth discussed local demographics. Anxious to get going, she finally tapped her watch. "Coz, I hate to break up this—"

"Okay, okay," Renie snapped. "We're out of here. Thanks, Garth. Let me know when SuperGerm is ready for delivery."

"Will do," Garth replied.

Making hasty farewells, the cousins left the studio and walked back to the car. A few drops of rain were falling, but not enough to daunt native Pacific Northwesterners. Indeed, neither Judith nor Renie owned an umbrella. The rain was too unpredictable and rarely more than a drizzle. Umbrellas were only a nuisance, extra baggage that was often lost or mislaid by those who used them.

Parking was allowed on both sides of the street, creating a one-lane thoroughfare. Renie drove slowly, negotiating the traffic islands at each intersection. After two and a half blocks, she took a right-hand turn. At the next cross street, Judith spotted Renie's obsession.

The property took up the south end of the block facing Moonfleet Street. A rockery, now overgrown with large ferns, ivy, and Oregon grape, surrounded the lot on three sides. Tall firs and cedar trees obscured the house from view. Renie slowed the Camry to a crawl. Above the dense shrubbery, Judith could see beyond the peeling white stucco walls and the red-tiled roof, both of which sprouted large patches of moss. There was no lawn; there was no garden. A dirt track separated the property from its neighbors.

"I've never driven up that alley," Renie said as they pulled to a stop. "I don't know if Cammy would like it," she added, using the Joneses' nickname for their car. "It doesn't look as if it's ever used."

Judith put on her glasses for a better view of the house, which faced south on Moonfleet. The cousins were on the east side. The first thing Judith noticed was that the dwelling was a two-story structure with a one-story wing jutting from the main building. The wing had an arched passageway, a grilled window in the front, and one on the side. Ornamental tiles formed a pleasing pattern above the window that looked out onto the street. A tower almost in the center of the house rose slightly higher than the red-tiled roof. There was a balcony on the second floor of the main structure, and the only chimney was at the west end. Even though the stucco was peeling from the exterior and the roof was badly faded, the house was still impressive.

"The shades are drawn and the drapes are pulled," Renie noted. "It's always been that way."

Judith was still staring through the car window. "It's not a huge house—four bedrooms at most. And even though the land goes from corner to corner, it's a narrow block. Three legal lots at most. What do you figure the place would sell for, even without improvements?"

Renie considered. "Langford isn't as pricey as Heraldsgate Hill, but it's an up-and-coming area. I'd guess maybe seven, eight hundred thousand?"

Judith nodded. "That sounds about right."

Renie pointed to the yard. "The woodpile's down, but it's June. There aren't any toys that I can see, but if there were ever kids living in the house, they'd be grown up by now. There's a detached garage on the far side of the house that you can't see from here. In fact, you can't see it at all anymore because the trees and shrubs have grown so high since I was a teenager."

Movement nearby caught Judith's eye. She turned to look out the other window. Two women in their thirties were coming out of a modest Craftsman-style house across the street and heading for an SUV parked at the curb.

"Quick," Renie said as she rolled down Judith's window, "ask them who lives here."

"Hi," Judith called. "Could you tell us something?"

The taller of the two came into the street and stood by the SUV. "Are you lost?"

"No," Judith replied with her friendliest smile. "Do you know who lives in this wonderful old Spanish house?"

The woman frowned slightly. "Why do you want to know?"

Judith shifted into her small-fib-in-a-good-cause mode. "It's exactly the kind of house my husband and I've been looking for. That style is very hard to find in this city. I wondered if it might be for sale. It looks deserted."

"Heavens, no," the woman replied. "I doubt very much if the owners would want to sell. They've lived there for years."

"Then," Judith said, keeping her smile fixed in place, "they might be thinking of moving to a smaller place. I mean, if they're getting up in years."

"Doubtful," the woman said, opening the SUV's door.

The second woman was already in the passenger seat. She leaned over, calling to her friend. "Come on, Glenda, let's go. We're supposed to meet Maddy at one."

Judith waved a hand. "Please—wait. Do you know the owners' names?"

Glenda, who had started to get into the SUV, shot Judith an exasperated look. "Yes. They're Dick and

Jane Bland. Now will you please move your car so we can get out of here and go to lunch?" She sat down hard in the driver's seat and slammed the door.

"Twerp," Renie growled as she took her time starting the Camry.

"Well, now you know." Judith took off her glasses and slipped them back into their leather case. "An elderly couple named Bland live in your so-called mystery house. Are you satisfied?"

The question was met with an ominous silence. On the way back from Langford, Judith deliberately steered the conversation in directions other than the Spanish house. Renie's responses were terse, however, and her short chin was set at a pugnacious angle.

They had crossed the bridge over the ship canal when Judith realized that Renie wasn't in the right-hand lane to make the turn onto Heraldsgate Hill.

"Hey!" she cried. "Where are we going? I've got to get home."

"Open the glove compartment," Renie commanded. "Get out the phone book I use for my cell."

"Dammit," Judith began, but obeyed. "I really don't have time for this. Whatever *this* is," she added.

"It may only be a detour," Renie retorted. "Look up the Blands."

As fast as she could, Judith flipped through to the residential *B* section. There were a handful of Blands but no Richard, Rich, Rick, Dick, or any initials that might be the couple on Moonfleet Street. "Drat," said Judith, returning the directory to the glove compartment. "Now I *am* getting mad at you."

"Oh, be a sport, coz," Renie urged. "How many

times have you dragged me into all sorts of weird situations, not to mention occasionally risking my life and all my limbs?"

Judith grimaced. Renie had gone far beyond the call of kinship to help Judith solve her own mysteries, most of which had exposed them both to danger. It was not yet one o'clock. None of the guests were due until four at the earliest. Joe was over on the Eastside helping to sort out an insurance scam. Phyliss was used to working unsupervised. Gertrude wouldn't care if her daughter was tardy. The old girl was too wrapped up in her movie script.

"Okay," Judith said, leaning back in the seat. "Where are we going?"

"Downtown," Renie replied, sailing along at ten miles over the forty-mile-an-hour speed limit. "I want to check the rolls at the county courthouse."

It took ten minutes to get to the courthouse, another ten to park, and a quarter of an hour to find the right department and the proper records. Judith's artificial hip was beginning to ache, but she kept her mouth shut. Renie, who was carrying a large, worn binder, would retaliate with complaints about the shoulder that still bothered her even after extensive surgery.

Fortunately, the cousins found a place to sit down. "You do have the address," Judith said.

"No," Renie admitted. "I've never been able to see the house numbers. But since it's the only residence on that side of Moonfleet, I can't miss. The houses across the street are in the twenty-one–hundred range, odd numbers. Ah!" In triumph, she looked up from the big binder. "I got it! It's two-one-oh-eight."

Judith scooted her chair around for a closer look. The yellowed page showed the original plat, with a floor plan for the house and the garage. The date was April 11, 1925.

Renie moved on to the information about ownership. "The house was completed in March of 1926. The builder was somebody named L. R. Engstrom, and the first owners were Preston D. and Eleanor F. Conway, who paid thirty-five hundred dollars for it." She moved her finger down the page. "They sold the place in 1933 for five thousand dollars. Maybe they couldn't keep up the payments during the Depression. Anyway, the new owners were Ruben C. and Ellen M. Borbon. Ruben must have passed on by the time it was sold again for seventy-five hundred dollars in 1947 by Mrs. Borbon to..." She paused and took a deep breath. "To Richard L. and Jane C. Bland."

"You're right." Judith swiftly calculated the years. "They've lived there for well over a half century. Goodness, they must be old."

"Fairly old," Renie amended. "We aren't spring chickens, either. It's possible that they bought it as newlyweds. They might be in their early seventies."

"That's not old anymore," Judith said wistfully. "It used to be, though."

Renie stood up. "Let's go."

"Home?" Judith asked hopefully.

"No. Back to Moonfleet Street."

Judith did her best to catch up with Renie, who was sprinting toward the elevators. "Why?"

"That disagreeable neighbor is probably still out to lunch," Renie said, entering the elevator and poking the button for the street level. "I want a better look at the house."

"Coz—" Judith began in a pleading tone.

"It's only two o'clock," Renie interrupted. "I'll have you back at the B&B by three. I promise."

The elevator doors opened onto the lobby. "Okay," Judith said with a sigh. "I guess I owe you."

"You bet you do," Renie retorted as they waited for the light to walk across the street to the parking garage. "Besides, this is just a little harmless fun."

"True," Judith allowed.

Or maybe not.

TWO

ON THEIR RETURN trip to Moonfleet, Renie found a parking place across the street from the front of the house. "We can't see much of anything from here except for that path that goes up from the sidewalk," she said. "We'll have to get out and walk."

"Walk?" Judith responded. "How about carrying me? I'm getting gimpy from all this walking."

"Nonsense," Renie snapped. "We haven't walked any farther than you'd do at home, especially going up and down all those stairs. Furthermore, I can't carry you. My shoulder, remember?"

The drizzle had stopped, though the sky remained cloudy. As the cousins got out of the car, they saw a postal van pull up at the corner.

"Aha!" Renie exclaimed under her breath. "We can interrogate him."

"Why not?" Judith said in an indifferent voice. "Maybe I can spare my hip by riding around in his pouch."

Crossing the street, the cousins peered up through the narrow path that was flanked by towering camellia and lily-of-the-valley bushes. They could see the arched front entrance. The door was made of vertical mahogany planks with three ornamental hinges and a matching knocker. Faded multihued tiles surrounded the door. The large arched first-story window was made of tinted glass. There were two smaller rectangular windows in the tower, one on the first floor, the other on the second. There was no lawn—only dirt, rocks, and a few weeds. Despite the secluded setting and beauty of design, the overall impression was bleak. Judith sensed that this was not—perhaps never had been—a happy house.

"It's terribly sad," Judith declared. "It's not just the feeling of neglect. There's despair, too, and hopelessness."

Renie nodded. "I'm becoming depressed just looking at it. But doesn't it make you curious?"

The human element—or lack of it—moved Judith, who was always intrigued by other people. "Yes. Yes, I have to admit it does."

Renie turned to watch the mailman come across the street. "Good grief!" she exclaimed under her breath. "I don't believe it! That's Morty! I thought he would have retired by now."

"Morty?" The name rang a bell with Judith. "The one who always left a trail of mail behind him and read all the magazines before he delivered them?"

"The very same," Renie replied. "And here comes his awful dog, Zip Code."

"Son or grandson of Zip Code," Judith murmured.

Morty stopped at the curb, peering at Renie. "Do I know you?"

It had been going on forty years since Renie and Morty's last encounter. Both had been in their early twenties. Renie had bawled out Morty for delivering her copy of *Vogue* with mustard and ketchup smeared on its summer bathing-suit layout. Drool, too, she'd told him at the time.

"I don't think so," Renie lied. Then she smiled. It was a big mistake.

"Those teeth!" Morty shouted, recoiling so fast that he dropped several pieces of mail. "You! It's Fang!"

Zip Code, a shaggy golden retriever, hid behind his master and growled.

"Okay, okay," Renie said in an impatient voice. "Skip the past history. We're both older and hopefully wiser." Indeed, Morty's blond hair was almost white and his ramrod posture had deteriorated into a sorry slouch. "Have you always been on this part of the route?"

"Why do you care?" Morty shot back. "How many times did you report me to the Langford post office?"

"I only did that once," Renie said, "after I found my IRS refund in the hydrangea after the leaves fell off in the fall. It was my folks who called the post office about a dozen times. Dad hit the roof when you tore the fishing-hole maps out of his *Northwest Angler* magazine."

"So I had a hobby on my days off," Morty shot back. "What did you expect me to do? Play golf and walk eighteen holes? You should see my feet, they look like corncobs."

"*Please.*" Renie put her hands over her eyes. "Why haven't you retired?"

"I will," Morty replied, "end of the month."

"Congratulations." Renie smirked. "To the people on your route, that is."

Judith tapped Renie's arm. "Coz . . ." None too gently, she pushed Renie out of the way. The ungroomed Zip Code came out from behind Morty and warily approached the cousins. "That's a"—there were times when Judith couldn't tell a fib even in a good cause—"a real doggie dog. How long have you had him?"

"This guy?" Morty leaned forward to pat the dog's scruffy rump. "Twelve years. Fourth generation. I've always taken a Zip Code with me. Keeps the other dogs at bay."

"So you've had this whole route all these years?" Judith inquired.

Morty glanced at Renie, then looked back at Judith. "Why are you two asking me these questions?"

"It's this place," Judith replied, gesturing at the house. "Doesn't it seem kind of spooky to you?"

Morty, who was now standing on the sidewalk, glanced up the path that led to the front door. "Spooky? Gosh, I've never noticed. It's just another house, another stop on the route, another slot to fill, twenty-five steps to three stairs, back down again, twenty-five to the street, fifty-seven steps to the corner, then—"

Judith interrupted, though quietly. "Have you ever seen anybody around the house?"

"Like people?" Morty shook his head. "I don't see many people. Most of 'em work. Like me. Besides, I've only been doing this end of the route for the past year.

My supervisor finally decided I'd had enough of that other part of Langford." He paused to glare at Renie. "What I put up with all those—"

"So," Judith said to prevent another monologue from Morty, "whoever lives here does get mail."

Zip Code was sniffing at Renie's shoes. Renie was doing a little dance to get away from the animal.

"Oh, they get mail," Morty replied with a shake of his head. "They all get mail, every day, except Sundays and holidays, rain, shine, snow, hail, heat, cold, earthquakes—"

"Lots of mail?" Judith interjected, ignoring Renie, who had stepped—not too hard—on Zip Code's paw.

Apparently, Morty didn't notice. "Well—no." The hint of a smile played at his thin lips. "I'll say that for them. Oh, they get the usual bills—utilities, mostly— and the flyers everybody else gets." He bent down to retrieve the pieces he'd dropped, but Zip Code had grabbed one of what looked like a personal letter and was chewing it to bits. "Never mind," Morty said, "that wasn't for these folks. It was for somebody in the next block." He stroked the dog's neck. "Yum-yum, huh, Zippy? What he really likes are those big manila envelopes that look so important but probably aren't."

Renie twirled around and wandered off down the street.

"At least," Morty went on, sorting through the rest of the mail he'd picked up, "these people here don't get all those horrible catalogs. Two years ago, I ended up in traction after I threw my back out. No more of that, I said to myself. I load those blasted things into the van, but I dump 'em off at the nearest recycling bin. Who needs all that junk? I figure I'm saving folks a lot of money. Besides, if they ordered the stuff, guess who'd have to deliver most of it?" He poked himself in the chest with his thumb.

"So they don't get actual letters here?" Judith asked, beginning to feel weary.

Morty scratched his chin, which looked as if it could use a shave. "Once a month, maybe. That's it."

"I assume everything's addressed to Mr. and Mrs. Bland," Judith remarked.

"Oh, yeah. Except for the stuff marked 'Resident' or 'Addressee' or—here's the one that really gets me. 'To Our Friends at . . .' Now, you know danged well, they aren't friends. They don't even know each other. It's just a—" This time, Morty interrupted himself. "Hold on. A while back, there was a letter addressed to somebody who wasn't named Bland. I noticed, 'cause I pay close attention to names and addresses. In fact, I think there've been some other letters to whoever it was."

Judith spoke loudly and quickly to drown out Renie's strangled cry of disbelief. "What was the name on the envelope?"

"I don't remember offhand," Morty replied, "but it was the right address."

"Maybe someone lives with them," Judith ventured.

Morty shrugged. "Could be." He glanced at his watch. "I'd better be on my way. Don't want to get behind." He scrutinized his watch more closely. "Gee, I'm already an hour or so off schedule. Guess I shouldn't have had that second cup of coffee."

Morty sauntered up the path, with Zip Code trailing behind him. Judith joined Renie at the corner.

"Did you hear that?" Judith asked. "There's a third party living in the house."

"I heard it," Renie replied grimly. "I heard all of it. I can't believe that after all these years, I had to run into Morty the Mailman."

"I wonder who else is living there," Judith mused, ignoring Renie's complaint. "A sister of Mrs. Bland? A child who's returned after a divorce? A friend?"

The cousins had turned the corner and reached the unpaved alley. "Any of the above," Renie said. "Are you coming with me?"

Judith studied the dirt track. "There are too many potholes and rough spots. I don't want to risk a fall. Go on without me. I'll wait here."

Renie paused several times during her mission. Upon reaching the garage, she went out of sight, apparently exploring from every angle. It seemed to Judith that the alley wasn't intended for communal purposes, but belonged to the Blands. There were tall trees and big shrubs on both sides. Through a thicket of blackberry vines, Judith could make out a wire fence that probably marked the property line.

All she could see of the garage was part of a red-tiled roof. She shifted her gaze to the house itself. From the side angle, the only windows she could see were two casements upstairs and the one with the grille in the arched wing. Heavy curtains drooped behind the small panes on the second floor; fusty drapes sagged behind the tinted glass at ground level. Judith swore she could almost smell the dust and mold inside the house.

And then, to her amazement, she saw movement behind the upstairs curtains. Ever so slowly, they parted. An inch, no more, not enough to allow her to see a person. But someone was there. Judith looked away, turned in every direction, and whistled shrilly.

"Renie!" she called loudly. "Come, Renie! Come, nice doggie!" Judith moved beyond the alley, toward the adjacent property with its one-story frame house.

A minute later, Renie came running down to the sidewalk. "What's up?" she asked, a bit breathless.

Before Judith could reply, Zip Code came bounding down the street, barking his head off. He leaped on Renie, almost knocking her down and licking her face. "Hey!" she yelled. "Cut it out! You've got letter breath!"

Judith firmly grasped Zip Code's collar and pulled the animal away from her cousin. "Zippy! Nice doggie! Go find Morty."

Panting, Zip Code eyed Judith for a brief moment before trotting away.

"You should have called for a cat," Renie said, taking a tissue out of her purse and wiping her face. "What's up?"

"Someone's peeking through the upstairs window," Judith replied, explaining how she'd seen the curtains move, but couldn't make out a face or a figure. "We'd better get out of here." She gazed up at the house on the other side of the wire fence. "Should we call on these neighbors?"

Renie pointed to the empty attached garage. "Their car's gone. It doesn't look as if they're home. We might have better luck with the guy on Moonfleet that Garth talked to."

"But he didn't know anything," Judith pointed out.

"True," Renie agreed. "I don't suppose canvassing the entire neighborhood would help, either."

It was starting to rain again. The cousins stood on the sidewalk, contemplating their next move.

"I really should get home," Judith finally said. "We can always come back."

Renie grinned. "You're hooked, aren't you?"

Judith winced. "Well . . . I guess. Now that we've put names to the owners and know that somebody's inside and the place feels so forlorn and sad—"

"Ha!" Renie rocked back and forth on her heels. "I knew it. You're a sucker for a sob story."

"Don't rub it in," Judith retorted. "We'd better go. I doubt that whoever was watching us is still at the window. They can't see us from there and won't know where we parked."

"Probably not," Renie agreed, "unless they've been on the lookout all along."

The cousins went back down the street and crossed over to the other side. Before getting into the Camry, they both looked back at the house.

"The mail's still in the mailbox," Judith noted. "There's a milk box on the porch, too."

"So I see," Renie said. "We could wait until somebody comes to get it."

"Like Joe on a stakeout?" Judith shook her head. "What do you bet they don't come out until after dark?"

"Could be." With a shrug, Renie got into the driver's seat.

"Tell me what the view from the alley was like," Judith said after they were under way.

"Not much," Renie answered with a scowl. "I could hardly see anything of the house. It's blocked off by the trees and shrubbery. They've got rhododendrons that must be ten feet tall. I could just barely make out a small storage shed and what might have been a greenhouse, but it's in a state of virtual collapse. Near the fence on that side was probably once a fishpond—you can see the rectangular concrete outline, but it's full of moss and weeds and scilla. There must be a back door, but I couldn't see it. As for the garage, it's locked up. There are two small windows, but they're covered with what looks like cardboard and chicken wire, not to mention cobwebs."

"Any sign of car tracks in the dirt alley?" Judith inquired.

Renie shook her head. "I don't get it. If these people are old, don't they ever go to a doctor? That's what old people do, right?"

Judith grimaced. "We ought to know."

"We're not *that* old," Renie retorted, flipping on the windshield wipers. "We've just had some weird medical problems."

"More than our share," Judith conceded. "But we started out as sickly kids."

Allergies and asthma had plagued the cousins from early childhood. Renie had suffered severe sinus problems as well. Judith had always been prone to hip troubles, exacerbated by using a pogo stick during a growth spurt. Judith had often thought that their mutual illnesses had helped cement their bond. They had been only children, growing up two blocks away from each other until Renie's family moved to Langford just before she started junior high. The cousins had always been close, even closer than some sisters. When they quarreled, both of them could retreat to their own homes instead of being forced to share the same roof.

"I'll drop you off and then stop in to see Mom," Renie said as they once again crossed the high bridge over the canal. "As usual, she insists I'm neglecting her."

"When were you there last?" Judith asked.

"Yesterday," Renie replied. "Twice. And I've talked to her on the phone three times since I stopped by. Today she needs ice cubes."

"Is Aunt Deb's refrigerator broken?" Judith inquired.

"No," Renie answered, turning onto Heraldsgate Hill. "But she complains that her arthritis is so bad that she can't get the ice-cube trays out of the freezer compartment. The trays are stuck."

"What does she need the ice cubes for?"

"Her water. You know Mom—she drinks about a gallon of water a day," Renie said. "And then she wonders why she has to go to the bathroom so often."

"Water's good for you," Judith declared. "I drink quite a bit myself."

"I don't," Renie said in a stubborn tone. "I drink Pepsi. Water tastes like . . . water."

Judith didn't argue. The cousins had had that discussion many times, and neither of them won—or lost. "It's a blessing that our mothers got those motorized wheelchairs. The walker was okay for my mother as long as she stayed in the toolshed. But when she'd go out, it was getting very hard on her. She almost gave up bridge club."

"Heaven help us if Aunt Gert and Mom had to stop playing bridge," Renie asserted. "Though I'll have to admit that Mom's work as a consultant for Wirehoser Timber helps keep her occupied."

"Ditto for Mother's movie script," Judith said. "I still can't believe those two old girls have managed to start new careers in their old age."

"More power to them," Renie responded as traffic slowed on Heraldsgate Avenue. "I'm still thanking my lucky stars for sending Mom to that graphic design conference to take my place. All her old-fashioned, commonsense ideas really struck a chord. She still can't believe she gets a twenty-five-hundred-dollar retainer every month even if she doesn't have to do anything. But being Mom, she feels she has to earn her keep. Thus Wirehoser gets their money's worth when she comes up with one of her quaint little ideas. The latest is Bucky Beaver. I think she named it after me." Renie bared her prominent front teeth.

"What does Bucky do?"

"He beaves," Renie replied, "as in 'behave.' 'Beave Like Bucky' is her slogan. It's to promote good manners for campers and hikers. Bucky will wear a napkin around his neck and spats."

"Cute," Judith remarked as they started down the steep counterbalance. "Frankly, I think it's wonderful that our mothers can still contribute. People live so long these days, and the younger generation has always tended to disregard the old folks' wisdom and ideas. It's not only a shame, but a waste."

"Speaking of the younger generation," Renie said as

she turned onto Judith's street, "isn't that your son's Range Rover pulling into the cul-de-sac?"

Judith leaned forward. "It looks like it. But there are plenty of Range Rovers and Land Rovers and every other kind of Rover on Heraldsgate Hill these days."

However, the beige-and-brown Range Rover had stopped in front of Hillside Manor. Sure enough, as the cousins pulled up behind it, Mike McMonigle got out.

Hurriedly, Judith removed her seat belt and all but lunged out of the car. "Mike!" she cried, hurrying to embrace her son. "How good to see you! Can you stay for dinner?"

Mike didn't answer right away. In fact, he clung to his mother much longer than usual.

"Hi, Mike," Renie called as she came toward the pair. "How are you?"

"Not good," Mike replied, finally stepping back from Judith. "Kristin and I've split up."

"What?" Judith cried, a hand at her breast.

"Mike!" Renie put her arms around her nephew. "What happened?"

"It's just not working." Mike hugged his aunt, then wiped at his eyes.

Judith was too stunned to speak and suddenly sick to her stomach. She stared at her son, realizing that he was pale and haggard. Even the red hair he'd inherited from Joe seemed to have lost its luster.

"Let's go inside," Renie said as the rain began to come down even harder. "Where are Kristin and the boys?" she asked.

"They're still up at our place at the ranger station," Mike replied in a heavy voice. "They're packing."

The trio entered through the front door. Judith felt dazed as she led the way into the living room. Mother and son sat down across from each other on the new matching navy blue sofas in front of the fireplace. Renie remained standing.

"I can make a discreet exit," she offered.

Mike shook his head. "No." He attempted a smile. "You're my favorite aunt."

"I'm your *only* aunt," Renie reminded him. "Can I get you two something to drink?"

Mike hesitated. "A beer, maybe?"

"Sure," Renie replied. "Coz?"

Judith was staring at the carpet. "What? No, I don't feel so good."

"I'll bring you a little brandy," Renie said. "Frankly, I could use a stiff bourbon." She hurried out of the room.

"Has this been coming on for some time?" Judith finally asked. "You all seemed so happy when you were here at Easter."

"I thought we were," Mike responded. "But that was the end of March. It was about a week later that Kristin told me she didn't think things were working out. She feels stifled up at the summit. She wants to have more of a life than chasing two little kids through the snow."

Kristin, like Mike, was a forest ranger. But she hadn't worked since their wedding six years earlier. It was difficult to post married couples to the same place. Little Mac was now five; Joe-Joe was going on three. Kristin was a big, hearty young woman with enough energy and endurance to run an entire wilderness area. Judith could understand that she'd feel frustrated, and said so.

"But," Judith continued, "she knew what she was getting into when you got married. Furthermore, she's only an hour from the city, and much less than that from the Eastside, with all its stores and restaurants and other things to do. What on earth does she plan on doing as a single mom? It's going to be harder than it is right now."

Mike looked bleak. "She wants me to keep the kids."

"Oh, dear." Feeling a headache coming on, Judith rubbed her temples. "Really, Kristin is going through a serious crisis."

Renie entered with the drinks. "I heard most of that." She looked at Judith. "You need some aspirin, right? I'll get it." She left the room again.

"Do you still love her?" Judith inquired softly.

Mike nodded emphatically. "Yes. Yes, I really do."

"Does she still love you?"

He grimaced. "She says she does. But she says she needs her space."

Judith frowned. "Does that mean this is only a trial separation?"

Mike sighed. "I guess. My head's so messed up I don't know what anybody means." He waited until Renie had delivered the aspirin and the glass of water to Judith. "I thought if it's okay I'd spend the night here and then go back tomorrow and get the kids."

Judith swallowed the pills and stared at her son. "And what?"

Mike looked upward. "There's room, isn't there? I mean, there's my old room on the third floor along with the guest room, right?"

"Wrong," Judith said, realizing she sounded harsh. "That is, we've rearranged things upstairs. Your old room is Joe's office. Granny's room is a sitting room. There's not much space for you and the boys."

"Don't look at me," Renie said as Mike turned toward his aunt. "Uncle Bill and I just spent thirty-odd years shoving our kids out of the nest. We're enjoying a little peace and quiet. Maybe that sounds selfish, but," she added wistfully, "there's always the chance that our children may come home to visit."

Judith looked at the grandfather clock across the room between the bookcases. It was almost three-thirty. Phyliss had left for the day, which was a good thing. Judith wouldn't want her cleaning woman to overhear this particular conversation. "I wish your father would come home," she said. "Maybe I should call him on his cell phone."

More than thirty years earlier, after Judith and Joe's engagement, she became pregnant. But Joe was a rookie cop at the time, and had become distraught after seeing his first teenage OD fatalities. To ease his pain, he'd gotten drunk in a cop watering hole and run off to Vegas with Vivian, the bar's hard-drinking chanteuse. Vivian—or Herself, as Judith had always called her—had somehow managed to get Joe to a justice of the peace.

The next day, Joe awakened in horror, not remembering exactly what had happened. He'd phoned Judith at once, but Gertrude refused to let him talk to her, informing him that her daughter never wanted to see or speak to him again. The old lady never mentioned his call. In desperation, Judith accepted a proposal from Dan McMonigle to provide a father for her unborn child. Dan had died at forty-nine, having eaten and drunk himself into a four-hundred-pound machine of self-destruction. When Judith and Joe finally met again, his marriage was on the rocks—bourbon-rocks, Vivian's favorite hobby. When she remembered to add the rocks.

Judith's memory of her nineteen miserable years with Dan made her angry. "You took a sacred vow," she asserted, snapping out of her dumbfounded state. "If your father—your stepfather, I mean—and I could stay married, so can you."

Mike sighed. "It takes two."

"No, it doesn't," Judith shot back. "Sometimes it only takes one."

"You don't understand, Mom," Mike began. "It's a—"

Judith cut him off. "I understand all too well. Don't you remember how it was before Dan died?"

"He was a good father," Mike asserted. "I loved him."

Judith's shoulders slumped. "I know. I give him credit for virtually raising you—since he wouldn't work and I had to have two jobs to support us. I went from being a librarian by day to a bartender by night. Sometimes I feel as if I missed out on much of your childhood. But yes, we had some good times—though I wouldn't call it a happy marriage."

"Gruesome," Renie noted.

Mike wore a surprised expression. "I always thought you two got along pretty well."

"We tried to, in front of you." Judith took a big swig of brandy. "Look—give yourselves some time apart. Think things over. Consider what's best for the boys.

Come up with ways that Kristin can have more of a life outside of the house."

"Like competing in tractor pulls," Renie murmured.

Mike turned toward his aunt, who was sitting on the arm of the opposite sofa. "What did you say, Aunt Renie?"

"Like meeting with actor girls," Renie said. "I mean, *actresses*. And actors. You know—amateur theatrics or something."

Mike shook his head. "She isn't interested in that kind of stuff."

The phone on the cherrywood table rang. Renie, who was closest to it, answered. "It's for you," she said to Judith. "A Mrs. Beecroft."

"Oh. She's one of our guests for tonight." Judith stood up and took the receiver from Renie.

Mrs. Beecroft had called to say that their car had broken down on the other side of the mountains. She and Mr. Beecroft would have to cancel. Could they stay tomorrow night instead? Judith informed her that wasn't possible, but she'd check with the state B&B association to find another nice inn for them. Would Mrs. Beecroft please call back in a couple of hours?

"Okay," Judith said to Mike as she resumed her place on the sofa. "You can stay in the empty room tonight."

Mike brightened slightly. "Gee, thanks, Mom. I really appreciate it. I'll get my gear."

When Mike was gone, Renie shook her head. "I suppose I can look forward to some of that, too. Damn, why does this generation have to be so egocentric? Kristin feels stifled, and her reaction is to bolt. Whatever became of holy matrimony? Whatever happened to remembering that 'we' isn't spelled with an 'I'?"

"I don't know," Judith replied. "It must be partly our fault. We were so intent on making sure they grew up with more than we had as kids that we spoiled them rotten. Maybe this bunch will figure it out before it's too late for their own children."

"Call me tonight," Renie said, picking up her purse. "Good luck."

Judith was certain she'd need it.

THREE

JUDITH DIDN'T SLEEP well that night, tossing and turning, fretting and fussing. She'd gotten up early, but in her muddled state had managed to drop two raw eggs on the floor, set fire to the bacon, and step on Sweetums's tail; the cat retaliated by shredding the new dish towel Judith had left on the counter. It was a rocky way to start a Wednesday.

Mike, as well as the guests, left by ten-thirty. Joe had stayed home, having another heart-to-heart talk with his son. The results hadn't pleased Joe any more than had the session the previous night.

"He's got an answer for everything," Joe grumbled, helping Judith clean up the kitchen. "Hell, I'm twice his age, and I still don't have the answers for anything."

"Yes, you do, Joe," Judith responded. "They're just not the answers Mike wants to hear."

Joe sighed. "I guess. God knows I mucked up my life when I was young."

"You were younger then than Mike is now," Judith pointed out. "I didn't do much better."

"That was different," Joe pointed out. "I did something very foolish, but it could've been mended if your mother hadn't interfered. Then you did something foolish, too. But the point is, once we'd married a pair of drunken sots, we tried to make a go of it. We wouldn't break our vows, even though we had damned good reasons to do it."

"You and Herself were drunk as skunks and got married by an Elvis look-alike, yet you managed to do your best to stay together," Judith declared. "Dan and I were married at SOTS," she went on, using the nickname for Our Lady, Star of the Sea. "To me, divorce wasn't really an option. Making marriage work, no matter what it took, was what most of my family believed in."

"Murder was considered, as I recall," Joe said with a bemused expression.

"I stabbed Dan in the rear end with a meat fork after he threw the Thanksgiving turkey, dressing and all, out onto the sidewalk," Judith replied, putting paper products in the recycling wastebasket. "He was so fat he didn't even feel it."

Joe shook his head. "We both had a hell of a lot to put up with."

"You finally got out, though," Judith noted.

"Leaving Vivian was my last attempt to get her to save herself," Joe declared, shutting the dishwasher with unnecessary force. "It didn't work. She kept right on drinking. And, of course, there was Caitlin," he added, referring to the daughter he'd had by his first wife.

"And there was Mike," Judith said. "He needed a father, especially since he was a boy."

The phone rang. Judith picked up the receiver from the counter by the sink.

"Hi, Mom," Mike said. "Guess what? Uncle Al says the kids and I can stay with him for the next few days while Kristin decides where she wants to go."

Uncle Al had never married, despite plenty of chances. By coincidence, he lived in a bungalow in the Langford district, about a mile from Renie's mystery house.

"That's very generous of Uncle Al," Judith said. "But what about your job?"

"I've taken the week off for family reasons," Mike replied. "If Kristin hasn't moved out by next Monday, I'll just have to commute for a while. It's less than an hour and we won't have snow on the pass this time of year. Say, can you do me a favor?"

"Sure," Judith said in a dull voice. "What is it?"

"I'm not going to get out of here with the boys until lunchtime. That means I'll have to stop along the way to feed them. By the time we get to Uncle Al's, Joe-Joe will have to take his nap. I left in such a hurry this morning that I forgot most of my stuff. Can you bring it over to Uncle Al's? He probably won't be home—he was going to the racetrack. Just leave it on the front porch."

"Sure," Judith said, sounding even less enthusiastic. "Have you thought any more about what Joe and I said to you?"

"I really haven't had time," Mike replied.

"Okay. Be careful. When will I see you again?"

"Dinner? Uncle Al will still be at the track," Mike explained. "He always stays for the last race."

"Fine." Recognizing the apathy in her voice, Judith

tried to make amends. "It'll be fun to have the boys here, too. What do they like to eat?"

"Fried chicken," Mike responded. "They love your fried chicken."

"Okay, that's what we'll have. See you later."

Joe was watching Judith. "Now what?" he inquired.

Judith related Mike's end of the conversation. "I'm going to Uncle Al's. Mike needs his gear."

Joe tucked his shirt into his pants. He still wore a size thirty-four belt, but it rode much lower on his torso than it had in years past. "Do you want me to go over there?"

"I thought you had to go back to the insurance company," Judith said.

"I told them I wouldn't be there until one," Joe replied.

"Well . . ." Judith paused. It would only be a few blocks out of her way to swing by Moonfleet Street. Focusing, however briefly, on something else would be good for her. "No, I'll do it. I need to get out of the house. The fresh air might wake me up. I still feel kind of out of it. But I could use your help loading the stuff into the car."

After collecting their son's belongings from the guest room and evading Phyliss's questions about why Mike had spent the night, Judith and Joe headed for the Subaru.

"We'd better put it in the trunk," Joe said. "Why did he have to bring a sleeping bag along with all this other stuff?"

"Maybe he thought he'd have to camp out," Judith replied.

Joe unlocked the trunk. "Since Uncle Al's out wheeling trifectas at the track, you be sure to carry each of the heavy items one at a time. Forget the stairs. Just dump it all on the lawn." He winced as he tried to open the trunk. "This damned thing's sticking. Why didn't you tell me? I'd have taken it in to be fixed."

"It's even harder to close," Judith pointed out as they loaded Mike's gear. "It just started doing that in the last couple of days."

"I'll make an appointment with Jim at Nabobs Auto Shop," Joe said. "You sure you can manage?"

"I'm sure." Judith gave Joe a quick kiss on the lips. "If I'm not back before you go to the insurance office, good luck. I've got errands."

Backing down the drive, Judith waved to her neighbors, Carl and Arlene Rankers, who were working in their impeccable garden. Impeccable, that is, except for the laurel hedge that seemed to grow a couple of feet every year. Judith wouldn't dream of complaining—Carl and Arlene were wonderful, kindhearted people. And Arlene, with her insatiable curiosity, had often proved an invaluable ally to Judith when it came to keeping track of any criminal doings on Heraldsgate Hill.

Reaching the avenue, Judith drove another five blocks before pulling over next to the Presbyterian church. She took out her cell phone and dialed Renie's number.

"Want to do a drive-by on Moonfleet Street?" she asked.

"Ohhh . . ." Renie sounded flustered. "I can't. Guess who gets to draw Bucky Beaver? Mom recommended me, probably figuring I could do a self-portrait. Wire-hoser called this morning. They have a Monday deadline."

"You can use the money," Judith pointed out.

"That's very true," Renie replied. "How are you doing?"

"Upset. Sad. Tired." Judith gazed out at the church's playground, which was shared with Pooh Pals Preschool. The sun was out from behind the clouds, and the children were playing on the slides and swings and a small merry-go-round. They looked so happy. With a pang, Judith thought of Mac and Joe-Joe, who were the same ages as most of the preschool kids. She shook off the thought, and told Renie about Uncle Al's offer of hospitality. "I decided another visit to the Moonfleet house might distract me."

"Go for it," Renie said. "A good mystery always takes your mind off your own troubles. Keep me posted—on all fronts."

Judith went directly to Uncle Al's. Ignoring Joe's advice, she placed Mike's belongings behind a porch pillar that was shielded by a huge red geranium. But she made three trips to do it, not risking an overload on her artificial hip. The trunk stuck again, but she finally managed to get it closed. Or so she hoped. At least it didn't fly open when she started down the street. Backtracking for much of the way, Judith reached Moonfleet in less than five minutes.

To her surprise, there was activity in front of the house. A Dairyland milk truck was parked there, and the milkman was coming down the path carrying an empty delivery basket.

Judith parked behind the truck, hopefully out of sight from the house's prying eyes. "Hi," she called just as the milkman reached the sidewalk. "Can you spare me a moment or two?"

The milkman, who was middle-aged and slim as a reed, grimaced. "I'm already running late, ma'am. My truck broke down this morning. Can you make it quick?"

Judith noticed that his name, Vern Benson, was stitched on his blue jacket. "I'll try, Mr. Benson," she said, offering him her warmest smile. "Have you ever met the people who live in this house?"

"Call me Vern," the milkman said, looking somewhat surprised by the query. "No, I can't say that I have. I guess they aren't home much."

"I understood the Blands never left the place," Judith said.

"Then maybe that's why I never see them." Vern brushed a leaf off the front of his striped overalls before moving toward his truck. "All I know is they get the same order every week." He glanced at the checklist in his hand. "Half gallon of milk, pint of cream, pound of butter, dozen eggs. They pay the bill on time. The money's always in the milk box. That's all I need to know. Sorry, got to run."

Vern hopped into the truck and drove away. Briefly, Judith considered marching up to the door and knocking. But she had a feeling no one would respond. Maybe she'd try it another time when her spirits weren't so low. With one last look at the desolate house, she started back to her Subaru. Before she could open the car door, a UPS van pulled up where the Dairyland truck had been parked.

Judith retraced her steps. The driver was still inside, wrestling with a large parcel. As soon as he emerged, she greeted him with a friendly smile.

"Is that for the Blands?" she asked.

The driver, who was a good-looking black man of about thirty with close-cropped hair and a tidy mustache, nodded. "Excuse me, it's kind of heavy. I'll be right back with you."

With bated breath, Judith watched the brown-clad young man go up the path. She noticed he didn't use the knocker, but leaned the parcel up against the wall on the opposite side of the door from the milk box. A moment later, he was back on the sidewalk.

"How can I help you?" he asked.

"Ah . . . do you have any supplies on the truck?" Judith inquired.

"Sure," the young man replied. "What do you need?"

"Some forms—a half dozen will do," Judith replied. "And a half dozen of the standard overnight letter-size envelopes."

The deliveryman nipped back inside the truck, then reappeared with the forms and envelopes. "Here you go. Anything else?"

"Thanks. Actually, I do have a question. My name's Judith, and I'm a . . . neighbor. That is, my uncle is a neighbor," she amended for fear that the deliveryman might someday show up on the Heraldsgate Hill route. "Uncle Al is worried about the Blands. He heard they were very ill."

"I'm Kevin," the deliveryman replied with an attractive smile. "Gosh, I wouldn't know. I've been on this route almost four years, and I've never met them."

"Do you come by here often?" Judith queried.

Kevin chuckled. "No. As a matter of fact, they get one delivery a year, always around this time. They've waived the signature, so they never have to come to the door. Frankly, I worried a bit about them last year. While I was driving along Moonfleet, I noticed that it took three or four days before the parcel was removed from the porch. But before I got around to checking on them, the next time I came by, it was gone. Maybe they'd been out of town."

"That's kind of odd, though," Judith commented. "Are the parcels always so big?"

Kevin nodded. "Pretty much. They come from Austria."

"Really." Judith tapped at her chin. "Are they from a business or a person?"

Kevin made a face. "I can't tell you that, Mrs. . . . Judith." He winked. "You'd have to find out for yourself."

"Yes," she responded in a musing tone, "I suppose I would. Thank you, Kevin."

Judith waited for the UPS van to pull away before she went back to her car to slip the mailing supplies onto the floor on the passenger's side. Hesitating only briefly, she walked back down the street. Gazing up at the house, she waited to see if anyone was watching from the windows. There was no sign of movement. *No sign of life*, she thought. That seemed more apt. In fact, all of Moonfleet Street seemed deserted. But, as Morty the Mailman and the others had mentioned, most of the homeowners worked.

As a precaution, Judith decided to move her car. She drove it around the corner and backed up onto the dirt track just enough to keep the sidewalk clear. Then she walked around the corner and boldly approached the house. If she got caught, she'd have an excuse. Judith could invent a dozen pretexts on short notice.

She reached the porch. The parcel was at least a yard long, two feet wide, and four inches in depth. It was wrapped in plain, heavy brown paper with plenty of strapping tape. Judith bent down to read the return address on the UPS shipping label.

The sender's handwriting was hard to decipher. Judith surmised that the cramped, somewhat shaky printing had been done by an older person. The name was Bachman; the place of origin was Kopfstein, Austria; the air bill was for second-day delivery, dated Monday, June 17; the signature was illegible.

Judith was about to read the rest of the information when she was startled by a noise that seemed to come from inside the house. As fast as her hips would take her, she hurried down the path and moved out of sight behind the shrubbery next to the sidewalk.

Judith searched for an opening in a big rhododendron bush. With any luck, she might be able to spot someone removing the parcel from the porch. At last, she managed to part some of the glossy leaves, allowing a silver-dollar-size view of the front door.

The parcel was still there. A car went by on Moonfleet, but apparently the driver paid no attention to Judith. A second noise, very close by, gave her another start. A moment later, she saw a squirrel dart from under some blackberry vines and dash toward the house. The small gray animal climbed up a tall cedar tree and disappeared.

After at least five more minutes, there was no activity on the porch. A car, a pickup truck, and a gas-company van drove along the street. Judith shifted from one foot to the other. She was about to give up and go back to the Subaru when she heard what sounded like a door being closed. Hastily, she again looked through the shrubbery. The parcel hadn't budged. Could the sound have been made in the house? Maybe someone was coming to the porch. Another three minutes passed. Nothing happened.

Discouraged, she gave up. Moving quickly beyond the path, she walked to the end of the block and turned the corner. Telling herself she hadn't completely wasted her time, she got into her car and eased it down the dirt track and onto the street. At least she'd learned a few things about the residents of the Spanish house. And the yearly parcel from Austria was certainly intriguing.

But heading back to Heraldsgate Hill, her mood shifted back into gloom. She should stop at Falstaff's Grocery to shop for Mike and the boys. A cut-up fryer with extra drumsticks—Mac and Joe-Joe both loved drumsticks—along with fresh corn on the cob, an orange punch drink, and chocolate-chip ice cream were on her mental list. Those were all her grandsons' favorites. She had potatoes on hand, but decided to get some special Yukon golds. And, since it was on the way, Toys-O'-Joy might have some items the boys would like. They were probably tired of the stash of playthings their grandparents kept for them at Hillside Manor.

Judith had to drive around the block four times before a parking space opened up near the toy shop. Heraldsgate Hill had grown in population the past two decades, making for crowded streets and sidewalks in the commercial area. But twenty minutes and a hundred and fifteen dollars later, Judith was satisfied with her purchases of the primate zoo, the freight train, and the battery-run fire engine complete with siren and flashing red lights. With a small smile, she put the toys in the backseat and drove on to Falstaff's, two and a half blocks away.

It cost less but took almost as long to finish her shopping there. Kippi, the freckled courtesy clerk who had often helped Judith, carried the groceries to the car.

"It's going to rain again," Kippi said with a frown. "As soon as school gets out, it always rains. Darn."

"But never hard," Judith pointed out.

"Right." She smiled at Judith, revealing new braces on her teeth. "What do you think? Do I look too totally geekish?"

"Of course not, Kippi," Judith assured the girl. "And you'll look downright gorgeous when you get the braces off."

They'd reached the Subaru. "There's only three bags," Kippi said. "Do you want them in the car or the trunk?"

Judith considered. "I've got a bunch of toys for my grandsons in the car," she said. "We'd better put them in the trunk."

"Sure." Kippi waited for Judith to turn the key.

"This lid's a problem lately," Judith remarked. "We're getting it fixed. It's at an age where little things go wrong with it every now and then."

"But not nearly as old as Mr. Flynn's MG," Kippi noted. "He really loves that car, doesn't he?"

"Oh, he does indeed," Judith said, struggling a bit to open the back of the Subaru. "The problem is, it's hard to get replacement—"

The lid of the trunk sprang open with a labored creaking noise. Judith and Kippi both screamed.

Someone was lying inside the trunk, curled up in an awkward manner. Kippi screamed again and dropped the grocery bags.

Judith clapped a hand over her mouth and stared. There was blood by the man's head, not much, but just enough to scare the wits out of Judith. The man didn't move. As she kept staring, she was overcome with a feeling of horror. She knew the person who was stuffed into her trunk. She recognized the blue jacket and the striped overalls.

Vern Benson, the milkman, looked to Judith as if he were dead.

FOUR

JUDITH KNEW SHE shouldn't tamper with evidence, but she slammed the trunk shut anyway. Kippi was shaking like a leaf, her plump body huddled over.

"I'm calling 911," Judith said, taking out her cell phone and putting a hand on the girl's back. "You go back into the store and tell the front end manager what's happened. After that, you may want to lie down in the employee break room."

Kippi looked up, tears in her blue eyes. "Do you know who that is?"

"No. Yes." Judith motioned for Kippi to go as she heard the 911 operator's voice on the line. "I'd like to report an . . . accident. There's a milkman in the trunk of my car. I'm parked at Falstaff's—"

"Excuse me," the female voice interrupted. "Did you say there was a milkman in your trunk? What's he doing?"

"Nothing," Judith gulped. "I think he's dead."

There was a pause on the line. "Is this Mrs. Flynn?" the operator asked.

"Well . . . yes," Judith admitted. "And it's not a joke. I—"

"Of course it's not a joke," the operator broke in, sounding resigned. "You never joke about finding dead people. We'll have someone there right away."

Judith felt like an idiot. Customers were coming out of the store; a couple of cars pulled into the lot. Not wanting to attract attention, she picked up the Falstaff bags and managed to fit them onto the backseat floor. So far, no one had noticed anything out of order. She was about to get into the driver's seat to wait when Phil Erickson, one of the store managers, came striding out of the side entrance.

"What the hell's going on?" he asked, keeping his voice down. "Kippi said you've got a dead body in your trunk. Is it one of our customers?"

Judith grimaced. "Of course not. It's a milkman."

Phil's face had gone red. "You mean one of our delivery guys?"

"No," Judith answered, beginning to feel indignant. "Not unless your milk deliverers also do residential routes."

"They don't," Phil said, looking relieved. "You didn't run over this guy, did you?"

"Of course not!" Judith glared at Phil.

"Okay." Phil sighed and put a hand on Judith's arm. "I'm sorry. Like any business, we worry about all our people."

And your liability insurance, Judith thought. But her reaction was harsh. She could empathize with Phil after the death in her own kitchen sink. If the Flynns had been liable, they would have been sued into oblivion.

"Really," Judith said, "this has nothing to do with your store. I wish I could move my car out of your lot, but that's impossible."

"You ought to know," Phil retorted, then attempted a commiserating smile. "That is, with your husband being an ex-cop, and telling you all sorts of war stories."

"Yes." Judith knew that Phil was avoiding mention of her own involvement in several homicides on Heraldsgate Hill. The manager wasn't about to offend one of his best customers.

The cops, in fact, were driving into the parking lot. They hadn't turned on their siren or their lights. As Heraldsgate Hill grew in prestige and affluence, discretion had become a byword except for obvious emergencies or when drivers didn't move their brand-new Beamers out of the way.

The patrol officers were unknown to Judith. A husky dark-skinned male and a copper-haired female got out of the police car and walked tentatively toward Judith and Phil. So did two women who had just come out of the store and were staring with curious eyes.

"Do you need me?" Phil whispered.

"No," Judith murmured. "Only for customer control."

"Got it," Phil said, blocking the women's passage. "Hi, there, Ms. Farris, Ms. Ryan. Nothing to see here, nothing to see here. By the way, did you sample the local strawberries in the kiosk? They just came in this morning."

"Mrs. Flynn?" the female officer inquired. "You reported a corpse. Where is it?"

Fortunately, Phil had drawn the two women back toward the store. Judith noticed that there was an eager gleam in the young officer's hazel eyes. *Her first body. But not mine.* The broad-shouldered Samoan didn't look any older than his partner. He, too, seemed to be keeping a taut rein on his excitement.

"In there," Judith said, pointing to the trunk. "I know I shouldn't have closed the lid, but I didn't want to upset people coming through the parking lot. So many parents shop here with their children."

The Samoan officer, whose name tag read JASON PAO-LUSOPO, looked curiously at Judith. "I see."

Judith wondered how much he saw. She caught a quick glimpse of the redhead's name tag: COLLEEN O'-DONAHUE. She had her hands pressed to her sides, as if bracing herself. But she didn't speak.

"It may be hard to open," Judith warned Jason. "We've had a problem with the trunk lately."

"I guess," Jason said under his breath. But he was young and strong. The trunk opened on his first attempt.

"Oh!" Colleen cried, clapping her hands to her cheeks. "It *is* a body! Ohmigod!"

Seeing the young woman sway slightly, Judith put a steadying hand on her back. "It's all right. There's not much blood, at least as far as I can see. I didn't touch anything, of course."

"Gosh." Jason had removed his regulation cap and held a hand to his short black hair. "Shouldn't we have medics here? I mean, maybe he's not dead. Maybe he just passed out."

"Yes," Judith said, "medics as well as firefighters should have been sent. I imagine a homicide unit has been dispatched, or soon will be. In fact," she went on, hearing the rumble of a heavy vehicle coming along the avenue, "here come the firefighters now. If you have crime-scene tape, you'd better cordon the area off at once. We're already drawing a bit of a crowd."

At least a half-dozen people, including two young children, had stopped to see what was going on. Taking a deep breath, Colleen walked over to them and asked that they move back. Jason apparently had gone to the squad car to get the tape.

"Sorry," one of the firefighters apologized as he jumped off the truck. "We had a heart attack victim on the other side of the hill. The medics should be here any minute. What's going on?"

Once again, Judith offered an explanation. She recognized two of the firefighters. They recognized her. After checking the body, one of them shook his head. "Man, how do you do it, Mrs. Flynn? Do you find them or do they find you?"

Judith was spared an answer by the arrival of the medics. She also recognized one of them, a woman who had shown up at Hillside Manor when the movie producer had been killed two years earlier. It was no wonder that Jason and Colleen were staring at her. Judith figured that they must feel as if they were at some kind of macabre homicide reunion.

"You've done this before?" Colleen whispered in awe.

Judith nodded.

"We haven't," Jason said. "This is our first. No wonder you're so calm."

"I'm not, really," Judith protested. "If you could see my insides, they'd look like boiling pasta. But I do know the drill. My husband's a retired police detective."

"Wow," said Jason.

"Golly," said Colleen.

"Drat," said Judith.

As she'd predicted, an unmarked city car entered the parking lot, where minor chaos was erupting as customers tried to leave and newcomers were waved off. Phil reappeared, looking distressed.

"How long will this take?" he asked one of the firefighters.

"An hour, maybe two," the young man replied. He explained to Phil that the car would be towed after the detectives and the crime-scene experts checked it out. Photographs would have to be taken. Shoulders slumping, Phil went back inside.

"We can give you a ride home when they're finished here," Jason offered.

"Thanks," Judith said, "but I really have to leave before then. Maybe they'll let me go as soon as I answer some questions. By the way, I want to get my belongings out of the car. I hope that's not a problem."

If only, Judith thought, Woodrow Price, Joe's former partner, or one of the other detectives she knew would show up. But Woody and his wife, Sondra, were vacationing in Quebec. As the doors to the unmarked police car opened, she didn't recognize either of the men who got out. One was tall and slender, forty or so, neatly dressed and moving with precision. The other was a little older, but short, pudgy, and his shoes didn't match.

They brushed past Judith and went straight to the

Subaru. "What have we got here?" the taller man inquired in a brisk manner.

"Deceased male, forties, Dairyland logo on back of jacket," one of the medics replied. "I think he's been dead for less than an hour, Glenn."

"We'll let the ME decide that," Glenn snapped. He turned to his partner. "Camera ready?"

The other detective grunted a reply before producing the camera from under his rumpled raincoat. "Where the hell are the regular photographers?" he groused. "They get vacation—I don't, not until August."

Glenn beckoned the patrol officers. "Who found the body?" he inquired.

Jason pointed to Judith. "She did, sir."

Glenn's cold gray eyes rested on Judith. "What's your name?"

"Judith Flynn," she said.

"Address?" He turned to his partner, who was clicking off pictures at a rapid rate. "Get out your notebook, Trash."

"Hold your water," the man called Trash shot back. "I'm doing all the work. As usual." Clicking off a few more pictures, he unfolded the camera strap and slung it over his left shoulder. "Okay, okay, let's do it. What did you say your name was, lady?"

Judith had taken her wallet out of her purse. "Here," she said, pointing to her driver's license. "See for yourself."

Trash gave her a wary look. "You're a bundle of fun. Watch your mouth, Mrs."—he glanced at the license—"Flynn. Hey," he said to Glenn, "there used to be a

Flynn in the squad, but I heard he croaked. You remember the guy?"

"Only the name," Glenn replied. "It was before my time. Wasn't his wife a drunk? You're no relation, I assume, Mrs. Flynn?"

"Not to his drunken wife," Judith snapped. "I'm the second Mrs. Flynn, and I assure you, Joe is alive and well."

"Oh." Glenn seemed unfazed. "Where and when did you find the victim?"

"Here." Judith pointed to the Subaru, where the trunk was now closed. More than two dozen people, including Falstaff employees, were standing beyond the yellow tape. Out on the avenue, vehicles were slowing down to rubberneck. "Kippi, the courtesy clerk, and I found the body when we went to load my groceries."

"Where's this Kippi now?" Glenn asked, scanning the bystanders.

Phil spoke up. "She's resting in the employee lounge. She's barely sixteen, and she's had a terrible shock."

Glenn, as seemed to be his wont, was unmoved. "We still have to talk to her. Trash," he said over his shoulder, "go into the store and interrogate the Kippi witness."

"Stairs," Trash muttered. "Why don't you interview her?" He didn't wait for answer. "Right, right, you're the big shot, direct from L.A. I'll bet I'm going to have to climb stairs." With his raincoat flapping behind him, Trash lumbered toward the entrance.

Judith tapped Glenn's shoulder. "May I get my belongings out of the car now?"

Glenn shook his head. "We can't permit that. Your car is a crime scene."

"But there's fresh chicken and corn and . . ." Judith took a deep breath. "They're not in the trunk, for heaven's sake! They're inside the car and they were put there after Vern got killed."

"Vern?" For the first time, Glenn's expression altered slightly. "You know the victim?"

Judith looked pugnacious. "I'm not telling you another thing until I get my food and those toys. I refuse to disappoint my grandsons!"

"Disappointment's good for children," Glenn declared. "It builds character. Your car's off-limits. You ought to know that, being married to a cop."

Judith narrowed her dark eyes. She was almost as tall as Glenn and stood on her tiptoes to look at him head-on. "Okay. But may I leave for a few minutes to replace my purchases?"

"No." Glenn's lean jaw was set.

Judith squared her wide shoulders. "May I sue you for harassment?"

"If you like. Everybody else does," he added on a sour note.

"May I use the bathroom?"

Glenn considered. "Yes. But be back here in five minutes."

Judith returned in fifty-five minutes, huffing and puffing. She had gone into Falstaff's via the parking lot, acquired a shopping cart, and exited through the street entrance. Feeling like a bag lady, she walked the block and a half to Toys-O'-Joy. Fending off queries from the salespeople, she had bought duplicate presents for the grandchildren, returned to Falstaff's, and replicated the grocery purchases.

Additional patrol officers had been brought in for crowd control. After being thoroughly checked, customers were being allowed to leave, but no one was permitted to enter. Phil was at the parking-lot entrance, wringing his hands and making profuse apologies. Glenn and Trash were standing by the Subaru with a half-dozen men and women. Judith figured they were the crime-scene unit and perhaps backup from the homicide division. She stood off to one side of the entrance with her cart and fervently hoped Glenn wouldn't notice her. The store's overhang sheltered her from the drizzle, but she was growing more anxious by the minute.

Her hopes were in vain. Glenn saw her out of the corner of his eye and immediately marched in Judith's direction.

"Where have you been, Mrs. Flynn?" he demanded in a chilly tone.

"Here," Judith replied.

Glenn gestured at the cartful of purchases. "That's not true. Trash and I looked everywhere for you when you didn't show up after the first ten minutes."

"Men can never find anything," Judith said. "And why do you call your partner 'Trash'?"

"Because that's his name," Glenn replied. "Or rather, the short version. Jonathan Parker Trashman."

"What's yours, besides Glenn?" Judith demanded.

"Glenn Morris," the detective answered, exhibiting a hint of dignity.

Neither of the detectives' names rang any bells with

Judith. There had been so many changes and new hires at headquarters since Joe's retirement.

"Don't badger me," she said, shaking a finger. "I've had a terrible shock."

"You don't act like it, Mrs. Flynn," Glenn asserted.

"I tend to keep things bottled up," Judith retorted. *At least my reaction to things that happen to me far too often.* "When can I go home? Vern wasn't killed here, so I don't see any point in hanging out in Falstaff's parking lot. Besides, it's bad for business."

Glenn Morris didn't respond. Instead, he walked over to the patrol officers and exchanged words with them. Mostly *his* words, Judith noticed. Jason and Colleen seemed cowed by the detective's presence. But all three of them were distracted by the arrival of a beige Toyota Camry, horn honking and driver yelling. Judith didn't have to look twice to know it was Renie.

"Move it, scumbags!" Renie screamed. "I have to get Bill's snack!"

"Coz!" Judith cried, trying to hurry to the Camry before Renie drove right through the yellow tape. "Stop! You'll never guess what's happened!"

Renie stopped honking. She got out of the car and gaped at Judith. "You wrecked your car again?"

Renie was referring to the demise of Judith's previous vehicle, a Nissan with bad brakes. No brakes, actually, which had caused the car to crash into the concrete wall in Falstaff's parking lot.

"No," Judith replied. "Much worse. You'll never guess what I found."

"No!" Renie looked stunned. "Not again!"

Judith nodded. "I'm afraid so. It's a milkman. He's in my trunk."

"He's dead?" Renie asked in a bleak voice.

"I'm afraid so. It looks as if . . . Renie! Your car's still moving!"

Sure enough, the Camry was slowly but surely going forward through the tape and heading straight for the outdoor floral display.

"Yikes!" Renie cried, and jumped back into the car. "I forgot to set the emergency brake!" She stopped the Camry just short of dahlias and delphiniums. "Are you going home?" she asked when disaster had been averted.

"When they let me. Will you give me a lift? I'd rather not ride with the police," Judith said, then pointed to her cart. "I bought some things. Twice."

"Sure. I'll wait. Let's load your stuff now."

This time, Renie remembered to set the brake, though some of the yellow tape now decorated the Camry's hood. "Who's the stiff?" she whispered, glancing at Glenn. "I mean, the one who's still alive?"

"Glenn Morris," Judith murmured. "His partner's a guy named Trash. Never mind why. They thought Joe was still married to Herself and had died."

"Joe? Or Herself?" asked Renie.

"Joe. Or maybe both of them," Judith said, still keeping her voice down as they passed Glenn. "I didn't tell them that Herself was at her condo in Florida."

Vivian Flynn had had the gall to move into a house in the cul-de-sac several years earlier. But she also owned a condo on the Gulf, and her efforts to sell it had come to naught. Thus, to Judith's great relief, she was gone for much of the year. As Vivian put it, she preferred drinking on the beach instead of on the hill because she wouldn't roll when she fell in the sand.

Renie gathered up the toys; Judith took care of the groceries. Once again, Glenn was heading their way. This time, however, he advanced on Renie.

"Do you own this beige Camry?" he asked in a voice that barely concealed his fury.

"You bet. We paid cash for it. And no, it's not for sale. Excuse me, I'm busy." Renie elbowed Glenn out of the way and headed for the Camry's trunk.

"Hold it!" Glenn shouted. "Get that car out of here right now before I arrest you for impeding a homicide investigation!"

Renie turned to gaze at the detective. "That's what I'm doing. Leaving, I mean. I'll have to get Bill's snack later. But," she continued, folding her arms and looking mulish, "I'm not going to budge an inch unless my cousin comes with me."

Glenn glanced from Renie to Judith. "You're cousins?"

Renie nodded. "We have been, since we were born. Do we have a deal or not?"

Glenn shot Renie a menacing look. "You're impertinent," he snapped.

"I'm also impatient. Hurry up, time's a-wasting."

Glenn shifted his gaze to the Subaru. It appeared as if the law officers had concluded their examination.

"Very well," Glenn conceded in an irked tone. "Move along. Now." He turned to Judith. "We'll meet you at your house."

"Fine." Judith got into the car while Renie put the toys in the trunk and removed the yellow tape.

"Okay, tell me all," she said, reversing somewhat recklessly out into the street.

During the short drive to Hillside Manor, Judith was able to sum up what had happened from the time of her arrival on Moonfleet to the discovery of Vern Benson's body in the trunk of her car.

"Wow!" Renie exclaimed, stopping in the Flynn driveway. "Now I feel terrible. The Moonfleet house was my idea. You didn't want to get involved, but I insisted. It's my fault you're in another mess."

"No, it's not," Judith said with a weary sigh. "Joe's right. I'm a murder magnet. You know how it is— some people are lucky at cards, some keep making bad choices when it comes to mates, some have endless problems with everyday dealings, even though it's usually not their fault. A store clerk overcharges them, their mail goes awry, the bank makes a mistake and withdraws money from their account instead of the person who asked for it—it's like Job. One piece of trouble after another. I just happen to be the kind who finds dead bodies. Why couldn't it be stashes of diamonds and pearls?"

Renie opened the car door. "Some of it *is* your own doing. You're extremely curious, especially about people. That's bound to lead you into trouble."

Judith collected her groceries. "I suppose. Not to mention all the varieties of guests who come to the B&B. There's bound to be a clinker now and then."

"That's one way of putting it," Renie said from behind the pile of toys. "Tell me where I'm going. I can't see."

Judith led Renie down the driveway and to the back

porch. "Joe's gone," she said, unlocking the door. "He's going to have a fit when he finds out what's happened."

Renie stumbled slightly as she entered the house. "Don't tell him."

"That's impossible!" Judith cried, setting the grocery bags down on the kitchen floor. "It'll be in the newspapers and on TV."

Renie carefully placed the three toy boxes under the counter next to the computer. "They don't have to identify you."

"But they will, won't they?" Judith said, unloading the groceries.

Renie turned as the doorbell rang. "That must be the Grim Reaper and his sidekick, Trash. Let me handle this."

"Coz . . ." But Renie was already hurrying to the front door.

"Come in," Judith heard Renie say. "Take a seat. I'm the one you should be talking to. This is all my fault."

Despite her uneasiness at letting Renie take over, Judith stayed in the kitchen, finishing her tasks with the groceries.

"Here's how this all started," Renie was saying. She launched into her fifty-year obsession with the house on Moonfleet. "I coerced my cousin into going over there to have a look. She didn't want any part of it, but I insisted. Naturally, she became interested—who wouldn't? This morning, she had to go to Langford, where our Uncle Al lives. She wanted me to go with her, but I had to do a beaver. So on her way—"

"Excuse me," Glenn broke in. "*What* did you have to do with a beaver?"

"Draw him," Renie retorted. "Never mind. Anyway, she passed by the house just as the milkman was making his delivery. They got to chatting. My cousin is a very social being. Before she could leave, a UPS man arrived. She needed some supplies, which he gave her. After that, she left. End of story until Falstaff's parking lot."

Judith was slowly and silently approaching the living room. She'd reached the dining room archway that led to the entrance hall. Judging from the direction in which their voices were coming, Renie and the detectives must be sitting on the matching sofas.

"It seems as if you're leaving out some important facts," Glenn said stiffly. "For one thing, you weren't at the Moonfleet house this morning. Mrs. Flynn was. We still have to talk to her."

"That's not a good idea," Renie said. "She's not well. She suffers from anthurium sprue."

Renie didn't often tell lies, but when she did, it was usually a whopper. "Very sad," she murmured.

"I've never heard of it," Glenn replied, though given his controlled manner, Judith couldn't tell if he believed Renie or not.

"It's quite rare," Renie replied. "Judith contracted the disease when she was working as a missionary in Honduras. An attack—they're so severe—is usually caused by emotional distress. Anthurium sprue victims can be easily set off, especially when they're the center of attention. They tend to live very shy, withdrawn lives."

"Hey," Trash broke in, "I thought you told us your cousin was the social kind."

Glenn glared at his partner. "I'm asking the questions here. You're supposed to be taking notes."

Trash glanced down at the notebook in his lap. "I was, until I tried to spell 'anthurium.' You're so smart, you spell it for me, genius."

"Use shorthand," Glenn replied loftily. "Nobody can ever read your notes anyway. On our last case, they were covered in pizza sauce."

"I can spell it," Renie said, looking smug. "But I won't."

"Let's get back to Mrs. Flynn's problem," Glenn said. "Before I could speak, Trash asked how your cousin could possibly be outgoing when her condition is so delicate."

"That's part of the problem," Renie answered. "She has these relapses, when she thinks she's her former self. That," she added with a heavy sigh, "is when the trouble begins."

"Very strange," Glenn remarked. "Very."

"So," Renie continued, "I'd appreciate it if you'd be extremely gentle with her. And of course there must be absolutely no mention of her name in the media. That could easily finish her off." Renie choked on the last few words. "Excuse me, I must get a handkerchief out of my purse. I'm tearing up at the mere thought of what could happen to my poor cousin."

Some sniffing ensued, then a loud blowing of Renie's nose. "In fact," she finally went on, "it wouldn't be wise to tell Mr. Flynn what's happened. He worries about Judith so much. It's not good for him, especially in his present state of deteriorating health."

"I heard he was already dead," Glenn said.

"Not quite," Renie replied. "But it's just a matter of time." She blew her nose again.

A noise from the stairs made Judith jump. She turned quickly, seeing Phyliss Rackley on the landing. The cleaning woman had arrived late, having had one of her many medical appointments in the morning. Judith motioned for silence. Phyliss, who was carrying garbage from the guests' wastebaskets, looked puzzled.

Judith moved to the bottom of the stairs. "Police," she whispered. "They're talking to Renie."

"Ha!" Phyliss nodded approval, her gray sausage curls bobbing up and down. "About time, if you ask me!" she said in a low voice. "Have they arrested her?"

Judith shook her head. "Go on," she urged. "Keep working. But stay out of the living room."

With a snort, Phyliss went on her way. Judith picked up the conversation in Renie's midsentence:

". . . to be very patient with her. I'll bring her in here now."

Renie rounded the corner into the entrance hall and gave a little start when she saw Judith. "Oh, dear coz," she exclaimed, winking like mad, "did you hear me explain about your pitiful state?"

Judith shot Renie a disparaging look. "Yes. I'm feeling very feeble."

"Good," Renie said. "I mean, that's awful. You do get confused when you're having a spell. Come along, talk to the nice policemen."

Judith obeyed, but what she really wanted to do was kick Renie in the rear end. Fibs were fine, especially when no harm would come of them. Outright deception was wrong when Judith could foresee the tangled web into which Renie had plunged them both. On the other hand . . .

Docilely, Judith sat down on the sofa next to her cousin. "I feel better now," she said softly.

"You seemed fine in the parking lot," Glenn noted. "In fact, you acted quite unmoved."

"That's her defensive mechanism," Renie asserted. "She has to respond that way, to ward off the . . . attack and eventual collapse."

"I see." Again, Glenn's stiff manner made his words impossible to interpret. "So tell us about meeting this milkman."

"We talked," Judith said. "I asked if he knew anything about the people who lived in the Spanish-style house. He didn't, except for their weekly milk order. He left. I was about to drive off, too, when I saw the UPS van." Judith's voice had become more normal as she related her story. "I needed supplies." *Only a wee white lie, nothing to match Renie's monstrous fabrication.* "I decided to ask him about the people who lived in the house. He didn't know anything, either. He made his delivery and left. Then I walked around a bit before I got in my car and came back to Heraldsgate Hill." *Stretching the truth, maybe, that was all.*

"Was your car in view the whole time?" Trash inquired, bumping his knees against the new oak coffee table and ignoring his partner's baleful glance.

"Uh . . . no," Judith admitted. "I'd moved my car. Moonfleet seemed so busy. I pulled into the dirt alley in back of the house. I probably didn't see the car for maybe ten minutes or so."

Glenn cocked his head to one side. "Ten minutes? You were wandering around the property for ten minutes?"

"No," Judith responded. "I was just . . . mostly strolling along the sidewalk." *No need to mention going up to the door unless specifically asked.*

"Did you see anyone in or around the house?" Glenn queried as he smoothed his patterned silk tie.

"No," Judith repeated. "But I did hear a couple of noises—like a door being slammed. Oh!" She clapped her hands to her cheeks as she realized that what she'd heard wasn't a door in the house, but probably her trunk.

"What now?" Trash asked, hiking up his pants.

"The sound," Judith said with a little shudder. "It must have been when the body was put in my car. Whoever did it was closing the trunk."

Trash looked disbelieving. "You left your trunk open, lady? That's a bad habit." Again, he paid no attention to Glenn's look of disapproval.

"It's been acting up the last couple of days," Judith explained. She tried not to wince as she saw Phyliss lurking outside the French doors at the other end of the living room. "I probably didn't get it all the way shut when I left Uncle Al's."

"So," Trash said, leaning back on the sofa and again bumping the coffee table as he crossed one leg over the other, "whoever conked the milkman just happened to know you had a faulty trunk and decided to stash the body there. That's pretty far-fetched."

"Hey," Renie said loudly, "whatever happened to Good Cop–Bad Cop? Aren't you both being jerks? Don't make my cousin froth!"

Trash looked aghast. "Froth?"

"Froth," Renie said again. "Foam at the mouth. Take it easy, you two."

A cell phone rang. Judith knew it wasn't hers, which was in the kitchen inside her purse. But Renie and the detectives all reacted. The call was for Glenn. He listened for a few moments before saying, "Yes. We'll be there shortly."

Glenn disconnected and stood up. "The Langford Precinct has dispatched two patrol officers. They're at the Moonfleet house now. We're going to check the place out. Come on, Trash, let's move."

"Aw . . ." Trash, who looked as if he'd finally made himself comfortable, clumsily got to his feet. "Actually, I was kind of hoping to see her froth."

Glenn ignored the comment, addressing Judith, who, along with Renie, was accompanying the detectives to the door. "I trust you aren't planning on leaving the city," he said.

"No, I'm not," Judith replied.

"She can't," Renie put in. "She's far too frail."

"Good." Glenn waited for Trash to open the door for him. "Because as of now, we consider you a suspect in the murder of Vern Benson."

FIVE

GREAT!" JUDITH CRIED, slamming the door behind the departing detectives. "That's all I need! What the hell will Joe say about *this*?"

"Calm down, coz," Renie urged. "I repeat, why does he have to find out?"

"How can he not?" Judith fumed, going in the direction of the kitchen.

"Think about it," Renie said. "Being a suspect is the best thing that could happen to you. Even if my ruse didn't work, these days the cops rarely release names of suspects to the media unless they're holding someone in custody. If you don't tell Joe, who will?"

Judith considered. "That may be true about releasing names, but Joe still has ties to the department. Woody, for instance. He and Sandra are due back from Canada in a few days."

"I'll call him," Renie said. "Woody and I've always bonded because we both love opera. I'll tell him to keep mum."

"Woody's not the only one Joe knows at headquarters," Judith pointed out.

"But he doesn't keep in contact with most of the others except for the occasional reunion or holiday party," Renie replied. "Besides, the force has grown so in recent years, it sounds to me as if the cops don't know each other as well as they used to. Didn't Glenn say he thought Joe was dead?"

"Yes, he did," Judith admitted. "They thought Joe was still married to Herself. Maybe there's something in what you say. But it's risky."

"There's one other thing," Renie said with a sly smile.

"What's that?"

"You solve the case."

Judith leaned against the sink. "Oh, swell!"

"Well? Aren't you tempted?"

Judith took a deep breath. "Of course. But with Mike and Kristin splitting up and the B&B at its busiest, I don't know when or how I could do any sleuthing."

"But you will," Renie said.

Judith's shoulders slumped. "I don't know . . . but maybe I'll have to, if only to get myself off the hook."

"That's right." Renie slung her huge black purse over her shoulder. "Got to run. I still have to buy Bill's snack, remember?"

"Why doesn't Bill buy it himself?" Judith inquired. "I thought part of his snack ritual was the pleasure he gets from choosing which delicacy he's going to eat that night."

"It is. He does. But he's had a cold, and he coughed so hard this morning that he pulled a muscle in his side. I'm babying him." Renie headed down the narrow hallway to the back door. "I'll be in touch. I should be done with Bucky by tomorrow morning."

Renie went out as Phyliss came in. There was a brief hostile exchange, but Judith didn't hear the specifics. She was too absorbed in the task that lay before her.

"Police, huh?" Phyliss said as she entered the kitchen. "I just happened to—"

"How much did you hear, Phyliss?" Judith demanded.

"Well . . . not as much as I'd have liked," the cleaning woman admitted. "Those Dooley kids were playing out in their yard behind your place and they were making an awful racket. How many do they have now? About twenty?"

"Or more," Judith replied. "There are grandchildren and even a great-grandchild, I think."

"You wrecked your car, huh?" Phyliss remarked.

"What? Oh. Yes, in a way." Judith patted the other woman's thin shoulder. If the only thing Phyliss had heard pertained to the Subaru's trunk, Judith would leave it that way. "We won't tell Joe, will we?"

"How're you going to explain why it's not here?" Phyliss asked. "I saw that fiendish cousin bring you home. What did she do with Beelzebub?"

"She bested him, four out of seven," Judith murmured.

Phyliss cupped her ear. "What?"

"Never mind. He's gone." Judith was absorbed in thought. There was too much else bothering her: Vern Benson's murder, the Moonfleet house, being a suspect, dealing with Mike's dilemma, keeping secrets from Joe. She didn't know where to start. It seemed as if there were bells and buzzers going off in her head.

"Are you going to answer the phone or shall I?" Phyliss asked.

"Oh! Sorry!" With an apologetic look, Judith snatched up the receiver. Joe was on the other end of the line.

"I've got a problem," he said.

You've got a problem? Judith thought. "What is it?"

"I have to go to Omaha," he said. "The insurance company's home office wants me to come back there on this fraud situation. I'll have to leave tonight. I tried to get out of it, but I can't, not at this stage of the investigation. I'm really sorry, leaving you in such a mess."

You don't know the half of it. "Don't worry, I'll be fine. How long will you be gone?"

"Hopefully, we can wrap the whole thing up by the weekend," Joe said. "The insurance carrier wants to avert a trial, so they're trying to get plenty of evidence to either discourage the lawsuit or settle out of court. I'm thinking I could be home late Saturday or early Sunday, depending on the airline schedules. I'll swing by the house and stuff a few things in a suitcase. I have to be at the airport by seven."

Judith's reaction was mixed. She was relieved that Joe would be gone for a few days, but she'd still have to explain why the Subaru wasn't in the driveway. And of course she would miss him.

"Will you have time to eat dinner with Mike and the boys?" Judith asked.

"Maybe," Joe said. "It depends on traffic. You know what it's like getting across the floating bridge this time of day."

Judith, in fact, had lost track of time. She looked up

at the old schoolhouse clock, which informed her it was going on four. The commute between the city and the Eastside seemed to start earlier and earlier, even in midweek.

"I'll see you soon," she said, and rang off.

Staring through the kitchen window at the Rankerses' hedge, Judith put her thoughts in order. Logic was her byword. First things first. She had guests due soon, another full house. Phyliss would have to make up for lost time if she intended to finish cleaning before the first arrivals. Meanwhile, Judith would prepare the guests' appetizers and make a start on dinner. Murder must be put aside until she'd taken care of her family and her business. She also had to check on Gertrude, but that could wait. Wednesday was bridge club, and the old girl probably hadn't gotten back yet. Judith's mother had put a horn on her motorized wheelchair, and usually honked when she got dropped off. Sometimes she honked just for the hell of it.

Half an hour later, as Judith was husking corn, Phyliss announced she was finished. Putting on her long black raincoat and a plastic rain bonnet, she headed out into the June drizzle.

"I'll see you tomorrow if I don't get pneumonia," she called from the back door.

Ten minutes later, Gertrude honked. Judith put the corn on the counter and went outside.

"Did you win?" she asked, descending the steps to the backyard.

" 'Course I did," Gertrude replied, going pell-mell for the toolshed. "I got all the quarters, four dollars and twenty-five cents, despite having Deb as a partner. She goes to bridge club to visit, not to play cards. Talk, talk, talk. She drives me crazy."

"Mother," Judith said, opening the door, "there's something I have to tell you."

Gertrude twisted around in the wheelchair to look at her daughter. "You aren't expecting, are you?"

"No, Mother," Judith replied. "I'm a few years beyond that."

"You never know these days," Gertrude said, moving up to the card table. "I read about a goofy woman in *The Inquisitor* who had twins at your age. Their father was an alien. Like Lunkhead."

"I wish you'd stop calling Joe 'Lunkhead,' " Judith said.

"Fair enough," said Gertrude, allowing Judith to help her out of her coat. "I always called that first loser of yours that. How about 'Knucklehead' for this one?"

"Don't. Please." Judith sat down on the arm of the sofa. "I have some sad news."

"Knucklehead croaked?" Gertrude asked hopefully.

"No, Mother," Judith said through clenched teeth. "Mike and Kristin have separated."

Gertrude's wrinkled old face sagged. "Holy Mother!" she breathed. "That can't be! You don't mean a *divorce*?" The word came out sounding like a dread disease.

"Not a divorce," Judith said optimistically. "They need to be apart for a while, to straighten things out."

"I could straighten 'em out with a hammer," Gertrude asserted, but her chin trembled and her voice shook. "What's wrong with them?"

Judith reached out to take her mother's frail hand. "Frankly, to people like you and me, it sounds silly. Kristin wants more space."

"More space?" Gertrude scowled. "She's living up in the mountains, isn't she? How much more space could she want? Montana?"

"It's an expression," Judith explained. "I think she means she wants more opportunities for herself as a person. A career, maybe."

"She's got a career," Gertrude retorted. "A husband and two kids. That was enough of a career for most women in my day."

"You worked, at least part-time," Judith pointed out.

"It wasn't because I wanted a stupid career," Gertrude shot back. "We needed the money. That's why Deb worked, too. And your Aunt Ellen and your Auntie Vance and—"

"Yes," Judith interrupted, "I realize that most of the women in our family worked. But there are also two sides to any marital story."

"As Deb never tires of reminding me," Gertrude said. "She worked in a law office. She saw one divorce after another. I guess she ought to know," the old lady added grudgingly.

"That's true," Judith allowed. "Mike may be being unreasonable, too. Anyway, it's possible they can work things out. The problem is, the younger generation is self-absorbed and isn't very good at compromise. Or so it seems to me."

"You're right about that, kiddo," Gertrude said, still clutching at Judith's hand. "I'm too old for all this." She paused, shaking her head and looking off into the far corner. "You got married, you stayed married," she declared, her voice a bit stronger. "The only time I threatened to divorce your father was when he got that brand-new Chevy and drove like Barney Oldfield. A real speed demon he was in that car. It scared me. And then less than a year after he bought the car, he died of heart trouble. Maybe it'd been better if he'd run us both off a bridge. Then I wouldn't have had to be alone all these years."

Judith noticed tears in her mother's eyes. "But then I wouldn't have had you around to bully me," she said to Gertrude. "I wouldn't have missed it for the world." Judith bent down and kissed the top of her mother's white head.

Gertrude didn't say anything for a long time. The two women sat in silence, knowing their thoughts were the same, and finding quiet comfort in it.

Where's your car?" Joe asked as he breezed through the back door. "I thought you weren't home."

"The car?" Judith paused to wipe corn tassels from her hands. "It's gone," she said, kissing Joe.

"Gone where?"

"To . . . the shop. The trunk was driving me nuts. I had trouble loading the groceries." That was true enough. "I couldn't wait for the appointment you made with Nabobs. They'll work it in." Not true. But it sounded plausible.

"Oh." Joe started for the back stairs. "I'm going to pack. It's a good thing I called the shuttle to pick me up. You can drive the MG while I'm gone. Just treat it kindly." He disappeared around the hall corner.

The B&B guests seemed normal. So did Mac and Joe-Joe. But Judith, Joe, Mike, and Gertrude knew that their fried chicken dinner was anything but typical. The chair where Kristin usually sat had been pulled back from the oak dining-room table, but her absence hovered over the room like a phantom. The mood was so gloomy that even Gertrude kept her mouth shut.

Mike stayed on after dinner for a few games of cribbage with his grandmother. Joe skipped dessert. The airport shuttle arrived exactly at six-thirty. Judith's farewell kiss was fervent.

"Hey," he said, looking into her black eyes, "do you think I'm going to be taken hostage by terrorists?"

"You never know these days," Judith said somberly.

He kissed her high forehead. "I'll only be gone for a couple of days. What could go wrong in that short a time?"

Judith merely smiled. Weakly.

Upon leaving around eight o'clock, Mac and Joe-Joe were heartbroken when their great-grandmother informed them that their new toys couldn't go with them to Uncle Al's. The items Judith had purchased must stay with their other stash of playthings at Hillside Manor.

"Oh, go ahead," Judith said to Mike. She couldn't, of course, mention that the original purchases were at police headquarters. "We can always get them something else."

"Spoiled," Gertrude muttered, but for once, she didn't sound as if she meant it.

Two of the guests forgot their keys that evening and

had to be let in around midnight. Judith always handed out two keys—one for the room and one for the house. She locked up at ten. Late arrivals could let themselves in. Unless they left the keys in their room.

Another woman, one of four teachers on holiday, came down with a cold. Judith offered her aspirin, nasal spray, and cough drops. As always, when dispensing over-the-counter medications, she cautioned guests to read the labels carefully.

A Methodist minister lost his glasses and couldn't read his Bible before going to bed. He was sure he'd had them after he arrived at Hillside Manor. After a twenty-minute search, Judith found them between the window-seat cushions in the living room. The minister promised to pray for her. Judith said she could use all the prayers she could get.

She expected another restless night, especially since Joe wasn't lying beside her. But emotional and physical exhaustion had set in. Judith slept like a rock.

At nine o'clock Thursday morning when she was serving breakfast to her guests, Glenn Morris called. "Trash and I are coming by to ask you some more questions," he announced. "We'll be there in half an hour."

"Could you wait until eleven?" Judith asked. "I'd rather you come after my guests leave."

"Sorry," Glenn replied, sounding not the least apologetic. "We have a schedule to keep." He hung up.

All but the four teachers were checking out that morning. Hopefully, they'd leave early. When Phyliss arrived shortly after Glenn's call, Judith had to explain that the police were paying another visit.

"What for?" Phyliss demanded.

"It's a long story, Phyliss," Judith said. "I don't want to tire you with it. You look peaked." It wasn't true, but mentioning the cleaning woman's health always diverted her.

"I'm sure I do," Phyliss declared with a heavy sigh. "It's my chest. It feels as if an elephant sat on it." For emphasis, she pressed her hands to her flat bosom and gasped several times.

"Then take it easy," Judith cautioned. "I'll let you get started right away."

The Methodist minister and his wife left immediately after breakfast. A few minutes later, the couple who had forgotten their keys also departed. But the honeymooners from Oregon lingered upstairs and the grad students from UCLA decided to have coffee in the living room. As for the teachers, they were biding their time, waiting to see if their colleague with the cold felt like sightseeing.

At a quarter to ten, Glenn and Trash showed up at the front door. Judith ushered them into the parlor, making sure that both doors were shut tight.

Trash eyed the empty fireplace. "Damned near cold enough for a fire. Hell, October's warmer around here than June." With a grunt, he sat down on the settee and looked at his partner. "I suppose you're going to tell me how it's always seventy degrees and sunny in L.A."

Glenn ignored the other detective and assumed his place on the hearth, one elbow casually resting on the mantelpiece. "I have some questions about your car," he said to Judith, who had sat down in one of the two matching armchairs. "When did you last look in your trunk before arriving at the grocery store?"

Judith answered promptly. "Tuesday morning. I shopped for groceries to fill up the larder."

"Did you take the car out again that day?" Glenn inquired.

"Let me think—no, I didn't."

Glenn glanced at Trash. "Are you taking this down?"

"Down where?" Trash's expression was ingenuous—until he scowled at Glenn. "Yeah, sure, smart guy. Why do you think I have this notebook and pen? Or am I signing autographs?"

Glenn scowled right back before resuming his queries. "Why did you go to the Bland house yesterday?" he asked Judith.

"My cousin told you why," she retorted. "Mrs. Jones has been obsessed with the house for years. She used to live in the neighborhood. I went along with her Tuesday to humor her. But I'll admit, the place made me curious, too."

"Hey," Trash interrupted, "you got any coffee around here?"

"Yes," Judith said. But she'd be darned if she'd offer it to the detectives.

"How well do you know Mr. and Mrs. Bland?" Glenn inquired.

"I don't know them at all," Judith replied. "I didn't even know their names until day before yesterday when my cousin and I asked one of the neighbors who lived across the street."

"But you went back by yourself yesterday," Glenn remarked.

"Yes. I told you, I had to go to Langford to my uncle's. While I was in the area, I decided to have another look at the house. My cousin and I've already told you this."

Glenn gazed up at the ceiling. "Let's see. Mrs. Jones claims she's been fascinated by the Bland house since her early teens. Fifty years go by, but despite her alleged all-absorbing interest, she does nothing. Suddenly she convinces you to join her in surveying the premises. A day later, you go back—and end up with a dead man in your trunk. Tell me," he continued, his tone now deceptively benign, "does this make sense?"

"Of course not," Judith snapped. "I mean, it wouldn't make sense to most people. But it's simple curiosity. My cousin and I are both interested in people. And you have to admit, just looking at the house and its condition, it's certainly unusual."

"Unusual, perhaps," Glenn conceded. "But hardly a subject of repeated visits and querying of deliverymen. We understand you and Mrs. Jones also accosted the postman on Tuesday. He claims you're both very peculiar, particularly Mrs. Jones."

"Renie and Morty have a history," Judith said, exasperated. "They go way back. How did you happen to run into him so late in the day? You must not have gotten to Moonfleet Street until four o'clock."

"Mr. Mortimer told us he was running a little behind," Glenn replied.

"I like the guy," Trash put in. "He seems like good people."

You would, Judith thought.

"Let's go over yesterday's visit one more time," Glenn said.

"What's wrong?" Judith retorted. "Did Detective Trashman spill beer on his notes?"

"Hey!" Trash cried, looking offended. "It wasn't beer, it was a pork chop!"

Judith sighed. "Okay, but I'm going to tell you exactly what I told you yesterday." And she did, though again omitting a couple of details.

"I don't think you're telling us everything," Glenn said when she'd finished. "The crime scene people found damp earth in your tires, the same kind of dirt that's in the alley at the Blands' house."

"I told you—I backed up into the alley," Judith admitted. "With all those delivery people, I didn't want to take up a parking place on the street."

"Why did you get out of the car?" Glenn asked.

"I'm a gardener," Judith asserted. That much was true. "There's some very interesting vegetation on the property, including a camellia bush that's gone wild." Also true. "I was wondering what it looked like when it bloomed earlier in the year." Still true. Judith had noticed the tall, gangly bush, along with a couple of trees she couldn't identify.

Glenn's face was impassive. "What size shoe do you wear?"

"A ten." Judith knew what was coming next. "I was wearing these shoes yesterday." She pointed to her black loafers. "Do you want them?"

"Yes," Glenn said. "We'd like to make a cast."

Judith started to refuse, then reconsidered. The cast would prove that she'd gone to the front door. But she hadn't walked behind her car while it was parked in the alley.

"Go ahead," she said, slipping the shoes off and handing them over. "But I want these back as soon as possible. I have an artificial hip, and there are only certain kinds I can wear because I can't bend down too far."

"Pity," Glenn commented in an indifferent tone. He turned to Trash. "Bag them."

"Do you want me to shine 'em, too?" Trash grumbled.

"See here," Judith said, "the least you can do is tell me about the Blands. Are they elderly? Are they ill? Why have they let that house go to pot in the last half century? They had to be young when they moved in."

A gleam of amusement shined in Glenn's gray eyes. "My, my, Mrs. Flynn, you seem to be holding up remarkably well for a woman with a dread disease. Are you sure you don't want to rest now?"

"I'm having one of my good days," Judith asserted. "Come on, please tell me what they're like. And," she added a bit slyly, "who lives with them."

"They're quite old," Glenn replied.

"Older than dirt," Trash muttered, stuffing Judith's shoes into an evidence bag.

"But," Glenn went on, "they seem in relatively good health."

"For a couple of drunks," Trash put in.

Glenn gave his partner a warning look. "I believe Mrs. Bland may have a drinking problem. Or perhaps it's her inner ear. She doesn't have very good balance."

"And what about the third party?" Judith pressed.

"That would be Mrs. Bland's sister," Glenn replied. "She's elderly, too, though in rather good shape. Sprightly, you might say."

"Does she have a name?" Judith asked.

"Yes." Glenn gave Judith a nasty smile. "We'll be going now, Mrs. Flynn. Thank you for your time." He started for the parlor door that led into the entry hall. "And remember, stay within reach. Easy reach, that is."

"I have to," Judith said. "You've got my shoes."

SIX

As soon as Glenn and Trash had left, Judith called Renie. "How's Bucky?"

"He went away," Renie replied. "He said he didn't give a dam. Ha-ha."

"So you've finished the Wirehoser project?" Judith inquired.

"For now. They may require some changes. Most executives do, if only because they want to think they've made a contribution, other than cheating at golf or cooking the books."

"Can you come with me to Moonfleet Street? I want to meet the Blands."

"Jeez." Renie paused for almost a full minute. Stentorian moans and groans could be heard in the background. Bill uttered a few feeble monosyllables. "Which pills?" Renie inquired, away from the phone. "The mauve, the baby blue, the orange, or the yellow one shaped like a PEZ?"

Bill's voice grew stronger. "That *was* a PEZ you gave me," he shot back.

"Did it help?" Renie asked.

Some obscenities emanated from Renie's husband; Judith filtered them out to hear that Bill wanted the orange pill. Two, in fact.

"I'm not sure I can get away right now," Renie finally said to Judith. "Bill is near death. Can you hear him?"

"I could probably hear him without the phone," Judith remarked. "Dare I ask how he's feeling?"

"No," said Renie. "What's worse, he didn't like the snack I bought for him. He fed it to Oscar."

Oscar was the Joneses' stuffed ape, who had sat in splendor on the arm of their sofa for going on thirty years. Bill and Oscar shared a special bond, including Victoria's Secret catalogs and X-rated movies on premium cable. Renie humored both husband and ape. Her own in-house obsession was Clarence, a dwarf lop bunny that roamed free in the basement. The bunny had a varied wardrobe, including an angel costume with wings, a tutu, a smoking jacket, and bathing trunks. The only problem was that Clarence preferred eating his clothes instead of wearing them.

"Can you drive us?" Judith inquired.

"No," Renie replied as Bill bellowed from the living room. "I'm getting the damned pills," she informed her husband. "I'm on my way upstairs. Can't you see me? The moving feet on the steps are attached to the rest of my body." She spoke again into the phone. "Bill has a doctor's appointment at one. Why can't you drive Joe's MG and pick me up?"

"It scares me to drive that car," Judith admitted. "He's had it a lot longer than he's had me. He's so fussy that I don't think I've driven it more than twice since we got married. Besides, it's got a stick shift."

"Don't be silly," Renie said. "Driving a stick is like riding a bicycle. You never forget how to do it. We're only going a couple of miles to Langford. But what makes you think you'll be able to meet Dick and Jane Bland?"

Judith told Renie about the visit from Glenn Morris and Jonathan Trashman. "It's not fair," Judith griped. "They didn't even know about the Blands until yesterday, and now they can see them anytime they want. I'd be surprised if either of those two jerks has any idea of the house's history."

"Or its atmosphere," Renie noted. "Okay, I'm more or less conscious since it's well after ten. You know the old song—'Waking Up Is Hard to Do.' What time do we go?"

"An hour? I still have guests. By the way, did you see the brief article in the paper this morning?"

"Yes," Renie replied. "It didn't say much, just that a deliveryman from the Langford neighborhood had been found dead in the trunk of a car on Heraldsgate Hill. No names, including yours."

"They didn't even say he was murdered," Judith said. "I suppose they hadn't finished the autopsy before the newspaper deadline. All they mentioned was that foul play hadn't been ruled out."

"Now that we have two morning papers instead of only one and no evening edition, we get short-changed," Renie complained. "The deadlines must be for around six in the evening. Maybe I should start watching the news on TV. Of course, I'm not up early enough to see it."

"But you're definitely awake now?" Judith queried.

"We're going to have to be on our toes when we try to see the Blands."

"Oh, yeah," Renie answered. "I have been, for about the last fifteen minutes. It took a while, though. I poured milk on Bill's grapefruit. Unfortunately, he was eating it at the time."

The cousins agreed on leaving at eleven-thirty. When Renie got into the MG, she broached the obvious question.

"How are we going to meet Dick and Jane? By claiming that Spot and Puff are running amok in their yard?"

"I'm working on it," Judith said, struggling with the MG's gearshift. "Just follow my lead."

The sun, which had sneaked a peek at the city earlier in the morning, had now gone behind dark clouds. Renie, however, kept her sunglasses on. Not only did she have a chronic eye problem, she was a typical Pacific Northwest resident who insisted she was so unused to the sun that its irregular appearances bothered her eyes. Judith never argued. They lived in a city that bought more sunglasses per capita than any other place in the United States. Renie referred to the locals—especially the natives—as Mole People.

As the cousins crossed the bridge over the ship canal, they could barely see the foothills, let alone the two mountain ranges that flanked the metropolitan area. Summer was only a day away, but it felt more like January.

Judith drove slowly and carefully along the narrow residential streets. To her surprise, orange cones and wooden sawhorses barricaded both ends of Moonfleet

Street, blocking off the property from east to west. There was yellow tape starting at the wire fence and apparently encircling the entire grounds.

"This isn't going to be easy," she said with a grim expression. "I'm trying to think of a plausible excuse to get us inside the house."

"Termite inspectors?" Renie suggested. "Jehovah's Witnesses? Campfire Girls?"

Judith found a parking place around the corner of the block where the brusque neighbor lived. "I don't see any police cars," she said, "not even the unmarked kind. I can't quite figure this. If Glenn and Trash believe me—*big if*—then they're assuming that Vern Benson was killed on the Blands' property. Or if he wasn't murdered on the site, his body was put in my trunk while I was parked at the end of the alley. The Blands—as well as Mrs. Bland's sister—could be suspects, too. It looks like the police are considering this a crime scene. But it doesn't appear that any cops are on duty. They probably patrol frequently, though." Judith chewed on her thumbnail, a childhood habit she'd never overcome. "Thus we become the police."

Renie shook her head. "That's a crime. It's called 'impersonating a police officer.' "

"I didn't say what kind of police, did I?" Judith responded.

"Swell." Renie brightened. "Why police? Why not investigative reporters? You're FATSO, aren't you?"

The nickname was a corruption of FASTO, Female Amateur Sleuth Tracking Offenders. Some locals who had admired Judith's publicized skills in uncovering a murder on Heraldsgate Hill had created a Web site featuring her abilities as an amateur sleuth. Somehow, FASTO had turned into FATSO. It rankled Judith, who had fought a weight problem for years. The entire notion of the Web site also annoyed her to the point that she never ever looked at it. It was tempting, however, in that she had managed to lose twenty pounds in the past two years—not by dieting, but by wearing herself out while trying to recover from hip surgery and keep the B&B running.

"Maybe you're right," she conceded. "Have you got a notepad?"

"I think so," Renie replied, digging and delving into her huge purse. "Yes. It's kind of beat-up, but it'll do."

"It'd help if we had their phone number," Judith said as she got out of the MG.

"We don't," Renie said. "It's unlisted, remember?"

"Of course." Judith examined the car from every angle, making sure that there was sufficient space in front and in back of Joe's precious classic automobile. "Does it look safe?"

"You're no more than an inch from the curb," Renie noted.

"Okay." The cousins crossed the street. "Have you noticed," Judith said as they started down the sidewalk, "how Glenn hardly lets Trash speak?"

"Yes," Renie said. "If Trash wasn't such a bigmouth, you wouldn't know Glenn had a partner. The man's all ego."

"Plus, Trash seems like a screwup," Judith pointed out. "I have a feeling he's been passed around from partner to partner. I suppose you can't blame Glenn in a way. The police have to be so careful these days about how they interrogate witnesses. And suspects, of course."

Approaching the yellow tape, Judith paused. "This may be a wasted effort. I have a feeling they won't answer the door."

"Let's hope they do," Renie said, looking up at the low gray clouds. "It's starting to rain."

Judith lifted the tape just enough so that the cousins could duck under it. By the time they went up the path and reached the porch, the rain was coming down much harder than usual.

"This is a downpour," Judith declared. "We certainly get some weird weather in June."

"It's turning into hail," Renie declared as frozen drops bounced off the porch steps and the barren ground. "It shouldn't last long."

Judith banged the knocker three times. Nothing happened. She banged again. No response.

"You're not loud enough," Renie asserted. Disregarding her bad shoulder, she whacked the knocker so hard that Judith's ears rang.

The cousins waited as the hail pelted down and the temperature seemed to drop twenty degrees.

"They won't answer," Judith said with a shake of her head.

But she'd barely finished speaking when the door opened a scant two inches.

"What it is?" a high-pitched female voice demanded.

Before Judith could speak, Renie leaned closer to the door. "We want to offer you money," she said.

The door opened another inch. "For what?" the woman inquired, sounding suspicious.

"For your story," Renie replied. "We're freelance journalists. We have an opportunity to sell an article about what happened here. Do you mind discussing our proposal?"

"Yes. I mind very much." But the door opened another three inches.

To Judith's surprise, the woman was in her forties, blond, trim, with small, precise features, and wearing a tailored linen suit.

"It won't take long," Renie said. "We'll focus on what it's like to be innocent bystanders in what appears to be a murder case."

"I'm not a bystander," the woman said. "I don't live here."

Thinking quickly, Judith relied on her patented logic. "You're the daughter-in-law, right?"

The other woman looked surprised. "Yes. I'm Lynette Bland. How did you know?"

Judith shrugged. "Who else could you be? You're on your lunch hour, I assume. As my . . . colleague mentioned, we won't take long. I'm sure your in-laws would want you to hear about this opportunity."

Lynette Bland tapped her foot on the tile floor. "Possibly." She hesitated, assessing the weather. The hail was turning back into rain, leaving the front yard dusted with melting pellets. "Okay, come inside. But all I can give you is five minutes."

Judith felt as if she were entering the Holy of Holies. But Lynette stopped just inside the gloomy entry hall.

"Let's hear it," Lynette said, folding her arms across her chest and leaning up against the stucco wall. As far as Judith could tell, the entrance area was bare except for a quartet of wrought-iron wall sconces with un-lighted flame-shaped bulbs.

"How are Mr. and Mrs. Bland doing?" Renie inquired. "This situation must be hard on them at their age."

"Frankly," Lynette replied, "they aren't paying much attention to it. Why should they? It has nothing to do with them."

"Does Mrs. Bland's sister feel the same way?" Judith asked.

An ironic expression flitted across Lynette's face. "She ignores intrusions from the outside world. It's her way of coping."

Judith was about to ask why she needed isolation in order to cope, but Lynette wasn't finished. "So what's your proposal? You have four minutes left."

Renie took a deep breath. "Okay. Here it is. We interview Mr. and Mrs. Bland and Mrs. Bland's sister—" Renie stopped. "I'm sorry, I don't know her name."

"Sally Steiner," Lynette said. "Go on."

"Mrs.?" Renie queried.

"Yes. She's a widow."

"We'll ask them what it's like to have this invasion of their routine," Renie continued. "I gather they're up in years, and probably lead a quiet life. Suddenly this random act occurs, apparently on their property. Do they feel threatened? Fearful? Indifferent? Excited? Intrigued?"

Lynette glanced at her watch, which looked expensive. "You have three minutes."

Judith had the impression that Renie's approach

was a flop. "We're aiming the article for the senior citizen market," Judith broke in. "Like AARP or URP."

Lynette frowned. "URP? I never heard of it."

"United Retired Persons," Judith replied. "There are many organizations that are lesser known than AARP, but their publications still pay decently."

Lynette's hazel eyes narrowed. "How much?"

"We can't say," Renie replied. "It depends on the buyer. Of course, if we get into a bidding war . . ." She raised her hand and wiggled it in an upward motion.

"I'll have to talk to them," Lynette said without enthusiasm. "They're very private people. They had to be coaxed into speaking to the police."

"All three of them?" Judith said. "Goodness, you'd think at least one of your relatives would be more . . . social."

"They aren't," Lynette declared, with another look at her watch. "Time's up. Don't call me, I'll call you."

Renie scribbled both of the cousins' names and phone numbers on a sheet of her mangled notebook. "Here. My home phone is also my work phone. I'm listed under CaJones Designs."

"I thought you were a writer," Lynette said, still suspicious.

"I'm the artist." Renie pointed to Judith. "Mrs. Flynn's the writer. She's very good at fiction."

"Hunh." Lynette studied the phone numbers. "I'll let you know if they're interested. Good-bye."

"Maybe we should have been the cops," Renie muttered as they walked through the heavy rain. "My idea sucked scissors."

"Not completely," Judith said. "At least we got inside the house and we met a family member. We also learned the name of Mrs. Bland's sister, the alleged drinker. That's a start."

"Now what?" Renie inquired as they crossed the street.

"As long as we're this close," Judith replied, "maybe we should swing by Uncle Al's and see how Mike and the boys are doing."

"Uncle Al's probably teaching Mac and Joe-Joe how to handicap the horse races," Renie said as they got into the car. "It's your call."

Judith inspected the MG before getting in. Heaven help her if another vehicle had sideswiped Joe's car. But its red exterior looked as pristine as ever. "Okay," she said. "Let's go."

They'd driven five blocks when Judith spotted a Dairyland truck parked in the middle of the block. The milkman was going up the front steps of a house with a rose-covered trellis.

"Let's have a little talk with him," Judith said, carefully pulling into the house's driveway. "He must have known Vern Benson."

Renie, who seemed to be in one of her more affable moods, shrugged. "Go ahead. I'll stay in the car. It's still raining, and I might shrink. I'm already small enough."

The rain, however, was dwindling into a mere drizzle. Indeed, there were patches of sun in the western sky. Judith almost expected to see a rainbow.

"Hi," she called out as the milkman made his return journey to the truck. "I'm Judith Flynn. My uncle lives about six blocks from here. He saw the brief article in the paper this morning about one of Dairyland's employees getting killed on this route."

The milkman, who didn't have his name stitched on his blue jacket, grimaced. "I'm not supposed to talk about it. All of the Dairyland employees have been warned to keep quiet while the investigation's under way."

"Oh, of course," Judith said, looking sympathetic. "I should have realized that." She tried to think of some way to get the young man to open up, but nothing clever came to mind. He seemed like the earnest type, with his clear blue eyes, square jaw, and sandy crew cut. "Well. Please convey my condolences to Vern Benson's family."

The milkman winced slightly. "Thanks, but there's no need." The hint of a smile played at his mouth. "You see, *I'm* Vern Benson."

SEVEN

JUDITH WAS SPEECHLESS. "I d-d-don't understand," she stammered at last. "I th-th-thought . . ." Raking a hand through her salt-and-pepper hair, she stared at the young man in confusion.

"I'm sorry, ma'am," the milkman said. "Honest, I can't talk about it."

Judith decided to go on offense. "How do I know you're Vern Benson?" she demanded, and pointed to his jacket. "You don't have your name sewn on. You could be an impostor. How do I even know you're a milkman?"

Renie, aware that something extraordinary was happening, had gotten out of the MG.

"Somebody peddling phony buttermilk around here?" she inquired.

Judith turned to her cousin. "This person claims he's the late Vern Benson."

Renie looked startled. "That's impossible. Vern Benson is dead as a dodo."

"So if you insist you're Vern Benson, prove it," Judith challenged.

The young man looked miserable. "I can't. All my—" He cut himself off. "I just can't."

A light went on in Judith's brain. "Is that because someone stole your wallet, your driver's license, your jacket, and maybe even your truck?"

Several emotions seemed to cross the self-proclaimed Vern Benson's face. Finally, he spoke. "I can't talk about any of this."

Renie pointed to the truck. "If I were to hop inside and check the registration, would it be made out to somebody other than Vern Benson?"

The young man sighed. "Yes. I can't drive my own truck today." Suddenly he brightened. "Hey—I *can* prove I'm Vern Benson. Hold on." He fairly galloped down the street and zipped up the stairs to a small brown house with beige trim. The cousins trailed behind him. A few moments later, the front door was opened by a stout, white-haired woman.

"I was just coming out to get my milk," the woman said. "Did you forget something, Vern?"

"No, Mrs. Harmon," he said with a big grin. "Just tell these ladies who I am."

Mrs. Harmon stared at Judith and Renie. "Why do they want to know? Are they on your route?"

"I can't explain exactly," Vern replied. "Just tell them."

Mrs. Harmon eyed the cousins with suspicion. "This is Vern Benson. He's been my milkman for the past two years. He and his wife, Cindy, had a darling baby boy last month. Vern showed me pictures."

Judith gave both Vern and Mrs. Harmon a sheepish smile. "Thank you. I'm sorry for the trouble. It's just that Vern looked so much like—"

"He looks like Vern to me," Mrs. Harmon snapped. "What's going on in this neighborhood lately? First, the police going by, not just one car, but two or three. Then I walk my little dog, Doodle, this morning, and there's that yellow tape around that wreck of a house where the Blands live. Now you two, acting as if Vern were some kind of impostor. I've lived here for over fifty years, and I've never seen the like."

As Vern returned to the sidewalk, Judith held out her hand. "I feel terrible," she declared. "Please forgive me. I'm going to send you a baby present care of Dairyland to make up for being such a nuisance."

"Oh," Vern said with an awkward little laugh, "that's not necessary. But we could use another fitted crib sheet."

"Done," Judith said. "I'll send two." She shook Vern's hand before he hurried back to the truck.

"I'll pay for one of them," Renie said. "We can order them online and save a trip to Babies Be Wee."

"Fine." But Judith wasn't thinking about baby gifts. Rather, she was looking up at the brown-and-beige house. Mrs. Harmon had gone inside, but Judith had a feeling she was still watching the cousins. "Maybe we've just been given an opportunity."

"Mrs. Harmon?" Renie glanced at the house. "Hold it. I didn't catch everything that went on with you and the real Vern. What do you figure? The dead guy stole his truck and uniform and delivered something other than milk to the Blands?"

"Possibly," Judith allowed. "Or he went to collect. But what and why?"

"Did you see him deliver the milk?" Renie asked.

Judith shook her head. "No. He was coming back with an empty carrier. But he reeled off a list of items the Blands had ordered. Or that he claimed they ordered." She looked again at Mrs. Harmon's house, with its colorful splash of snapdragons and marigolds. The rain had stopped and the sun was peeking out from behind drifting clouds. "Come on, let's apologize."

"I thought you wanted to see how Mike and the kids were getting along," Renie said.

"I do. I will. But," she went on, "I can't dwell on them. It breaks my heart. Mike and Kristin have to solve their problems themselves. They know that Joe and I love them, but we can't interfere, especially these first few days."

Judith had already started for Mrs. Harmon's front door. Renie trotted along behind her. "Not to mention that you're a suspect," Renie noted. "Okay, I suppose you'll be more help to Mike and Kristin if you're not behind bars."

"You got that right," Judith said, ringing the doorbell.

Mrs. Harmon answered almost immediately, indicating that she had kept her eye on Judith and Renie all along.

"This is awkward," Judith said with an apologetic expression. "May we come in and explain ourselves?"

Mrs. Harmon surveyed her uninvited guests from head to toe. "You look harmless enough," she murmured as a black-and-white Pekingese with floppy ears came running to the door and began to bark. "Who are you?"

Judith introduced herself and Renie. "We grew up in this neighborhood," she said. "Our uncle still lives here. Al Grover. Do you know him?"

A twinkle came into Mrs. Harmon's blue eyes. "Al? That scamp! I've known Al Grover forever. Does he still ride in the sheriff's posse parades?"

"Not lately," Judith replied, relieved at making a connection. "But he keeps busy."

"Playing the ponies, no doubt," Mrs. Harmon replied, ushering the cousins inside and shushing the dog. "My late husband and I owned the little grocery store three blocks from here on the corner. It's a dry cleaners now, but Al used to buy his racing forms from us. He always made Jess and me laugh. Such a kidder!"

"I remember your store," Renie put in. "When I was a kid, I bought comic books there."

For the next five minutes, the cousins and Mrs. Harmon reminisced about the old days and how much the neighborhood had changed. Mrs. Harmon recalled Cliff and Deborah Grover.

"You were a skinny little thing with such big teeth," Mrs. Harmon said to Renie. "Looks like you've still got them."

Judith was growing impatient to steer the conversation around to the Blands. "Tell Mrs. Harmon about your fascination for the Bland house, coz," Judith said, nudging Renie, who was sitting next to her on a chintz-covered couch in the small but tidy living room.

Renie took the suggestion and ran with it. "Then," she said, "I managed to get Judith interested, too."

She paused. Judith understood why. Renie wasn't sure if she should reveal what a strange twist Judith's interest had taken.

Judith, however, felt there was no point in withholding the truth. She told Mrs. Harmon the entire story, bringing it up to the point where she'd accosted Vern Benson on the sidewalk.

Mrs. Harmon listened with only minor interruptions, including a couple of admonishments for Doodle, who seemed fascinated with Renie's purse. Instead of shock or even surprise, the old lady absorbed the information as if she'd heard far more outlandish tales in her time. Which, Judith realized, she probably had.

"My, my," Mrs. Harmon said with a sigh. "There was a mention of a body in a car trunk on TV last night, but it was very brief, and I didn't pay much attention. It didn't happen in our neighborhood, after all. I'm afraid that as I get older, I become more isolated from the rest of the city." She offered the cousins an apologetic look. "There's so much evil these days, you become hardened to it. Crime. Violence. Murder. Robbery." She sighed heavily. "Jess and I were held up three times in four years." She glanced at Renie. "Not while you lived here, but later. That's why we finally decided to give up the store almost twenty years ago. The new owners couldn't keep it going. So the dry cleaners moved in. Anyway, I can see why you'd be fascinated by the Bland house. We were, too. We'd take walks—Jess and I were always great walkers—and we'd often go by it. They moved in before we did. The first few times we went by, the house was very nice—beautiful, really, and so unusual for this neighborhood. There was a greenhouse and a pond and such lovely plantings. But after a time, it all began to go downhill."

"When would that have been?" Judith inquired.

Mrs. Harmon smoothed one of the crocheted antimacassars on the arm of her chair. "We moved here in '51. I heard the Blands had bought their house in '47, '48, not long after the war. As I recall, it was only a year or two after we moved to Langford that the place began to deteriorate."

"Did you know Mr. and Mrs. Bland?" Renie asked.

Mrs. Harmon chuckled softly. "I never met them. But they had two children—a boy and a girl—who went to school with our twins. I think one of them was adopted. That's the reason I know the name. Nice children, but quiet. They never played with our kids. But then we were a few blocks away, and ours were in between the Blands'."

"I mentioned," Judith put in, "that we met Lynette. She must be married to the son."

"Yes," Mrs. Harmon replied. "Yes. Now what was his name? Something biblical . . . Matthew, Mark . . . No, Luke. That's right, Luke Bland." She laughed, a merry sound. "It's coming back to me now. Luke was adopted. Now this is all hearsay, of course, from the other parents in PTA. I believe Mr. Bland served in World War Two. Mrs. Hermanson—or was it Mrs. Bruce? Anyway, whoever it was told me that Mr. Bland had been wounded in the war and couldn't have children. That's why they adopted. Then, when our twins were in second grade, the Blands had a baby girl. Unless there was some monkeyshines on Mrs. Bland's part, I guess it was just neighborhood gossip about Mr. Bland. He was wounded, though." She paused, holding up one finger. "Ah. I remember now. Anna, that was the daughter's

name. I've no idea what became of her. Our Sharon and
Roy were out of grade school before she entered kinder-
garten." Mrs. Harmon scooted forward in the armchair.
"Could I make you some tea? Or coffee?"

"No thank you," Judith replied. "We should be
heading for Uncle Al's shortly. Tell me, do you know if
Mr. Bland had a job?"

"No, I don't." Mrs. Harmon settled back in the chair.
"He may not have. It's possible that he had a disability
pension from the army."

"Weird," Renie remarked, shaking her head.
"Surely the neighbors must have speculated about
why the Blands were such recluses. Not to mention
why they let such a lovely house deteriorate."

"Of course the neighbors talked," Mrs. Harmon
agreed. "At least, at first. Everybody had a theory. But
that's what they were—theories. Like the army pension. If that's all they had in the way of income, they
couldn't keep up such a grand house. Some thought
they took in boarders. I understand someone else has
been living there for quite a while. A few gossiped
about a drinking problem. My husband figured there
was money in the family, but either it wasn't enough to
maintain the house or else they were just plain lazy."

"They had to shop for groceries," Judith pointed
out. "Didn't anyone ever see them coming in or out?"

Mrs. Harmon smiled sadly. "Maybe the old-timers
did. But most of them are gone now, in retirement or
nursing homes—or passed away. The neighborhood
has changed a great deal in fifty years."

"Except for the Blands," Renie said.

"Isn't that the truth?" Mrs. Harmon sighed. "I didn't

hear all of the gossip, of course. You must remember, I'm several blocks away. And if I'd seen them at the grocery store, I wouldn't have recognized them."

Judith started to rise from the sofa. It was very deep and very comfortable, but not easy to get out of with hip problems. "Do you know anyone near the Bland house who has been around for the past fifty years?"

"Oh, dear—let me see." Mrs. Harmon also rose as Renie gave Judith a shove. "Yes, Mrs. Bruce. Elsie Bruce. She must be almost ninety and is very crippled with arthritis. She has help, or she couldn't stay in her own home. And believe me, Elsie isn't going anywhere else until they take her to the mortuary."

"Do you know her address?" Judith inquired.

"I can look it up." Mrs. Harmon bent down to reach into a shelf on the end table. "Let me think—Elsie's husband has been dead for years, but his name was Elmer," she said, flipping through the White Pages. "I imagine she's kept the listing that way. Elsie's not one for change. Yes, here it is—Elmer Bruce, twenty-oh-nine. Do you want the number?"

Renie got out her notebook. "That'd be great."

Mrs. Harmon recited the phone number, but added a caution. "She's very deaf. We both attended the Presbyterian church, but she can't go to services anymore. She hasn't, for close to ten years, but she was deaf even then."

Offering their profuse thanks, the cousins made their exit. Behind the wheel of the MG, Judith cogitated. "Uncle Al or Mrs. Bruce?" She grimaced. "Uncle Al, for now. But we won't stay long."

Their visit was shorter than they'd expected. No one

was home at Uncle Al's, and Mike's Range Rover was nowhere in sight.

"I'll bet they went out for lunch," Judith said.

Renie suddenly looked wistful. "Speaking of which, I'm kind of hungry."

Judith frowned at her cousin. "Since when are you not?" Renie was one of those annoying people whose metabolism allowed her to eat like a pig and never gain weight. "We'll pick up burgers and fries at Doc's Drive-in. I'd like to call on Mrs. Bruce before I head home to get ready for tonight's guests."

"I want a vanilla shake, too," Renie said, pouting just a bit. "Maybe two hamburgers."

"Fine, but don't you dare trash Joe's car," Judith warned.

It was still the lunch hour when the cousins pulled into the drive-in that had been a landmark for almost fifty years in Langford. The lines were long.

"Let me do this," Renie said. "What do you want?"

"A plain burger and fries," Judith replied.

"Okay. Keep the motor running and watch this."

Renie got out of the car, walked toward the busy windows, and held up both hands. "Free Megabucks tickets across the street! Five minutes only! Don't miss out!"

All but three people turned to look at the convenience store across Langford's busy main artery. Sure enough, there was a partly visible banner over the store's entrance that read Free Mega . . . The mob took off like a shot, practically falling all over themselves to get to the crosswalk at the corner. Renie scooted up to the nearest vacant window and put in her order.

"Are they really handing out free Megabucks lottery tickets at the convenience store?" the teenage boy with purple hair asked Renie after he'd called out her request.

Renie turned around. The customers who had raced off were all standing at the corner, frantically pushing the "Walk" button on the traffic control post.

"Hunh," she said to the young man. "I guess I made a mistake. It says 'Free Megaphones.' I think I heard about that. It's a promotion for the baseball team."

Doc's fast food was really fast, one of the reasons the drive-in had prospered for almost half a century. Renie's order was up just as the light finally changed and the crowd started racing across the street.

"Thanks," she said, and ran back to the car. "Hit it," she ordered Judith.

After a brief glitch trying to shift into reverse, Judith sped out of the parking lot and down the side street. In the rearview mirror, she could see the now-irate customers storming around in front of the convenience store.

"Ah," Renie said complacently. "Food. Pull over when we get around the corner. We want to eat this while it's hot. Otherwise, the fries go limp."

"What," Judith asked as she found a parking place under a big maple tree, "would you have done if they hadn't fallen for your ruse?"

Renie paid no heed to the lettuce that had dropped onto her faded tee. "I suppose I'd have had to stand in line with the rest of the suckers. By the way, did you notice one of the three people who didn't rush off?"

Judith shook her head. "I was too busy watching the ones who did—and you."

Renie giggled, causing her to spew out a couple of diced onions. "Morty the Mailman. He was reading somebody's *Sports Illustrated* while he was in line."

"Morty," Judith murmured, tapping her fingers on the steering wheel. "I wish he'd been more helpful."

"I wish he'd retired," Renie said, sprinkling salt on her fries. "Like forty years ago."

"Still..." Judith let the sentence trail off. Morty hadn't been on the Moonfleet route for all that long. Maybe he honestly didn't have any information. He certainly wasn't the curious type.

"I'm done," Judith declared, wiping off her hands with a paper napkin. "You can finish my fries, along with the rest of your large quantity of food. We have to get going."

The cousins were only about six blocks from Mrs. Bruce's house, but they took a longer route to ensure that nobody coming from the drive-in would see them. Joe's MG was too easily identifiable. Judith had visions of a wild-eyed mob descending upon them and wreaking havoc with the car. And with the cousins.

Twenty-oh-nine Moonfleet was on the southwest corner, across the street from the Bland house. Elsie Bruce's home was a modest brick Tudor, showing signs of genteel neglect.

A plump, pretty Hispanic woman with a dish towel over her arm came to the door. *"Hola, señoras."*

"Is Mrs. Bruce at home?" Judith asked.

"Sí," the woman replied but didn't budge.

"May we talk to her?" Judith inquired. "I'm Mrs. Flynn and this is Mrs. Jones."

"Sí," the woman repeated, and still made no move.

Renie cranked up her rusty Spanish. *"Donde está Señora Bruce?"*

"Aquí," the woman said, stepping aside and pointing to a sitting room just off the hall.

"Gracias," Renie responded as the cousins entered the small, cluttered room where a TV was tuned into one of the shopping channels.

"Hello," Judith said in her friendliest voice.

Mrs. Bruce, who was small and wizened, didn't move. There was no sound coming from the TV set. Noticing the old lady's hearing aids and remembering that Mrs. Harmon had said Elsie was deaf, Judith raised her voice several notches.

"Hallooo!"

Elsie turned slowly. She straightened her glasses and adjusted the afghan on her lap. "What?"

Judith moved to stand in front of Elsie and leaned down so that their faces were practically touching. "I'm Judith." She pointed to Renie. "This is my cousin, Serena."

Elsie made a shooing gesture with one of her hands. "I can't see the TV," she declared in an irritable voice. "I want that ruby ring. Teresa, write that down." Elsie tried to peer around the cousins. "Where's Teresa? I want that ruby!"

"Aquí, señora," Teresa said, moving into Elsie's range of vision.

"The ring, Teresa! Call them! Act now!" The old lady pointed to an 800 number at the bottom of the screen. "Hurry up! They may sell out."

"Sí, señora," Teresa replied, and hurried out of the room.

"Stupid girl," Elsie muttered. "She'll get it all mixed up, as usual. She can hardly speak a word of English. Ah!" She pointed again at the screen. "Pearls! I adore pearls! Take down that number."

"It's the same one," Renie pointed out, all but shouting. "Shall I tell Teresa to order the pearls, too?"

"Yes, be quick." She dismissed Renie with a wave of her hand.

Fortuitously, the channel went to a commercial break. "I'd like to ask you some questions about your neighbors the Blands," Judith said, pulling up an ancient armless rocker next to Elsie's chair.

"Bands? What bands?" Elsie looked mystified.

"Blands," Judith said loudly.

Elsie merely stared at Judith. "You're mumbling," she finally said.

"I can't keep screaming at you," Judith asserted. She pointed to Elsie's hearing aids. "Are they turned on?"

"What?" Elsie scowled at Judith. She fiddled with the devices. "Hunh. I guess I turned them off. I don't need to hear when I watch TV. And I don't need to hear Teresa, either. She won't speak English. Imagine!" She stared at Judith with filmy blue eyes. "Who are you? An undertaker selling plots? A social worker? A burglar?"

Renie had come back into the room. There were no other chairs, so she leaned against the wall.

"My cousin and I are interested in the Spanish-style house across the street," Judith said. "Do you know the owners?"

"Those snobs?" Elsie sneered. "No, and I don't want to. They keep to themselves and that's fine with me.

They drink. The Lord abhors drunkenness. I see the police were there yesterday. I hope they arrested the lot of them. It's a good thing Arthur's dead. He was the only decent one in the family."

"Arthur?" Judith echoed.

"Yes, Arthur, Arthur Craig." Elsie scowled at Judith. "Are you deaf? Arthur was married to Anna. Died young about fifteen years ago. He couldn't have been more than thirty."

"Was it an accident?" Judith inquired.

"So they said," Elsie replied, her gaze again fixed on the TV screen. "Diamonds! Five carats! Teresa!"

"I'll tell her," Renie volunteered with a wink for Judith.

"What kind of accident?" Judith asked after Renie left the room.

"Arthur drowned." Elsie paused, admiring the twinkling stone on TV.

"A boating mishap?" Judith suggested.

"Ha! Where would Arthur get a boat? He drowned in the fishpond by the house." Elsie removed her glasses, exhaled on the lenses, and wiped them clean with a handkerchief. "The fishpond's gone now. The Blands never tended to it, or to much of anything else. That's why their place is such a wreck. Dirty, too. I've seen the exterminator there twice in the past year or so. Rats, if you ask me. And why not? The place is so overgrown, they could have a zoo living behind those big fences. Oh, I know my house is a little run-down, but I do what I can to keep it from falling apart. Those Blands—they never cared."

"Do you know Arthur's wife, Anna?" Judith asked.

Elsie wrinkled her nose. "Anna was always a spoiled brat. Fancies herself a fashion plate. She's some kind of buyer for Nordquist's. The second time around, she married a man named Philip French. Sinister fellow, if you ask me."

"What about Lynette?"

"Cold. Distant. Selfish." Elsie cocked her head to one side. "You're not asking me about the house. You're asking about the family. Come clean." With effort, she moved around in the chair and eyed Renie, who had just returned from her latest errand. "And clean up. You've got garbage all over your bosom."

Renie offered the old lady a strained smile as she haphazardly brushed off her tee. "People *are* houses," Renie said. "If somebody other than the Blands lived across the street, it could be a showplace."

Elsie considered Renie's words. "Yes, that's so. But I still don't—" She halted for a moment. "Go on, I'm not trying to get rid of you."

Judith assumed that the old lady was happy to have company, especially guests who seemed interested in her opinions. In fact, before Judith could speak again, Elsie said as much.

"I don't get many callers. Both my sons live out in the suburbs. Do you think they ever come into town? Too much traffic, they say. And the grandkids— they're all over the place, some with children of their own. What's all this soccer and swimming and gymnastics about? They want to be in the Olympics? Everybody's running around in circles. No time for old folks. Why can't children just *play* like we used to do? Or read. The Bookmobile still comes here, but it's getting so I can only read the large-print books. Maddy—the library lady—says I should try those Books on Tape things. I don't know—I've heard too much in my life already. A book, you can put it down. I don't want to fiddle with some crazy machine. I probably couldn't hear it anyway."

Judith was afraid the conversation was going too far afield. "I suppose," she said in an effort to steer Elsie back on track, "the Bland children aren't any better than most about calling on their parents."

"Oh . . ." Elsie again cocked her head to one side, eyes darting to the window that looked out onto Moon-fleet Street. "They come by now and then. They never stay long, though. Who would want to in such a gloomy old house? I don't think those upstairs drapes have been opened in twenty years. They must be rot-ting to pieces. The downstairs isn't much better. If the sunlight ever got inside that place, it'd probably blind the whole bunch of them."

"But," Judith said, "you actually know the younger generation. Lynette, Anna, Philip, and . . . Did you mention Luke?"

"The son?" Elsie shook her head. "He's a bit touched, if you ask me. Always wears sunglasses, even when it's raining. Must think he looks like a movie star. Luke invents things."

"Such as what?" Renie inquired.

"I couldn't say. But that's what I've heard he does. Or does he develop things? I forget, something you can't put your finger on. Rube Goldberg contraptions, probably." Elsie sniffed with disdain. She pointed to the window that provided a sidelong view of the path to the front porch. "I see the young'uns coming and going once in a while. Alan—that's Lynette and Luke's son—he was here a week or so ago. I suppose he's close to thirty by now. When I could still work in the yard, I'd speak to them. I didn't care if they didn't want to speak to me. I call that bad manners, and I've no time for it." She looked at the back of her hands, which were covered with liver spots. "Luke was always polite, though. So was his son, Alan, even though he tended to be tongue-tied in his teens. Typical of adolescents."

"What about the older folks?" Renie asked. "Do you ever see them?"

"About once every five years," Elsie retorted. "Look! Sapphires! I've always wanted earrings like that! Go tell Teresa!"

Renie whisked around the corner, though there was no sound of her walking away. For the first time, Judith realized that Elsie Bruce wasn't wearing any jewelry, not even a wedding ring. Her joints were too swollen from arthritis, and the hearing aids would make it difficult to wear earrings. It was a game, harmless, and sad.

"What was I saying?" Elsie mused, her gaze still glued to the sapphires. "Oh—Dick and Jane Bland. Years would go by when I never saw them. Jane went from a willowy brunette to an overweight white-haired old lady. Dick was always nondescript, but when I did see him, little by little, he lost his hair. For a while, he had one of those terrible comb-overs. The next thing you know, he bought a toupee! Imagine! He looked like he was wearing a dead chipmunk on his head. Of course," she added on a gentler note, "I heard he had a terrible scar from the war. Shot by the Germans, just missing his brain. No doubt that's why he couldn't hold down a job. Sad, I suppose, but at least he got to come home, unlike so many of our other brave boys."

"What about Mrs. Bland's sister, Sally?" Renie asked as she reentered the sitting room.

Elsie bristled. "She moved in with them years ago, when the children were still small. A moocher, no doubt, though the few times I've seen her, she was all gussied up. I could see her jewelry from here. Why should she have all those emeralds and diamonds and such instead of me? I figure she married a rich man and was left a wealthy widow." Elsie leaned closer and lowered her voice. "Or a merry widow, maybe. Two, three times a long time ago I saw her sneak out at night and get picked up in fancy cars. Once, I saw her being dropped off in the wee small hours. What was I to think but that she was up to no good?"

"How recent was that?" Judith inquired.

Elsie made a feeble wave with her crippled right hand. "Five years ago? Ten? I lose track of time. I haven't seen any of the older bunch in maybe a year."

"What do you think they do inside all the time?" asked Renie.

Elsie sighed. "Who knows? I hardly ever see more than one light on at a time. Maybe they have séances. Maybe they really are all blind. Maybe they've turned into moles." She leaned forward in her chair. "Topaz! I love that color! It looks good enough to eat! Get Teresa."

The cousins decided they should also get going. Thanking Elsie Bruce, they headed for the front door, meeting Teresa on their way.

"Topaz this time," Renie said.

"Gotcha," Teresa replied.

Judith stared. "You speak English?"

"Sure," Teresa said with a puckish little smile. "I was born in Medford, Oregon."

"But," Judith began, "why do you pretend not to understand?"

"Because," Teresa said, still with the quirky smile, "it makes life easier."

Judith understood. "Does Mrs. Bruce ever ask what's happened to her jewelry orders?"

"Never." Teresa opened the door for the cousins. "She understands, too. And by the way," she went on, speaking to Judith, "I saw you at the Bland house yesterday. You had a different car, but I recognized you anyway. I don't know what you're really up to, but if I were you, I'd keep away from that Bland house."

"Why is that?" Judith asked.

Teresa's face grew solemn. "Don't ask. It's a scary place."

"Emeralds!" cried Elsie from inside the house.

"*Sí, señora,*" Teresa called back. She lowered her voice and spoke to the cousins. "I'm not joking. Something strange is going on across the street. It's best that you forget all about it."

For Judith, the advice was worthless.

EIGHT

DOES TERESA KNOW more than she told us?" Renie asked as they headed back to Heraldsgate Hill.

"Yes," Judith said. "If she didn't, she wouldn't have warned us. We're going to have to get back to her. Meanwhile, our original mission has been thwarted. We may have learned a few things about the Blands, but except for Lynette, we still haven't met any of them."

"I have a feeling," Renie said, "that we never will. If it weren't for what those detectives told you about interviewing them, the Blands might not exist."

Judith, who had just turned onto the main thoroughfare that led across the bridge, darted a glance at Renie. "That's an interesting idea."

"Interesting, but unlikely," Renie said. "The cops wouldn't lie about it, and Mrs. Bruce sees them every now and then."

"She sees *somebody*," Judith allowed. "Damn!" she burst out halfway across the bridge.

"Watch it, coz," Renie said in alarm. "You're almost in the other lane. What's wrong?"

Judith focused on her driving until they reached the turnoff to Heraldsgate Hill. "I'm an idiot," she declared as they reached the six-way stop. "Why didn't I look at the customs declaration slip on that UPS box? All I checked was the postmark, from Kopfstein in Austria. The form would have told me what was in the box."

"Which," Renie said dryly, "would have solved the entire mystery."

"Okay, maybe it wouldn't have," Judith said as they crossed the little bridge above the gully, "but it might have been a clue. Isn't it odd that UPS delivers to the Blands only once a year and always at the same time?"

"Odd?" Renie looked aghast. "It's unthinkable. If I didn't get a delivery from one of the stores or catalogs every week, life would have no meaning."

Judith had turned down Renie's street. "Oh? And who delivered that outfit you're wearing now? The Pony Express? It looks like it's been on the road a long time."

"You know I don't wear my good clothes except for business and social purposes," Renie countered. "I bought this tee for eight bucks ten years ago. As for the pants, somebody gave them to me."

"Who? Noah?"

"Funny coz," Renie murmured as Judith pulled up in front of the Joneses' Dutch Colonial. "I'm going inside and tend to my sickly spouse."

As she headed back to Hillside Manor, Judith's spirits plummeted. It wasn't likely that a doddering trio of senior citizens would kill a milkman. Or someone pretending to be a milkman. The real Vern Benson was a pleasant young man with a wife and baby. So why did the murder victim dress up like a Dairyland employee and make a stop at the Blands' house?

It made no sense. Had the Blands been younger, Judith would have considered that they could be involved in drug dealing.

But the Blands *had* been younger fifty years ago. Maybe they'd bought the Spanish-style house for that purpose. The city was a Pacific Rim seaport; drugs had been a problem for much longer than in other metropolitan areas. Renie recalled seeing a deal go down when she was barely in her teens.

Austria, however, seemed like an unlikely source. And what did the Blands do with the money they'd made? Not much, judging from the house and their reclusive lifestyle.

Judith was still mulling after she got home to find Gertrude in the kitchen, ransacking the refrigerator.

"Why did you get this great big stainless-steel piece of junk?" the old lady rasped. "It looks like a spaceship, and I can't find anything! Where's the dill pickles?"

"There's a big jar inside the door," Judith informed her mother.

"Where?" Gertrude leaned forward in her wheelchair. "Oh. Now, why would you put dill pickles *there*?"

"All the condiments are in the door," Judith pointed out. "Mustard, mayonnaise, olives, capers—"

"Capers!" Gertrude snarled. "Who wants to eat something that looks like dried-up dingleberries? Ugh!"

"I use them with lox and cream cheese," Judith explained. "They're really delicious."

"They can't be." Having taken two dill pickles out of the jar, Gertrude resumed rummaging in the fridge. "Where've you been? You forgot my lunch."

"Oh, Mother, I am sorry!" Judith apologized. "I've got too much on my mind."

"And not enough room for most of it," Gertrude snapped. "Somebody brought my lunch. Somebody didn't forget a poor old crippled woman. Somebody *cares.*"

"Who?" Judith inquired.

"Al and Mike and the grandkids, that's who," Gertrude replied, adding a couple of cheese slices to the plate in her lap. "They showed up about one with fish and chips. They'd been to the lake to feed the ducks."

"So that's where they were," Judith murmured. "Why are you eating now? It's only a little after two."

"Because I'm still hungry. Aha! Cantaloupe. Can you slice this for me?"

Judith complied. To her daughter's dismay, Gertrude shook at least two tablespoons of chocolate sprinkles on the cantaloupe. She was wheeling herself out the back way when the doorbell chimed. She stopped in the hall while her daughter answered the front door.

"We'd like you to come downtown," Glenn Morris announced without preamble.

"I can't," Judith protested. "I have guests coming in a couple of hours. In case you haven't noticed, this is a B&B."

"What's that stand for?" Trash put in. "At our house, it'd be Bed and Boredom."

"I'll bet it would," Judith retorted. "Really, if you

don't mind, I'd prefer answering your questions here. I honestly don't know what else I can tell you."

"Don't cause a problem," Glenn said without inflection. "You should know this is police procedure."

"Police?" Gertrude rolled into the entry hall. "What now, terrorists blowing up Rankerses' hedge?"

Judith put an arm around her mother's shoulders. "No. These two detectives think I killed a bogus milkman."

"Ridiculous!" Gertrude scoffed. "We don't have a milkman here. And what do you mean, 'bogus'?"

"The victim was posing as a milkman," Judith explained.

"Why would anybody do that?" Gertrude demanded. "That's hard work. Why not pose as a lawyer—or a policeman?"

Glenn was trying to ignore Gertrude. "Come along, Mrs. Flynn. We can't waste time arguing about this."

"Come along?" Gertrude snapped. "She's not coming along with you. She has to get my supper. If she goes, I go with her. She's my daughter. She does what I tell her to. You want two for the price of one?"

Clearly, the ultimatum gave Glenn pause. "It's not up to you to decide, Mrs. . . . ?"

"Grover. Gertrude Grover. I'm part of the Greatest Generation. You'd better not tangle with me, buster. We beat the pants off of Hitler." She turned in Trash's direction. "And stop looking at my pickles."

Glenn glanced at Trash, who seemed to be enjoying the confrontation immensely. "All right," Glenn said with a sigh. "But I don't like making exceptions. The living room or the parlor?"

"The parlor," Judith said. "But let me help Mother back into her apartment."

"Oh, no you don't!" Gertrude exclaimed. "I'm staying right here. I know about police brutality. I wouldn't abandon my little girl for anything."

Glenn didn't argue. Judith led the way into the parlor. Glenn positioned himself as before, in front of the fireplace.

"Now," he began, "I want you to go over everything that happened yesterday from the time you left this house until you finished your shopping at Falstaff's Grocery."

"I'd kind of like to hear this myself," Gertrude put in, casting a reproachful eye at Judith. "Sometimes my daughter keeps things from her mother. 'Course she couldn't stop me from seeing the dead gangster lying outside my door."

"Is that so?" Glenn remarked with indifference.

"Or the fortune-teller who dropped dead at the dining-room table," Gertrude went on.

"Really." Glenn didn't bother to look at Gertrude.

"Having that movie big shot drown in the kitchen sink was a blessing in disguise," Gertrude declared. "Some of the people who worked for him are making a moving picture about me."

Glenn's facial muscles had tightened. "I'm sure they are," he said through gritted teeth.

"But I'm glad I missed that killer Easter Bunny up at church," Gertrude said. "Hop, chop, hop—"

"Mrs. Grover!" Glenn was getting red in the face. "*Please.* We're trying to conduct an investigation here." He moved a step closer to Judith, who was seated next to Gertrude. "Could you please make your mother stop talking nonsense?" he requested in a low voice. "I realize she's elderly and delusional, but she's impeding our interrogation."

"She's elderly, but she's not delusional," Judith said softly.

"Then you both must be crackers," Trash asserted. "Is that part of your alleged disease, Mrs. Flynn?"

"No," Judith said, then turned to Gertrude. "Mother, you'd better let me tell these detectives what happened or we'll never get rid of them."

Seeing the wisdom in her daughter's words, Gertrude shut up. Judith began to recount the events that had led to the discovery of the ersatz milkman in the trunk of her car. Sweetums wandered into the parlor just as she was getting to the part she hadn't mentioned the previous day.

"The UPS man told me that the parcel for the Blands was a once-a-year delivery," Judith explained. "Naturally, I was curious. I went on the porch to look at the box. It came from Kopfstein, Austria."

"Why didn't you mention that yesterday?" Glenn demanded as Sweetums wove between his feet.

"I didn't want you to think I was a snoop," Judith replied.

"But your whole story involves snooping," Glenn pointed out, trying to sidestep the cat.

"I know," Judith admitted. "It was stupid of me. But it didn't seem important at the time."

"Are you certain you're telling everything now?" Glenn asked, taking a couple of steps away from Sweetums.

"Yes."

Sweetums was undeterred. He rubbed up against Glenn's neatly pressed trouser leg and purred loudly. The detective jumped, knocked over the fire tools, and stepped on Sweetums's tail. The cat growled and took the offensive, clawing the fine trouser fabric. In an instant, Sweetums had torn four six-inch rents, from midcalf to cuff. Glenn swore out loud as he tried to grab the cat, who eluded him by ducking under Gertrude's wheelchair.

"This is an outrage!" Glenn shouted. "That animal ought to be put to sleep!"

"I could use a nap myself," Trash said, feigning a yawn. "Are we done yet?"

Glenn examined the rips in his slacks. "We are now," he huffed. "I'll send you a bill for this," he added, pointing to Judith.

"If you do, I'll report you to the SPCA," Judith shot back. "You deliberately stepped on Sweetums. No wonder he got upset. And what was the point of all this anyway?"

"To learn those details you conveniently forgot or omitted yesterday," Glenn asserted, trying to ignore the growls and hisses coming from Sweetums.

Judith had gotten to her feet, though Trash still lolled about in the window embrasure. "You have the whole story now," she said, annoyed. "Tell me who I was carrying around in my trunk. I don't like giving rides to strangers."

"You wouldn't know him," Glenn responded. "He's nobody, just some lowlife."

"But he's got a name, and I want to know it," Judith argued, "especially if you think I killed him."

"You killed somebody?" Gertrude asked. "That's a switch."

"You heard what I just told the detectives," Judith retorted. "Somebody put the body in my trunk while I was looking around the house and grounds."

Gertrude grunted. "Is that why you're cruising around in Lunkhead's jalopy?"

"You promised not to call him 'Lunkhead' anymore," Judith admonished.

"Okay, Knucklehead, then. So where's your car? At the mortuary?"

"Later, Mother," Judith said impatiently. "I'll fill you in after these detectives have gone. But," she continued, turning to Glenn, "I insist upon knowing the victim's name. I also insist on knowing whether I'm still a suspect."

"A person of interest," Glenn replied. "How's that?"

"Dumb," Judith declared. "If you really thought I murdered the guy, you'd probably figure out that I knew who he was. Come on, give me the dead man's name."

Glenn sighed. "I'll tell you because the name won't mean a thing. The man was Frank Purvis, address unknown."

Glenn was right. The name meant nothing to Judith.

Well," Gertrude huffed after the detectives had left, "it looks like you got yourself into another big mess." She cocked an eye at her daughter. "You can tell me—did you really bump off the milkman?"

"Of course not, Mother," Judith replied. "And he

wasn't a milkman. I never heard of anyone named Frank Purvis."

"I did," Gertrude asserted, wheeling herself back to the kitchen. "He worked for one of the lumber mills. He was a Freemason and had a glass eye. I went to school with his wife, Charlotte. Carrie, she was called. Homely girl. She got to that gawky stage and never left it."

"Did they have children?" Judith asked.

"I hope not." Gertrude had retrieved her snack and was about to take a bite out of a dill pickle. "The results would have been fearsome." The old lady loudly crunched her pickle and swallowed it before speaking again. "I lost track of Carrie after she got married. I think they moved away during the Depression."

The tiny speck of hope was snuffed out. Gertrude's recognition of the name was a coincidence. But someone must have known the Frank Purvis who had ended up dead in Judith's trunk. The "address unknown" troubled her. The bogus milkman she'd met on Moonfleet Street didn't look homeless. He'd appeared well nourished and well kempt. If the police knew the victim's name, there must have been some kind of identification on his person.

"It could have been a Social Security card," Renie suggested when Judith called her half an hour later. "Or credit cards. They don't list addresses."

"But the credit-card company would know where to send the bill," Judith pointed out.

"Yes," Renie said in a sour voice, "they always know where to find you. I changed our address once to

Buckingham Palace, but it didn't work. The queen said she wouldn't be caught dead in a Notre Dame sweatshirt. She especially hated the Fighting Irish logo."

"But no driver's license, no checkbook, no voter's registration," Judith said, ignoring Renie's flight of fancy. Or possibly, reality. Sometimes it was hard to tell with Renie. "It's as if Frank Purvis didn't want to be traced."

"Then why have any ID at all?" Renie queried.

"That's my point," Judith said, holding the phone between her jaw and shoulder as she sliced cucumbers. "I wonder if Glenn Morris didn't make up a name just to shut me up."

"Why would he do that?" Renie asked.

"Just because," Judith said. "I looked Frank Purvis up in the phone book. Like the Blands, there was no listing. I even called directory assistance to see if someone by that name lived in the suburbs. No luck."

"Did you try the Internet?"

Judith sighed. "Yes. I found three men named Frank Purvis. One in Baton Rouge, another in Sherman Oaks, and the third in Duluth. I've hit the wall."

"Maybe it's an alias," Renie suggested.

"The police must have taken his fingerprints," Judith said. "Glenn referred to Purvis as a 'lowlife,' which indicates some kind of criminal record. Maybe they know more than they're telling us."

"I assume they'll release his name to the media," Renie remarked. "It'll be interesting to see if there's an obituary in the paper in the next couple of days. Maybe we should visit the morgue."

"To do what? Go through Frank Purvis's meager belongings?"

"I meant the newspaper morgue," Renie clarified. "And not for Purvis, but the Blands. You can go back only a few years into the archives on the Internet."

"I suppose it could be helpful," Judith allowed. "Were you thinking of marriage, births—that kind of information?"

"Yes, but I also wonder if they haven't made the news in a less mundane way," Renie said. "I'm thinking feature articles, like an unusual hobby or rescuing a child from a vicious dog."

"They don't strike me as publicity hounds," Judith noted. "I picture them as going out of their way to avoid the limelight."

"Except sometimes people can't escape it," Renie pointed out. "It's up to you. I could go tomorrow morning. After ten, of course."

The cousins agreed on the time. The rest of the day passed swiftly. Besides her guests, Judith had to prepare another meal for Mike and the boys, as well as Uncle Al. The group seemed in high humor, having gone to the zoo after their trip to the lake and visit to Gertrude. Judith was put off by Mike's attitude. It seemed to her that he should be wallowing in misery. She also felt that Mac and Joe-Joe didn't seem to miss their mother very much.

As they were all leaving, Judith cornered Mike, dragging him into the parlor. "I want a progress report," she demanded. "What are you and Kristin doing to solve your problems?"

Mike shrugged. "She's going home to stay with her folks on their wheat ranch for a while. She's leaving Saturday. The boys and I'll go back to the ranger station Sunday."

"That's not progress," Judith noted.

"Yes, it is," Mike replied. "She feels claustrophobic up at the summit. She needs to get back to her roots to think."

Judith didn't comment on Kristin's needs. "I would expect the children to miss her," she said.

Mike grinned. "They're having a ball. This is all one big holiday to them. Tomorrow we're going to the aquarium and then to do the rides at the civic center. Not to mention that Uncle Al spoils them rotten. You know how he is with kids."

"Yes." Not having children of his own, Al Grover doted on his various nieces and nephews. "But," Judith went on, "I'll bet Mac and Joe-Joe will miss their mother when you get back to the ranger station."

Mike's expression turned glum. "Probably. We all will."

"Then," Judith said, putting her hands on her son's shoulders, "you'd better think very hard about what the rest of your life is going to be like. Not to mention the boys'. I've seldom seen the yo-yo effect on children do them much good."

Mike looked puzzled. "Yo-yo?"

Judith nodded. "Pulling them back and forth. A weekend with Dad, a workweek with Mom, summers and other school breaks up for grabs. And by the way, your father and I are too old—and too busy—to be babysitters."

"That's harsh." Mike sounded resentful.

"No, it's not. Oh, I'm not talking about the occasional day or overnight," Judith explained. "I mean having to help raise them. Children are supposed to be brought up by their parents, not their grandparents. It's called *a family.*"

"It's not a family when there's conflict," Mike declared. "It's a war zone."

Judith kissed her son's cheek. "Then make peace."

Mike's mood was still gloomy when he left. Judith felt both sad and frustrated. She understood that it was impossible to read what was in another person's mind and heart, even when that person was her own child. But Mike didn't know everything about Judith. It was strange, she thought, how once having left the nest, children seemed to think that their parents had no life without them. Mike probably never thought much about what running a B&B required or considered the physical pain Judith still suffered. Mothers were always mothers to their children. *One role fits all,* Judith thought as she finished cleaning up from dinner.

She wondered what Mike would think if he knew his mother had been suspected of murdering a milkman who wasn't a milkman.

Not much, Judith realized, as long as a rump roast was on the dinner table.

Joe called that night around nine. Progress was being made on the insurance case, and the company hoped to have the lawsuit dismissed. He expected to be home late Saturday. Judith evaded his questions about what was happening at Hillside Manor. She didn't dare tell him about the police investigation, and there was no need to burden him with her distress over Mike and Kristin. He was already upset about the breakup. Judith wouldn't distract him further. Joe had to focus on the business at hand.

At eleven, she tuned into KINE-TV, watching her old acquaintance, Mavis Lean-Brodie, deliver the news. Neither she nor her new coanchor, John Shinn, mentioned the murder. It seemed to be a slow news night. A lengthy feature on the upcoming first day of summer provided some lovely photography of sunlit beaches, verdant parks, and gurgling mountain streams. The reporter, a handsome young man named Adam Blake, made it sound as if there hadn't been a moment of bad weather since the first of June. Apparently, he'd been spending too much time inside the studio.

At the broadcast's conclusion, Judith switched off the TV and tried to go to sleep. She tossed and turned for almost an hour. When she finally drifted off, she dreamed of tennis balls flying back and forth over a steel net. The balls had faces. They belonged to Mac and Joe-Joe.

A division of labor?" Renie asked in a sleepy voice when Judith suggested they split up the next morning. "Okay, I'll do the newspaper thing. You call on Anna French at Nordquist's. We can rendezvous at one o'-clock for lunch at the Crab House."

"When I woke up," Judith said into the phone, "it dawned on me that if we can't get inside the Blands' house, the next best thing is talking to the other family members. At least we know where Anna works. Let's hope she can lead us to the others."

"Right." Renie yawned. "Ah. The digital clock on

my oven just turned to ten-oh-one. I think my brain's in gear. I suddenly remembered that Garth Doyle called me last night."

"About what? SuperGerm?"

"No," Renie replied. "Garth takes a walk every day, around noon. Yesterday he saw the yellow tape around the Moonfleet house. He called me to ask if I knew about it. I feigned innocence. He asked a couple of neighbors what was going on, but all they could tell him was that the police had been there just a few minutes before he came by."

"Did you still pretend to be ignorant?" Judith inquired.

"I didn't have to try too hard," Renie admitted. "But Garth said when he saw the crime-scene tape, he tried to remember if he'd noticed anything unusual in the neighborhood the previous day. He'd taken a different route, so he hadn't passed by the Blands' house. But around the corner on the west side—the opposite of the end of the alley where you parked your car—he noticed a Dairyland truck pulled in at the curb down the block. Bear in mind that Garth is a very visual person. As far as he could tell, there was no one in the truck and the engine had been turned off."

Judith considered Renie's words. "So what you're saying is that the phony milkman was somewhere else, probably up to no good."

"That's right," Renie agreed.

"Like, for example," Judith said slowly, "being murdered."

NINE

JUDITH REMEMBERED TO fix Gertrude's lunch before leaving. Although Phyliss was on duty, it would never do to have the cleaning woman deliver a meal to Judith's mother. Indeed, Judith kept the two women as far apart as possible, as if there were a Maginot Line between the house and the toolshed. They always ended up in a shouting match over religion, with Phyliss threatening to quit and Gertrude informing her she was already fired.

Arriving at Nordquist's, Judith asked the concierge where she might find Anna French. The smiling, impeccably garbed young woman behind the desk asked if she had an appointment.

"Yes," Judith lied. "For eleven-fifteen. It's about the fall sportswear line. We have a problem."

The concierge looked alarmed. "Nordquist's can't have problems. Go right up."

The corporate offices were on the top floor; the buyers' section took up at least a third of the space. Upon meeting the receptionist, Judith expressed indignation when her name wasn't found in Anna's appointment book.

"New York won't be happy," she declared. "I'm sure Ms. French is as anxious to salvage our account as we are."

The receptionist, who was also chic and attractive, momentarily looked put-upon, but quickly resurrected her smile. "I'll show you in at once," she said, and led Judith to the designer-sportswear buyer's door.

Anna French's office was small and crowded with catalogs, fabric samples, and designer sketches. When Judith came through the door, Anna was on her hands and knees, sorting microfiber swatches. She looked up in surprise.

"Excuse me," Anna said, "who are you?"

"I'm a fraud," Judith replied. "My name's Judith Flynn. I don't want to waste your time or mine. The man who was killed at your parents' home was put in the trunk of my car. I need your help."

Frowning, Anna got up, brushing off her straight black skirt and adjusting the collar of her pale yellow silk blouse. "Is this a joke?"

"No," Judith responded. "Far from it. As you must know, the police think that the man named Frank Purvis was killed on your family's property."

Anna French sat on the edge of her desk, which was piled high with more catalogs and sketches. She didn't offer Judith a seat.

"I don't see how I could possibly help you," she declared. "That man certainly wasn't murdered by my elderly parents or my feeble aunt. How the body managed to get into your trunk seems to be your problem, not ours. In fact, why was your car parked on my parents' grounds in the first place?"

Briefly, Judith studied Anna. She was fortyish, dark, rail thin, and of medium height, with striking features so artfully enhanced that she could have been a mannequin. But unlike a dress dummy, she moved with grace and confidence.

"Wait a minute," Anna said before Judith could speak. "Are you one of the women who came by the house yesterday with some tall tale about writing a magazine article?"

Obviously, Lynette had related the cousins' visit to her sister-in-law. Judith felt trapped. "Yes," she finally confessed just before inspiration struck. "I'm FATSO."

"What?" Anna was taken aback. "You don't look very fat to me. You're tall. You can carry a few extra pounds. I can't. You'd look particularly good in Max Mara or Donna Karan or—" She clamped her lips shut. The fashion maven in Anna had momentarily taken over. "What the hell are you talking about?"

As much as Judith hated referring to her semi-celebrity, she explained about the Web site and her work as an amateur sleuth. "So you can't blame me for wanting to find out as much as I can about the circumstances of this Purvis's death. I'm implicated. I have to try to figure out what happened. And you can't blame my cousin for being intrigued by your parents' house. It's certainly an anomaly."

"Perhaps." Anna was frowning again. "But I don't know what to tell you. My parents have never been social. When Dad came back from the war, he was a wreck. Mom was always shy. They preferred their own company."

"Didn't your father have to work?" Judith asked.

Anna shook her head. "He had a disability pension from the army. We lived frugally." She glanced down at her expensive black pumps. "I guess that's why I went into fashion. I was always the worst-dressed girl in my class."

"My family didn't have any money, either," Judith confided. "I had to wear my cousin Renie's hand-me-downs. They were pretty worn out by the time I got them, because they'd been passed on to her by our cousin Sue. The only nice clothes I owned were sewn by our grandmother. But she used the same pattern for all the granddaughters, so we all dressed alike, except sometimes she'd change the fabric colors."

Anna's expression softened. "I had a weight problem when I was young. I've spent my entire adult life counting calories."

"Who hasn't?" Judith responded. "I weighed over two hundred pounds in high school."

"At least you were tall," Anna noted. "I looked like a basketball."

Relieved that a bond seemed to have been created, Judith steered the conversation back on course. "Growing up can be so difficult. I was an only child. That can be very isolating. Did your family ever have company?" It would have been impossible to feel isolated in the Grover clan. There were always visitors when she was a child—relatives, friends, neighbors. Grandma Grover had laughed about it, saying she felt as if she were running a hotel. It had only seemed natural for Judith to turn the family home into a hostelry.

"Not really," Anna replied. "A knock on the door caused anxiety with my parents. Sometimes it was the Fuller Brush man or the insurance agent making his monthly collection or somebody with a petition."

"You had no other family nearby?"

Anna shook her head. "Only Aunt Sally. She came to live with us before I was born. Dad was from Kansas. He never went back after the war." Sliding gracefully off the desk, she pointed to the piles of fabric on the floor. "Look, I'm sorry I can't help you. I'm under the gun right now. I leave next week on a buying trip to Milan."

"I'd like to explain myself to your sister-in-law," Judith said. "Where does Lynette work?"

"The phone company," Anna replied. "She's just a couple of blocks away in the Qwiver corporate headquarters. She might have gone to lunch by now."

Judith thanked Anna for her time. The words were acknowledged with a brief nod. Anna was again fingering fabrics, completely wrapped up in her work. It struck Judith as odd that Anna seemed undisturbed about a man being murdered on the grounds of her old family home.

It was ten minutes until noon when Judith reached the head offices of Qwiver. Maybe she could catch Lynette Bland before she went to lunch. The building had strict security. Judith went up to the desk in the lobby and asked after Ms. Bland.

"I don't have an appointment," she admitted. "Just tell her I'm here about the milkman."

The buxom uniformed woman behind the desk gave her a curious look, but picked up the phone. Judith's message was relayed. The response at the other end was brief.

"I'm sorry," the woman said as she hung up the phone. "Ms. Bland can't see you. She's tied up in meetings all day."

Judith thanked the woman and walked out of the building. But she lingered by one of the pillars, keeping her eyes on the entrances. Lynette was avoiding her, Judith was sure of that. A steady stream of employees exited the building as Judith's watch registered exactly noon. She found it difficult to keep track of all four double doors. The seconds and then the minutes ticked by. The exodus began to dwindle. Maybe Lynette really was in a meeting that would go past the lunch hour.

But at twelve-oh-six, Judith spotted her prey. Lynette Bland was wearing a different linen suit, white, with a mauve blouse showing at the collar of her jacket.

Lynette walked briskly past her. She was headed for the south corner. Judith forced herself to keep up, though maintaining a six-foot distance. They both made the light; Lynette continued south for another block before turning the corner by a florist's shop. Two doors down, she entered a crowded café. By the time Judith came in the door, Lynette was sitting down at a table for two where a man wearing what looked like expensive designer sunglasses was studying the menu.

"Drat!" Judith breathed. There were no vacant tables and a line had already formed. Lynette and her companion exchanged a few words, but seemed more interested in the menus than in each other.

The hostess inquired after Judith's needs. "I'm waiting for someone," she said in response. "There's no rush."

Judith wondered if the man was Luke Bland, Lynette's husband. He was the right age, late forties, with graying brown hair. Average size, Judith guessed. It was hard to tell, since he was seated. The navy sport coat, white shirt, and tie indicated he was a professional. When he put the menu aside, he picked up a thick binder from under the table and began studying it. Lynette spoke to him, but he merely shrugged. After their order was taken, she stared across the busy room with unseeing eyes. Luke—assuming it was Luke— made notations in the binder.

Judith felt she was wasting her time. She could approach the couple and explain herself, but there was no room for her to sit down. Standing up would make it awkward to apologize for the fabrication of writing a magazine article or for explaining about the body in her trunk. Judith surrendered and left the café.

Inspiration struck as she walked by the florist on the corner. If she couldn't explain, she could still apologize. She couldn't take time to have something made. A striking arrangement of yellow gladioli, bells of Ireland, and baby's breath caught her eye.

"How much?" she asked the curly-haired young woman behind the counter.

"Forty-five dollars, plus tax and delivery."

"I'll deliver it myself," Judith said, trying not to shudder at the price. "I'm taking it just down the street to Qwiver Towers."

Judith reached the phone-company lobby by twelve-thirty. The buxom security guard had been replaced by a dark-skinned youth who couldn't have been more than twenty.

"I want to take this bouquet to Lynette Bland," Judith said, offering the guard her most ingratiating smile. "It's a surprise."

The youth looked uncertain. "We can deliver it for you."

Judith shook her head. "I just saw Lynette at lunch. I want to have it on her desk when she gets back, and I haven't had time yet to write the note."

Apparently, Judith didn't look like a terrorist or an industrial spy. The young man shrugged. "You know where her office is?"

"No," Judith said. "We're social friends, not business associates."

The guard checked his directory. "She's in fiber optics, fifteen twenty-two."

"Thanks," Judith said, and hurried to catch an elevator that was about to go up.

There was no receptionist in the area and the only employee Judith saw was a woman absorbed in eating lunch at her desk in a nearby cubicle. Judith walked past several offices until she found the one with Lynette's nameplate beside the door.

Lynette's office was as spartan as her sister-in-law's was cluttered. A watercolor of the Grand Canyon hung on one wall; her framed MBA from the University was displayed on another. A single file folder sat in the middle of her desk. A couple of pens, an in- and an out-basket, a telephone, a company directory, and a day calendar were the only other items. There was plenty of room for the floral arrangement. Judith hastily scribbled on the notecard provided by the florist:

Lynette—Sorry I missed you. This is my peace offering. I have something very important to tell you. Please call me.

Judith added her name and phone number. Glancing at the day calendar, she saw that Lynette did indeed have a meeting at one, but it was to be held at another of the phone company's buildings, some six blocks away. There was no point in waiting.

She took one last look around the office. Atop a filing cabinet was a thick notebook that almost but not quite obscured the tops of a double picture frame. Carefully, Judith reached around the notebook and picked up the photos. Lynette and her companion from the café were standing on a windswept beach. They were both much younger, perhaps not yet thirty. Judith had guessed correctly. Lynette had lunched with her husband, Luke. They looked much happier in the picture than they had in the café.

The other photo was of a handsome young man in commencement regalia. He was blond and wore an engaging smile. No doubt it was their son, Alan. Judith looked more closely. There was something familiar about that face, especially the smile. She tried to picture him ten years older.

Judith knew him. Not as Alan Bland, but as Adam Blake, KINE-TV reporter.

Excuse me," said a rich masculine voice. "Are you looking for something?"

Startled, Judith almost dropped the picture frames. She turned around to face Luke Bland in the office doorway.

"I was admiring your photos," Judith replied, struggling with her composure. "Your son's on television, isn't he?"

Luke moved closer to the desk. "Yes, but he uses a different name. I'm sorry—do I know you?"

"No," Judith admitted, recovering from her surprise. "But I recognized you from the photo with Lynette."

"I'm afraid you have me at a disadvantage," Luke replied, looking bemused. "Do you work with Lynette?"

"No." Suddenly Judith remembered something Renie had told her about seizing control in a business situation. Abruptly, she sat down in Lynette's chair. Now, according to Renie, Judith was in charge. Or was it the other way around? Did the person who was standing up have the upper hand because he or she was looking down on a presumed inferior? Judith was befuddled.

"I'm the one with the body," she blurted, casting power plays aside. "I brought Lynette some flowers because my cousin and I pestered her yesterday about what had happened at your parents' house."

Putting one foot on a visitor's chair in front of the desk, Luke Bland chuckled. "I heard about that. You pretended to be writers. Well, that's understandable. You must have been shocked when you discovered what was in your trunk. That would be enough to make anyone behave a bit recklessly. No hard feelings, I'm sure."

Up close, Luke was good-looking in a worn, craggy kind of way. His manner was smooth, pleasant, and not quite sincere. Certainly his demeanor was much less austere than it had been with his own wife.

"Yes," Judith said, "I was stunned when I opened my car. I hope this whole situation hasn't been too hard on your parents."

Luke smiled softly. "We've played it down with them. With Aunt Sally, as well. At their age, it wouldn't be right to let them get upset. And really, it has nothing to do with them. It was just one of those freakish accidents."

"But the man was murdered," Judith said.

Luke shrugged. "I gather that may be so. But he was some sort of impostor, probably running from the law. That type of person is often done in by his own kind. The fact that he may have been killed near my parents' house is irrelevant. It's no different than if a pedestrian had been run over out on Moonfleet Street."

Judith didn't argue. "I'm glad your parents haven't been too affected by the tragedy," she remarked.

"A blessing," Luke replied, removing his foot from the chair and moving around the room to straighten the Grand Canyon painting. "Still, it's one more reason why they shouldn't stay in that big old house. In a way, it's a magnet for crime."

Judith figured she might as well stand up. "How is that?"

Luke's smile struck Judith as disingenuous. "Teenagers, mainly. They see a place like that and think maybe it's abandoned. They try to climb over the fence, throw rocks at the windows, party out in the alley. I've been trying to talk Mom and Dad into moving to a retirement home. They're at a point where they need assisted care."

"There must be stairs," Judith remarked, "and quite a distance from one room to another in such a big house. It must be difficult for them to get around." She put aside her own fears for the future, when her hip might not allow her to manage the four stories of Hillside Manor. "I assume they must be rather crippled at their age."

"They have their bad days," Luke allowed. "There are plenty of other problems. The gas furnace is very old and the heating bills are outrageous. They've had problems with animal life, too—raccoons chewing on the exterior and getting into the basement, squirrels entering the attic to set up housekeeping, bees making nests in the walls, even the occasional rat—and mice, of course. The grounds are a sanctuary for small creatures. Still, my parents don't want to leave."

"I take it Aunt Sally doesn't want to, either?"

"Aunt Sally doesn't know what she wants," Luke said with a hint of disparagement. "But she's certainly not fit to stay there." He stopped roaming around the office and approached the desk. "Excuse me, but I have to get Lynette's keys out of the drawer. I'm borrowing her car this afternoon. Mine's in the shop."

"Oh." Judith came around to the other side of the desk. "I mustn't keep you. In fact, I'm late for a luncheon appointment."

Luke had opened the drawer. "It was nice meeting you. By the way, I should give you one of my cards." He reached inside his jacket. "Here. If you're ever in the mood to buy or sell, give me a call. Enjoy your lunch."

As soon as Judith was in the main hallway, she looked at the card. It read:

LUKE BLAND
REAL ESTATE AND PROPERTY INVESTMENT
COMMERCIAL AND RESIDENTIAL
Our Professionals Meet All Your Needs

Judith should have guessed that Luke Bland was some kind of salesman. Knowing that, it was easy to understand why Luke wanted his parents out of the big house on Moonfleet Street. Despite its state of disrepair, the family home with its three legal lots would fetch a bundle on the real-estate market.

I was beginning to worry," Renie said as Judith was shown to their booth at the Crab House. "You're twenty minutes late."

"I've had a few encounters," Judith said, noting that Renie had thoughtfully ordered her a Scotch rocks. "But not necessarily of a beneficial kind."

"Tell me all," Renie urged.

Judith did, although it took a quarter of an hour and several sips of Scotch. When she finished, she leaned back in the booth and, for the first time, looked out at the marina next to the lakeside restaurant. The sun was shining and the water sparkled. Suddenly it looked like the first day of summer. The yachts and catamarans and smaller craft bobbed gently at their moorage while a four-man crew plied the lake. A float-plane landed close by; another took off farther north. From this vantage point, Judith could look straight ahead to the Langford neighborhood some three miles away.

"In other words," Renie said drolly, "you struck out."

Judith took umbrage. "What do you mean? I found out several things, especially about the Bland family."

Renie paused as their server arrived to take their orders. Judith hadn't had time to read the menu, so she asked for the same entrée Renie requested—Dungeness crab and melted cheddar on an English muffin, with coleslaw and fries on the side.

"What I mean," Renie explained, "is that they sound pretty normal. Old folks who don't want to give up their home, a son in real estate who'd like to make a big profit off the house, a grandson in TV news, a daughter-in-law who works for the phone company, and a daughter who's a buyer for Nordquist's. Her husband—Phil, is it?—probably holds down a perfectly normal job, too. They hardly sound like candidates for committing homicide."

Judith eyed Renie over the rim of her glass. "Come on, coz—you know that we've come across plenty of so-called normal people who've turned out to be murderers. I'll admit, on the surface, everything sounds ordinary. Even the house itself, if you accept the fact that some people are reclusive by nature and don't give a hoot about appearances. But you're the one who got me started on all this in the first place. I expect more support."

"True." Renie sighed. "I blame my overactive imagination."

"Your imagination didn't kill Frank Purvis."

"No." Renie was looking somber, the expression that Judith always called her cousin's "boardroom face." "Let's leave the Blands out of this for a minute. They're old, they're feeble, they're eccentric. But that doesn't make them killers. So who would want to murder a phony milkman?"

Judith pondered Renie's question. "What was Frank Purvis doing there in the first place? Why was he pretending to be a milkman?" She wagged a finger at Renie. "Purvis was doing the same thing I was doing. He was watching the house. I was there by chance, but he wasn't. He knew that a parcel was being delivered to the Blands. That's why he was lurking around the grounds."

Renie nodded. "That makes sense. You say Purvis arrived before the package did. He couldn't be sure when the UPS van would show up. Purvis pretends to deliver the Blands' order. Maybe he looks inside the milk box, thinking the delivery might already be there. It's not, so he has to wait. He parks the truck around the corner and down the street, where Garth Doyle spotted it. Then he hangs out around back, maybe in the alley. He must have been killed there, though the police certainly haven't verified that information."

Judith nodded slowly. A cabin cruiser was being untied from its moorage, getting ready to sail. Judith noticed that there were several "For Sale" signs along the piers. That was not uncommon. As someone had once said, the two happiest days in a boat owner's life were the day of the purchase and the day of sale. Boats were expensive to buy and expensive to maintain. Judith was glad that Joe had never had a hankering to ply the local waterways.

But the concept of luxury made her wonder what was so valuable about the package that had been delivered to the house on Moonfleet Street. Yachts weren't the only costly items that people coveted. Jewelry, art, rare coins, even postage stamps were of great value. And drugs, of course. But somehow, Judith still couldn't see the Blands involved in dealing illegal substances.

"No one notices a milkman—or a mailman or a UPS deliveryman—coming and going," Judith finally said. "Not even at the Blands'. Purvis used a good cover for whatever he was up to. Except somebody figured it out. Who?"

"I suppose," Renie ventured, "the police interviewed the other neighbors, especially the people who live in the houses across the alley. Of course they're both cut off from the Bland house by all the trees and shrubs as well as the fence."

Judith finished her drink and took a sip of ice water. "You're suggesting those neighbors might be involved?"

Renie shrugged. "It's not impossible. Maybe we should talk to them."

"The ones on the east side weren't home the other day," Judith noted. "They probably work. I really didn't pay much attention to the house on the other side of the block."

Renie was silent for a moment. "Austria," she said at last. "Why Austria? I looked up Kopfstein on a map last night. It's located in the Bavarian Alps, and it's tiny. In fact, it's not even listed in my *Webster's Geographical Dictionary.*"

"Tiny or not, somebody must live there," Judith pointed out as their orders arrived. "Did you turn up anything of interest at the newspaper morgue?"

After her first bite of crab and cheddar, Renie was looking ecstatic. "A few small items," she finally said. "Richard and Jane—her maiden name was Goss—took out their marriage license August third, 1947. They were married two weeks later in the old Langford Lutheran Church, which, I believe, was torn down and is now the site of an East Indian restaurant and a used-book store."

Judith smiled wistfully. "Think how this city has grown in just over fifty years. Back in the forties—and into the sixties—the newspapers ran all the marriage licenses, birth announcements, and even the divorce decrees. Not to mention that almost everybody could get their wedding notice—including photos—into what was called the society section."

"Engagements, too," Renie recalled, "though I didn't find one for the Blands. However, the wedding story was fairly complete. The bride wore silk trimmed with seed pearls, a fingertip veil, and so on. Her maid of honor—Lucille Almstead—had a pink dress with a sweetheart neckline. They both carried roses—white for Jane, pink for Lucille. She was the only attendant."

"That's odd," Judith commented. "What about Sally, Jane's sister? It's unusual when sisters aren't included in the wedding party, especially as attendants. Cousins we may be, but you were mine and I was yours."

"That's true," Renie said. "Jane and Sally were local girls. Maybe Sally had moved away and couldn't make it to the wedding."

"Maybe," Judith allowed, "but I still think it's strange. Who was the best man?"

"Steven Carnofsky." Renie spelled the name out loud. "He was from Wichita, Kansas. That's where Dick Bland grew up, right? Steven was probably a boyhood chum."

"That's it?" Judith inquired.

"Not quite," Renie responded, removing a piece of shredded cabbage from her sleeveless chartreuse sweater. "Remember how they used to list college degrees and current employment of the bride and groom? Jane was a secretary for the Great Northern Railroad. No college, but a secretarial school was mentioned. Dick attended the University of Kansas for a year before he went into the service. He was discharged as a first lieutenant in '46 after serving with the Seventh and Third Armies in Europe. The article said he was self-employed."

Judith frowned. "Or unemployed. According to Anna, her father was a nervous wreck after the war. Maybe he couldn't work. In fact, somebody told us— was it Mrs. Harmon?—that Dick Bland had been wounded."

"He had a disability pension," Renie reminded Judith. "I don't know how much that would've been—or still is—but they had enough money to buy the house on Moonfleet Street, apparently right after they were married."

Judith nodded. "So far, all this fits with what we've heard about the Blands. Did you check birth announcements?"

"For Anna?" Renie speared a couple of french fries. "Yes. Born in April of '58."

"So Dick's wound did, in fact, permit him to conceive a child," Judith mused. "Unless . . ." She gave Renie a meaningful look.

"Always a possibility," Renie said. "Dick doesn't sound like the most exciting man in town. Jane may have strayed."

"Jane doesn't sound too exciting, either," Judith said. Then, after finishing her coleslaw, she asked if Renie had found anything else of interest.

"No. Luke's adoption wouldn't be in the daily papers," Renie said. "But it occurred to me that it might be worthwhile to check out the neighborhood weekly newspaper. It's still around, and even if they don't have microfiche, they probably have bound volumes. Do you think it's worth the trouble?"

Judith considered. "Not really. There's no secret about the adoption."

"I was thinking of other things as well," Renie said. "For instance, don't you remember the police-beat column? It was written in a flippant but factual style. Even when they didn't mention names or addresses, you could still get an inkling of who was doing what to whom."

"I don't remember it, in fact," Judith admitted. "I guess I was too young when we moved to Heraldsgate Hill."

"It was a comprehensive paper, too," Renie said. "They covered everything in the neighborhood. When I was in fourth grade, I was on the front page for getting first prize in the city with my drawing of our chicken, Madame de Pompadour."

"I do remember that," Judith said with a smile. "You were so skinny that some of the readers thought you were a war refugee and sent food."

"I was allergic to most of it," Renie said, "which was why I was so skinny in the first place. The only thing I could eat was the two dozen Hershey bars. I polished them off in three days and got hives."

"But you still didn't gain weight," Judith said with an ironic expression. "I would have turned into a blimp. Of course I had my own set of allergies, but luckily—or not—to food. We were a pair of sickly—" She stopped suddenly, staring out the window. "Coz!" she cried, lowering her voice. "Look discreetly at the three men on the dock by that very large yacht. Do you see who I see?"

Casually, Renie turned in her seat. "Good Lord!" she whispered. "It's Glenn Morris and the Trashman. What are they doing here? And who's the other guy with them?"

Judith didn't answer right away. The trio was going aboard the yacht, which had a "For Sale" sign on its starboard side.

"I'm guessing," Judith finally replied. "The unknown person is in his forties, well dressed, and—this is a stretch—could have a sinister look. Do you suppose that could be Philip French, Anna's husband?"

"It could," Renie said slowly, "but are the three of them here for police business or boating pleasure?"

"A good question," Judith murmured as the men disappeared inside the yacht. "I think I know how to find out."

TEN

JUDITH WAS DIALING a number on her cell phone. Renie was licking mocha residue off of her upper lip.

"Hello?" Judith said with a thumbs-up sign for Renie. "Yes, I'm calling about the"—she paused, grimacing as she tried to calculate the length of the yacht that was for sale—"forty-foot yacht that's moored by the Crab House. How much is it?"

Renie didn't take her eyes off Judith even as she accepted the bill from their server.

"Three-fifty?" Judith said. "You mean . . . Yes, that's what I thought. Three-hundred and fifty thousand dollars." She gave Renie a look of incredulity. "How many previous owners? . . . Oh, just one. Good . . . Is that right? How interesting . . . Yes, I would like to look at it. If possible, I'd prefer that the owner shows me around. Mr. French would know the yacht intimately. When would be a good time? . . . He is? Can you reach him? I could be there in . . . ten minutes . . . Certainly. My cell phone number is . . ."

Renie was holding her head.

"Have another mocha," Judith advised. "We're in for the long haul."

"So Philip French owns that very expensive yacht?" Renie inquired, dumping the contents of her fourth raw sugar packet into what was left of her mocha.

"Philip French of French's Fleet," Judith replied, looking a bit smug. "It's a tugboat company. I've heard of them. Haven't you?"

"Sure," Renie replied. "My dad worked for a big tugboat company after the war."

"That's right," Judith remarked. "But it wouldn't be French's outfit. The person who answered the phone said Philip was the owner and founder."

"He must have found some money in it along the way," Renie said. "He had to come up with a bundle to buy that baby brand new."

Judith was staring out the window. "Here they come. Glenn and Trash don't look very happy. Phil, however, seems unperturbed."

"And sinister, no doubt," said Renie, resolutely not looking toward the window behind her.

"I can't really say that," Judith replied. "He's fairly tall, balding brown hair, goatee, Nordquist's finest men's casual wear. I'd opt for 'urbane.' "

"People who own big yachts have to act urbane." Renie slipped her credit card inside the leatherette folder. "You know, ascots and captain's caps and navy blazers with gold buttons."

"Right," Judith said vaguely as she watched the men move out of sight. "I hope French's Fleet calls back soon. It's almost two-thirty. I have to get home to prepare for my guests."

"Viewing the yacht is your idea," Renie responded. "If we stay here long enough, I can order seconds."

"Glenn and Trash must have been interviewing Phil," Judith surmised. "Cops can't afford yachts. You have my word on that."

The server came to collect the bill. Renie refrained from ordering another mocha. "Are you really going through the charade of being a potential buyer?" she asked. "Surely Phil French must know who you are by now."

Judith considered. "Only to toss out the bait. After I reel him in, I'll be candid," she said as her cell phone rang.

It was Phil himself who was making the call. "Yes," Judith said. "In fact, I'm already here. In the restaurant, that is. Ask for Jones. The reservation is in my cousin's name."

Renie waited for Judith to disconnect. "Is he biting?"

Judith smiled. "He said he could be here in two minutes."

"Did he recognize your name?"

"I don't think so," Judith said as their server returned with Renie's receipts. "I'm not the only Mrs. Flynn in town."

Renie's eyes twinkled with mischief. "At least one Mrs. Flynn is in Florida."

"Thank heavens," Judith murmured. "That's the worst thing about summer. Herself usually comes back to town for a few months."

"Phil should sit on my side of the booth," Renie declared. "You'll want to face him."

"Yes." Judith looked up as the hostess arrived with Philip French.

"Good afternoon," he said with a congenial smile. "Which of you is Mrs. Flynn?"

The hostess moved away. Judith raised her hand. "That would be me. Please call me Judith. This is my cousin, Serena Jones."

"Take a seat," Renie said, patting the place next to her in the booth. "Can we order something for you?"

Phil eased himself onto the upholstered banquette. "A martini would do, but it's on me. What will you two be having?"

"Drambuie, straight up," Renie said without hesitation.

"Galliano on the rocks," Judith responded.

Phil, with a subtle show of long practice, signaled for the server and relayed the drink orders. "So," he said, after the server had gone off to the bar, "you're interested in the *Moonfleet*."

Judith gave a little start. "Ah . . . yes, I am." Confused about whether Phil was referring to the yacht or the family home, she decided that silence was her best ally.

"Great ship," Phil said. "I wouldn't sell it, but we need something a bit larger. I use the *Moonfleet* for company business. Two staterooms aren't enough when you take her out with a group of potential business prospects."

The drinks arrived. Now that she knew which Moonfleet Phil was talking about, Judith decided it was time for candor. "I'm not a buyer," she confessed. "I'm trying to keep out of jail."

Apparently, Phil thought she was joking. "So are a few of my business associates. Do you want to buy the

Moonfleet to sail to some country that doesn't have an extradition treaty with the United States?"

"No," Judith replied, vigorously shaking her head. "I mean it. Those detectives you were with this afternoon think I may have killed the man who apparently died on your family property. He ended up in the trunk of my car."

Phil threw back his head and guffawed. "This," he said when he finished laughing, "is a unique approach to bartering. I'm not coming down in price, Mrs. Flynn. It's firm and it's fair."

Renie was looking irked. She was swinging her feet under the table, and accidentally kicked Judith. "Sorry," Renie apologized before she turned to Phil. "I'm just sitting here listening to an incredible conversation and wondering if I should set my hair on fire to put an end to it. Please take my cousin seriously. Or do you honestly not know about the murder of Frank Purvis?"

Philip French's olive skin turned pale; his hand shook as he put down his martini. "Frank's been murdered? You're kidding!" He reached inside his jacket, then suddenly withdrew his hand. "Damn! There's no smoking here. I could use a cigarette. And another one of these." He tapped his half-empty glass.

"Did you know Frank?" Judith asked, recovering from her surprise at Phil's reaction.

"Yes. Yes, he was interested in the *Moonfleet.*" Phil's color had returned, but he was starting to perspire. "We looked at the yacht Monday. He said he'd get back to me by the end of the week."

"It looks like you lost a potential buyer," Renie said. "Didn't the cops tell you his name just now?"

After a gulp of his drink, Phil shook his head. "They didn't mention a name." He stared at Judith. "You *are* serious. Frank's body was found in your trunk?"

"Yes. I've no idea how it got there. I mean," Judith clarified, "I don't know who put it in my car. It certainly wasn't me. The detectives seem to think otherwise, or at least haven't eliminated me from their list of suspects. Did they mention my name by any chance?"

Phil shook his head again. He still seemed dazed. "We didn't talk long. They got kind of interested in seeing the boat."

"How long had you known Frank Purvis?" Judith asked.

"Not long," Phil replied, indicating to their server that he could use another round. "I met him a couple of months ago on the golf course. It turned out he was interested in buying a yacht. I hadn't made up my mind to sell yet, so I told him to call me in a month or so. He did."

"He must have been well-heeled," Judith said, wondering why Glenn Morris had referred to Frank as a "lowlife." "How did he make his money?"

Phil finished his first martini just as the second arrived. "Investments. I guess he was one of the lucky stiffs—excuse the expression—who didn't bomb out in the market."

"Were you playing a private course?" Judith inquired.

Phil nodded. "Broadwood. I'm a member."

Judith knew that Broadwood was one of the most exclusive—and expensive—courses in the area. "Did Frank belong?"

"I don't know," Phil replied, lapping up some of the new martini. "I guess so."

"I don't suppose," Judith said, "you'd have any idea why Frank would impersonate a milkman?"

"I sure don't." Phil devoured half of the olive. "It must have been a prank."

Phil didn't look as if he believed his own words, and Judith certainly didn't. "You have no idea why Frank Purvis would have an interest in your in-laws' house?"

"Well . . ." Phil was beginning to look a trifle bleary-eyed. Maybe, Judith thought, these weren't his first drinks of the day. She guessed that the *Moonfleet* had a well-stocked bar. For three hundred and fifty grand, it should come with a bartender and a case of Hangover Helper.

"Yes?" Judith urged as Phil faltered.

"The only thing I can think of," Phil said slowly, "is that maybe he was interested in buying the house. Luke and Lynette—Anna, too—have been pressuring the old folks to move to a retirement home. Maybe Frank wanted to look around the place without being noticed. I mean, who pays any attention to a milkman?"

"Because they can't afford yachts?" Renie put in.

"No, of course not," Phil said, giving Renie an unpleasant look. "What are you—the semicomic relief?"

"I'm not 'semi' anything," Renie shot back. "And 'comic' doesn't exactly describe my present mood. Besides, only a nutcase would wear a disguise to check out a house. Frank Purvis must have been up to something other than real-estate speculation."

Judith glanced at her watch. It was after three o'-clock. "We have to go, I'm afraid. I'm sorry about the deception, but it was the only way I could think of to meet you."

"Yeah, sure, fine." Phil was more than halfway through his second martini. Grudgingly, he got out of the booth so that Renie could make her exit. "Say," he said to Judith as she stood up and slung her purse over her shoulder, "if you think you could swing it, you'd find yourself in a whole new world if you bought the *Moonfleet*."

"Like a world of debt," Renie muttered.

"We'll keep in touch," Judith said.

The cousins left Phil just as he signaled for a third hit.

What's wrong with that picture?" Judith asked as they walked to their cars. "As in how much coincidence can you accept?"

"You mean Phil knowing Frank Purvis?"

"That's just part of it," Judith declared. "Why did Glenn Morris say that Frank was a lowlife? Granted, there are some wealthy people who are sleazes, but that's usually not the way they're described. And how did Frank meet Phil? Did Frank plan it? Or was it the other way around? And why was Frank so interested in the Blands' house?"

"It *is* possible," Renie said as they reached the Jone-ses' Camry, "that he may have been checking it out as a potential real-estate project. If the place is as dilapi-dated inside as it is outside, it could be a teardown and at least three houses could be built on the property.

Didn't Phil say that Frank had made his money in investments?"

"That's what he told us," Judith replied, "but it all sounded vague to me. I think Frank was casing the joint with a plan to steal whatever was being delivered to the Blands. Surely everyone in the family knows they get only one UPS delivery a year. They may not know what it is, but it would be the kind of thing you'd talk and speculate about."

"How could the younger generation know?" Renie asked, digging into her purse for her car keys.

"Think about it, coz," Judith responded. "Luke and Anna wouldn't be any less curious than other kids. A big box arrives. Being children, they hope it's something for them. But it never is. They're disappointed. Not to mention that the family leads a very dull life. Eventually, they realize that the annual delivery is strictly for the grown-ups. But they never forget."

"That's true," Renie agreed. "The box always comes in June. Luke and Anna would be out of school. They played outside—I do remember seeing wagons and tricycles and other toys in the front yard. It was one of the few signs of life I ever noticed around the place. It's likely that they might have seen the deliveryman come to the house."

"Exactly." Judith squinted up into the bright sky. "I gather that Phil and Anna are childless. I wonder how they get along. Judging from what I saw at the café, Luke and Lynette seem to be on rather frosty terms. I couldn't help but think that if Mike and Kristin stayed married for the sake of the children, they'd end up like

Luke and Lynette—couples who are strangers to each other."

"Maybe you just caught the younger Blands on a bad day," Renie said, opening the door to her car. "Remember, there are no easy answers."

"No," Judith agreed. "Not for Mike and Kristin, not for any of us, really."

And, she thought, waving Renie off, certainly not when it came to the house on Moonfleet.

The hors d'oeuvres were prepared; the first four guests had arrived; and Mike had left a message saying that he and Uncle Al and the boys were eating out. With one ear cocked for the doorbell, Judith dialed the Broadwood Golf and Country Club's number. Having once dealt with residents of an exclusive community, she knew that protecting members' privacy was a priority. Thus she was forced to invent a ruse.

"I'm a friend of the late Frank Purvis," she lied to the smooth-voiced woman who'd answered the phone. "I've lost his address, and I want to send a sympathy card to his family. If you can't release that information, then I'll send the card to you and you can forward it. If it isn't too much trouble."

"One moment," said the voice. "I'm sorry," she said after a full minute had passed, "we have no Frank Purvis listed as a member. There must be some mistake."

"Is it possible that he lives in the gated community next to the golf course?" Judith inquired. "I know he has some connection to Broadwood."

"I'm sorry," the voice apologized again. "I checked

the residential listings as well as the membership rolls. We have no one named Purvis connected to Broadwood."

Judith thanked the receptionist and hung up. Frank had somehow finagled an invitation to play at Broadwood. Was it for the sole purpose of meeting Phil French? Was it possible that Phil was an accomplice in whatever scheme Frank had concocted?

It was Friday. Joe would be home the following day, or Sunday at the latest. Judith had to act fast. Anna French was the only Bland family member with whom she'd established any sort of rapport. And Anna was about to leave town. She'd probably be working late. Six more guests—sorority sisters from Missouri—arrived and had to be settled in before Judith was able to dial Anna's office just before six o'clock.

Anna was in. "Yes, I'm stuck here until nine at least," she informed Judith. "Can you make this quick?"

"Actually, no," Judith said. "May I buy you dinner when you get off work?"

"Dinner?" Anna sounded surprised. "I don't know . . . I'll probably just want to go home and crash. I have to be back at the store by nine tomorrow."

"This is important, Anna," Judith said. "I met your husband today. I'm worried about him. Did you know that he knew the man who was killed?"

There was an audible gasp at the other end of the line. "No! I haven't talked to Phil since breakfast. Okay, where shall we meet?"

"Where do you live?" Judith inquired. "I'd like to make this easy for you."

"We live over in Hamilton Park," Anna said, referring to the upscale neighborhood near Broadwood. "We have a condo on the lake. It would be just as easy if you met me downtown. How about Julio's? It's close to the street I take to go directly to Hamilton Park."

"Fine," Judith said. "I'm on the south slope of Heraldsgate Hill. It'll take me less than ten minutes to get there. How about nine-fifteen?"

That worked for Anna. It didn't work quite so well for Judith, since she wouldn't be at Hillside Manor to lock up at ten. But time was of the essence. And if Anna was worn out, her defenses might be down.

"You call this dinner?" Gertrude demanded, looking at the tray Judith had brought to her. "I don't recognize anything but the plate."

"I made a casserole out of the leftover chicken from the other night," Judith replied. "It has noodles and broccoli and peas in it. That's a cheese sauce for the filling."

"Cheese sauce?" Gertrude snorted. "It looks like motor oil. What kind of cheese did you use? Part of the moon? It's green."

"You're looking at the vegetables," Judith said. "You've got peanut-butter cookies, too."

"They're stale," Gertrude asserted. "When did you make them? April?"

"Monday," Judith responded. "There wouldn't be any left if Renie wasn't allergic to peanuts and Joe hadn't left town. As it is, those are the last three. Mike and the boys love them."

Gertrude fingered one of the cookies. "Too bad I can't skate anymore. I could use these for hockey pucks. By the way, do you remember when I was in the Olympics?"

Judith stared at her mother. "As in mountains? Yes, of course. Daddy had his first teaching job in the area."

"Oh. Sure he did." But Gertrude looked bewildered. "Maybe they didn't understand."

"Who?" Judith was feeling as confused as her mother.

"The movie people. I guess they thought I meant I'd been in the Olympic Games, not the Olympic Mountains. Anyways, they've got a part in the script where I won a silver medal in the 1928 Olympics in Amsterdam for the hundred-meter backstroke. I may be great, but I don't remember being that great."

"You weren't. I mean," Judith added hastily, "you didn't swim in the Olympics. You'd better tell them to take that out of the script."

"Yes." Gertrude rubbed at her wrinkled cheek. "I'll them it was the 1936 Olympics. That was in Berlin, right? Then I could say I beat the pants off of Hitler's Nazi amazons."

"Why not?" Judith had given up arguing over the accuracy of the script. Apparently, so had Gertrude. Both the writer and the agent had told them that the character of Gertrude—who might actually be called by another name in the film—was a composite of several women who had been part of the Greatest Generation. For all Judith knew, her mother could end up being Eleanor Roosevelt.

Judith left the house at nine after asking Arlene and Carl Rankers to keep an eye on the place. In their typical good-hearted manner, Arlene and Carl readily agreed to house-sit and to entertain Gertrude. Judith said she owed them—again.

Julio's was an intimate Italian restaurant with valet parking. Arriving first, Judith waited to order. Five, ten, fifteen minutes passed before a waiter came over to her corner table and asked if she was Mrs. Flynn. Judith said she was. The waiter asked if she'd please take a telephone call at the maître d's desk.

"I'll bet my friend's still stuck at work," Judith said to the waiter as he led the way to the front of the restaurant.

The maître d', who was appropriately suave, offered a cordless phone to Judith. "For privacy, *signora*," he said, pointing to an alcove near the coatroom.

"*Grazie*," Judith replied, proud of herself for remembering the word from her travels in Italy. "Anna?" she said when she reached the alcove. "It's Judith."

"I can't make it." The words were rushed and barely audible.

Judith frowned at the near wall, which was decorated with a poster of La Scala in Milan. "Did you say you can't make it? Are you still working?"

"No." There was a pause. "I'm being followed."

"*What?* Where are you?"

There was no reply. The phone went dead in Judith's ear.

ELEVEN

JUDITH WAS FLUMMOXED. There was no Caller ID feature on the phone she'd been given. She hurried back to the maître d', but he was showing a couple to their table. She tried hitting *69 on the cordless phone, but the call had been blocked. Then she looked at the main console on the desk. It did have Caller ID, so she pressed the button. An Eastside number came up. That couldn't be Anna; the area code was outside the city. Judith figured that another customer had phoned the restaurant after Anna called. Going on to the next listing, she saw "Security Screen—000-000-0000." The time of the call was nine thirty-one. It was now nine thirty-six. The screened call must have come from Anna. Judith swore under her breath, then wondered if she should contact the police.

But what could she tell them? That a dark-haired five-foot-six well-dressed woman in her forties was somewhere downtown and thought she was being followed? That wouldn't do.

Judith had her purse with her. She had gotten her

valet parking stub out of her wallet when the maître d'
returned.

"I'm so sorry," she apologized. "There's been an
emergency and we'll have to cancel."

The maître d' nodded in understanding and was
about to say something when Judith bolted through
the front door. She handed the parking stub and a ten-
dollar bill to the young attendant on duty.

"Hurry, if you can," she said. "It's an emergency."

Judith had no idea where the MG had been parked,
but it careened around the corner and to the restaurant
entrance in less than a minute. Thanking the attendant, she jumped into the car and headed uptown to
the large underground parking garage across the street
from Nordquist's.

The garage had four floors, each marked by a different Pacific Northwest symbol—a salmon, a deer, a
spotted owl, and a wild rhododendron. It was the log-
ical place for Anna to park, since the four-story shopping plaza aboveground was connected to the store by
a sky bridge. Anna had mentioned that she wanted to
eat at Julio's because it was on the street that led directly to her Hamilton Park neighborhood. Thus, Judith figured, she'd planned to move her car to the
restaurant so she could head straight home.

But had Anna called from the parking garage by
Nordquist's or from somewhere along the six-block
route to the restaurant? Judith had no idea what kind
of car Anna drove. Going on ten o'clock, traffic was
light, but Judith still couldn't have spotted Anna's vehicle even if she'd known what it looked like. It might
be the longest day of the year, but darkness had almost

settled in over the city. Judith's only chance was to ask someone at the garage if they'd seen Ms. French drive out. She must be a regular; somebody ought to have recognized her leaving.

Judith pulled into the valet parking lane. Two attendants were chatting near the curb. The younger one, a Hispanic with a name tag that read TOMAS, hurried over to the MG.

Judith gave the young man Anna's name and a brief description.

"Sure," Tomas replied. "We all know Ms. French on this shift. She works late quite a bit. But no, we haven't seen her drive out."

"Does she valet park?" Judith asked.

Tomas shook his head. "All the Nordquist employees have a special area on the deer level. They pay by the month. But Ms. French uses the east exit," he went on, pointing to his right. "I guess that's quicker for her. She probably comes in that way, too."

Judith thanked the attendant. "She may be having car trouble. Could you notify security? Meanwhile, if you don't mind, I'll drive down to the second level to look for her."

Tomas grimaced. "We'll have to charge you the minimum."

"No problem." With effort, Judith smiled and started down the winding ramp to the deer level.

Since the garage had entrances on both sides of the block, there was some confusion about where one level ended and the other began, not to mention that each level seemed to be split into separate halves. On several occasions, Judith had had problems locating her car, and Renie had once been forced to ride around on the security guard's cart to find Cammy.

With the stores closed and only the building's movie theaters and restaurants open for business, the parking places were sparsely occupied. Judith realized she was already befuddled when she passed the bank of elevators for the spotted-owl level. She had gone too far. Feeling frustrated and panicky, she managed to get back to the second level. So far, she had seen no one— not even a security guard. The gray concrete walls, floors, ceilings, and pillars struck her as vaultlike, evoking the stone crypts under an ancient cathedral. Even the handful of parked vehicles looked as if they'd been abandoned and should have been shrouded in dust and cobwebs.

She returned to the deer level. Except that it wasn't. She saw the salmon on the door to the elevators and realized she'd somehow missed the second level entirely. Reaching the second floor again, she felt as if the entire garage was full of echoes. But it wasn't just an echo. A car was coming down the ramp behind her. In the rearview mirror, she could see a dark blue—or maybe black—sedan. The windows were tinted. She couldn't tell who was driving.

But she was sure it wasn't Anna. There would be no reason for her to be coming back down into the garage. Judith pulled into a vacant parking place. The sedan— an Infiniti, she noticed—passed by. Slowly. Too slowly. Judith tensed and waited for the car to keep going.

To her relief, it did. Judith slumped over the wheel, gathering her composure. Her quest for Anna seemed doomed. Maybe she'd already left, and the attendants hadn't noticed. It was absurd to try to find someone in a parking garage that made searching seem like looking for a needle in a haystack. Judith rubbed at her temples where a headache was incubating, and decided to go home. Assuming, of course, she could find her way out.

The thud on the passenger window wrenched a scream from Judith's throat. Anxiously, she looked up and turned to her right. A disheveled Anna French stood next to the MG.

"Let me in! Please!" she cried.

Judith reached over to unlock the passenger door. Anna virtually fell into the bucket seat. "Get us out of here! Quick!"

Judith reversed into the exit lane, driving at a speed most unsuitable for a parking garage. "What happened?" she asked Anna. "Are you okay?"

Anna, who was breathing hard, nodded. "I am now. Or will be, when we're out on the street. Thank God I saw you pull in! I couldn't believe it was really you!"

"It was. It is," Judith said as they approached the pay box near the exit. Only then did she remember that parking stubs had to be taken to the cashier inside the building. "Damn! We can't get out of here unless we run through the barrier! I don't dare do that in the MG!"

"Here," Anna said, groping in her handbag. "Use my monthly pass."

The pass worked. The automated arm swung up. Three seconds later they had exited the garage.

Anna leaned back in the bucket seat. "Oh, my God! That was horrible!"

Rattled, Judith offered to pull over into a loading zone in the next block. "What happened to you?"

"Don't stop! Keep going!"

Judith pressed down on the accelerator and automatically headed for Heraldsgate Hill. "Can you talk about it?" she inquired of Anna.

The other woman nodded. "I walked out of the store and over the sky bridge, like I always do, since our offices are on the top floor. I took the garage elevators down to the second level."

"Deer, right?" Judith asked, keeping her eye on the rearview mirror. It didn't appear as if anyone was following them, but with normal traffic moving along the same route, she couldn't be sure.

"Yes, deer," Anna said. "I'd seen a bearded man in that kind of headgear they wear in the Middle East by the elevators before I got in." She uttered a lame little laugh. "I know, it's silly, but these days you can't help but notice someone who reminds you of a terrorist. It's sad. Naturally, I didn't want to stare."

To reach the bottom of Heraldsgate Hill, Judith had to change lanes. She noticed that the third car behind her—a sedan—also made the switch. She didn't mention it to Anna. It was probably a coincidence.

"No one else got into the elevator," Anna continued. "We stopped once to let on some people who got off on the main floor where the cashier is located. By the time I got to the deer level, I glimpsed the bearded man exiting the elevator area. He must have taken one of the other cars and it hadn't had to stop. I didn't think much about it, so I started walking to my car, which is always parked at the far end. Before I got there, I heard another car start up. I kept going, but before I could get to my parking place, the car came roaring up behind me, veering into the pedestrian walkway. I ducked behind one of the pillars, thinking that whoever it was must be drunk. I waited for the car to keep going, but it suddenly stopped and reversed. It was slowing down. I ran around the other side of the aisle and headed for the elevators." Anna paused and sat up straight. "I was scared. I hadn't seen a security guard anywhere. There's an emergency phone by the elevators, but when I picked it up and pressed the button, nobody answered. I looked out into the lot and the car had stopped again. I pushed one of the elevator buttons, and luckily, the doors opened right away. I got in and poked the first button I could hit. Unfortunately, it was for the third level. I didn't know what to do. That's when I called the restaurant. Then I tried 911, but the battery had gone out on my phone, probably just as I hung up from talking to you. Oh, God, it was awful!"

Judith had turned onto the street that led up to Heraldsgate Hill. The sedan was still behind her, keeping its distance. But she still didn't mention the possible tail to Anna.

Instead, she interrupted Anna with a question. "There's a fire station at the top of Heraldsgate Hill. Shall we go there to report what happened?"

Anna emphatically shook her head. "No. Not now. I just want to get home. I'll call from there. In fact, I'll call Phil right now. Do you have a cell?"

"It's in my purse," Judith replied. "Dig down as far as you can. It's always at the bottom."

"After that, it was cat and mouse," Anna said, delving into Judith's handbag. "I wasn't thinking properly. I felt dizzy and confused. I should have gone up to the main floor, but all I could think of was reaching my car and getting the hell out of there. I was still ducking and running when I spotted you. I didn't recognize your car, of course, but I could see you in the driver's seat. I couldn't believe you'd come to rescue me. It seemed like a miracle."

"It seemed like the thing to do," Judith replied. "Was the car a dark sedan with tinted windows?"

Anna nodded. "I'm not even sure if the driver was the man with the beard. Whoever it was started to open the car door just as I got into the elevator, but I didn't wait to see who got out. I was too terrified."

"Naturally," said Judith, though her attention was distracted by the sedan that wasn't going away. She couldn't take a chance on whether the driver was an innocent or a villain. The hill was honeycombed with dead ends and winding streets that would eventually lead her in the direction of Anna's Hamilton Park address. Thus she avoided Heraldsgate Avenue, heading instead for the main street on the east side of the hill. Anna seemed too caught up in figuring out how to use Judith's phone to notice the strange route.

"I'm so muddled I can't remember my own phone number," she exclaimed in frustration. "I'll call Phil on his cell. He always leaves it on in case of a business emergency."

Fillmore Street was wide, a good place to pick up speed. Halfway up, Judith shifted down, gunned the engine, and without signaling, turned up a side street that went in two directions at the top. Instead of going straight ahead, she took a sharp turn to the right. If the sedan had followed her, the uphill climb was so short and so steep that the driver couldn't see where she'd gone. On the flat, she took a left, racing up another hill for two blocks, then taking a right. Changing gears on the level ground, she zipped along the residential thoroughfare until she had to stop at an arterial. To her relief, no one was behind her.

Anna had gotten in touch with her husband. "I can't explain right now," she told Phil, "but I'm on my way home. A . . . friend is driving me. And no, I didn't wreck the car. I'll tell you everything when I see you."

Judith had reached the six-way stop that led onto the bridge. "Is he upset?" she asked.

"Worried," Anna replied, returning the cell phone to Judith's purse. "He probably thinks I had a crisis at work." She took a deep breath. "That was some piece of driving! Do you always go so fast in this MG?"

"Never," Judith admitted. "It belongs to my husband. I'm scared to death to drive it at all, but we've been followed since leaving the garage. I lost whoever it was on the side of the hill."

"No!" Anna swiveled around, looking out the rear window. "All I see now is a Jeep. I should have guessed."

Judith took her turn at the arterial. "I know how to get to Hamilton Park. Once we're there, you can tell me how to find your condo. Don't forget to call the police right away. Morris and Trash—the detectives handling the case—probably won't be on duty. But the homicide squad will want to know what hap-

pened so they can pass it on to the investigating officers. I'm going to call, too, after I get back to Hillside
Manor."

"Hillside Manor?" Anna looked at Judith. "Oh—
that's right. You run a B&B. I know that from your
FATSO Web site."

"Yes," Judith replied. "It's questionable advertising
for an innkeeper."

"Some people say any advertising is good advertising," Anna remarked. She shivered. "But a Nordquist
buyer being chased by a lunatic wouldn't be good for
the store's image. We're all about *nice*."

"Have you any idea who it could have been?" Judith
asked as they took the turn onto the bridge.

"Of course not." Anna sounded offended at the idea.
"The fashion industry's cutthroat, but nobody tries to
whack a competitor."

"That's not a very likely theory," Judith replied. "In
fact, when you think about it, your bearded man with
a elaborate headgear presents other possibilities."

Anna seemed puzzled. "Like what?"

"What else was he wearing?"

"Oh—you know, those baggy pajamalike pants and
some sort of loose top. Typical attire for that culture."

"How tall?"

Anna grimaced. "I tried not to stare. Average, I
think. Or maybe a little taller than that. What's your
point?"

"My point is that your description could be a disguise," Judith replied, exiting at the far end of the
bridge to head for Hamilton Park. "Your pursuer

could have been an ordinary—if terrifying—American man. Or a woman."

"Good grief!" Anna put both hands over her mouth as she stared out through the windscreen.

"Think about it," Judith said. "Those loose-fitting clothes, the beard, the headgear—they could cover up just about any kind of person. The question is why would anyone try to harm you?"

"I've no idea," Anna said in a breathless voice. "I don't know anything, I haven't done anything—I'm the original innocent bystander."

Judith's expression was ironic. "So am I. But the cops may not agree with me."

"This is all so strange," Anna declared as they passed by the University's medical center. "I can't figure out any of it. What could it possibly have to do with anyone in our family?"

"I have to ask what may be a very important—if prying—question," Judith said, recrossing the canal and turning toward the arboretum. "Have you any idea what's in the UPS box that comes once a year to your parents' house?"

Startled, Anna turned to look at her. "No, I honestly don't. How did you find out about that?"

"I'm FATSO, remember," Judith replied with a quirky little smile. "The delivery was made the same day that Frank Purvis was killed. I know, because I was there. I've already explained that part to you."

"I have to admit," Anna said, "that it seems odd you showed up on that very day."

"Curiosity and coincidence," Judith said, not wanting to discuss the many situations that she'd encountered by chance. "As you should know from my Web site, I have a knack for finding trouble," she added as they wound their way through the verdant arboretum. A half-moon rose high above the tall hemlock, yew, and cedar trees. "Well? What do you know about the annual delivery?"

"I'd almost forgotten about it," Anna murmured, "not having lived at home for so long. It's the third week of June. That's when the box always arrived. The only thing I remember is that my mother said it came from Uncle Franz."

"Uncle Franz in Austria?" Judith inquired.

"Yes." Anna looked surprised. "He lives in a small town near the German border."

"Kopfstein," Judith said, but spoke again before Anna could interrupt. "Have you ever met Uncle Franz?"

"No," Anna replied. "He must be quite old by now."

"An uncle or great-uncle?"

Anna hesitated. "I'm not sure. I've never known a great deal about our relatives. None of them live around here. Except for Aunt Sally, of course."

They had reached the main street that led to Hamilton Park. "Take a left?" Judith inquired.

"Yes, all the way to the lake," Anna replied. "Go right at the boulevard."

Judith glanced to her left. "Broadwood Golf and Country," she noted, "and Broadwood itself. The woman who answered at the country club had never heard of Frank Purvis."

"Why should she?" Anna inquired.

"Because that's where your husband met Frank," Judith said. "That's why I wanted to talk to you tonight. Did Phil ever mention Frank to you?"

"I don't think so," Anna replied. "Phil meets so many people in his business. Frankly, I don't pay much attention. They come, they go."

"Frank went," Judith remarked, "permanently."

"That can't have anything to do with Phil," Anna said, sounding defensive.

"The police might think differently," Judith responded. "They questioned Phil today. I saw them with him at the marina."

"Good Lord," Anna gasped, "you seem to be everywhere."

"Another coincidence," Judith said, turning right onto the boulevard. "My cousin and I like crab. Where to now?"

"Take the next left," Anna directed. "There's a gate to the condo building. Can you poke the keypad buttons to open it?"

"Sure," Judith said, rolling down the window as they stopped by a brick pillar. "Do you trust me to know the code?"

Anna laughed softly. "It seems I've trusted you with my life." She ticked off the numbers to Judith.

"Have the police talked to you yet?" Judith asked, working the keypad.

After a moment's pause, the gate slowly swung open. "No," Anna replied. "Do you think they will?"

"Yes," Judith said, "to cover all the bases. By the way, did you happen to see the license plate on the sedan that was chasing you?"

Anna shook her head. "I was too panicked."

"And I couldn't see it after we got out of the garage because the car was always too far back," Judith said. "When do you leave for Milan?"

"Wednesday," Anna replied, opening the passenger door. "Hey, I can't thank you enough. You may have saved my life. It's only beginning to sink in now. What can I do to repay you?"

"How about a deep discount on Max Mara?"

Anna smiled. "You've got it. We'll be in touch."

You're right about that, Judith thought. But all she said was, "Give my regards to Phil."

Joe had phoned while Judith was out. He'd left a message saying that they'd hit a snag. He wasn't sure when he'd be able to come home. "I hope everything's all right at your end," his recorded voice had said with a touch of anxiety. "It isn't like you to be gone this late when you've got guests. Call me when you get a chance."

Joe had called at a little after eleven, Omaha time. It was now one in the morning in the Midwest. But she didn't want him worrying about her. After several minutes of arguing with herself, she dialed his hotel's number. When she was connected to his room, he answered in a sleep-fogged voice.

"I'm so sorry," she apologized. "I'm fine. I must have turned off the phone by mistake. Go back to sleep."

"Unhh," Joe said, and clicked off.

Judith reasoned the fib was for a very good cause. She was exhausted. Suddenly it occurred to her that

Arlene or Carl should have answered the phone. They'd arrived at the B&B a few minutes before Judith left at nine. She looked out through the kitchen window. The Rankerses' lights were still on. They were early-to-bed, early-to-rise. She'd assumed that once the guests had all returned, the Rankerses would go home. Judith dialed their number, but got their answering machine.

There was another possibility. The lights had been on in the toolshed when Judith had put the MG in the garage and entered the house through the back door. Gertrude always stayed up to watch the eleven o'clock news, so there'd been no cause for concern.

Judith went back outside and knocked once on the toolshed door.

"Come in," Arlene called in her cheerful voice.

Gertrude, Carl, and Arlene were playing three-handed pinochle.

"As usual," Arlene said with a merry laugh, "your mother is taking us to the cleaners. Carl and I've lost two dollars between us."

Gertrude chortled. A green visor sat atop her white hair and she puffed on a cigarette. All that she needed to complete the picture were garters on her housecoat sleeves. "These two are real suckers," the old lady asserted. "I've won four out of five games, and put both of them way down in the hole twice."

"Amazing," Carl murmured. "Mrs. G, you've got one of the best heads for playing cards that I ever ran into. You ought to join my poker club."

"They're all men, Carl," Arlene snapped. "And I

don't think our sweet darling here likes beer that much. She certainly wouldn't enjoy the belching contests."

"I just might," Gertrude put in. "I can belch with the best of 'em. And I can touch my nose with my tongue. When I take out my dentures, that is. Want to see?"

"No!" Judith cried. "Please, Mother, don't be crude."

Arlene patted Gertrude's arm. "This dear lady couldn't be crude if she tried."

"Damned tootin'," Gertrude replied. "Which reminds me——"

"Mother, stop it!" After glaring at Gertrude, Judith looked at Arlene. "Did everything go smoothly at the B&B?"

Arlene nodded. "Beautifully. Everyone was tucked in before ten o'clock. Except for the man with the heart attack, of course."

Judith blanched. "What man? What heart attack?"

Arlene was studying her cards. "His name is . . ." She looked at Carl. "Griffin? Griffith? Gervin?"

Carl shrugged. "Something like that."

"Greenwalt," Judith said, feeling panicky as she recalled the names on the guest registry. "George and Lucy Greenwalt, from Nashville. Is he okay?"

Arlene shrugged. "The doctors will know more by morning, after he has some tests."

"He's in the hospital?"

Carl nodded. "Norway General. Mrs. . . . Greenwalt is spending the night with him there."

"Did he have the heart attack *here*?" Judith asked.

"Yes," Arlene replied. "In the entrance hall. He

and his wife came in just a few minutes after you left." She looked at Carl. "Who dealt?"

"Mrs. G," he replied. "I'm in. The bid's up to you."

"Please," Judith implored, "what happened to Mr. Greenwalt?"

"What?" Arlene turned to glance at Judith. "Oh. We were chatting by the elephant umbrella stand when Sweetums leaped off the banister and landed on Mr. Greenwalt's head. The poor man collapsed. Just like that." Arlene snapped her fingers. "I *think* Mrs. Greenwalt said her husband had a phobia about cats. When he was very young, he was chased by someone wearing a Sylvester the Puttycat costume at a Halloween party."

"Hey," Gertrude interrupted, "are we going to talk or play cards?"

Arlene patted the old lady's arm. "Just give me a teensy minute, sweetheart. Your daughter seems impatient."

Gertrude scowled through her visor. "What else is new? She knows I don't like to mix cards with a lot of blah-blah. She's just trying to get my goat."

"Anyway," Arlene went on, with an apologetic expression for Gertrude, "Carl called 911. Naturally, they came right away."

They would, Judith thought. All the emergency personnel knew the way to Hillside Manor. She sat down on the arm of the sofa. "Good Lord! I hope he recovers quickly." Visions of lawsuits danced through her head.

"The EMTs didn't seem to think it was too serious," Carl said, then nudged his wife. "Are you going to bid or what?"

"Two hundred," Arlene said.

"Two-ten," Gertrude responded.

"Pass," said Carl.

"Hold it," Judith interrupted. "Nothing else happened that I should know about?"

"Nothing important," Arlene replied, concentrating on her cards.

"Oh, go ahead and tell her," Gertrude rasped. "Otherwise, she won't go away and we'll never finish this game."

Arlene turned to Judith. "They arrested Sweetums."

Judith almost fell off the sofa. *"What?"*

Carl made a face at Arlene before he spoke. "They didn't actually arrest him. They took him to a vet to see if he's rabid. If he isn't, you can pick him up in the morning."

"Two-twenty," Arlene said.

"Two-thirty," Gertrude shot back.

Since Carl had already passed, Judith stood up and leaned over to speak into his ear. "Which veterinarian?"

"I don't know the vet's name," Carl said softly, "but it's the Cat Clinique. You know, over in the Langford district."

"Thanks," Judith replied, giving Carl's shoulder a squeeze. "Thanks for everything."

"Sure." He looked up. "Who got the bid?"

"I did," Gertrude retorted. "For two-eighty." She sorted her cards, discarded three, and laid down fifteen-hundred trump in clubs. "I'm out again. Pony up those quarters."

Judith left quietly, following the concrete walk to the house. But the path that loomed in her mind led to Sweetums and the veterinarian in Langford. Fate was pushing her in that direction, and Judith wondered if she'd eventually find a killer at the end of the journey.

TWELVE

WHEN JUDITH FINALLY had time to look at the morning newspaper, she turned first to the obituary section. There still wasn't a death notice for Frank Purvis. But, as had become her habit in recent years, she scanned the rest of the obits. Judith was at an age where occasionally she'd find one of her peers, often an old school chum. More numerous were the parents of the youngsters she'd grown up with or met later in life. Occasionally it was a guest who'd stayed at Hillside Manor, a fellow SOT—as our Lady, Star of the Sea parishioners called themselves—or some other resident of Heraldsgate Hill. It didn't strike Judith as morbid. Rather, it was her interest in people and sense of community that compelled her to find out who had passed on. The city had grown a great deal since she was a child, but making a connection, even to the dead, enforced the idea that she didn't live in a faceless metropolis.

One surname tweaked her memory: Pettibone, Alfred Earl. She had gone to school with an Albert Pettibone, who was listed as a surviving brother.

One of four children, Alfred was several years younger than his brother. Judith vaguely recalled an Alexis Pettibone, one of two sisters mentioned. Alexis had been a couple of years behind her in school. She was only a blurred memory, but Judith did recall Bert, as he was known—a bright, skinny student with curly brown hair and a shy manner. Alfred, a longtime federal government employee, had also left behind a wife, Andrea, and two sons. Remembrances were to be made to the local humane society.

Just as Judith was about to call Renie, Mrs. Greenwalt phoned from Norway Hospital. George was doing well, Lucy Greenwalt reported, but he'd have to stay until Sunday. She, however, would return to Hillside Manor, since they'd booked their room for two nights.

"You will," Lucy said in a soft but firm manner, "have that horrid animal put to sleep. He could have killed my husband."

Judith winced. "I'm taking care of the matter this morning," she said. Maybe the vet could keep Sweetums at the clinic until the Greenwalts were gone. At least Lucy Greenwalt hadn't mentioned a lawsuit. Yet.

Having planned to collect Sweetums as soon as the other guests were out and about, Judith called the Cat Clinique.

"Your pet isn't rabid," the woman at the other end said, "but he should be enrolled in an anger management program. There are three different groupings— Ill-Natured, Bad-Tempered, and Incorrigible. Your pet would be put in the third group. You'd be amazed. He could emerge with a Happy Cat Award."

"I'll think about that," Judith said.

"You really should. Soon. How soon can you collect him?"

"Well—I was wondering if you could keep him overnight," Judith said.

"Are you kidding?" the woman retorted. "He already bit Dr. Pettibone twice."

"Dr. Pettibone?" Judith echoed. "What's his first name?"

"Albert," the woman replied. "He was on emergency call here last night when your animal was brought in. Believe me, he has enough troubles already. His brother's funeral is Monday."

"Oh!" Judith couldn't keep the surprise out of her voice. "I went to school with Bert. I saw his brother's obituary in this morning's paper. I'm so sorry. He was only in his late forties. Was it sudden? The notice didn't mention cause of death."

"Fred Pettibone died very suddenly," the woman replied. "I have two other calls on hold. Please come get your cat as soon as possible."

As soon as the sorority sisters had bounded out the door, Judith called Renie to bring her up to speed on the latest developments.

"A car chase?" Renie cried. "What are you trying to do? Get a part in an action movie? The next thing I know, you'll be hanging by your thumbs from a thirty-story window somewhere."

"It *could* have been a coincidence," Judith said lamely. "It may not have been the same car that tried to run down Anna in the garage."

"Ha! You should be so lucky!" Renie paused. "Well, you *were* lucky—to escape unscathed."

"So," Judith went on after having finished filling Renie in, "would you mind taking Sweetums just until tomorrow?"

"Are you nuts?" Renie shot back. "What would he do to Clarence?"

"Sweetums could stay outside," Judith suggested.

"Outside our immediate neighborhood," Renie retorted. "Really, coz, I couldn't take that chance. If anything happened to our darling bunny . . . well, I can't even think about it. Try Arlene and Carl. They haven't had any pets since their dog Farky met an untimely—and mysterious—end."

"Farky was a bit of a pest," Judith allowed. "But I couldn't ask them. They've already had to bail me out this weekend. And don't suggest the Dooleys. They have such a menagerie of kids and pets of their own that they'd probably let Sweetums out by accident and he'd be right back here. In fact, that could happen with any of the neighbors in the cul-de-sac. Sweetums is very sneaky."

"Hey," Renie said, her voice brightening, "what about Uncle Al? Mike and the kids are going to be there one more night. I'll bet they'd like to have Sweetums around."

"Brilliant," Judith enthused. "I'll call them right now before they take off on their round of playtime pleasure."

It was Mike who answered. After getting Uncle Al's approval, he told his mother she'd better hurry. They were leaving before noon to go to a farm that had pony rides and a petting zoo.

Judith left the B&B a few minutes after eleven. The feline veterinarian clinic was located only a few blocks away from Uncle Al's. The woman behind the desk, whose nameplate identified her as Alma Burke, eyed Judith suspiciously.

"You wouldn't happen to be Mrs. Flynn, would you?" she asked.

"Yes," Judith replied. "I've come to collect my cat."

"Good," Alma said. "I'll go get him."

Judith remained by the desk, discreetly observing the people in the waiting room. An older woman stroked a long-haired calico; a teenage girl had a black kitten in a carrier; a young woman in workout attire held a sleek Siamese. Judith wondered if Bert Pettibone was still on duty.

Alma returned carrying a cardboard box that had holes punched in it. "Here he is," she said, shoving the box at Judith. "That'll be one hundred and forty dollars. Cash, check, or credit card?"

Startled by the large sum, Judith stammered her reply: "C-c-credit c-c-card." She leaned her head closer to the box. "I can't hear Sweetums. Are you sure he's okay?"

"Define 'okay,' " Alma shot back. "Yes, he's just fine."

Judith was skeptical. She put the box down on the floor and began to open it.

"Don't!" Alma shouted. "Wait until you get outside!"

"Hey," Judith said, anger replacing astonishment, "I want to make sure before I fork out a hundred and forty bucks."

The first thing she saw was Sweetums's yellow eyes, glaring like traffic warnings. Then she saw the muzzle on the lower part of his face and the restraints on his legs.

"My God!" she shouted. "My cat looks like Hannibal Lecter! What have you done to him?"

"Precautions," Alma responded. "Let's see that credit card."

Judith fumbled in her wallet, finally producing the card. "I'm paying this under protest," she announced. "Sweetums better be in perfect condition when I get him home."

"Perfectly horrific." Alma sneered as she scanned Judith's card. "Really, even though he's not a young cat, you should train him. Indeed, if there's an elderly person in your family, you ought to let him or her help. It's a fact that dogs and cats and older people bond very quickly, and the animal often takes on the characteristics of its owner."

Judith narrowed her eyes at Alma. "That," she asserted, "is why Sweetums is Sweetums."

Mac and Joe-Joe were delighted to see Sweetums, whose restraints had been removed as soon as Judith arrived at Uncle Al's. She'd hated to keep him fettered, but was afraid he might go on a rampage in the MG and do some serious damage to the leather upholstery.

The boys wanted to take Sweetums with them to the farm, but Mike said no. Judith, however, worried about leaving the animal in Uncle Al's house.

"Stop fussing," Uncle Al said. "We made a litter box. He'll be fine."

"But he might destroy your furniture," Judith protested. "He's not in a good mood after his stay with the vet."

Uncle Al, who was tall, burly, and had a perpetual twinkle in his sea blue eyes, glanced at Sweetums, who was permitting himself to be petted by the boys. "He looks happy to me. Besides, there's nothing here that can't be replaced. I'll bet you ten bucks he doesn't do any damage."

Judith smiled sheepishly at her uncle. "I'd never bet against you. You're too lucky."

Uncle Al shrugged. "I suppose I could ask Tess to come over and stay with him," he said, referring to his longtime lady friend, who had money as well as looks and lived in an elegant condo only a few blocks away.

"I wouldn't want you to bother her," Judith said. "Besides, as I recall, she's not a cat person."

"She doesn't hate cats," Al said. "She just doesn't want to be bothered with pets. You run along now. We'll work it out."

Judith kissed the boys, hugged her son and her uncle, and headed off in the MG. Five blocks away, she reached the intersection where she could turn right for Heraldsgate Hill—or keep going straight to Moonfleet Street. But, she asked herself, waiting for the light to change, what would be the point of driving by the Blands' house? None, really. She put on her turn signal to take the usual route home.

Only then did she realize that vehicles were backing up on the cross street. The light turned green. Judith followed the two cars ahead of her and looked to her left. Six blocks down, at a five-way traffic signal, she saw flashing red and green lights. Apparently, there had been an accident, not uncommon at such a major intersection.

Judith went straight ahead to avoid the tie-up. She turned onto the main artery through Langford, going less than a block before she had to stop at the next traffic light. As she waited, she admired the floral display in front of the grocery store on her left. There was a special on gladioli, nine stems for ten dollars. The glads in Judith's garden wouldn't bloom for another month. She had the perfect vase for them—tall, curving slightly, with a glazed green finish—which she always put in the entry hall near the guest registry. When the light changed, Judith moved up a space and turned into the parking lot.

It took her a few minutes to decide on the colors. Finally, she decided on a combination of yellow, purple, and chartreuse. Upon entering the store, she noticed three cardboard boxes filled with groceries. One box was marked GONZALES; another read JOHNSTON; the third was inscribed with BLAND.

Judith hurried into the express lane. Impatiently, she waited for the man ahead of her to pay for his six-pack of beer and bag of potato chips. As soon as he left, Judith accosted the frizzy-haired blond checker whose name tag identified her as Jaimie.

"Is that box by the door being picked up by the Blands?" Judith inquired.

Jaimie glanced toward the entrance. "It should be. Why? Are you the designated driver this week?"

"Yes," Judith replied glibly. "Anna couldn't make it."

"Anna?" Jaimie's high forehead wrinkled. "Is that the one who looks like she stepped out of *Vogue*?"

"Right," Judith agreed. "Is everything there?"

"Let me find out," Jaimie replied before calling over to the clerk at the next checkout stand. "Is the Bland order ready to go?"

The clerk, a young man with close-cropped hair, studied what appeared to be a list next to the register. "No. They need a pound of hamburger, a cut-up fryer, and a turkey breast."

"I'll take that order to them," Judith volunteered, aware that at least two people were in line behind her. "Go ahead, Jaimie, I'll pay for my flowers now."

"One of the courtesy clerks will bring the meat order," Jaimie said, ringing up the glads. "You're not one of the regulars, are you? Do you have the address?"

"Yes, on Moonfleet, right?"

Jaimie nodded as she accepted Judith's money. "Personally," she said with a puckish grin, "I like it when the young guy comes in. He's on the TV news, you know."

"Yes, that would be Adam Blake, as he calls himself," Judith said.

"His first name is really Alan. He changed his name for television," Jaimie went on. "He's the Bland grandson. But there's nothing bland about his looks." She smiled some more. "He wasn't on last night. Mavis Lean-Brodie mentioned that he'd been sent on a special assignment. Frankly, he's the only reason I watch KINE-TV instead of KINK or one of the other channels. Thanks. Enjoy your flowers."

The courtesy clerk had put the late additions into the carton and picked it up. "Your trunk?" he asked as they went out into the parking lot.

Judith winced. Even though it was the Subaru's trunk that had held Frank Purvis's dead body, she wasn't keen on any semblance of a reenactment. "You can put it in the bucket seat next to me," she said.

"Will do."

It took Judith less than five minutes to reach the Blands' house. The yellow tape was gone. That didn't surprise her. The murder was now four days old. Morris and Trash's crime-scene experts should have finished collecting evidence from the Bland property by now.

Since it was Saturday, on-street parking was hard to find. Judith went around the block twice without spotting an open space. She couldn't carry the heavy box of groceries very far. In addition to the meats, there was a loaf of bread, a head of lettuce, three bottles of wine, and several cans of soup, vegetables, and fruit. Judith had no choice but to pull into the rutted alley and park near the back door.

Her next problem was getting through the overgrown shrubbery while carrying the box. She stumbled over roots and deadwood, got scratched by blackberry vines, and narrowly avoided being poked in the eye by a forsythia branch. Out of breath, she proceeded through the tall grass, weeds, ferns, and rocks.

Still panting, she set the box down on the small moss-covered stone porch that rose only a few inches from the ground. The door was arched and made of solid wood with a tile surround, two wrought-iron hinges, and a handle to match. Judith wound up like a pitcher and pounded the door as hard as she could.

Looking at her watch, she decided to wait at least a

full minute for someone to respond. Sixty-eight seconds later a curious Alan Bland stood in the small entryway.

"Excuse me?" he said.

Judith pointed to the groceries near her feet. "I'm Judith Flynn. I didn't think Anna would be able to collect the order, so I thought I'd drop it off for her."

Alan's handsome face grew puzzled. "It wasn't Anna's turn. It was mine. I was going to the grocery store in just a few minutes. Who are you?"

"It's a long story," Judith said with a sigh. "May I come in for a moment? I had a hard time cutting through from the alley. There was no place to park out front."

"Everybody in this neighborhood seems to have two cars," Alan remarked, still eyeing Judith with curiosity. "Did you say you're a friend of Aunt Anna's?"

Judith avoided a direct answer. "I took her home from work last night. Have you spoken with her today?"

Alan shook his head and stepped aside. "Come in. I'll get the groceries. Is Aunt Anna okay?"

"Yes, she's fine," Judith said, going into the kitchen. One glance made her feel as if she'd moved back in time. Even though the sun was coming through the single window with its colored panes, the room seemed dark. The green gas range looked as if it had been installed in the twenties; so did the matching refrigerator. The tiles on the counter and the walls were faded and chipped. The old-fashioned sink and the tiled floor also showed considerable wear and tear. There was no dishwasher, no microwave, no garbage disposal. Only the wooden table and chairs looked as if they'd come from a later era by about twenty-five years. Even the quartet of metal canisters on a wooden shelf appeared to be at least a half century old. The musty air and the tomblike silence in the rest of the house gave Judith a chill.

Alan noticed. "Are you all right? Your arms are bleeding. Can I get you some Band-Aids or antiseptic?"

"A towel will do," Judith replied. "They're only scratches."

Alan pulled out a drawer that seemed to stick just a bit and handed Judith a dish towel thin enough that she could see through it. She had to be careful walking across the floor. The tiles were so grooved and cracked that they upset her balance. At the sink, she turned on the warm water tap. It sputtered a bit, then released the water in fits and starts.

"I know what you're thinking," Alan said with a wry chuckle as he stashed groceries in the ancient fridge. "You're wondering why my grandparents haven't done some renovating. The truth is, they don't have the money and they don't care."

"Really." Judith dabbed at her scratches. "So even though your folks and your aunt and uncle—and you—are doing quite well, your grandparents don't want to be bothered?"

"You got it," Alan replied. "Too much hassle, they say. Workmen all over the house, lots of noise, confusion, being inconvenienced—the whole gig. But hey— as long as they don't care, it's their home after all."

"It's such a beautiful house," Judith said. "That is, it could be a real showplace if it were fixed up."

"That's what my dad says," Alan responded. "He

keeps trying to talk them into moving to a retirement place. But they refuse to budge."

"Aunt Sally concurs, I assume," said Judith.

Alan looked amused. "Aunt Sally—well, she goes along with whatever my grandparents want."

"Aunt Sally is your grandmother's sister, right?"

Alan nodded. "In her younger years, she was quite the adventurer," he replied, taking the towel from Judith. "For her time, of course. She was a photographer. She even had some of her photos published in *National Geographic*."

"She must have traveled widely," Judith remarked.

"She did," Alan replied, placing the worn towel on the counter. "Africa, Asia, Europe, South America— somehow she never got to Australia or New Zealand. That's one of the reasons I went into TV. I want to work my way up to reporting from the field. See the world and be where the action is."

"I understand you're on special assignment right now," Judith said. "I assume—since you're here—you don't have to travel for this job."

Alan looked away. "No. But sometimes I do. I've been to L.A. and San Francisco and Vancouver, B.C."

"What are you investigating?" Judith asked.

Alan hesitated, then looked again at Judith. "I'm sorry, I can't talk about it. At this stage, it's confidential."

"Oh." Judith was edging toward the door that led out of the kitchen. "I understand. My husband's been a private detective since he retired from the police force. Once in a while he gets a case he can't discuss. In fact, he's working on one right now. All I know is that it's some insurance scam. At least that's what the carrier is trying to prove."

Alan's keen blue eyes were regarding Judith with apprehension. "Were you thinking of going out the front way?"

She was standing on the threshold, which led to the dining room. The drapes were pulled. All she could glimpse was a table and a couple of chairs.

"No," she replied. "I was wondering if the rest of the house was furnished in Spanish-style furniture."

Alan laughed. "It's furnished with whatever my grandparents could get at secondhand stores. It's just plain old-fashioned furniture. I think some of it came with the house. The previous owner didn't want it, I guess."

"It's so dark," Judith noted. "Why don't they open the drapes on such a nice day?"

"My grandmother has very weak eyes," Alan replied. "So does Aunt Sally. It runs in the family. I hope I don't inherit it when I get older."

Desperately, Judith was trying to figure out an excuse for seeing more of the house and at least one of its inhabitants. "You know," she said in a wistful voice, "I've never met your grandparents. I understand they're very private people. But as long as I'm delivering their groceries, I thought it might be polite to introduce myself."

Alan looked regretful. "They're resting right now. They always take a little siesta after lunch."

"Oh. Aunt Sally is resting, too?"

"Aunt Sally is always resting," Alan replied in an ironic tone. "She's very frail."

"How old are they?" Judith inquired. "My own mother is quite elderly. She doesn't take regular naps, but she does tend to doze off now and then."

Alan tapped his cheek, apparently calculating ages. "Grandpa is in his eighties. Grandma is up in her seventies. Aunt Sally is a few years younger."

Compared to Gertrude, the trio was still fairly young. But, Judith realized, her own mother couldn't be compared to other human beings. "I understand your grandfather never really recovered from his war experiences," she said. "My Uncle Corky never has either. He was in the army, serving in Europe. At least once a week, he still feels a need to shoot at crows and seagulls and an occasional piece of garden statuary. Twice, he's used his pickup to take out a couple of utility poles. He calls his truck 'Tank.' "

Alan nodded. "Grandpa served in Europe, too, under General Patton. The carnage was horrendous."

"Really? That's who Uncle Corky served under. Patton may have had his flaws, but my uncle adored Old Blood and Guts."

"Grandpa didn't feel the same way about Patton," Alan said. "Of course, he doesn't like to talk about his war experiences. I wanted to interview him a while back for a feature on World War Two veterans, but he turned me down. I guess it stirred up too many bad—"

A phone rang somewhere nearby. Judith didn't see one in the kitchen, but before she could peek into the dining room, Alan removed his cell from his back pocket.

"Hi, Aunt Anna," he said in a bright voice. "What? . . . Oh, no, everything's fine. A friend of yours stopped by. Judith Flynn." He glanced at Judith to confirm that he'd gotten her name right. "Yes, she's here with me in the kitchen. She picked up the week's supply of groceries . . . Really?" Alan shot Judith a curious look. "I didn't know that . . . Yes, of course I will. Talk to you later."

Alan clicked off the phone. His expression had grown troubled. "Aunt Anna said to say hello." He hesitated, wincing slightly. "She told me who you really are. You're FATSO. I'm afraid you'll have to go."

THIRTEEN

IT DID NO good to try to explain it was Mavis-Lean Brodie's fault that Judith had gained such notoriety. Alan was polite but firm. The Blands were private people. They didn't want some amateur sleuth—especially someone whose car had held Frank Purvis's corpse—lurking around the family home.

Unencumbered by the heavy groceries she'd delivered, Judith managed to reach the alley without doing any more damage to herself. She settled in behind the MG's steering wheel, then suddenly thought it might be a good idea to take a look in the boot. She didn't want to cart around another body in a Flynn automobile. Judith lurched out of the car and apprehensively raised the boot's lid. Except for some of Joe's belongings, it was empty. She sighed with relief.

Driving home, she grew angry with Anna French. After rescuing the woman, Judith expected a more gracious response. Anna had acted grateful the previous night, but now she seemed to have turned her back on her savior.

And yet . . .

Judith had come away from the house on Moonfleet feeling as if she had missed something. It might have been a remark by Alan, the conversation between him and his aunt, or the house itself. Whatever it had been, she felt an immediate need to talk to Renie.

Carefully parking the MG on the steep hill in front of the Joneses' Dutch Colonial, she spotted her cousin in the front yard. Half-hidden by ornamental evergreens, Renie was wielding a broom and cussing. A fat gray squirrel fled through a patch of St. John's wort.

"Coz!" Judith called from the parking strip. "It's me."

"Yikes!" Renie cried, almost falling over a cherub statue that had been a birthday present from Judith. "You startled me! I'm obsessed with those damned squirrels since they got inside our attic and set up a condo two years ago. They've been lurking around all spring, trying to get back into the house. I don't trust them an inch. What's worse, they're smarter than I am."

"I thought Bill had screened off all the areas where they could come in," Judith said as Renie came out of the garden and down to the sidewalk.

"He did," Renie replied, keeping a wary eye on the squirrel's path of flight. "They removed the duct tape and ate two of the screens."

"They keep digging up my bulbs," Judith complained, before changing the subject. "You got a minute?"

"Sure," Renie replied. "Let's go out on the deck, where I can exercise vigilance if Squeldon the Squirrel tries to attack from the rear. Do you want something to drink?"

"Water will do," Judith said as they went inside and down the hall to the kitchen. "Where's Bill?"

"Running his usual Saturday errands," Renie responded, taking two glasses out of the cupboard. "You know—the Swedish bakery, the German deli, the Japanese market. Bill's very global."

Judith accepted a glass of ice water; Renie removed a can of Pepsi from the fridge. The cousins went out onto the deck, where they had a clear view of the mountains and the northeastern section of the city.

"So what's up?" Renie inquired, putting on her sunglasses.

In detail, Judith explained about the impromptu visit to the Blands' house and her chat with Alan. Then, with equal precision, she related Alan's conversation with his aunt.

Renie, who had listened without interruption, frowned and stared down into the big backyard. Atop the garage, which faced the street in back of the house, stood Squeldon—or one of his cohorts. Renie glared at the squirrel; the squirrel glared back.

"Beat it!" Renie yelled.

But Squeldon—or his henchman—skittered to the near end of the garage and jumped into a mountain ash tree. "Now what?" Renie muttered as the squirrel climbed down the tree and disappeared behind the tall rockery that separated the upper garden from the lower section. "What were you saying? Oh! That darkness—it does seem very strange. I mean, even if you've got weak eyes—and I do—you'd think that as you got older you'd need some natural light to help you move around."

"Blind people get used to their surroundings," Judith pointed out. "After all, the Blands have lived there for over fifty years."

"Fresh air's another matter, though," Renie noted. "Did the place feel stuffy?"

"Very," Judith replied. "As if it hadn't been aired out in fifty years."

"Hunh." Renie became pensive again. "Go over that one part again—about the elder Blands being feeble."

Judith repeated what she'd already told her cousin. "Except for Jane Bland and Aunt Sally's eye conditions, Alan didn't mention any other specific physical problems."

"Inertia," Renie said. "Lack of exercise and fresh air. Can you imagine how you'd atrophy in such a house?"

"Except that it's very big and they must have plenty of stairs," Judith pointed out.

"But that's about it," Renie said. "They obviously aren't gardeners." She sighed. "Talk about dysfunctional families—the senior Blands don't seem to function at all. Luckily, it seems that their two children haven't inherited their parents' reclusive traits."

"That's true," Judith allowed, waving off an inquisitive bee. "But remember, Luke was adopted."

"Yes," Renie agreed. "I'd forgotten." She turned abruptly in her lounge chair to face Judith. "Alan is Luke's son. Why would he worry about having the same eye problems as his grandmother and his aunt? They're not related by blood."

Judith stared at Renie. "He wouldn't. But the only time I saw Luke Bland was in that café, and he was wearing sunglasses."

"Lots of people do that," Renie said, "especially around here, or if they think they look cool."

"Luke was reading," Judith responded. "First the menu, then something from a big binder. He kept the sunglasses on the whole time."

"They might be prescription sunglasses," Renie pointed out.

"Damn!" Judith breathed. "Adoption papers are sealed. How do we find out? And why would someone lie about adopting a child?"

"Because the child belonged to someone near and dear?" Renie suggested.

"Like Aunt Sally?" Judith scowled. "Sally's a widow. Not that we can't rule out an illegitimate baby. Maybe she had an affair."

"Maybe this has nothing to do with Frank Purvis's murder," Renie pointed out. "But often there's a mystery within a mystery."

Squeldon, accompanied by two accomplices, was on the stone stairs that led to the lower part of the garden. They had surrounded a wooden planter next to the steps and were attempting to tip it over.

"You vile wretches!" Renie shrieked, jumping up from her chair and running from the back porch toward the stone stairs just as the planter was upended. The villains fled, furry tails a-flying.

"They're smirking, I swear it!" Renie called up to Judith. "That's the fourth time they've done that this week!" She stooped down, using her bare hands to scoop the plants and the soil. "They've just about ruined this planter. Dad made it for us when Bill and I moved into this house years ago. I'm taking it into the basement."

Renie disappeared under the deck, where the basement door was located. Two minutes later, she reappeared, brushing her hands off on her jeans.

"Land mines," she muttered as she returned to the deck. "That's what we need. They know about traps and such. They can even deactivate them and remove the nuts. They probably think it's just a game on my part." With a sigh, she sat down again. "Have you heard from Morris and Trash?"

Judith shook her head. "For being their original suspect, they've kept me at arm's length. It makes me wonder if they have a line on who really did it. There's been nothing in the paper, not even an obit for Purvis."

"I know," Renie said. "I've been searching the papers, too, and even—gag—watching the local TV news."

"I've caught the late news on KINE," Judith said. "I often do, especially when Joe's home. I figure he's got a thing for Mavis. By the way, I tried to find out what kind of special assignment Alan—or Adam Blake, if you prefer—had been given, but he couldn't talk about it."

"Sounds like city politics," Renie said. "Somebody's got a hand in the till, I'll bet."

Judith glanced at her watch. "Good grief! It's after one! Mother must be starving. I'd better get home."

"Doesn't she have about a six-month supply of microwave foods in the toolshed?" Renie asked. "Why do you have to knock yourself out to wait on her hand and foot?"

Rising from her chair, Judith shot her cousin a challenging look. "How many times have you talked to your mother today?"

"Uh . . ." Renie also stood up. "Twice. I'll drop by her apartment for a bit after Bill gets home with the car." Grinning, she put a hand on Judith's arm. "They spoiled us, we spoil them. I guess it's only fair."

"There's fair," Judith murmured as they entered the kitchen, "and there's unfair. I still can't understand how Anna French could be so uncooperative after what I did for her last night."

"You know perfectly well that life is not fair, and neither are people," Renie declared, walking Judith to the front door.

"It's not just that," Judith said, "it's that she told Alan to say hello to me. I'm getting a mixed message there. I wonder what else she had to say to her nephew."

Renie shrugged. "You'll probably never know."

Reaching the porch, Judith eyed her cousin closely. "If I have anything to do about it, I will."

Uncle Corky and Aunt Theodora lived on an island across the bay. The surroundings were rural; their A-frame house was set among tall firs and other varieties of evergreens. They rarely took the ferry into the city, but far from being reclusive like the Blands, they remained active in community affairs and frequently traveled abroad. Uncle Corky particularly enjoyed going to Europe and visiting the sites where he'd served during World War II. He was smart, outspoken, and profane. In fact, he was not unlike his hero, General Patton.

On a whim, Judith decided to call her uncle. After a greeting of hearty expletives, Uncle Corky asked why Judith was calling.

"We don't usually hear from you unless it's the annual invitation for Christmas, Easter, and Thanksgiving," he said in his rich baritone. "What's up? Don't tell me my freaking sister-in-law bought the Big One?"

"No, Mother's fine," Judith answered. Briefly, she considered telling her uncle about Mike and Kristin's estrangement. But for now, the less said, the better, Judith decided. "I'm doing a little research. I know you were in Innsbruck at the end of the war. Have you ever heard of a town in Austria named Kopfstein?"

"Kopfstein." Uncle Corky was obviously turning the word over in his agile mind. "Yes, as I recall, it's closer to Salzburg than it is to Innsbruck. In fact, it's right on the German border in the Bavarian Alps, near Berchtesgaden."

"That's interesting," Judith said. "I mean, being so close to Hitler's mountain retreat."

"Beautiful country," Corky noted. "Too freaking good for that crazy bastard."

"So Kopfstein is just a dot on the map," Judith said. "That is, there's nothing unusual about it?"

"Not that I know of," Uncle Corky replied. "Along with the freaking French, we overran that whole part of Austria, accepting the surrender of the German freaking soldiers. Then it was balls-up with a lot of our soldiers. They really cut loose. Who the hell could blame those poor SOBs after all they'd gone through? To the victor go the spoils, as they say. They raided the Nazi big shots' liquor cabinets and wine cellars, they snatched up a bunch of souvenirs, they traded loot with each other, and took everything with a swastika on it. One big item was the Hitler freaking Youth daggers. I wouldn't have used one of those freaking things to cut up a seagull. But besides the souvenirs, our men got to sleep indoors, take showers, wear clean uniforms. And when it came to women, well, there were plenty of lonely broads in Europe after the war. Our guys were more than happy to console them."

"They had free time on their hands," Judith remarked. "That must have been a terrific adjustment."

"You bet your butt it was," Corky retorted. "I had an office on the third floor of a seventeenth-century building in Innsbruck. The town had been shot up pretty goddamned well, but that Baroque beauty survived. Anyway, I'd sit on my dead ass and watch the GIs down in the street. Sometimes it seemed as if they were wandering around in a freaking daze, not quite sure how to act without some crazy Kraut bastard shooting from a roof or a window or a doorway. Fear's hard to shake. We didn't just liberate Europe, we liberated ourselves. Sudden freedom is heady freaking stuff. It's no wonder some of our guys got out of control."

"Those of us who've never been through it really can't understand," Judith said, then paused before continuing. "I've got a silly question for you, Uncle Corky. Does the name Dick Bland mean anything to you?"

"In connection with the war? Not offhand," Corky replied. "Who *is* the bastard?"

"Someone I know who served under Patton, maybe in the same places you did," Judith replied.

"He could have," Corky said. "But he wasn't in my

company. Hey—I've got a perfect freaking shot at a seagull. The SOB's about to crap on Tank. Keep your pecker up, as my mom used to say."

Hanging up the phone, Judith smiled. Grandma Grover had been a true lady, but her favorite words of encouragement to her children and grandchildren had been given without regard to gender—or delicacy. It was her only vulgarity, but the phrase had served Judith well.

As she prepared various cheeses and a crab dip for the guests' appetizers, Judith considered how she could approach Lynette and Luke Bland. But what was the point? Nobody in the family seemed willing to surrender any kind of useful information. Still, Judith reasoned as she melted cream cheese for the crab dip, casual conversation often elicited revealing tidbits that the speaker unwittingly let slip.

She was bringing the hors d'oeuvres tray into the living room when the phone rang. Juggling the tray, Judith swore under her breath. Luckily, none of the guests had come downstairs yet for the social hour. Before she could safely set the tray down on the oak buffet, the call switched over to Voice Messaging. Judith fetched the chafing dish with the crab dip before dialing her mailbox's number.

"This is Lynette Bland," said the brisk recorded voice. "I wanted to thank you for the lovely bouquet you brought to my office. I'm sorry I missed you. You don't need to call me back."

Judith, however, immediately dialed the Blands' home number, which had shown up on her Caller ID. Lynette answered on the second ring.

"Really," she said, "you didn't have to return my call. This is probably a busy time for you."

"I have everything under control," Judith assured Lynette. "I'm so glad you liked the flowers. I bought some glads for myself today. In fact, I got them at the grocery store in Langford and ended up delivering your in-laws' weekly order."

"I heard about that," Lynette replied in an ironic tone. "You certainly cover all the bases."

Judith sat down in one of the kitchen chairs. "Do you blame me? If you'd found a dead man in the trunk of your car, wouldn't you want to know why?"

"Maybe." Lynette sounded unsure.

"I can't help it," Judith confessed. "It's my nature. That's how I got to be . . . FATSO."

"I suppose it is," Lynette said without enthusiasm. "Frankly, I've always felt that the less you know about certain things, the better."

"Sometimes that's true," Judith agreed. "Ignorance can protect you. It can save you from worry and heart-break. Yes, I see what you mean. We've all had the op-portunity to seek Truth, but couldn't face it because it was too painful. Don't you wonder, though, if not knowing eats away at your insides?"

"Well . . ." Lynette paused. "Perhaps."

"Or what's worse," Judith went on, forcing herself to sound long-suffering, "it can build barriers between people who should be close. You might think you're protecting someone else, for instance, when, in fact, you're only creating mistrust. Goodness, I ought to know," she continued, now speaking from the heart as she recalled the years she'd let Mike believe that Dan

McMonigle was his biological father. "I've been through that with my own son. Can you imagine what anguish it caused?"

"Really?" The indifference had seeped out of Lynette's voice. "Did he resent you for it?"

"Not in the long run," Judith admitted. "He'd sort of figured it out on his own after he became an adult. But he was almost thirty by that time. In retrospect, it was more painful for me than it was for him."

"Did it cause a rift between you?" Lynette asked.

Judith winced. "Yes," she lied, her mind's eye recalling the chilly scene between Luke and Lynette at the café. "He knew I was keeping something from him, something I was too ashamed to tell him. We grew apart for many years." Not a complete lie; Mike had been posted to Montana as a forest ranger. "I can't tell you how difficult it was to let my wretched secret come between us."

"Yes. I mean," Lynette amended, "I can see how that might happen."

"Before I forget," Judith hurriedly put in when Lynette didn't seem inclined to speak further, "your own son seems like such a nice young man. I've seen him on TV, of course, but he made an even better impression on me when I met him at your in-laws' house this afternoon. You must be very proud of him."

"I am," Lynette asserted. "Luke and I both are."

"I was trying to figure out who he resembles," Judith said as she heard bouncing footsteps and giggles from the front staircase. The sorority sisters had descended for the social hour. "He has your blond hair, of course, but his facial features resemble your husband."

"He looks a little like both of us," Lynette said, "but he mostly takes after my father."

No help there, Judith thought. Lynette's family didn't seem to play any part in the little drama going on at the house on Moonfleet.

"I'm afraid I have to go," Judith said with reluctance. "My guests are gathering in the living room."

Lynette thanked her again for the flowers and hung up. All Judith could hope was that her surmise was right: Luke Bland was keeping a big secret from his wife. Maybe Judith's discourse on the agony of withholding information would spur Lynette to discover the truth. More likely, she'd often tried and always failed. But Frank Purvis's murder may have brought matters to a head. Judith could but hope.

"Good evening," she said to the young women. "There's wine and other beverages in the dining room." Hillside Manor's bar was a converted washstand that had once stood in an upstairs bathroom. "That dip is crab. Just a warning in case anyone has allergies."

The foursome giggled some more and headed straight for the dining room. Mrs. Greenwalt and a middle-aged couple from Dallas named Durning came down the stairs and entered the living room. Mrs. Greenwalt zeroed in on Judith.

"The cat, I trust, is dead," she said, her plump face a mask of disgust.

"The cat's gone," Judith replied, looking forsaken.

"How is Mr. Greenwalt? Are you going back to the hospital tonight?"

"Yes, for an hour or so." Mrs. Greenwalt sighed heavily. "I spent much of the day there. Fortunately, my husband is recovering. We'll be able to leave for home tomorrow. You'll receive the airline and hotel bills directly."

"Airline and hotels?" Judith gulped.

Mrs. Greenwalt nodded stiffly. "Of course. Our original plans were to travel for another week. Now we've had to cancel everything because of your homicidal pet. It's only fair that you should pay for our return fare. Obviously, we couldn't get a decent rate on such short notice. There's no direct flight from here to Nashville, which means we'll have a layover in Chicago and another in St. Louis. Obviously, George can't wait around in airports. We'll have to spend two nights in hotels. It will take us three days to get to Nashville."

Judith was speechless. The Durnings, meanwhile, were plundering the appetizers while the sorority sisters guzzled wine in the dining room. Before Judith could think of something to say, the doorbell rang.

Mike and the boys stood on the front porch. All three of them were carrying bags and boxes from KFC. "Hi, Mom," Mike said with a big grin. "I hope you haven't started dinner. We brought it with us. Is Dad home yet?"

"Uh . . . no," Judith responded. "He's stuck in Omaha for a couple more days. I forgot to tell you."

Mac and Joe-Joe made a beeline for the kitchen, scattering the sorority sisters, who proclaimed the little boys' adorability in high-pitched admiration.

"Chicken! Let's eat now!" Mac cried. "I'm hungry!"

"Cluck-cluck!" Joe-Joe exclaimed. "Cock-a-doodle-doo!"

"Go ahead," Judith said to Mike. "But get Granny out of the toolshed. She loves fried chicken. And she'll love seeing all of you."

"That's what I figured," Mike replied, heading for the kitchen. "Since the boys and I are going back to the ranger station tomorrow, I'm not sure when we'll—"

Mrs. Greenwalt had come into the entry hall. "You keep your mother in a *toolshed*? What kind of a place *is* this?"

"The toolshed's been converted—" Judith was interrupted again by the doorbell. "Excuse me." She turned away from Mrs. Greenwalt.

"Police," Glenn Morris announced, flashing his badge just in case Judith might have forgotten.

"Ah!" exclaimed Mrs. Greenwalt, who had traipsed after Judith. "It's about time! I hope you're going to arrest her."

"Who's this broad?" Jonathan Trashman asked, pointing to Mrs. Greenwalt as he lumbered into the entry hall.

"*I beg your pardon!*" Lucy Greenwalt huffed. "*You* look like last week's laundry!"

Judith stepped between the pair. "Mrs. Greenwalt is one of my guests," she said through gritted teeth. "Shouldn't we adjourn to the front parlor?"

"No need," Glenn said airily. "We wanted to tell you in person that you're no longer a homicide suspect."

"Not as far as I'm concerned," Lucy Greenwalt put in, moving her plump figure in front of Glenn and Trash. "I knew I should have called the authorities myself, but it seems some other concerned soul did it for me. Mrs. Flynn's culpable of attempted murder at least!"

Glenn eyed Mrs. Greenwalt with interest. "Really? Who is the victim?"

"My poor husband," Mrs. Greenwalt snapped. "As if you didn't know!"

Glenn's gaze turned to Judith. "Is there something you haven't told us?"

"Plenty," Judith retorted. "But it has nothing to do with Frank Purvis. Believe me, this is all a silly—"

"Old fart coming through!" shouted Gertrude, wheeling herself into the entry hall. "What's all this commotion? I want to have my supper in peace!" On the run, Mac and Joe-Joe led the way, crashing into Glenn and Mrs. Greenwalt.

"Cluck-cluck!" Joe-Joe shouted, tugging at Mrs. Greenwalt's too-tight green slacks. "Big fat chicken!"

Lucy Greenwalt yanked Joe-Joe's small hands from her slacks. "Mind your manners, little boy! They should keep *you* in the doghouse!"

"Woof, woof," Joe-Joe barked, scampering away.

The sorority sisters stared and the Durnings gaped. Mike started toward his mother, but she waved him off.

"Later," Judith mouthed.

"What's with these two bozos?" Gertrude asked, gesturing at the detectives.

Judith grasped the handles on Gertrude's wheelchair

and started to turn the old lady around. "Never mind, Mother. You'd better eat your supper while it's hot."

Gertrude, however, set the wheelchair's brake. "I don't like the looks of 'em. Don't let those two get near Grandma Grover's breakfront. They might steal her Royal Doulton gravy boat."

Glenn, whose composure had previously seemed unflappable, began to look slightly dazed. "Yes," he informed Judith, "the parlor. Now."

"Pat 'em down before they go!" Gertrude shouted as Judith moved quickly through the parlor door with Glenn and Trash on her heels. Mrs. Greenwalt attempted to follow, but Trash slammed the hall door in her face while Glenn secured the door to the living room.

"We won't keep you from your . . . whatever they are," Glenn said, assuming his accustomed stance in front of the fireplace. "We merely wanted to advise you that you're no longer a suspect. In fact, you're no longer a person of interest."

"As in"—Trash chuckled—"you're really boring! Ha-ha!"

Judith felt like rolling her eyes, but she already had a throbbing headache. "Does that mean you have an actual suspect?"

Glenn gave Judith a thin smile. "We can't reveal that information. But you may claim your car from the impound lot Monday morning. We're finished with it."

"Good," Judith said. At least she'd have the Subaru back before Joe came home. "Did you find anything helpful?"

Glenn shook his head. "I can't say."

"How was he killed?" Judith persisted.

"The classic blunt instrument to the skull. A garden tool, in this case." Glenn made a dismissive gesture. "I can't go into details."

"Did Frank Purvis leave any survivors?" Judith asked.

"Not that we could find," Glenn replied. "No one has stepped forward to claim the victim."

"What happens to the body?" Judith inquired, vaguely recalling that Joe had once mentioned that the county or the city was responsible for disposing of the remains in such cases.

"We take care of that," Glenn answered with an appropriately grim expression.

Judith wasn't satisfied with the response. "I realize that, but how?"

"We roast 'em and toast 'em," Trash said. "The ashes go in a metal box and get sent to a crypt someplace. Purvis is a done deal. Well-done, I might add. Ha-ha."

"What information goes on the metal box?" Judith asked.

Trash shrugged. "Name, date of death, and, if we know it, date of birth. That's it."

"Does that happen often?"

Glenn gave Judith an impatient look. "Too often these days, with all the homeless."

Judith cringed. "That sounds so . . . awful."

"It's reality," Glenn stated flatly.

"I suppose it is," Judith murmured. Then, in a stronger voice, she posed another question: "Why are you working on a Saturday?"

"We're shorthanded," Glenn replied. "We'll leave

you now. Thanks for your cooperation." The detectives went out of the parlor the way they'd come in.

Judith remained in the room, staring at the fireplace's empty grate. The explanation jibed with what Joe had told her. Except for the part about Purvis having already been cremated. If she remembered correctly, homicide victims were kept in the city morgue for some time if the body had not yet been claimed.

But maybe it had. Maybe somebody out there wanted Frank Purvis's earthly remains destroyed.

Judith wondered who—and why.

FOURTEEN

JUDITH HAD TO choke back tears when Mike and the grandchildren left around seven-thirty Saturday evening for the ranger station. They weren't going more than fifty miles from Hillside Manor, and they were only a phone call away, but she felt as if a new distance had grown between her and Mike. It was an emotional gap, a generational chasm, a disparity in values.

At least Mike had managed to find a sitter for the boys. But Kristin was headed for her family's wheat ranch across the state, presumably to mull over her options. Judith wanted to shake her Valkyrie-like daughter-in-law. But that would be like a willow trying to move an oak. Nor would it be wise to interfere or offer advice to Kristin. Maybe her parents would be able to make her see reason. Unfortunately, Judith wasn't optimistic.

"They're gone," Judith said to Renie over the phone. "And Joe's not here to help me cope with my emotions. I feel miserable."

"How do you think I feel with all three of our

kids in far-flung places?" Renie shot back. "Bill and I waited forever for them to get married and leave home. Then, when they all did it at the same time, I was bereft. I still am."

"But none of them are breaking up," Judith pointed out, sounding bitter.

"Not so far," Renie replied. "Heck, they've only been married for a little over a year. Cheer up. Get your mind back on murder."

"That's hard to do," Judith declared, but promptly regaled her cousin with the latest homicide-related news.

"What are you saying?" Renie asked after Judith had finished. "That someone did in fact claim Frank Purvis's body, but it's a big secret? Isn't there a record of who the body was released to?"

"Maybe. Maybe not."

"In other words, money passed hands," Renie speculated.

"It's not impossible," Judith said, "though bribes were almost nonexistent in the homicide squad when Joe was there. Or so he insisted."

"No city is immune to police corruption," Renie remarked. "I wouldn't trust Glenn and Trash an inch."

"Neither would my mother," Judith said, "but she doesn't trust most people. As she puts it, if you can't trust the weather around here, who can you trust?"

"Maybe that's why so many of us natives are skeptics."

"Maybe," Judith conceded. "But it wouldn't have to be Glenn or Trash who were coerced into releasing the body. It could have been a higher-up or maybe even somebody in the morgue. The question is, who would want to dispose of Purvis's corpse and why? And who *was* Frank Purvis in the first place?"

"What about checking with the people at Dairyland?"

"The police must have done that already," Judith said. "Dairyland keeps its trucks in a lot a couple of blocks from Emerald Lake. That neighborhood adjoins the Langford district. How hard would it be to steal a truck and a uniform? It'd take some daring, unless Purvis arrived earlier than the other drivers and employees."

"Who's awake at four in the morning?" Renie remarked. "I'd be a zombie. I wouldn't notice a woolly mammoth in the bathtub."

"People who work those shifts are used to getting up early. On the other hand, they probably do things by routine, each employee in his or her own little world."

"Purvis had to know Vern Benson's route," Renie noted. "Maybe the drivers keep their route and schedule in their trucks. All Purvis would have to do is scout the Moonfleet area and take down the truck number when Vern made his deliveries."

Judith sighed. "The one thing we know is that Frank definitely stole Vern's truck and jacket. I saw him with my own eyes, both alive and dead."

"I suppose we can dismiss any complicity on the part of the real Vern Benson," Renie said.

"I think so," Judith replied. "He seemed like a nice, hardworking young man. Still . . ."

"Still what?"

"You never know—as we've discovered before," Judith asserted. "The real question is how and why did Frank Purvis show up on the day of the UPS delivery? Where does he fit into the picture with regard to the Blands? Was he really going to steal the package on the porch?"

"Teamsters?" Renie suggested.

"Huh?"

"I was thinking—I assume UPS and the Dairyland drivers belong to the Teamsters," Renie explained. "If Frank Purvis was an actual truck driver, maybe he heard about the peculiar annual delivery to the spooky house. It's the kind of oddity that people would talk about."

"That's true," Judith responded slowly. "If not at union meetings, then with other UPS drivers." She paused, testing her memory. "Kevin, that was the driver's name." She paused again. "Drat—the office wouldn't be open on a Saturday night except to take pickup orders or trace deliveries. I'll have to wait until Monday to find out Kevin's last name. Why didn't I think of this before?"

"You've been kind of busy," Renie said dryly. "As for me, I'm out of work at the moment now that SuperGerm's been delivered and I finished the Bucky Beaver art for Mom. All I did today was work in the yard, chase squirrels, and run some errands. Which reminds me, I should put the sympathy card I bought for Alyssa Barnes in the mail tomorrow on the way to Mass."

"Who's Alyssa Barnes?" Judith inquired.

"She works for the gas company in marketing. I've

done some projects for her and we have lunch together a couple of times a year. Her brother, Fred, died this week. I'm not going to the funeral Monday, so I figured the least I could do is send her a card. Good PR on my part."

"You might have mentioned kindness," Judith said as something clicked in her brain. "Is Barnes her maiden name?"

"No, it was Pettibone. In fact," Renie went on, "Lyssa's—that's what she goes by—other brother is the vet at the Cat Clinique where you collected Sweetums. When are you bringing him home from Uncle Al's?"

"Tomorrow," Judith said tersely, her mind veering in a different direction. "This Pettibone thing is curious, but I'm not sure why. I saw Fred's obituary in the paper. In fact, I sent my condolences to Bert through his receptionist or whatever she is at the clinic. I went to school with Bert. I also remember an Alexis Pettibone."

"They're an old Langford family," Renie noted. "Lexis teaches nursing at the University. I don't recall her married name. Why are you so intrigued?"

"I'm not sure," Judith said. "Maybe I'm just obsessed with Langford these days. Or maybe I'm losing my mind."

"We've got roots in Langford," Renie pointed out. "Uncle Al still lives there. Heck, Morty the Mailman's still on a Langford route. You've said it yourself, this city may be big in some ways, but for those of us who go back a few generations, it's still a small town. You ought to know—how many times have you met somebody, gotten them to open up a little, and discovered that their first cousin is somehow related to you on your mother's side of the family?"

"Twice, actually," Judith admitted.

"And what about our Anne? We go back to visit Bill's relatives in Wisconsin, she takes one look at a graduation photo on his sister's endtable, screams, and runs out of the house because she'd made out with the guy at a high-school party. By coincidence— or what you will—he's our brother-in-law's nephew whose family moved here years ago."

"I remember that," Judith said. "Yes, it's true. If we've lived here for any length of time, we all seem to be interconnected."

"Ask my mother," Renie responded. "She's like you, she knows everybody."

"Maybe I should ask her," Judith said in a musing tone. "She probably remembers the Pettibones. Uncle Al might, for that matter."

"Sorry, coz," Renie said with a sigh, "I'm not following your train of thought. I mean, why do you care about the Pettibones?"

"Because," Judith replied, "we've got a body that's disappeared. Or has it? Would you care to change your mind and attend Fred Pettibone's funeral with me Monday?"

Renie had hemmed and hawed, but finally said she'd go, even if she thought Judith was crazy. "Bert Petti- bone may not remember me," Judith had argued. "At least you've been in recent contact with the deceased's sister. You have a reason to be there. I don't."

Judith attended eight o'clock Mass Sunday morning, after setting up brunch for her guests. Mrs. Green-walt hadn't appeared when Judith returned a few minutes after nine. She still hadn't shown up by a quarter to eleven. The other guests had finished and were in the process of checking out. While eleven was the deadline for departure six days a week, Judith allowed an extra hour on Sundays.

Waving off the sorority sisters at eleven-fifteen, Judith decided to go upstairs and see if Mrs. Greenwalt was all right. A single knock on the door evoked a sharp response.

"What is it?"

"I was making sure you're awake," Judith said through the door. "Did you want to eat before you check out at noon?"

Yanking open the door, Lucy Greenwalt stood before Judith in a zebra-striped bathrobe and matching zebra slippers. "I'll leave when I leave," she declared. "George can't be released from the hospital until one. We'll go straight from there to the airport. Our flight's at three-fifteen. Our *first* flight, that is. I'd like a tray in my room. Three scrambled eggs, ham, hot biscuits with gravy, fried cornmeal mush, grits, and strong, hot coffee with sugar and cream. Frankly, I've been very disappointed with your breakfasts. Omelettes with fish? Crab on a muffin? And those bagels with very thin sliced . . . what is it, salmon? What kind of breakfast food is that?"

"Salmon omelettes and Dungeness crab and Nova Scotia lox are considered delicacies around here," Judith retorted. "I can do the scrambled eggs and ham, maybe even whip up some biscuits, but the grits and gravy are out. Sorry." She stalked off down the hall to the back stairs.

She reached the kitchen just as the phone rang. It was Uncle Al. "Your gang left here around ten," he said. "We went out to breakfast first. Tess came along, too. We had a swell time."

"Good," Judith said. "Thanks so much for letting them stay with you. I really appreciate it. I'll be over to get Sweetums in an hour or so. Is that okay?"

"It would be," Al said, his voice no longer so chipper. "The only problem is, Sweetums isn't here."

"What do you mean?"

"He took off right after Mike and the boys left," Al explained. "You'd better wait until he shows up again."

"But he might not," Judith said, sounding agitated. "He doesn't know the neighborhood."

"Hey, kiddo, he'll be fine," Uncle Al soothed. "He's probably exploring the alley out back. I'll give you ten-to-one odds that when he gets hungry he'll wander up to the door. I'll call you when he gets here. How's that?"

"That" had to be sufficient. But Judith was unsettled. Sweetums had never been let loose anywhere except in his familiar Hillside Manor surroundings. It was four miles from the B&B to Uncle Al's house. No matter how Sweetums might try to head home, he'd have to cross a bridge. To Judith's knowledge, the cat had never been on a bridge. Indeed, he'd never strayed far enough to confront a stream of traffic.

She wouldn't tell Gertrude about Sweetums's defection. There was no point in upsetting the old girl. Not yet, anyway. For the next twenty minutes she busied herself with baking biscuits, making more scrambled eggs, and reheating the ham that was left on the sideboard.

Lucy Greenwalt accepted the food with ill grace. "It took you long enough," she declared. "Will you please order a taxi for twelve-thirty?"

"There's a phone for guests by the wicker sofa in the hall," Judith retorted.

Mrs. Greenwalt glared at her hostess. "Will you please order a taxi for twelve-thirty?" she repeated. "I don't know the cab company's number. You do."

Rather than exacerbate the situation, Judith ordered the taxi from the downstairs phone. She felt like telling the dispatcher to send the company's most reckless driver, especially one who didn't speak English.

The last straw came when Mrs. Greenwalt asked Judith to carry her luggage downstairs. Lucy and George had two large suitcases, two carry-on bags, and a garment bag. There were also two shopping bags from local stores where the Greenwalts had made purchases.

"I simply can't pick up anything that weighs over ten pounds," Judith stated. "I have an artificial hip."

"As in 'phony'?" Mrs. Greenwalt snapped. "This whole place is phony, if you ask me. Well? If you can't, who will?"

"Ask the taxi driver," Judith shot back. "I'll take those shopping bags and I'm sure you can manage the carry-ons. The driver can get the suitcases and the garment bag."

"What about my purse?" Mrs. Greenwalt demanded, wielding a huge handbag decorated with sequined roses.

"Isn't that a shoulder bag?" Judith asked wearily.

"I don't like to carry it over my shoulder. That makes it too easy for purse snatchers."

"Inside the house?"

"You never know," Mrs. Greenwalt snapped. "Especially *this* house."

The doorbell rang. Judith hurried out of the guest room and down the hall to the stairs, taking the shopping bags with her. Opening the door, she faced the taxi driver, a huskily built platinum blonde with long dangling earrings.

"Hiya, hon," the woman said, chewing gum. "Are you Greenwalt?"

"No," Judith replied. "She'll be right down. Would you mind helping with her luggage?"

"Is this an airport run?" the driver inquired with an eager expression.

"I don't think so," Judith replied as Lucy Greenwalt came huffing down the stairs with the two smaller bags and her big purse.

Disappointment crossed the driver's florid face. "Rats. Oh, well." She shrugged. An airport trip cost at least thirty dollars. "Is the stuff upstairs?"

"Yes," said Mrs. Greenwalt. "Room Five. And be *very* careful with the garment bag. I have some extremely fragile items in it."

"Gotcha," the driver said, and took the stairs two at a time.

Mrs. Greenwalt turned to Judith. "I'm not paying our bill. You owe us, as I'm sure you're aware. Good-bye." She flounced out of the house, all three bags swinging this way and that.

Bag is right, Judith thought, watching her guest place her belongings into the taxi's backseat. Mrs. Greenwalt, however, waited at the curb.

"Piece of work, huh?" the driver said, coming down the stairs and easily managing the suitcases and the garment bag.

"Just awful," Judith replied, moving onto the porch.

"From around here?" the driver inquired.

"No," Judith said softly. "An out-of-towner."

The driver chortled. "Then I think I'll take her for a little ride."

"Good," Judith said, noting that Mrs. Greenwalt was watching them with a wary eye.

"Mind that garment bag!" she shouted.

"Gotcha," the driver called back, then spoke under her breath to Judith. "In more ways than one."

After the morning haze had lifted, the sun came out and the temperature rose. High sixties, Judith calculated. It was a lovely day. But somehow, it didn't feel like it.

It was after two before Judith had the rooms cleaned and ready for the next batch of visitors. Phyliss never worked on the Sabbath; she rarely worked on the day before the Sabbath, either, insisting that she had to get herself into the proper mood for worship. Over the past few months, Judith had considered hiring someone part-time to help with the weekend tasks. Now might be a good time. Students would be looking for summer jobs. She decided to put an ad in the paper.

Wanting to stay near the phone, she took it with her while she worked in the yard. But after two hours, there was no call from Uncle Al. It was likely that he'd gone out to the track for the afternoon. The ponies took precedence over all other animals, including Sweetums.

"Where's that wretched cat?" Gertrude asked, wheeling her way to the small patio. "I heard about his latest shenanigans from Arlene. Too bad he didn't claw that pain in the butt into shreds. I've no time for people like that. They think they're big shots, just because they can afford to travel. Phooey."

Judith looked up from the flower bed next to the fence that separated Hillside Manor from the Dooleys' property. Maybe it was best to be candid. "Sweetums decided to go exploring at Uncle Al's. I think Uncle Al went to the horse races. I'll call around seven. He should be back by then. The last race goes off at six."

Gertrude's face crinkled with worry. "You think so?" She gave herself a little shake. "Sure he will. He's too ornery to miss supper."

Like owner, like pet, Judith thought. Gertrude probably envied Sweetums's ability to take off and savor liberty. Maybe the old girl was vicariously enjoying the cat's escapade.

But when Judith got hold of Uncle Al at seven-thirty, Sweet-ums still hadn't shown up.

"I stuck around until almost four," he said, concern edging into his voice. "Then I drove out to the track to catch the last three races. When I got home a little before seven, he still wasn't here. I put some chow out for him on the back porch before I left, but it hasn't been touched."

"Maybe he'll come back after dark," Judith said hopefully. "The trouble is, it stays light so long this time of year."

"Let's bet on it," Uncle Al replied. "Seven-to-two odds. I'll call you as soon as your cat crosses the finish line at the door."

Judith had barely clicked off when the phone rang in her hand. It was Joe.

"I had the day off, being Sunday," he announced, sounding cheerful. "I called your Aunt Ellen and Uncle Win last night in Beatrice, and they offered to meet me halfway in Lincoln. I didn't realize they were long-time Cornhusker ticket holders. I guess the Nebraska supporters wear red even in the off-season. We had a good time touring the campus, and then we ate some excellent steak at a restaurant I'd found in the tourist guide."

"Not one recommended by Aunt Ellen?" Judith inquired.

"I knew better than that," Joe replied. "Your aunt's the only person I know who can still find a four-dollar buffet this side of Nevada. The part I don't get is that she insists on paying for seconds, even the coffee refills."

"Aunt Ellen is not only thrifty, but incredibly honest," Judith replied. "She once stood on a downtown street corner for twenty minutes with a nickel she'd found in the gutter and waited for someone to claim it. But she's also very moral. She wouldn't give it to a wino, and ended up putting it into an expired parking meter to save somebody a ticket."

"So how are things at home?" Joe asked.

Judith informed him about Mike's departure, but tried to keep her sorrow to herself.

She was unsuccessful. Joe knew his wife too well. "You can't let this thing eat away at you. Frankly, I'm glad I had to go out of town," he said. "It keeps my mind off of Mike's marital troubles. You should focus on something else. It's too bad you couldn't find a dead body someplace. Ha-ha. Only kidding," he added hastily.

"Right," Judith murmured. "So you think you'll be home Tuesday night?"

"I'll know for sure by tomorrow afternoon," Joe said. "I'll call you around seven your time, okay?"

Judith said that would be fine. Feeling desolate, she hung up. No husband, no cat, no reconciliation, no killer. It had not been a good day.

Here's my plan," Judith said to Renie over the phone the next morning. "The Pettibone funeral's at noon, Langford United Methodist Church. I can get out of here right after eleven. If you could pick me up, I can collect the Subaru from the impound and then we could drive separately to the service."

"Nuttier and nuttier," Renie muttered. "Okay, why not?"

"I take it Bill doesn't need the car today?"

"Not until this afternoon," Renie replied. "Right now he's in the basement, playing with his dirk."

Bill Jones had a limited but choice collection of swords, daggers, and other antique blades. At one point, Renie had urged him to buy a fifteenth-century pikestaff that she wanted to use as a hat rack. Bill demurred.

Renie picked Judith up at eleven-fifteen. Phyliss, who proclaimed that Sweetums wasn't really missing but had finally turned back into the Archfiend, was knee-deep in the weekend's accumulated laundry. The parish's senior-citizen bus had picked up Gertrude, who had gone off to bridge club with Aunt Deb.

To Judith's surprise, there was no problem retrieving her car. The officers on duty were courteous and efficient. Judith didn't mention Joe's name. She felt it was best to be discreet, lest the saga get back to Joe. The thought of him blowing a gasket wasn't pleasant.

Renie led the way to the church, which was located about a mile from Uncle Al's and a half mile from the Blands' house. The day was warm and the small church was packed. Dying young always attracted a crowd, Judith thought as she and Renie allowed an usher to find them places on the aisle in the next to the last row of pews. Unlike the elderly, those who were taken too soon left behind many friends and relatives.

Renie twisted this way and that in her seat, trying to look over and around the people in front of her. "Alyssa," she whispered to Judith. "Second row on the right, short dark hair, black suit with white trim on the collar."

Being almost a half-foot taller than Renie and on the aisle, Judith spotted Alyssa Pettibone Barnes with comparative ease. "I don't see Bert," she said under her breath. "He must be a pallbearer."

"He is," Renie replied, checking the memorial program the usher had given them. "There's a Barnes, too. That must be Lyssa's husband."

The soloist had concluded singing "The Old Rugged Cross." There was a pause before the minister appeared on the altar and the organ played the notes to begin the service. The mourners all stood as the casket was moved slowly into the church proper.

The six pallbearers seemed to come from two generations—young and middle-aged. Judith recognized Bert Pettibone, despite the forty years that had passed since she'd seen him last in grade school. He wasn't as thin, he now wore glasses, and his graying brown hair had receded, but the features were basically the same.

The casket, adorned with a spray of lilies and roses, rolled past the cousins. Judith bowed her head and said a prayer for Alfred Pettibone's soul and for his survivors.

The funeral was conducted with dignity and simplicity: hymns, prayers, and a eulogy by the pastor. Alfred— or Fred, as he was better known—had been a hardworking individual, a man of faith, and devoted to his family. Fred and his wife had a daughter and a son, now grown. The deceased had spent most of his life working for the government and earning high praise from his superiors. He had been taken before his time, but that was God's will.

"Bull," Renie muttered. "That's not how it works. God gets too much blame for humankind's flaws."

Judith nodded, but remained silent as the pastor concluded by announcing that the casket would be opened for viewing and that a reception would follow in the church hall.

"The only dead bodies I look at are the ones you find," Renie whispered to Judith. "I'm going to track down Lyssa and give her my condolences. Gawk, if you want to."

Doubts about her reason for attending the services began to assail Judith. Was there any point in viewing the deceased? The hunch had come from out of left field. Often, her intuition had been proved right. But she had also been wrong on numerous occasions.

Approximately two thirds of the mourners were queued up to pay their last respects to Fred Pettibone. Judith moved into her place near the end of the line. It was a slow process. The closer she got to the coffin, the more she heard sniffles and weeping. Fred must have been well loved. Certainly the minister had made him sound like a fine man. Maybe Renie was right. Judith was going crazy.

At last she approached the casket. Taking a deep breath, she looked at the dead man.

She was right.

He might be Fred Pettibone to the rest of the world, but he was Frank Purvis to Judith.

FIFTEEN

YOU'RE KIDDING!" RENIE exclaimed when she and Judith rendezvoused outside the church. "How in the hell did you figure that one out before you saw the body?"

A couple of older women apparently coming from the church overheard Renie and briefly stopped in their tracks on the stone walkway. Judith looked away from them and shielded her eyes from the midday sun. "It was the way the body was handled by the police," Judith said, keeping her voice down as other mourners trickled out of the church. "It didn't sound right, not according to what Joe has told me about unclaimed victims. Then it dawned on me that Alfred Pettibone was about the same age as Frank Purvis. There was no mention of how he died in the obituary, nor did the minister refer to it just now. Also, remembrances were to be made to the humane society. That's a good cause, but usually when someone passes away in their forties, it's heart or cancer, and the memorials are sent to related research associations or to a hospice."

"A lucky guess," Renie remarked drolly, but her expression became thoughtful. "Yes, not to mention that if it's cancer, there's often a brief account of the deceased's courage or the family's appreciation for caregivers. If it's an accident of some sort, there's a reference to the 'senseless tragedy.' But I still don't quite get it."

Judith and Renie had moved under the shade of a dogwood tree. "It was the initials, too," Judith said. "All of the Pettibones had names that began with *A*, but they were known by their nicknames—Bert for Albert, Fred for Alfred, Lyssa for Alyssa, and, as I recall, Lexi, for Alexis."

"So?"

"Fred Pettibone—the names start with the same initials as Frank Purvis," Judith pointed out. "And, by the way, what did Frank—I mean, Fred—do for the federal government? His résumé was far from complete."

"That's true," Renie said. "There weren't any memories from the congregation, either. Not that I mind—those things can go on until I want to jump in the casket and get wheeled away along with the corpse."

"You've got to introduce me to Lyssa," Judith declared. "Then maybe I can meet Fred's widow. Andrea, I think her name is."

"I assume they don't call her 'Drea,' " Renie murmured, then narrowed her eyes at her cousin. "Surely you don't mean meeting them now?"

"Why not?" Judith responded. "I'm not going to drill either one of them, but I'd like an entrée into the family."

Renie looked grim. "Okay, let's go back inside." Suddenly she brightened. "Maybe they have some decent food at the reception."

"You graze, I talk," Judith said as they returned to the church and headed down a flight of stairs.

"But you don't conduct an interrogation," Renie warned. "May I remind you, this isn't the place for it."

"I know, I know," Judith replied. "I'll be discreet."

The reception line had dwindled to a half-dozen people. The other guests were sitting at round tables, eating finger food from the buffet that was set up under a large painting of Jesus feeding the multitudes with loaves and fishes.

Renie started for the buffet, but Judith grabbed her arm. "Hold it. Introductions first, food second."

Renie frowned at the selection of fruit, raw vegetables, crackers, and cheese. She turned to a gray-haired woman wearing an apron and pointed to the picture of Jesus.

"Could I have what He's serving?" Renie asked.

Staring with disapproval at Renie, the woman stomped away in her sturdy shoes.

"And you criticize me," Judith muttered, hauling Renie over to the Pettibone family, where they were receiving condolences from the last of the funeral attendees.

"Lyssa," Renie said with a sympathetic expression that probably fooled everybody except Judith, "I couldn't leave without introducing you to my cousin Judith Flynn. We had a car problem, so she came with me. I'm sure you've heard me speak of her."

Lyssa Barnes's smile was about as convincing as Renie's sympathy. "Oh, yes. You run a motel, don't you?"

"A bed-and-breakfast," Judith replied. "I understand you work for the gas company."

Lyssa, a plump woman with auburn hair and deep green eyes, nodded. "That's how I met Serena."

"I went to grade school with Bert," Judith said.

"Really?" Lyssa gazed across the room to where her brother was now standing by the buffet table. "I was a few years behind Bert."

"I'm sorry about your other brother," Judith said, noticing that the Widow Pettibone was about to move on. "I must convey my condolences to your sister-in-law. And Bert, of course."

Lyssa called after Andrea, who had taken a few steps away from where the receiving line had formed. Andrea turned. She was a pretty woman, though pale and drawn. Lyssa made the introductions.

"I was widowed quite young, too," Judith said, putting out her hand. "Believe me, I know what you're going through."

"Thank you," Andrea said, her handshake limp. "You went to school with Bert?"

Judith nodded. "Grade school. I lived in Langford for a few years before my family moved to Heraldsgate Hill. How are your children coping?"

Andrea looked in the direction of the two young adults who were talking to Bert and a woman who might have been his wife. "They're still in a state of shock. When someone passes so suddenly, it's terribly hard. Excuse me, I should be with them."

Judith was left alone in the middle of the room. More people were leaving. Renie, in fact, had deserted Judith and was edging her way into the kitchen. Lyssa had also moved off, speaking with an older couple who were seated at a table toward the end of the church hall.

Having no idea of what Alexis Pettibone looked like, Judith figured Bert was her last hope. He was still with his presumed wife, niece, nephew, and Andrea. It would be gauche to breach the family circle.

But a moment later, Bert left the others and headed for the exit. Judith moved swiftly, catching her prey just before he left the hall.

"Bert," she said, putting a hand on his arm. "Do you remember me? I was Judith Grover in grade school."

Bert peered through his glasses, studying Judith's face. "I'm sorry, I don't, offhand."

"We lived on Hyde Park Place, that triangle block," Judith said as she heard loud noises coming from the kitchen area.

Bert peered some more. "Oh—yes, you look quite different. You used to be . . ."

"Fat," Judith put in, ignoring a couple of shouts that also emanated from the kitchen. "And my hair was jet-black, not silver. It started to turn gray when I was in my early twenties, just like my mother's did."

"You're looking well," Bert said in his studious manner. If no longer shy, he had retained a certain diffidence. "Did you know my brother?"

"No," Judith said, then explained about the connection between Renie and Lyssa. "I have a question for you," she continued. "It won't take a minute. My cat, Sweetums, was at your clinic the other night. He wasn't hurt, but he'd done some damage to one of my guests. I left him with my uncle in Langford until the guests checked out, but now the cat's run off. He doesn't know the neighborhood. What's the best way to find him?"

A hostile glint appeared in Bert's brown eyes. "Sweetums, did you say?"

Judith grimaced. "Yes."

"I heard about Sweetums," Bert replied, his forehead wrinkling. "From what I was told, it might be best not to find him."

If Judith had dared, she would've stamped her foot. But possible hip dislocation was always at the back of her mind. "Sweetums is our beloved family pet. We've had him for years. Of course he can be contrary, even ornery. He's a *cat*, for heaven's sake!"

"Unlike any other," Bert murmured. But he gave Judith a half smile. "Advertise. Put signs on utility poles near your uncle's house. A photo would help. If someone finds your cat, they won't want to keep him. That is," he amended, "they'd want to return him to his human."

"Thanks," Judith said, sounding sarcastic, but quickly remembering her hidden agenda. "Assuming Sweetums is found, I'd like to bring him in for a checkup. It's been a while. There may be a medical reason why he sometimes behaves so . . . aggressively."

Bert's expression was dubious, but his response was polite. "Call the clinic this afternoon. We can make the appointment for later in the week. If your pet doesn't show up by then, it's probably hopeless."

"Don't say that," Judith retorted. "I mean, he has to show up. Is it possible I could see you this afternoon? For grief counseling? I assume you provide such a service for bereaved pet owners."

Bert looked askance. "We don't. We give referrals, however. In any event, I won't be in the office today. I have some personal grief to deal with."

Judith was embarrassed. "Oh, please—I'm really sorry! It's just that I'm so upset. Not just about Sweetums, but the funeral service brought back so many sad memories. You see, I lost my husband when he was still in his forties. It was terrible." She managed to force tears into her eyes, not so much for Dan's loss, but for the waste of his life.

"I didn't realize that," Bert said, sounding genuinely touched. "Was it sudden?"

Judith shook her head, trying to ignore the ongoing commotion in the kitchen. "No. He'd been ill for some time." Drinking and eating for even longer. "But it was still a shock." Especially for the two slim undertakers who had practically had to bring in a crane to move Dan's four hundred pounds out of the house. "As I told your sister-in-law, I realize it's even worse when death comes so unexpectedly. That is, I assume Fred didn't have a long illness."

"No. He did not." Bert's thin lips clamped shut in a grim line. "His health was excellent."

"An accident?" Judith asked in her most compassionate tone.

"If you want to call it that." Bert remained grim.

"That's so sad. I hope it didn't involve a vehicle. That usually means a drunken driver or a reckless teen."

Bert made no comment.

"It's good that he worked for the government," Judith continued quickly, lest Bert start to move on.

"They have excellent benefits, I understand. I suppose, though, that it depends on what branch your brother worked for."

"I suppose it does," Bert said. "Excuse me, I have to find out when the funeral director will be ready to go to the cemetery. Nice to see you again after all these years."

Nice, Judith thought, *but not very helpful.* Her brooding was interrupted by the sight of Renie, holding a chicken leg, and being propelled out of the kitchen by two stout women.

"And stay out!" one of them ordered, letting go of Renie and swiping one hand against the other. "This food is for the poor!"

"Do I look rich to you?" Renie demanded, despite the fact that she was wearing a black bouclé summer suit from Neiman Marcus.

The women didn't bother to answer, but disappeared into the kitchen.

Taking a savage bite out of the chicken leg, Renie approached her cousin. "Sowadidufnow?" she asked with her mouth full.

Judith translated quickly. "Not much. Dr. Bert was very vague about how Fred died or what he did for a living."

"But we know how he died," Renie said after she'd swallowed her food.

It was pointless to chastise Renie for invading the kitchen. Judith surveyed the hall. "Yes." Only a couple of dozen people were left, and most of them seemed to be family members. "Let's go."

"How about some real lunch?" Renie said as they climbed the stairs to the main floor.

"I can't," Judith replied. "I've got to try to sort out this latest development."

"We can do it over menus," Renie suggested. "I can help."

"Let's do it at your house," Judith said. "You have to get your car back for Bill, right?"

Renie looked at her watch. "I've got almost an hour. He won't need it until after two when he finishes his leisurely lunch."

"Okay, then we can stop at Carlo's on the canal," Judith said as they walked out to the sidewalk. "I'll meet you there in five minutes. Unless the bridge is up."

Since it was after one o'clock, the restaurant customers were beginning to leave. The cousins had no trouble getting a window table where they could look out at the various craft that plied the city's only east-west waterway. Because of time constraints, they ordered their food along with their drinks. Judith and Renie requested the same items: screwdrivers, clam chowder, and small Caesar salads with smoked prawns.

"Working for the government can be a euphemism for other things," Judith pointed out.

Renie was buttering a large chunk of warm bread. "Such as serving five to ten in a federal penitentiary?"

"That's one thing," Judith agreed. "Sometimes spies use that expression, especially those employed by the CIA. It can also be a nice way of saying that someone is on the dole, maybe a disability pension or some other form of welfare."

"Did Fred looked disabled to you?" Renie asked as their drinks were served.

"He looked dead," Judith said, raising her glass. "To Fred, whoever he may have been." She took a sip, then shook her head. "No, the Fred I met appeared hale and hearty. But that can be deceptive. Some handicaps are hard to detect. I'm convinced the answer to all this is in the UPS parcel."

"How do you plan to find out what it contained?" Renie inquired.

Judith sighed and gazed at the eight-woman crew rowing a sleek shell under the bridge. "Heaven knows I've already tried. If only we could get inside the house and talk to the elder Blands. We've blown our cover, so that's out. I've run out of ideas."

"How about sending someone else?" Renie suggested. "Like . . ." She paused. "Like Bill?"

Judith made a face. "What does Bill do? Disguise himself as a termite inspector?"

"Squirrel man," Renie responded promptly. "With the problems we've had, he knows all about squirrels. The Blands have them, right? Bill could say that one of the neighbors—like Elsie Bruce across the street—complained."

"It's a wonder she hasn't," Judith murmured. "So what does Bill do when he gets inside? Psychoanalyze the Blands?"

"He's tried psychoanalyzing the squirrels, but it hasn't done much good," Renie replied, tugging at her short chestnut hair. "I don't know. But he'd do something. At least he'd meet the Blands and see more than the entry hall or the kitchen."

"Maybe," Judith allowed. "That place is harder to get into than a bank vault." She paused to smile at the waiter, who was placing steaming bowls of chowder in front of the cousins. "It's worth a shot. Will Bill do it?"

"I can but beg," Renie said. "I have to admit, he's never been very curious about the house, even though I've babbled about it for years."

"Does he know anything about what's been going on?" Judith asked as the salads arrived.

Renie speared a smoked prawn. "Well . . . kind of. I mean, I've told him some of it, but he doesn't always listen."

"A peculiar quality in husbands," Judith murmured. "Joe's the same way. What *does* Bill know?"

"I think the part about finding the body in your trunk registered," Renie said after devouring the huge prawn in one mouthful. "But you've found bodies before, so he didn't react very much. I backtracked then and told him how we'd been scouting the Moonfleet house, which is how you happened to be there when Frank—Fred— was killed. I don't think he heard all of that. But he realizes the situation has caused you concern."

Concentrating on the problem, Judith didn't speak until she'd consumed most of her chowder. "So you'll ask him? When?"

"When I get home," Renie said. "Of course, knowing Bill, he'll have to think it through. You know how he approaches dilemmas—from east, west, north, south, and several compass points in between. Anyway, I'll phone you as soon as I get an answer."

Judith didn't respond. She was watching a tugboat tow a barge out toward the sound. THE LADY JANE was painted on the tug's stern with smaller letters underneath reading *French's Fleet*.

"Doesn't Phil French have his headquarters a mile or so from here on the canal?" she asked Renie.

Renie also looked at the tug. "Yes. Turn right from the restaurant, and go about ten blocks. Which you will do, I assume."

"I shouldn't take the time," Judith said.

Renie smirked. "But you will."

Philip French was in his office, an airy space that overlooked the canal that connected the sound to the large lake that separated the city from the eastside suburbs. Several tugs were tied up along the bank, all named for women. Judith could make out *The Lady Anna* and *The Lady Charlotte*.

Phil tried to look pleased at seeing Judith. "What brings you this way?" he asked, inviting her to sit in a captain's chair on the other side of his teak desk.

Briefly, Judith admired the oil paintings of various French's Fleet tugs as well as the framed maps of regional waters. There were a couple of other handsome ship prints as well, including a Vermeer and a Monet that she recognized from art catalogs. A perfectly scaled model of a vintage tugboat sat on Phil's desk.

"What a wonderful view," Judith remarked, gazing across the canal at the tall poplars that lined the north bank. "I wouldn't mind coming to work in a setting like this."

"I enjoy myself," Phil replied, tapping a finger on the edge of his desk. "Don't tell me you want to lease a tug, Mrs. Flynn."

"No," Judith said with a little laugh. "I was wondering how Anna is getting along after her scare the other night. Is she still leaving for Milan this week?"

"Yes, Wednesday," Phil said, still tapping. "She's feeling fine now. In fact, she thinks it was all a trick of her imagination. You know how everyone is these days—edgy, wary, not trusting anybody who looks . . . strange."

"Yet she's not nervous about traveling to Europe?" Judith asked.

"Not to Italy," Phil replied, abruptly stopping himself from tapping. "That is, she knows Milan fairly well. Rome, too. But she *is* cutting her trip short. She'll be back Sunday instead of next Tuesday."

"Instead of going on to Rome?" Judith asked in an innocent voice.

"Ah . . . no, she'd planned to do a little sightseeing," Phil replied, starting to tap his fingers again. "The Italian hill country or Lake Como or somewhere around there." He cleared his throat, stopped tapping, and turned to look at the pictures on the wall.

"Do give her my bon voyage wishes," Judith said. "I haven't been to Italy for years."

"I will." Phil stood up. "I've got to see a man about a boat. If you'll excuse me—or is there something else you wanted to discuss? A nice little cabin cruiser, perhaps?"

"Ah . . . no, I'm afraid not." Judith was stymied. But she did have one last question for Phil. "Are the tugs named for women in your family?"

"Yes," Phil said, coming around from behind his desk. "Maybe you saw the *Anna* tied up outside. That's for my wife, of course."

"And *Lady Charlotte* would be who?"

"One of my aunts," Phil replied, walking Judith out of his office and down the hall to the reception area. "By the way," he said. "I sold the *Moonfleet*."

It took a moment for his meaning to sink in. "Oh— the yacht," Judith said. "That's wonderful. I'm glad to hear that the downturn in the economy hasn't affected everybody."

Phil shrugged. "There are still people who have money and want to spend it. Anyway, I'm glad to have the yacht off my hands."

"But you're getting another, bigger one, aren't you?" Judith inquired as they reached the company's entrance.

"What?" Phil seemed taken aback. "Oh, yes, when I find exactly what I want. That takes time." He gave Judith one of his urbane smiles. "Thanks for stopping by. I'll send along your good wishes to Anna."

Walking back to her Subaru, Judith had a foreboding that Anna would need them.

An hour after Judith got home, Renie called. "Bill agreed to play Squirrel Man," Renie announced, "if he has a semilegal document to show the Blands."

"Oh, dear," Judith replied, making way for Phyliss, who was wielding a dust mop around the kitchen ceiling. "How do we do that?"

"We already did it. We used Uncle Al," Renie replied. "Good grief, he's got an in with half the city."

It was true. Al Grover had been an outstanding athlete in his day, a well-known sportsman around town, and was a former saloon owner to the Influential, especially labor leaders and city officials. While many of his cronies had passed on to that great arena in the sky, there were still a lot of people who remembered, liked, and admired Al Grover, including at least three county sheriffs.

"I don't know," Judith hemmed and hawed. "It wouldn't be exactly ethical, would it?"

"Oh, put a sock in it," Renie retorted. "Uncle Al has had Bill designated 'Squirrel Man for a Day.' "

"Bill doesn't mind?"

"Bill will do anything to avenge himself on those squirrels," Renie said. "He might even catch one. He's bringing traps."

"He's going today?" Judith asked in surprise.

"Right after his nap. He's taking it early. Right now he's on his way downtown to pick up the license. The trip fits in with his other errands."

"I can't believe you talked him into it," Judith declared. "And so quickly."

"Bill has his routine," Renie said, "but he knows that it's wise to break out of it now and then. Besides, he hates squirrels and he loves nuts. As in the Blands, who must be. Nuts, that is. Reclusive behavior intrigues him. Frankly, it's a type of neurosis he's never dealt with much over the years."

"Are you going with him?" Judith asked in an envious tone.

"Of course not. Like you, I've blown my cover. Besides, this is a job for Squirrel Man. He doesn't need a sidekick."

"I can't wait to hear what he has to say," Judith said. "Why don't you two come for dinner? I'll barbecue some ribs," she added, knowing Bill's fondness for babybacks. "I've got some in the freezer."

"I'll let you know," Renie said, and rang off.

Judith was antsy for the rest of the afternoon. By five-twenty, she still hadn't heard back from Renie. The grill was heating out on the patio; the ribs had been defrosted. Finally, at five-forty, she phoned her cousin.

"Oh!" Renie sounded dismayed. "I'm sorry, I forgot. That is, I got on the phone with Anne and we talked for over half an hour. Then I decided to call Tom and Tony. It's really hard to figure out when to get hold of Tony because Guam is like a day ahead of us."

Judith didn't chastise her cousin. All three of the Jones children and their spouses had moved far away after their marriages. Renie—and even Bill, who otherwise wasn't fond of using the telephone—racked up big long-distance bills every month.

"Are they all okay?" Judith inquired.

"Yes, they're fine, but they're homesick. One of these days . . ." Renie's voice trailed off for a moment. "Yes, we're coming for dinner. Bill's at the Moonfleet house right now. He's been gone almost an hour. I'm really sorry I didn't let you know. I imagine we'll get there around six-thirty. Is that okay?"

"It's fine," Judith said. "I'll feed Mother earlier or she'll have a fit. And the guests should be heading out by then after the social hour. We may actually be able to eat and talk in peace."

Gertrude swore the ribs were underdone and that she'd get trichinosis. Judith assured her mother that pork was supposed to be slightly pink or else it would be like eating cardboard. Which, she added, would be difficult with her mother's dentures.

Gertrude wasn't convinced. "If I croak, I'll sue you," she muttered, using her fork to pick at the meat. "The least you could do is cut it off the bone for me."

Judith did, though she was clumsy.

"What's wrong with you?" the old lady demanded. "You act like Nervous Nelly. You going through the Change? Again?"

"No, Mother," Judith assured her, "I'm really just fine. Except for worrying about Mike and Kristin and the boys."

"Who isn't?" Gertrude retorted. "I've said the rosary so often in the last few days that I've run out of Holy Mysteries. Glorious, Sorrowful, Joyous, Miserable, Hilarious—how many Mysteries are there? I forget. And where's that darned cat?"

"Actually," Judith said, "I believe there is a fourth—real—Mystery of the Rosary. The pope decreed it recently, but I don't remember what it's called. As for Sweetums, I'm afraid I still haven't heard anything about him. He may be exploring new territory. I guess I should put up some signs around here and over by Uncle Al's."

"You'd better do something," Gertrude said in an ominous tone. "Do you want that cat carried off by ravaging wolves?"

Briefly, Judith pitied any wolf that might attempt such a feat. "Cats have instincts," she asserted. "He'll find his way back. I'm sure of it."

But of course Judith feared the worst.

Renie and Bill arrived just after six-thirty. Judith had considered eating outside, but clouds were beginning to gather in the east. She offered cocktails; the Joneses declined. They were both hungry, and Bill, who had suffered from an ulcer, preferred eating between six and seven.

With Renie's help, it took only a couple of minutes to serve the food. Judith could hardly wait to hear Bill's account of his visit to Moonfleet Street.

Bill, however, took his customary deliberate time. "Good ribs," he remarked. "Red cabbage, too. Excellent."

"Tell us," Renie urged. "I practically exploded with curiosity in the car."

Judith looked at her cousin. "You haven't heard what happened?"

Renie shook her head, dislodging a couple of wilted flower petals from her hair. Bill leaned over and plucked a dead leaf from his wife's bangs. "I was waiting in front of the house for him to pick me up," Renie said. "I passed the time working in the garden. When I got in the car, he told me he'd save it until he got here so he wouldn't have to repeat himself."

"You're here now, Bill," Judith said sweetly.

Bill cleared his throat. "I was able to park on the street not far from that dirt alley off Moonfleet. I went to the back door. After a minute or two, the young TV guy responded to my knock. Alan, Adam, Aaron . . . ?"

"Alan's his real name," Judith put in.

"Alan. Say," he said, using up most of the paper napkin to wipe off his greasy fingers, "I could use a warm damp towel." He shot his wife a critical glance. "I don't enjoy feeling as if I'm wallowing around in a pigpen when I eat."

With a sneer for her husband, Renie got up to fetch

the towel. Bill took another bite of ribs and chewed for a few seconds. "I introduced myself—using my real name since it's so common—and showed him my temporary license. He seemed upset, and said he couldn't let me in." Bill forked up a chunk of baked potato.

"So what did you do?" Renie asked.

Bill chewed again, then finally answered the question. "I told Alan that if I didn't check out the complaint, a team of inspectors could be sent to go over every inch of the house. It's not a lie—that's what happens when homeowners refuse admission." He began eating more ribs.

"So what did Alan do?" Judith queried, neglecting her own plate in her anxiety over Bill's visit to the Blands.

Another digestive pause. "He contended that the squirrels were all outside, that several years ago a squirrel remover had trapped a couple of them in the attic and sealed up the whole house. The squirrels had never come back inside." More ribs for Bill.

Renie twitched in her chair before leaning toward her husband. "So?"

"So," Bill replied a moment later after another wipe-down with the towel, "I asked to see where the work had been done. Alan started to stonewall again. That's when the alarm went off."

Judith stared at Bill. "What alarm?"

"They have an alarm system," Bill explained. "The control panel is inside one of the kitchen cupboards. Alan shut it off, but he had to make sure no one was trying to get in the front door or somewhere else in the house."

"He left you alone in the kitchen?" Judith asked.

Bill nodded. He was eating more cabbage.

"What did you do?" Judith urged.

"The rest of the house seemed very dark," Bill replied after another pause. "I went into the next room, the dining room, and saw that all the drapes were pulled and seemed stiff with age. Musty, too. I assumed they hadn't been opened in years. I could make out the table and chairs—good, solid stuff—along with a buffet, a breakfront, and a couple of floral paintings on one wall."

"What was in the breakfront?" Judith asked. "I didn't notice it when I was there."

Bill shook his head. "Dishes, I think. It was hard to tell. I was trying to focus on the house itself, the ambience, the atmosphere. Understand a house, and you understand the people who live there. My initial reaction was that the residents live in fear. But fear of what? Of other people in general? No, that's not necessarily the case." He paused to chew on another rib.

"Towel," Renie murmured, handing the soiled linen to her husband.

Bill shook his head again. "I need a clean one. That's a mess."

With a heavy sigh, Renie returned to Judith's kitchen drawer.

Judith was growing impatient. "They have eye problems," she pointed out. "Or so I heard. Light bothers Jane and Sally."

Bill took the fresh towel from Renie. "I'm not talking about physical ailments. I'm trying to get inside their heads. They're in hiding. They don't want intruders. Are they hiding themselves—or hiding something else?" He stared into space. "That's what I'm trying to work through now. It'll take some time."

"Oh, don't stop now," Renie said with a sneer. "Why don't you dissect your analytical process? We're hanging on every word."

"You have cabbage hanging on your lower lip," Bill noted. "Want to borrow the towel?"

Renie declined and used the back of her hand.

"Isn't there more to the story itself?" Judith urged.

"Let me think," Bill said, then ate some more potato. "Yes," he finally continued, "I heard Alan moving around, so I went back into the kitchen. He didn't sound as if he were coming any closer, but I decided to play it safe and waited. That was when I noticed the mail sitting on the counter."

"What sort of mail?" Judith asked eagerly.

"Three pieces," Bill replied. "A bill, a circular, and"—he paused, presumably for dramatic effect—"a letter from Kopfstein, Austria."

The cousins both gasped. "Who was it to? Was there a name on the return address?" Judith asked.

Bill nodded again. "Very shaky handwriting. The return was from a Franz Steiner. The letter was sent to Frau Franz Steiner. Do you know who that is?"

SIXTEEN

FRAU STEINER HAS to be Sally," Judith declared, "Jane's sister. The so-called Uncle Franz could be her husband. That's her married name, Sally Steiner."

"Then she's not a widow," Renie noted. "But why have she and her husband lived apart for so long?"

Judith turned back to Bill. "We're getting sidetracked. What happened after you looked at the mail?"

Bill wiped his hands on the towel. "Alan returned to the kitchen. He apologized for the interruption, adding that somehow the alarm had been tripped by accident. 'A squirrel, perhaps?' I said. He assured me it wasn't a squirrel, but that they did have an occasional mouse in the basement. 'A squirrel,' I repeated. I know squirrels, dammit. Nobody knows squirrels like I know squirrels."

Bill was getting very red in the face and looking grim. But he collected himself and continued. "Definitely a mouse, Alan insisted, and looked at me as if I were weird. In any event, he went on, the alarm had frightened his grandparents and his great-aunt. They were very upset. This wasn't a good time to check out the house. Perhaps I could come back later? Or better yet, he suddenly added, he'd call the city and make the proper arrangements."

"Eyewash," declared Renie.

Bill shrugged. "Probably. In any event, I had no choice but to leave. But," he added with an intense glint in his blue eyes, "by God, I still say it was a squirrel."

Frowning, Judith picked at her food. Except for the Steiner letter, she was disappointed in Bill's adventure. "Could you see what was beyond the dining room?"

"Just barely," Bill said. "It appeared to be the living room. Leather chairs, a fireplace, more closed drapes. I only got a glimpse." He stopped speaking to finish his last rib, but waved a finger as he chewed. "Wait," he said after he'd swallowed and wiped his chin. "There was one other thing about the dining room. A statue of the Blessed Virgin. It caught what little light there was coming from the kitchen. I didn't think about it until now because you expect to see religious artwork in a Spanish-style house like that."

Judith looked puzzled. "The Blands aren't Catholic as far as I know. Dick and Jane were married in a Protestant church. Lutheran, as I recall, in Langford."

"But Steiner could be a Catholic name," Renie pointed out. "Maybe Franz is Catholic. Sally could be a convert. That might explain why Sally wasn't an attendant at Jane's wedding. In those days, it was frowned upon for Catholics to participate in Protestant ceremonies."

"But it wasn't always enforced," Bill said. "It depended a lot on the parish priest. Some of them winked at those outmoded ideas."

"Maybe Sally was living in Austria at the time," Renie suggested.

"That makes the most sense," Judith agreed. "But when she came back to the States, why didn't she bring Franz with her? Were they estranged by then? If so, why didn't they get a divorce?"

"Because," Bill put in, "Franz is a Catholic? Maybe Sally converted. Hence the Blessed Mother statue."

"But they stayed in contact," Judith murmured. "Morty the Mailman told me that over the years, there'd been letters for someone not named Bland. Sally's lived there forever, according to Elsie Bruce."

"That's a long estrangement," Renie remarked, handing Bill another towel.

Judith stood up, starting to clear the table. Renie joined her cousin in the cleanup process. "I shouldn't have—excuse the expression—ribbed Bill when he started to drone on," Renie said after her husband went out to stretch his legs on the front porch. "He's right. What are the Blands hiding or hiding from?"

"You don't hide when you live in a house for over fifty years," Judith pointed out. "You can be found, even if you're not listed in the phone book. So if it's about hiding, and not just being crazy, then what have they got in the house that they don't want anybody to see? Glenn and Trash must have gotten a search warrant. They must know what's in there."

"They won't tell you," Renie said. "You seem to be completely out of their loop."

"What's for dessert?" Bill asked as he strolled back into the kitchen. "By the way, it's starting to drizzle."

"I made Grandma Grover's cream puffs," Judith replied. "Your favorite."

"Sounds good," Bill said.

To Judith, the cream puffs might sound as well as taste good, but they also brought back memories of the first time she'd encountered murder. Some of her guests had invited a fortune-teller who was subsequently poisoned. The cream puffs had undergone their share of suspicion.

During dessert, the topic changed from murder to marriage, specifically the unions of Mike and the three Jones offspring. The cousins did most of the talking, while Bill consumed every last crumb of his cream puff. He was thinking, of course, and as he pulled away from the table, he made his pronouncement.

"I'd suggest therapy for Mike and Kristin," he said, "but I don't believe in it. What they need is a good kick in the butt."

"Amen," said Judith.

Joe didn't call that night. Judith assumed he was working long hours and was probably worn out. She was tempted to phone his hotel but resisted the urge. With any luck, he'd be home in twenty-four hours. Judith wasn't worried about his return now that she was no longer a murder suspect and had the Subaru back from the police impound.

But the phone rang around eleven-thirty, just as Judith was undressing. It wouldn't be Joe; it was one-thirty in Omaha. Maybe it was Mike. Judith grabbed the receiver with one hand and her bathrobe with the other.

"Arthur," Renie said. "What about Arthur?"

"Arthur?" Judith echoed, sitting down on the bed. "Oh! Anna's first husband. What about him?"

"That's what I'm asking," Renie replied doggedly. "Did I wake you?"

"No, of course not," Judith said. "You know I usually don't go to bed until around this time."

"Neither do I," Renie said, "which makes it very hard for me to understand how you can get up so early in the morning and actually function. But back to Arthur. I know it's off-the-wall, but did you really believe Elsie Bruce when she told us that Arthur drowned in the Blands' fishpond?"

"No, I didn't," Judith answered after a pause to recollect the conversation with the Blands' neighbor. It had been less than a week since the cousins had called on Elsie. It seemed more like a month. "That is, I realized she was confused about some things, or making them up out of sheer spite. Luke, for example, being an inventor, rather than a developer. It also occurred to me that Arthur didn't drown in the fishpond. From the way you described it, the pond had been empty for ages."

"It wouldn't have been deep enough to drown a grown man," Renie pointed out. "I don't think it was more than a foot, if that. Someone would have had to hold Arthur down. Unless, of course, he was drunk and fell in. But you're right—Arthur's been dead for what? Fifteen, twenty years? I'd say that pond's been dried up for a good thirty. I don't remember seeing it more than a couple of times when I was a kid."

Judith grimaced. "You're evil. You're trying to make sure I can't get a good night's rest. Frankly, I hadn't thought much about Arthur. But now that you mention it . . ." She paused, trying to recall something else Mrs. Bruce had said. "His last name was Craig. I remember asking if he'd drowned in a boating accident. Elsie Bruce sneered at that, and said something about 'Where would Arthur get a boat?' I wonder if he got one from Philip French?"

"Ah." Renie laughed quietly. "Phil, in love with Anna, maybe having an affair with her, takes Arthur out on his yacht—and pushes him overboard."

"Assuming Phil had a yacht in those days," Judith said as the rain began to come down hard enough to make splattering noises on the tree near the bedroom window. "He would've just been getting started in the tug business." She turned to look outside at the rain. "Maybe we're going out on a limb."

"We can check the records on Arthur Craig tomorrow," Renie said. "That is, Bill can. He has to go to the courthouse to turn in his temporary license to make everything legal. It was good only for today."

"If we find the date of death," Judith put in, "we can look his obit up in the newspaper archives."

"Unfortunately," Renie pointed out, "the Internet archives don't go back that far. We'll have to go there in person. Unless, of course, I can con Bill into stopping on the way home from the courthouse."

After Judith had hung up, she wondered why they were going to such trouble to find out about the demise of Arthur Craig. He'd been dead for over fifteen years. It'd be much simpler to merely ask Anna or some other family member what had happened to him.

Judith finished getting ready for bed, and went to sleep with dreams about big orange koi swimming in an Olympic-size pool with Mark Spitz.

Tuesday was Allergy Morning for Judith. She was accustomed to allergies. Both cousins suffered from them. But on this particular gloomy day in June, four of her guests had submitted their lists of what they couldn't eat, including eggs, pork, wheat, and milk. Breakfast would have to provide alternatives. Rye toast, artificial eggs, hamburger patties, and fruit would fill the bill and, Judith hoped, the tummies.

"I need a vacation," Judith complained to Phyliss Rackley. "Unfortunately, that's impossible until fall. I can't leave Hillside Manor in the summer."

"Idle hands are the devil's workshop," Phyliss retorted. "Speaking of which, I don't see your wicked cat anywhere."

"I know," Judith said with a sigh. "As soon as I clear up from breakfast, I'm going to make some signs."

"Signs," murmured Phyliss. "There are many signs in the Bible and one of the bad ones is your furry familiar." She flipped a dustrag for emphasis and headed upstairs.

Renie called around eleven. Bill, who was an early-to-bed, early-to-rise type, had just gotten back from the courthouse. He'd found Arthur Andrew Craig's death certificate. He had died June 3, 1985, at the age of thirty-one. Cause of death was listed as accidental drowning.

"But not necessarily in a fishpond?" Judith remarked.

"Not necessarily," Renie replied. "I think we can save a trip to the newspaper if I coax my buddy Melissa to check the archives."

Melissa Bargroom was the newspaper's music critic. Judith had met her a few times, and considered her anything but the stodgy classical critic she had originally envisioned. If Melissa had to stand on her head, twirl like a dervish, and sing Lucia di Lammermoor's Mad Scene, she'd be up to the task.

"I'll let you know what she finds out," Renie said, "wild-goose chase, or not. Come to think of it, there's an opera about a goose girl, but it's kind of obscure."

"I should think so," Judith said, and rang off.

She got six feet from the phone when it rang again.

"Late lunch break," Joe said in a weary voice. "We've got a slight hitch. I won't be home until tomorrow."

"Is the hitch a serious problem?" Judith asked.

"No," he replied, "we're waiting for some expert to show up from New York and his flight was canceled. He won't get in until this evening."

"You've never mentioned what kind of case you're working on," Judith said. "Is it hush-hush?"

"Yes. That's why I never mentioned it." Joe sighed. "I'll be able to tell you when it's finally wrapped up and I get home. No big deal. It's not exactly dangerous. What's going on at your end?"

Judith kept her recital brief, though she did relay the worrisome news about Sweetums.

"You know," Joe said softly, "he's an old cat. He may have just crawled off somewhere and—"

"No!" Judith broke in. "Sweetums isn't *that* old! We got him after I moved back home. Some cats live to be in their twenties, especially the really pampered ones. And you can't say that Sweetums isn't that."

"No," Joe said in a musing tone, "I certainly can't. And he's tough. I'll give the little beast that much."

The phone call galvanized Judith into making up some signs on the computer. She had a half-dozen photos of Sweetums, but two showed him asleep; two more showed only his rear end and plumelike tail. In the pair of remaining pictures, he looked so ornery that she was afraid he might scare off would-be finders. Indeed, she thought as she printed out the signs, if there had been a "Ten Most Wanted" cat gallery at the post office, Sweetums would be Human Enemy Number One.

After making Gertrude's lunch, Judith spent the next half hour posting the signs in the immediate neighborhood and along Heraldsgate Avenue all the way to the turnoffs for the two nearest bridges. She had another dozen left, so she headed to Langford and Uncle Al's.

Her uncle was home, watching a baseball game on TV. Or four baseball games, since Al Grover had two TV sets, both of which had picture-in-picture inset features.

"You've struck out, haven't you?" Al said, not looking away from the games in progress. "I feel terrible about it. I'm not used to having pets."

"It's not your fault," Judith assured him. "Sweetums has never been out of our neighborhood until this. The person to blame is that Mrs. Greenwalt, who insisted on his absence from Hillside Manor. I didn't know what to do."

"He may still show up," Uncle Al said, grimacing as one of the four second basemen made a fielding error. "Did you know I've got an autographed ball from Jackie Robinson?"

"No," Judith said. "How'd you manage that?"

"I asked him for it," Uncle Al replied. "It's worth a bundle now, but I wouldn't part with it at any price. I keep it in a safe with my souvenirs from the war."

"I saw some of those when I was a kid," Judith said. "I think it was right after you got out of the navy."

"Probably," Al replied, pausing as one of the four batters smacked a line drive home run just over the right field wall. "I don't know how much that stuff is worth. Somehow, it seems as if the collectors' items from the Pacific don't gain as much in value as Corky's stash from Europe. I think I'll sell the stuff anyway. I could use the money to buy another TV. You know, one of those big jobs with the flat screen."

Judith laughed, as much in astonishment as amusement. "What on earth would you watch with so many sets?"

"Plenty of good stuff," her uncle replied, picking up a TV schedule. "I've got that special sports package that shows games and other events all over the world. It'd be a moneymaker in the long run. I'd be able to see more, and thus, bet more wisely."

"What does your bookie say about that?" Judith asked.

Uncle Al finally looked at his niece. "Not *bookie*. You

know they're illegal around here. I have a sports *broker*. In fact, he's also my stockbroker. A very versatile guy."

That figured, Judith thought. Uncle Al was also pretty versatile, at least when it came to making a buck.

She ran out of signs about a mile from Uncle Al's house. By that time, the rain had begun to soak through her clothes. But she was only a few blocks from Moonfleet Street. She couldn't resist driving by the Bland property.

The worn stucco and tiles looked even more dilapidated through the rain. Slowing down near the walkway to the front door, she saw Luke Bland leaving the house. Fortunately, there was a parking place behind what looked like a brand-new Toyota SUV. By the time Judith had turned off the engine, Luke had opened the SUV and was reaching into the back.

Judith got out of her car. "Hi," she called to Luke, whose upper torso was still inside the vehicle. "Are you delivering the groceries this week?"

Startled, Luke stopped whatever he was doing and stared at her. Despite the rain and gloomy clouds, he was wearing his sunglasses. "Ah!" he exclaimed, forcing a smile. "Mrs. Flynn. What can I do for you?"

"Nothing, really," Judith said, approaching him. "I just happened to be driving by on the way home from my uncle's place. I saw you coming out of your parents' and thought I'd say hello. How is everybody?"

"Fine, fine," Luke replied in a jovial voice that, to Judith's surprise, struck her as genuine. "Say, you shouldn't be standing out in this rain. It's coming down pretty hard."

Judith declined to take the hint. "I'm a native. I don't mind."

"I'm not," he replied, "and I want to get back under cover. Hold on." He rummaged around inside the SUV, finally pulling out a tool kit and what looked like a wooden sign with matching posts. Setting his burden down on the parking strip, he grinned at Judith. "As long as you're here," he said, picking up the sign and turning it around, "are you interested in buying a house? This one's for sale."

SEVENTEEN

JUDITH COULDN'T HIDE her astonishment. "For sale? What about your parents? And your aunt?"

Luke was still smiling. "We finally convinced them they'd be far better off in a retirement home. The police intrusion last week, and the possibility that a man was killed near the house, made them realize that it was time to move on. Lynette and I—along with Anna and Phil—are making the arrangements. We've found a very nice place for them not too far away."

Judith was still flabbergasted. She studied the sign, which read:

FOR SALE
By appointment only—contact
LUKE BLAND
REAL ESTATE AND PROPERTY INVESTMENT

"I'd love to see the inside of the house," Judith said. "When is it possible to do that?"

"Not until after the first of the month," Luke

replied. "I'll start setting up appointments as soon as I hear from prospective buyers. We have to get the old folks settled, move the belongings they want to keep, and do some cleanup."

"What about an estate sale?" Judith inquired, moving closer to the shelter of a tall cedar tree. "They must have some valuable pieces. Or at least items that would qualify as antiques after fifty years."

Luke shrugged. "My parents couldn't afford expensive furnishings. Oh, I know that with so much restoration of older homes these days, people will pay exorbitant prices for anything that fits their period decor. Anna keeps up with that kind of thing. She says the best way to handle it is to sell the whole lot to an estate auction house."

"That makes sense," Judith said, flinching as a large drop of rain dripped from a cedar branch onto her nose. "What's the asking price?"

"Four ninety-five," Luke replied, no longer smiling. "I'm afraid the house needs quite a bit of work."

"Yes," Judith murmured, moving another step or two to avoid the *drip-drip-drip* of the big cedar. "It'll have to be brought up to code."

Luke bent down to open the tool kit. "I'd better get this sign up before I catch pneumonia. If you're really interested in seeing the house, give me a call along about Friday."

"I will," Judith said as Lynette Bland came out of the house.

"What's taking you so long?" she called to her husband as she came down the walk.

Luke looked up from the post he'd started to pound

into the damp ground. "What? Oh, I was talking to Mrs. Flynn here."

Just before reaching the sidewalk, Lynette spotted Judith. "Oh." She didn't look too happy to see their visitor. "Are you in the market for a house?"

"Not really," Judith said, "but one of my cousins is. They're moving here from Nebraska. This might be just the right kind of property for them," she went on, elaborating on her fib. "Spanish style is unusual in Beatrice, where they live now. Not to mention that they're very handy at repair work."

Lynette's pale face brightened slightly. "Really? If they're still in Nebraska, they can take a virtual tour of the house once Luke has it ready to show on the Internet. Excuse me," she said, noting that Luke had almost finished his task. "I have to go back inside to get my purse. I took the afternoon off from work, so we're heading home."

"I'll get your purse," Luke said, adjusting the sign, which hung from two short chains. "I want to say good-bye to the oldsters." He headed for the house. The rain had almost stopped.

"Would you mind showing me something?" Judith asked Lynette.

"What?"

"My cousins have always wanted a water feature," Judith lied. "They're great gardeners, too, especially with wildflowers and native plants. Did someone say there'd been a fishpond here?"

Lynette frowned. "Yes, years ago."

"Does it still exist?"

"Sort of." Lynette had started walking down the

street toward the far corner. "You can see what's left of it from the side of the house."

Through the fence and next to the collapsed greenhouse covered with blackberry vines was the outline of a concrete pond. Two thirds of it was overgrown with scilla now past its prime, ferns, vetch, and weeds. All but the rim of the formation was covered with moss. Renie was right. It was no more than a foot deep, though it was five feet wide and about eight feet long.

"It could be salvaged," Judith remarked. "I assume the pipes are still underground."

"I wouldn't know," Lynette replied. "It was before my time."

"Just as well to leave it drained," Judith said, and then lied some more. "I once heard of a child who wandered into someone's yard and drowned in a pond that was unattended."

Lynette nodded once. "Like those refrigerators people leave in their yards. Kids can't resist exploring."

"Speaking of drowning," Judith said as they walked back down to the corner, "I understand Anna's first husband, Arthur, drowned. How awful. Was he swimming?"

"Fishing," Lynette said. "Alcohol and trout don't mix."

"Oh, dear," Judith said softly, "that's so sad. Was he alone?"

"No. He was with some shirttail relation visiting from out of town. They'd both been drinking. They were on a lake someplace up near Blue Mountain. The boat tipped over, I guess. The other fellow managed to save himself, but he couldn't rescue Art. It was very hard on Anna. They'd been married seven years."

"No children, though?"

Lynette shook her head. "Anna can't have children. I'm not sure she really wanted them. She's very career-minded, and neither Art nor Phil seemed to care."

"She was lucky to find Phil," Judith noted. "That is, another man who didn't insist on raising a family. Was the problem hereditary?"

Lynette looked blankly at Judith. "How do you mean?"

"Well," Judith said, feeling awkward, "her mother, Jane, apparently didn't think she could have children or they wouldn't have adopted Luke. But after several years, she got pregnant with Anna."

"Yes." Lynette glanced across the street toward Elsie Bruce's house. "But I don't think the medical conditions were similar. Anyway, she'd known Phil for years. I think they met in high school. They didn't date, in fact, they didn't run into each—" Lynette stopped just short of Judith's car. "Why am I telling you this?"

"People tend to do that with me," Judith said with a wry smile, though she knew the thaw between them was partially caused by her relations' alleged interest in buying the house. "I'm told I invite confidences."

Lynette shrugged. "Well, none of this is confidential. But I'm usually not a babbler. Ah," she went on, espying her husband coming across the sidewalk, "Luke's ready to go. Check the Internet in a couple of weeks. You can tell your relatives to watch for it, too."

Judith said she would. But of course the only relative she was going to tell was Renie.

*   *   *

They can't do that," Renie declared, insisting that Judith stand by the heat vent in the Joneses' living room. "Don't move. You're very dampish and likely to grow mold."

"What do you mean?" Judith asked. "If Mr. and Mrs. Bland have agreed to sell the house, why shouldn't they?"

"Because," Renie stated in a stubborn voice, "it's bad business to put a house up for sale shortly after a crime has been committed there. It's much better to wait six months. There's such a thing as 'disclosure,' you know."

"I thought it was one of those 'don't ask, don't tell' situations," Judith responded, shaking out her cotton slacks.

"That happens sometimes," Renie admitted, "but it's unethical and dishonest."

Judith slowly shook her head. "The problem is that no one except those of us directly involved know that a murder occurred on the Bland property. What little media coverage there was mentioned that the victim was found in the trunk of a car on Heraldsgate Hill. As far as the public is concerned, there's no connection with Moonfleet Street."

"Luckily," Renie noted with some asperity, "there's no public connection with you, either. But I still don't think it's right for Luke Bland to sell the house so soon after the tragedy. The neighbors know *something* happened there, or the cops wouldn't have shown up. You can bet Elsie Bruce would give prospective buyers an earful."

"That's true," Judith allowed. "Elsie's probably already jabbering her head off to Teresa about the 'For Sale' sign." She snapped her fingers. "Teresa! Why haven't I talked to her? She warned us to keep away from the house. Why?"

Renie looked thoughtful. "Superstitious? If I had to look at that house every day, I'd get the willies, too. As it was, I used to see it maybe once every couple of weeks during the school year. I merely became obsessed."

"We should ask her," Judith said. "Where did you last toss your phone?"

Renie tended to be careless with her cordless phone, leaving it outside in flower beds, on top of the garbage can, and inside the clothes dryer. Judith felt it was fortunate that her cousin had a lease agreement allowing her to have the phones replaced after they'd been on the spin cycle too long.

"Ah . . ." Renie glanced around the living and dining rooms. "The kitchen, I think. Yes, it's in the silverware drawer. Hold on, I'll get it."

"The directory, too," Judith shouted after her cousin.

Renie returned with both items and handed them to Judith. "Remember, Elsie's still listed under her late husband's name."

"I know," Judith said, moving from the heat vent to an armchair. Finding Elsie's number, she pressed the buttons. The "3" seemed to stick, but the call went through. "What did you spill on this?" Judith murmured.

"Pepsi," Renie replied, unconcerned.

Teresa answered on the fourth ring. *"Hola,"* she said.

Judith identified herself. "My cousin and I called on Mrs. Bruce last week."

"Oh, sure," Teresa said with a little laugh. "You were grilling her about the Blands."

"Yes," Judith responded, "and when we were leaving, you warned us to stay away from the Blands' house. How come?"

There was a pause at the other end. "Sorry," Teresa said, "I had to move into another room on the off chance Mrs. Bruce could catch a word or two." She cleared her throat. "I was probably being silly. But when I first came to work for Mrs. Bruce a couple of years ago, she told me—while I pretended not to understand, of course—that the house was haunted. She said there'd been strange doings there at night a long time ago, and she insisted she'd seen a ghost walking in the grounds after that." Teresa paused again. "Mrs. Bruce forgets some things, she gets them mixed up, she rambles. In any event, she never mentioned the house being haunted after that. But about three weeks before you stopped by, I had to get up in the middle of the night to go to the bathroom. Hold on."

Teresa apparently turned away from the receiver. *"Sí, señora!"* she called. *"Las esmeraldas, sí, sí. Ahora, pronto, sí."*

"More emeralds," Teresa said into the phone. "Gimme a break. Where was I?"

"Going to the bathroom," Judith said, anxiously waiting for Teresa to finish her tale.

"Right. The moon was out that night, and from the upstairs bathroom window, you can look out on the Bland place. I swear to God, I saw what looked like a ghost."

"You saw a ghost?" Judith said for Renie's benefit.

"You may think I'm nuts," Teresa said, "but I do believe in ghosts. Our neighbors in Medford had one when I was growing up. I never saw it—actually, it was a her—but it was all pretty convincing. Rumpled quilts, lights turned on by themselves, furniture moved—the whole bit."

"What exactly did you see from the bathroom window?" Judith asked.

"A white figure, moving slowly in front of the house and then disappearing around the other side. I'll admit," Teresa went on, "it was hard to see with all the trees and shrubs over there. But I caught several glimpses between the greenery until the figure went out of sight."

"The white figure was moving west or east?" Judith inquired as Renie stood rooted to a spot in front of the sofa.

"Is that important?"

"Just curious," Judith said.

"Umm . . . it would be to the west," Teresa replied. "Toward the back of the house where the garage is located, if you know where I mean."

"Yes," said Judith, "I know where the garage is. Did you see anything else?"

"No. I waited for several minutes," Teresa said. "Finally, the moon went behind a cloud and I couldn't see much of anything. Look, I'm probably being silly. I shouldn't have scared you. But that place is really creepy, ghost or no ghost. I couldn't get back to sleep the rest of the night."

"It's creepy all right," Judith agreed.

"I'll be relieved when they sell it and move out,"

Teresa declared. "On top of everything else, now their blasted alarm system keeps going off. You can hear it everywhere. Fortunately, Mrs. Bruce is immune as long as she doesn't have her hearing aids turned on. Oh—by the way, did you know the house is for sale?"

"I did, actually," Judith said. "I'm afraid I didn't heed your warning."

"Well, as long as you haven't seen any—*sí, señora! Oro, muy bonito!*" Teresa lowered her voice. "Now she's on the gold wagon. Gotta go."

"Ghosts, huh?" Renie said when Judith rang off.

"Ghostlike figure," Judith replied. "I suppose it could be one of the Blands in a nightshirt, getting some fresh air. They certainly don't go outside very often during the day."

"Chasing squirrels, maybe," Renie remarked. "Hey, you're pretty well dried out."

Judith didn't respond immediately. She'd stood up and put the phone down in the armchair. Pacing around the living room, she didn't hear Renie. "Prepare yourself, coz," she said suddenly. "We're going in."

Renie's brown eyes widened. "In where?"

Judith smiled grimly. "Into the Blands' house. Tonight, after dark. Wear camouflage."

Good grief!" Renie cried, collapsing on the sofa. "You're kidding!"

"I am not."

"Camouflage? What kind? Squirrel suits?"

Judith shook her head. "Just something dark."

"What about the alarm system?"

"Teresa says it's going off every so often," Judith

replied. "They'll think it's another false alarm. Squirrels, no doubt. Or," she added on an optimistic note, "they may have had to disconnect it. The alarm-system companies—and the cops—don't like it when those things get tripped by accident. The owners can get penalized."

"You're taking a big risk," Renie pointed out. "I mean, *we're* taking a big risk. Oh, hell," she fretted, "we aren't really going to do this, are we?"

But Renie saw the answer in the obstinate set of Judith's face.

Judith had her own qualms about breaking into the Blands' house. It was illegal, dangerous, and foolhardy. It was also the only way she could ever discover the truth about the mystery on Moonfleet. There were other things that disturbed her, too, or at least raised some important questions. Sitting in front of the computer, she began to type a list:

What are Blands hiding—or hiding from?

Uncle Franz Steiner—annual parcel; Kopfstein, Austria

Arthur Craig—accidental drowning or not?

Car chasing Anna in and from parking garage

Frank Purvis a.k.a. Fred Pettibone

Cops & media downplay FP's murder

There were other, smaller unanswered queries, but these were the ones that plagued her most. For at least five minutes, she stared at the notations on the screen.

Woody Price was still out of town. No help there from
the police grapevine. She'd talked to all of the younger
Blands, the neighbors, and the Pettibone family. What
if—the thought made Judith groan aloud—Frank
Purvis had been killed by someone who had no connection to the Blands? He might have been prowling
around the house while his stolen milk truck was
parked on the other side of the street. Or was he sneaking a peek at the houses lining the other side of the dirt
track?

Judith didn't believe that. For one thing, contact had
been established between Phil and Frank. To her, he'd
always be Frank rather than Fred, since it was in his
guise as Frank that she'd carted his corpse around
Heraldsgate Hill. It had to be Frank who'd sought out
Phil on the golf course. Frank Purvis wasn't a member;
he would've had to get someone to sponsor him. There
might be a record of the sponsorship at the country
club, but their privacy policy wouldn't allow her to
find out the member's name.

Interlocking her hands behind her head, Judith
sighed. Getting inside the house might help her solve
the mystery. It was a desperate measure, but she had
to try it. Otherwise, she seemed to have tapped every
resource, followed every lead.

But one.

A name jumped out at her from the past: Addison
Kirby, city-hall reporter, and widower of the actress
Joan Fremont, who had been murdered while staying
at Good Cheer Hospital. Addison had regular contact
with the police. Judith had found him to be a decent
man and they had parted on good terms. She dialed

the number for the newspaper's city desk and asked for Addison Kirby.

By luck, he was at his desk. "How could I ever forget you, Judith?" he asked. "You exposed the villain who killed my wife. Among others," he added grimly. "How's your hip?"

"Fairly good," Judith replied. "How's your leg?"

"Almost as good as new," Addison said, referring to the broken bones he'd suffered when the killer ran him down in the hospital parking lot. "Last night, I danced the tango. Joan taught me how years ago, but I never really got into it until I met Amalia."

"Is she a special friend?"

"Yes," Addison replied, his voice softening. "I'll never stop missing Joan, but Amalia has given me a reason to keep going."

"Good for you," Judith declared.

"You know how it is—you lost your first husband, right?"

"Lost" always seemed a peculiar way to describe Dan McMonigle's demise. Dan had been so huge that Judith couldn't have "lost" him unless he'd been fired off into outer space.

"Yes, Dan died young, too," Judith said. "You met Joe, of course. He's wonderful. Which," she went on, "is part of the reason I'm calling. Joe's not only retired from the force, but he's out of town, and so is his former partner, Woody Price. I have no real in with the police, and somehow I got involved with . . ."

Judith hit the high points of her story, not wanting to get off the track with details that would be out of Addison's purview. "So you see," she concluded, "I don't understand why Frank Purvis's murder has been played down in the media. Have you heard anything about it?"

"I did, in fact," Addison answered. "One of the new reporters on the police beat picked it up off the log. I can't believe you were the one with the body in your car."

"I can," Judith murmured. "That is, it was a terrible shock, of course. Do you know why your reporter didn't follow up on the story?"

Addison's laugh was bleak. "If you read the paper, you can see that there's almost a murder a day in this region. As for the city, maybe one a week. Most of them are fueled by alcohol or drugs. Who wants to read about a wife who wallops her husband with a cast-iron skillet while they're both drunk as skunks? Or a couple of guys in a bar shoot-out? It's horrible, it's sordid, and it's—unfortunately—too common to make big headlines. I'd seen the article, but figured a couple of bozos got into it during a midday drinking bout and one of them whacked the other one."

"So you don't find it odd that there wasn't a second story with more details?" Judith asked, disappointed.

"Well—no." Addison sounded apologetic. "For one thing, the police don't release names until they notify next of kin."

"But don't the original articles state cause of death?"

"If it's obvious—like a stabbing or a shooting— they do," Addison replied. "But I gather that in this case, the cops wanted to wait for an autopsy. Anyway, a day or so later, Chico—that's the new guy on the police beat—got assigned to a gang shooting in the south end. It involved two innocent victims, including a pregnant woman—a random act of violence. Chico, you see, is writing a book on the subject. Or trying to. There's only so many hours in a day and so much space in the paper."

Judith recalled seeing a couple of articles about the drive-by shootings, but hadn't paid much attention. Like the drug-related killings and the drunken domestic homicides, the gang murders hadn't piqued her interest. As Addison said, they were too common.

"But," Judith pointed out, "the rest of the media seemed to ignore Frank Purvis, too."

"Same thing," Addison said. "Thirty minutes less commercial breaks, weather, sports, and features—the broadcasters can't cover everything."

Judith was silent for a moment. "I still think it's odd. Would you mind asking Chico if he *tried* to do a follow-up on the original story?"

"I'll ask him right now," Addison replied. "He just walked into the newsroom."

Judith waited impatiently while she heard the murmur of masculine voices at the other end of the line. Finally, Addison again spoke into the receiver.

"Chico says he did try to find out if the guy was officially ID'd, but he was told that the victim was using an alias. That's when he gave up," Addison recounted before lowering his voice. "That's also about the time they had the gang shoot-out."

"Frank Purvis was using an alias," Judith stated. "He was really Alfred Pettibone, a solid citizen and a civil servant."

"No kidding!" Addison sounded intrigued. "How do you know?"

Judith told him about attending Fred Pettibone's funeral. "It was just a hunch until I saw the body," she added.

"You really are something," Addison said in an awed tone. "Maybe you should sell your B&B and take up detective work along with your husband."

"I'd rather not," Judith replied, "but thanks for the compliment."

"You know," Addison said, still speaking softly, "I owe you one. A big one, in fact. Chico won't mind. He's writhing his way through Chapter Three on why bad guys go badder. I think I'll do a little digging of my own."

"Would you?" Judith was excited at the prospect.

"Sure. I'll start now. City hall's budget crisis is beginning to bore me. And the readers, too. I'll let you know what I find out."

Judith expressed her gratitude and hung up. Turning back to her list on the monitor, she had another brainstorm. If Uncle Franz could call for a UPS pickup from Kopfstein, then he might have a telephone. Tiny Alpine village or not, no place on earth was too remote these days. According to the phone book, there was a nine-hour time difference, making it shortly after eleven at night in Austria. No matter. Maybe Uncle Franz kept late hours. She dialed international information, and after a couple of transfers, reached Salzburg and an operator who spoke almost flawless English.

Judith, however, didn't speak any German, flawed or unflawed. The gruff voice that answered after several rings was unintelligible to her.

"Is this Franz Steiner?" she asked, slowly and loudly.

"*Ja, ja,* so vot?"

"I'm Judith . . . Hoffman," she said, using Gertrude's maiden name in the hope of creating an Austro-Germanic bond.

"Are you a Chew?"

"What?"

"A Chew," Franz repeated loudly. "Of the Chewish race."

"No, I'm a Catholic," Judith replied, realizing that Franz meant "Jew." "Why does it matter?"

"Never mind. Vot about Sally? Is she dead?"

"No, she's fine," Judith asserted. "She doesn't see too well. She can't dial the phone. I'm calling for her."

"Vy not Lukas? Or Anna? Vere is Lukas?"

Judith assumed the old man meant Luke. "He's home, with Lynette."

"Oh." Franz sounded relieved, but resumed his gruff tone. "Vy so late? I vas abed."

"I'm sorry, but this is important." Judith swallowed hard before she spoke again. "Your last package was . . . lost."

"*Vot?*" Franz sounded as if he were going to explode.

"Was it insured?"

"*Nein, nein* . . . no, no. I never insure. You ring off phone. I call Sally. *Mein Gott,* I haven't heard her—" The call ended abruptly.

Judith frowned at the mute receiver. She wasn't sure she'd taken the right approach. Maybe she shouldn't have mentioned the parcel at all. But at least she'd found out that Franz Steiner was alive and grumpy in Kopfstein, Austria.

But maybe the expensive prime-time international call hadn't been wasted. Judith dialed Renie's number.

"What's up?" Renie asked, panting.

"Are you okay?" Judith inquired.

"Yes, yes, I'm okay, if you call 'okay' trying to re-plant the primroses the squirrels dug up last night. I'm under an azalea bush, retrieving a purple one that the little wretches tossed there. Fortunately, I brought the phone outside."

"Don't turn the hose on the receiver like you did a month or so ago," Judith cautioned.

"I didn't mean to," Renie replied, catching her breath. "I was aiming for the squirrels."

"Guess what," Judith said. "I just had a chat with Uncle Franz."

"You did?" Renie sounded aghast.

"It was brief, but more interesting than I thought at first." Succinctly, she recounted the conversation.

"Lord, you're a pathological liar," Renie said with a sigh. "You're getting out of hand. What was so inter-esting other than that you're probably going to hell?"

"Funny coz," Judith murmured. "I'll tell you what I realized after he hung up on me. He referred to Lukas, not Luke. Thus I don't think Luke Bland was adopted. I think he's Franz and Sally Steiner's son."

EIGHTEEN

OKAY," RENIE SAID with only a hint of skepticism, "tell me how you came to the conclusion that Luke is Sally and Franz's kid."

"Never mind that right now," Judith said. "Luke's eye problem has always bothered me."

"Not as much as it bothers him."

"Hush." Judith didn't need interruptions. She was running behind on her daily schedule and still had to prepare the appetizers for the incoming guests. "If it's hereditary, it may have come down from his mother's side. It'd be too much of a coincidence for Dick and Jane Bland to adopt a kid who had a similar eye condition. But Sally has it, too. Thus Sally is Luke's mother. When Luke and I were talking about the rain, he mentioned that he's not a native. I didn't think much of it at the time, assuming the Blands had gotten him from another state, or even from east of the mountains, where the weather is very different. Then Uncle Franz called him 'Lukas' and seemed more interested in him than in Anna. It finally all came together. Sally may have had her baby in Austria, and for reasons I still don't know, sent him to live with the Blands and they adopted him."

"Why couldn't Sally have come at the same time with the kid?" Renie asked as Judith paused for breath.

"Maybe she did," Judith replied. "She's been here for many years. But why stay married to Franz? Why didn't Franz come with her? Why is he still in Austria?"

"He likes it there?" Renie suggested.

"That's possible," Judith allowed. "The other possibility is that he couldn't join Sally and Luke because he wasn't able to get into the country."

"Hmm." Renie was silent for a moment. "Are you thinking 'Nazi'?"

"Nazi sympathizer, maybe," Judith said. "That came to mind when he asked if I was Jewish. Let's face it, some of those old folks in Europe still have anti-Semitic feelings, not to mention Nazi sympathies. Remember, Austria had its own National Socialist party before the war."

"I know that, I've seen *The Sound of Music* six times," Renie said. "So what you're saying is that Uncle Franz may not have *dared* to enter the U.S."

"Right," Judith responded, trying to ignore Phyliss, who had just come up from the basement and was groaning loudly while she massaged her left knee. "Sally, being an American, didn't have that problem. But because she wanted to be with Franz, she may have sent the baby here, using the ruse of adoption by the Blands."

"I hate to admit it," Renie said, "but you're making

sense." She paused. "How about your own son? Any word from Mike?"

"No," Judith replied as Phyliss hopped into the kitchen on one leg. Obviously, another attack of hypochondria had beset the cleaning woman.

"How about Sweetums?" Renie inquired.

"No." Judith couldn't ignore Phyliss, who was now sprawled on the floor. "I'm trying to keep distracted." She glanced at the twitching figure just a few feet away. "It's not as hard as you might think."

As Judith said good-bye to Renie, Phyliss raised her head. "I'm paralyzed," she declared.

"From what?" Judith asked, long accustomed to such complaints.

"Arthritis. Rheumatism. Lumbago." Phyliss groaned some more. "The Lord loves those He punishes."

"That's never made much sense to me," Judith said. "Do you want me to help you get up or would you like to just lie there for a day or two?"

"You could call an ambulance," Phyliss said between moans.

"I could," Judith agreed, "but over the years, we've had our share of emergency vehicles here in the cul-de-sac. What I can do is go out to the car and get the tire jack and lift you up with that."

"What? Are you crazy?" Phyliss shrieked.

"Not at all," Judith replied calmly. "I'm not sure I can manage to raise you without damaging my artificial hip."

"You could be real careful. I'm not heavy, I'm your hired help." Phyliss went limp.

Sighing, Judith pulled a chair away from the kitchen

table and sat down in an effort to spare her hip. "Did you twist your knee?"

"It twists itself," Phyliss replied, facedown again on the faux pine flooring.

Judith bent over just far enough to grasp the ties on Phyliss's apron. "Guess what," she said, unable to budge the cleaning woman without cooperation. "If you lie there like a rag doll, I can't help you. I suggest prayer."

Phyliss didn't react for several moments. Then she began to wail and shout hymns of praise. Or something. Judith couldn't be sure, but it seemed to work. Suddenly Phyliss bolted onto her knees, let out a few more worshipful paeans, and finally struggled to her feet.

"It's a miracle!" she cried, embracing Judith with fervor. "Hallelujah! I'm cured!" Phyliss hesitated. "For now."

"Good," Judith said, patting Phyliss's back before wriggling free. "I assume you mopped the kitchen floor earlier."

" 'Course I did," Phyliss said, a scowl replacing exultation. "Do you think I'd wallow around on a floor with ungodly germs? I'm almost done except for the living and dining rooms and the front parlor. I'd like to go home a little early so I can put together my miraculous witness for our Bible study group tonight."

"Fine, Phyliss," Judith said, opening the fridge and considering the possibilities for the guests' hors d'oeuvres.

After the morning and early afternoon's hustle and bustle, the rest of the day seemed to drag. Judith kept busy, but she was anxious to head for Moonfleet Street. Luckily, the weather had remained overcast, which meant that it should get completely dark around ten o'clock, instead of closer to ten-thirty.

Just before eight, she called Renie again. "I'll pick you up at ten," she told her cousin. "What are you telling Bill?"

"Not much," Renie replied, speaking in a low voice. "And don't come until after ten-fifteen. Bill should be heading for bed by then. If he misses me, I'll leave a note, saying I had to go over to the B&B to help you with some unruly guests."

"Let's make it ten-thirty," Judith said. "I can lock up the house at ten, and we want to make sure the Blands are in bed."

"How do we do that?" Renie asked.

"When all the lights are out," Judith said.

"*The* light, you mean," Renie noted. "I've never seen more than one on at a time in that house."

"Correct." Judith took a deep breath. "Are you nervous?"

"No. I'm drunk."

"Coz!"

"Just kidding," Renie said. "I'm not as much nervous as I am curious after all these years of wondering what went on inside that house. I can barely sit still. While Bill's watching De Niro and Pacino in *Heat* for the forty-third time, I told him I was going to organize my closet. I've been all over the house like a damned grasshopper."

"We'll be okay," Judith asserted. "What's the worst thing that can happen?"

"Getting arrested? Getting killed?"

"Either. Both. See you at ten-thirty."

Fortunately, all the guests except a thirtysomething couple from Little Rock, Arkansas, had returned to Hillside Manor by ten o'clock. The latecomers had their key and their instructions. After making sure Gertrude was all right, Judith put her domestic responsibilities behind her and drove off to collect Renie.

Misgivings began to overcome Judith by the time she reached the top of the hill. As she descended the north slope, the misgivings became qualms. By the time she reached the Joneses' house, doubts loomed large before her.

Renie, clad in black slacks, a black long-sleeved sweater, and a black watch cap covering her hair, slipped out through the front door and locked it behind her. She could have passed for a cat burglar if she hadn't tripped over the edge of the doormat and bounced off the porch railing.

"Don't try that at the Blands'," Judith warned when her cousin got into the Subaru.

"Shut up and drive," Renie snapped.

"I like the watch cap," Judith remarked as they took the turn to the bridge. "I settled for a head scarf to complete my all-black ensemble."

"You always did look good in black," Renie said. "Are you nervous?"

Judith decided to keep her fears to herself. "No. Why?"

"Because you just ran the arterial at the six-way

stop," Renie said. "It's a good thing there's not much traffic this time of night."

Judith grimaced. "Okay, so I'm a little on edge. Aren't you?"

"Anxious is more like it," Renie replied. "You don't think Teresa really saw a ghost, do you?"

"No," Judith answered. "I think it was a real person."

"Bill believes in ghosts," Renie said. "I allow for the possibility."

Judith didn't respond. They were turning off the bridge, heading for Langford.

"Do we have a plan?" Renie asked after another minute of silence.

"Yes," Judith replied in a solemn tone. "I pick the lock on the front door."

"Okay."

Renie didn't question her cousin's expertise. During Judith's marriage to Dan McMonigle, she'd been forced to learn how to pick various locks and even open a safe to find where Dan had hidden his gambling money. Though they might be stony-broke and unable to buy groceries, Dan had considered his betting stash untouchable. Judith hadn't agreed.

"What happens next?" Renie inquired, twitching anxiously in her seat.

"We'll have to wait and see." Judith didn't speak again until they were a block away from Moonfleet Street. "I'm going to chance it and pull into the alley."

"Okay," Renie said in a faint voice.

The Subaru crept across the intersection. On her left, Judith could see the outline of the tile roof and chimney through the big trees and dense foliage. All lay in darkness. No rain, no moon, no breeze, only a charcoal sky above them. She reversed slowly onto the dirt track, stopping the car just out of sight of any late-night passersby.

"I think I'll wait here," Renie said, folding her arms.

Judith looked stern. "Come on, before I lose my nerve, too."

Reluctantly, Renie got out of the car. Judith opened the back door on the driver's side and handed her cousin one of two police-issue flashlights. "These are Joe's," she said in a quiet voice before pointing to the shrubbery next to the alley. "Come on, we're going through here, but we don't dare turn on the flashlights until we're inside."

"Great. I should have worn armor." But Renie followed Judith, who was trying to keep to the same route she'd taken when delivering the Blands' groceries.

The rain had stopped early enough that the ground was now solid and the greenery was dry. But the cousins both stumbled a couple of times and felt the clawing of branches and berry vines on their arms and legs. Reaching the overgrown backyard, they stopped to collect themselves.

Neither spoke, but both gave a start when they heard a rustling noise nearby.

"Squirrel?" Renie breathed.

"Mouse?" Judith whispered back.

Slowly and quietly, they moved around the side of the house and under the arched wing wall. Reaching the front, they passed the jutting single-story section that could have been a den or a parlor. Creeping by the tower, they finally reached the arched mahogany door.

Unzipping the fanny pack she wore under her black sweatshirt, Judith removed a thin, flexible wire and inserted it in the lock.

"Damn!" she cursed under her breath. "It's a dead bolt. That's a bit trickier."

Renie leaned against the tower and kept her mouth shut. Judith let out a big sigh. "I'm going to have to turn on the penlight. Shield me."

Renie moved so that the small dot of light couldn't be seen from the front window on their left. Judith kept working, twisting and turning the wire. Finally, she shook her head.

"You're going to have to hold the penlight," she whispered. "See if you can crouch down in front of me."

Renie managed to squeeze in between her cousin and the door. Judith was beginning to pant with exertion; Renie's knees started to wobble.

Suddenly there was a click as the locks retracted.

"Ah!" Judith exclaimed softly. "Get in and lie flat."

The second the cousins crossed the threshold, the alarm went off. Quickly, but carefully, Judith dropped down onto the cold tiles and rolled to one side of the entry hall. Renie did the same, in the opposite direction. The alarm kept ringing. The cousins scarcely breathed.

The loud, jangling sound continued. Judith closed her eyes, as if that would deaden the cacophony. A minute, two minutes passed. Surely the noise would waken the dead. Unless, Judith thought . . .

But someone was alive in the house. After another

minute had passed, the alarm stopped. Judith figured
that whoever had hit the switch must have done it in
the kitchen. Listening intently, she heard faint, slow
footsteps. She braced herself, but the sound faded.
Whichever member of the household had disconnected the alarm was apparently going away. Upstairs,
Judith decided. She couldn't hear a door being closed,
and there didn't appear to be any space for bedrooms
on the main floor.

Clumsily, she sat up. Her eyes had grown accustomed to the dark and she could see Renie moving on
the other side of the entry hall.

"Living room," Judith murmured, realizing that her
legs had been blocking the open doorway.

The cousins got to their feet. "Thank God whoever
that was didn't use the tower stairs," Renie whispered.
"There must be a spiral staircase in there because it's
two stories high. If they'd come down that way, I'd
have gotten stepped on."

Judith didn't respond. The floor seemed to moan
under her footsteps. She turned on her regular flashlight and slowly aimed it around the room. Bill had
been right: the furniture was covered in leather, a
Spanish style appearing so old that Ferdinand and Is-
abella might have sat on it. There was wrought iron,
too, in the chandelier with its candle-shaped bulbs and
the heavy fire screen that reminded Judith of gates to a
country mansion. The odor of mold and age hung on
the air; the flashlight caught clouds of dust particles.
The house felt like a museum that had been closed for
years. Or maybe, Judith thought with a shiver, more
like a mausoleum.

Renie was examining a pair of lamps on a pecan de-milune chest. "Look," she said under her breath. "Real peacock feathers around the top, amber beads on the bottom—but the silk shades are rotting away. It's a wonder they don't catch fire."

"I'm beginning to doubt Alan's word when he told me his grandparents furnished this house on the cheap," Judith murmured. "Originally, this stuff must have been costly, even if some of it was left here by the previous owners." She aimed her flashlight onto the stucco walls. "See these urns on the mantel? The blue is beautiful on the plain one and the flowers on the other are so delicate."

Renie used her own flashlight to look at the urns. "The gold scrollwork on both of them looks real. These didn't come out of a factory. The craftsmanship is too good." She moved the beam of light to a pair of pastoral miniatures above the mantel. "These little guys are lovely, too. They almost look real."

The phone rang close by. Judith stifled a cry and Renie jumped. The phone rang again. Pointing her flashlight in the direction of the sound, Judith spotted the old-fashioned black dial phone on a small end table next to the sofa. Gingerly, she picked the receiver up in the middle of the third ring.

"Speak up," said a hoarse female voice on what Judith figured was an upstairs extension. "I can't hear you."

"It's me, *Liebchen*, your Franz."

Judith mouthed the caller's name to Renie, who hissed "Sally?" in response. Judith nodded.

"Why are you calling so late?" Sally demanded. "I was asleep."

"Ven are you not?" Franz retorted in an ironic tone. "Anyvays, it's morning here."

"You never remember the time difference," Sally scolded. "After all these years . . . Oh, what's the use? You never listen."

Renie had moved to stand next to Judith, trying to catch at least part of the conversation.

"You listen to me," Franz ordered in his gruff voice. "Vy didn't you telephone me about the package? Who is this voman who told me yesterday it vas lost?"

"I don't know what you're talking about," Sally declared. "I think you've finally gone crazy, Franz. And by the way, yesterday to you is still today to me."

"Vot?"

Sally emitted a deep sigh. "Never mind."

"I vaited to call until now so it vould be morning," Franz said doggedly. "I didn't vant to vake you."

"Fine, fine. What about the package? It arrived last week, safe and sound. And who is this woman you're jabbering about?"

"I don't know," Franz replied. "She didn't say her name."

"Tell me more about the woman," Sally demanded.

"I don't know more," Franz snapped. "She said she was a friend, and you were not able to speak. It vouldn't be the first time you couldn't talk on the telephone. But the package is there?"

"You're mean," Sally retorted. "Yes, the package arrived safely and on time, thank you," she went on, her tone growing more affable. "Porcelain candlesticks fetch a good price. The silverware needs polishing, but at least the settings are almost complete. I'm not sure about the wall plaque. Are you certain it came from an Italian palazzo?"

"I am alvays certain," Franz huffed. "It vas part of a ceiling. There are more panels, but I save them for later."

"All right." Sally cleared her throat. "But I still don't like this business about some woman calling you. Was she an American?"

"*Ja*," Franz replied.

"That's very interesting," Sally said in a musing tone. "But perhaps it doesn't matter."

"It mattered to me," Franz asserted. "She knew Lukas. And you and Anna, too. How is Lukas?"

"Very well," Sally assured him. "His eyes, of course, trouble him. You received my letter?"

"Letter? Not yet. Is one coming?"

"Yes. It should be there tomorrow or the next day. We have big news," Sally said in a smug tone. "I won't say more now, but I'll be seeing you very soon."

"*Vot?*" Franz's shout was so loud that both cousins gave a start.

"I'm hanging up now." Sally's voice had begun to slur. "I'm very tired."

Judith heard the dial tone. "Well." She set the receiver down in its cradle. "Do we know now what this is all about?"

"Black-market goods? Smuggling?" Renie suggested.

"There may be more to it than that," Judith murmured. "Let's check that other room across the hall."

The door was locked. Once again, Judith got out her wire tool. Unlike the first time, the lock to the single-story room clicked open after less than a minute.

Judith felt as if she had stepped outside. The air was fresh; the sense of decay had evaporated. And the room itself seemed empty. Judith pointed her flashlight toward the arched front window. There were no rotting drapes. Instead, a taut shade blotted out the light.

She began to scan the stucco walls. There were two paintings directly in front of her. "Golly," Judith said, "these are beautiful prints. They've even installed lights over them."

One was a Rubens nude, the other a Fragonard landscape. Moving closer, Renie reached up to touch the Rubens. Then she ran her fingers over the Fragonard. For what seemed like a long time to Judith, her cousin stared at the paintings. Finally, she turned around.

"Prints?" Renie said softly. "These are the real thing."

"What do you mean, 'real'?" Judith inquired in a low, puzzled voice.

"I'm not an art expert," Renie averred, "but I can tell a print from a painting. If these aren't originals, they're outstanding copies. Put your light up close, feel the texture. The canvas has small cracks. It's paint."

Judith followed Renie's instructions. Sure enough, she could feel the brushstrokes. Shaking her head in disbelief, she turned around to see what Renie was doing.

"Holy cats!" Renie breathed. "A Holbein, a Joos van Cleve, a Titian, a Van Eyck, a couple of small Monets—this is incredible!"

Her voice had risen with excitement. Judith waved

at Renie to tone it down. "Surely," Judith whispered, "these can't all be authentic."

Renie was hopping with excitement. "Then why go to such trouble to have a controlled atmosphere? Why, when the rest of the place is practically falling down, keep these in a special room?" She turned back to gaze at the Titian. "Stolen artwork? Stolen twice, that is? *By* the Nazis and *from* the Nazis?"

"It makes sense," Judith said, speaking in an awed whisper, "especially after what Uncle Corky told me about how the soldiers looted the area around Kopfstein, which happens to be very close to Berchtesgaden, where Hitler and his henchmen had their mountain retreats."

Renie seemed mesmerized. "I can't believe we're looking at genuine art treasures. It's like being in the Louvre or the Prado."

"How long have the Blands been selling this stuff?" Judith murmured.

"And keeping what they couldn't part with?" Renie gestured at the closed drapes. "No wonder they never let in any light. It wasn't just sensitivity of their eyes, but an effort to preserve their treasures."

"And keep them from being seen by other people," Judith pointed out. "That's something I don't understand. Great art should be shared with the world, but some collectors hide their masterpieces. It's so selfish and such a waste."

"But profitable, if you're able to sell some of it," Renie noted, still gawking at the paintings. "Now what do we do? Besides swipe the small Monets, of course."

Judith adjusted her head scarf, which had started to

slip off her hair. "We'll go out the back way so we can check out the dining room."

"We're tempting fate," Renie noted, "but it's worth it."

Going into the hall, Judith carefully closed the door behind her. "Sally sounded as if she were half-asleep when she hung up, so we may be safe for a bit. I'd like to see that statue of the Madonna that Bill noticed."

Renie was already at the door to the dining room. The pecan and wrought iron furnishings matched the living room, though the chairs around the long table had canvaslike leather backs and seats. They looked uncomfortable to Judith, but she had a feeling they hadn't been used in years. There were a half-dozen iron wall sconces, also with candle-shaped bulbs.

There were no more paintings, but the breakfront held some exquisite china and glassware, along with what appeared to be a quartet of Dresden figurines.

Judith gazed at the Madonna, a two-foot-high statue that might have come out of a seventeenth-century church. The stars in her halo sparkled like genuine diamonds; the gold trim on her blue mantle seemed real; the serpent beneath her feet had flashing emerald eyes. The work was very old, very lifelike, and very beautiful. Judith was compelled to say a prayer for safe passage out of the house.

Apparently, the Ave Maria worked. Or maybe, Judith thought as she quietly closed the back door, they just got lucky.

"Whew!" Renie exclaimed under her breath. "I can't believe we did it!"

"Neither can I," Judith admitted.

"We're middle-aged, soon-to-be-dowagers," Renie

said as they moved off the small porch. "We should be at home knitting or some damned thing."

"You can't knit," Judith pointed out.

"Neither can you," Renie retorted. "I'll never forget the dishrag you knitted for me when you were in high school. It was wool. When it got wet, the kitchen smelled like a dead sheep until I threw the blasted thing out. And speaking of kitchens," she added, pointing back to the house, "that furniture in there *is* old and crappy."

"Yes," Judith agreed, walking to her left. "I wonder—"

"Hold it," Renie interrupted. "Why are we going this way?" She gestured over her shoulder. "The car's over there. Aren't we done here?"

"I want to look at that fishpond up close," Judith said, almost tripping over a moss-covered rock.

"I guarantee there aren't any fish," Renie declared. "Let's make this quick. I'm getting nervous. *More* nervous, I should say."

But Judith kept going. A moment later, they'd reached the pond by the collapsed greenhouse. Playing the flashlight around the broken glass, shattered wood, and remnants of plant stands, she saw nothing of interest. Ivy and berry vines crisscrossed what was left of the roof. The small structure seemed to have caved in with age and disuse.

Judith turned the light onto the outline of the pond. "This will be completely overgrown in another year. In fact, the plant and lichen growth look even thicker than they did this afternoon. That's weird."

"The rain," Renie said. "This time of year, you can practically watch stuff grow."

"Not this fast," Judith responded. "I can't bend so well. Would you mind?"

Renie complied, dropping down to the pond's edge. "You're right. There's a whole patch of Irish moss and another of creeping thyme that looks as if it's just been planted. In fact," she continued, reaching down to pat the plants, "they're still wet, even though everything else has dried out from the rain."

Judith leaned over as far as she dared. "The thyme is blooming. It certainly wasn't there when I came by with Lynette."

A skittering sound from the side of the house startled the cousins. They both turned, but saw nothing. The noise stopped. Judith took a deep breath.

"More rodents," she murmured.

"Not rats, I hope," Renie remarked, her attention once more focused on the pond. "This is odd, too. Can you see how the cement at the bottom of the pond doesn't match the sides?"

Judith studied the seam near her feet. "You're right. And," she added on a sad note, "so am I."

"Huh?" Renie stood up, brushing leaves and other debris from her black slacks.

Judith's expression was bleak. "This pond was once much deeper. It had to be, for fish to survive." As a sudden breeze blew through the tall trees, she shuddered. "I hate to say it, but I think this is a grave."

Renie grimaced. "Any idea who's in there?"

"I can guess," Judith replied grimly.

"After all this time," Renie said softly, "the more I know of this house, the creepier it gets. But oh, those paintings!"

"They'd be worth killing for," Judith said, still gazing down into the pond. "There's definitely a sinister aura around here."

Renie, who was facing Judith, looked toward the house with a shocked expression. "There sure is," she said in a barely audible voice. "Don't look now, but I swear to God I see a ghost."

NINETEEN

BOTH COUSINS IMMEDIATELY switched off their flash-lights. Despite Renie's caution not to look at the apparition, Judith turned her head. A white-clad figure stood on the end of the second-floor balcony at the front of the house. A halolike aura glowed around the head.

"Holy Mother," Renie breathed, "if that's a real ghost, I'm one up on Bill. Let's get a closer look."

The wraithlike figure might have convinced most skeptics. But Judith, who relied on logic, shook her head. "Wait a minute. Let's see what your so-called ghost does next."

Even as Judith spoke, the figure moved farther down the balcony and out of sight.

"I don't believe in ghosts," Judith declared. "I wonder if whoever that was noticed us."

"It better be a ghost," Renie said stubbornly. "Then I can tell Bill. He'll be jealous."

"You're about to find out," Judith whispered. "Here comes your spectral buddy now."

The apparition was coming through the back

door. Clad all in white, with the luminous shimmer around the long white hair, the figure seemed to drift rather than walk toward the cousins.

Renie made a whooping sound. "Watch! I bet I can put my hand right through this ghost! Boo!" she shouted.

But Renie's waving fingers met with all-too-real resistance. Not only did she make contact, but a gun suddenly appeared from the folds of the diaphanous white fabric.

"Who are you?" the figure demanded in the hoarse, slightly slurred voice Judith recognized from the overheard telephone call with Franz.

Judith gulped before she spoke. "Mrs. Steiner? It's me, Judith Flynn."

"Flynn?" Sally Steiner stopped about ten feet from the cousins. "I know that name." While she kept looking at Judith and Renie, her expression became confused. "Flynn," she repeated to herself before speaking louder and moving a few steps closer. "You're trespassers. I can shoot you. Why are you here?"

"To see you," Judith replied, trying to focus not on the gun, but on Sally. She wasn't wearing a bathrobe as Judith had first assumed, but a long-sleeved chiffon evening gown. Or, judging from the seed pearls that decorated the bodice, a wedding dress—a very old wedding dress, dating from a half century earlier. The shimmer in her hair was a small tiara attached to a long veil. Both dress and veil were slightly tattered and yellowed with age.

"I can't visit with you right now," Sally said in the slurred voice that had become dreamy. "I'm going to meet my groom."

"How nice," Judith said. "Where is he?"

"Far away," Sally said. "But I can get there in time. The church is very pretty, with an onion-shaped dome. You have to leave now."

Judith noticed that although Sally looked glassy-eyed, the hand that held the gun didn't waver.

"Are Dick and Jane going with you?" Judith inquired in a voice that wasn't quite steady.

Sally slowly shook her head. "They're already gone."

"You mean they're dead," Judith said quietly, surprised at the calm in her voice. She waved an arm behind her. "They're buried in that fishpond, aren't they? Is Arthur there, too?"

"Arthur!" Sally's voice was tinged with contempt. "Arthur couldn't hold his liquor like I can. He fell out of a boat. A happy accident, I figured. Arthur had ethics. Anna has no sense when it comes to men."

"But you must have been shrewd at choosing a husband," Judith noted. "Why haven't you lived with Franz all these years?"

"Franz loves his homeland more than he loves me," Sally said in a sad voice. " I didn't like the village where he lived. I felt isolated." She frowned. "Like here. But it's different. I can do as I please. Now." .

Judith glanced at Renie, who was looking more annoyed than frightened. Sally was coming closer. Judith wondered how well she could see. Was her sight better in the dark than in daylight? The woman's skin was relatively unlined. She wasn't that old—late sixties, early seventies. She looked wiry and perhaps strong.

"Luke is your son, isn't he?" Judith asked. "Yours and Franz's."

"He's *my* son," Sally replied, her voice growing a trifle stronger. "I was only eighteen and naive, seeing the world right out of high school. I wanted to find a prince and a fairy-tale castle. It wasn't long after the war. There was plenty of royalty in those days. I thought that princes and dukes and counts must be everywhere. But alas, I met a cruel wolf—like Little Red Riding Hood instead of Cinderella—and I was violated and conceived a babe. Then I met Franz. His first wife had died young and left him childless. He wasn't royal, and he didn't own a castle, but he offered to marry me. Franz grew fond of Luke. But I couldn't let my boy be raised in a remote Austrian village. It wasn't like a fairy tale. For several years, after Dick and Jane had adopted him, I stayed with Franz out of loyalty and gratitude." She waved the gun, which Judith recognized as a Luger. "Now you must leave or I'll have to shoot you."

"This house," Renie said, speaking to Sally for the first time. "I grew up around here. I was fascinated by the place."

The sound of a car caught all three women's attention. It had stopped close by, perhaps at the opposite end of the alley from where Judith had parked.

Lunging across the five feet that separated the cousins from Sally, Renie dove at their adversary. Caught off guard, the other woman crumpled to the ground with Renie on top of her. But Sally managed to hold on to the gun.

"Wicked witch!" Sally shrieked as Judith hurried to help her cousin.

Going for the hand that grasped the Luger, Judith

tried to loosen Sally's grip. But her adversary was tenacious. Sally managed to wrench free, aiming the gun at Judith.

"Hold it!" a male voice called out. "Police!"

The cousins both froze. Sally went limp, though the gun was still in her hand. Judith turned in the direction of the approaching footsteps. Glenn Morris was striding purposefully across the grounds. There was no sign of his partner, Trash.

"I'll take the weapon," Glenn said, lowering his voice to its normal, cool level.

The Luger slipped out of Sally's grasp, but she didn't try to get up, even after the cousins were on their feet.

"Thank God you came by," Judith breathed. "She was going to shoot us."

Glenn nodded curtly. He quickly walked over to Sally and retrieved the Luger. "Can you stand? I can help you."

"I'll sit," she replied, allowing Glenn to give her a boost.

Judith let out a sigh of relief; Renie gave herself a good shake.

Sally was sitting up, her arms clasping her knees. She took several deep breaths before speaking again to Glenn. "You're late," she said in a sulky tone.

"Sorry," Glenn apologized. "The patrol car was responding to your alarm. The shift change is at eleven, so they were coming from the local precinct station. I sent them away." He turned to the cousins. "You look like burglars to me. I assume you got inside the house?"

Judith couldn't think of a fib that would cover their illegal activities. Despite her relief, she felt helpless—and confused. Which, she realized, was better than being dead. Still, something wasn't right. A shiver of fear crept up her spine.

"It's my fault," Renie declared to Glenn. "You know about my obsession with this house. I couldn't resist the opportunity of having a look inside before the place was sold."

"You could have looked when it went on the market," Glenn pointed out, still holding the Luger.

"No," Renie replied. "That would have been too late. I wanted to see it while the Blands still lived here."

Judith found her voice. "I don't think they do," she asserted. "Live, that is. Check out the fishpond. If you remove the concrete, you'll find Dick and Sally Bland's remains."

Glenn smirked. "You *are* inventive, Mrs. Flynn. But you can't talk your way out of this one. You two broke into the house, setting off the alarm system summoning the police. You may have stolen some of the family's prize possessions. The patrol officers didn't get here in time because of the shift change, not to mention the recent false alarms. Mrs. Steiner chased you out of the house, but you turned on her. She'll have the bruises to show for it. Thus she has every right to shoot you."

"Oh, do hush, Glenn," Sally broke in. "Now we must kill them. I'm taking a chill."

The realization struck Judith like a flash of summer lightning. "You're wrong!" she gasped at Glenn, who was now aiming the Luger straight at her. "I should have known!"

"You do now," Glenn said in his cool, calm voice.

"How did you get on the force?" Judith asked, still reeling from the shock. "How did you get assigned to this case?"

"Simple. I quit the LAPD and got on up here. As for this investigation, I happened to be in the area." He laughed low in his throat. "Cause and effect, you might say. Come, come, Mrs. Flynn, surely you don't think all of the local cops are lily-white? You're married to an ex-cop. You've heard stories."

"Yes." Judith was barely able to mouth the word.

Renie was wearing her most perverse expression. "You killed the man known as Frank Purvis," she said to Glenn. "You stonewalled the whole case. That's why we could never find out anything. But we discovered that Purvis was really Fred Pettibone. Why did you kill him?"

"Purvis was an alias," Glenn replied. "Frank Pettibone was an undercover agent, assigned to international smuggling operations. He was about to nail Sally. I couldn't let that happen. But more agents would come—we had to vacate the house. You see, I've bought a yacht, and tomorrow I'm sailing away with some very nice paintings. Asia, I think. The market in Japan and Hong Kong is good, despite the economy. There are always buyers for a true masterpiece."

"You bought the yacht from Phil," Judith said, recovering her voice along with some of her composure.

Glenn sneered. " 'Bought'? Phil French had no choice but to give me the *Moonfleet*. Like the rest of the family, he doesn't want to be charged with conspiracy to defraud or as accessories to murder."

"They're all in on it?" Renie asked in amazement.

"Of course not," Sally snapped, her vaporous mood hardening. "They're too stupid to handle such arrangements. They had to keep their mouths shut, though, or else they'd—" She clamped her lips shut.

"End up in the fishpond," Renie finished for her.

Sally shrugged. "They hadn't had fish in there for fifty years. Dick and Jane have only been there for two. They don't have to sleep with the fishes. Fish smell bad."

"What about Trash?" Judith asked, stalling for time. Maybe the regular patrol car would come by. Maybe Teresa was in the bathroom across the street. Maybe pigs would fly.

"Trash?" Glenn snickered. "That clod? He doesn't know anything. Last Wednesday, he was hungry, so I dropped him off at Doc's Drive-in before I caught up with the milk truck. The only one who might have worried me was Alan—word leaked out that there was a sting operation to uncover a smuggling ring in the area. Someone was being sent to confiscate a delivery."

"Fred Pettibone," Judith murmured, "disguised as a milkman."

Glenn ignored the comment. "Alan was given the assignment, but he was afraid it would lead him to his family. The poor twit's been putting the station off for days while he struggles with his conscience. By the time he makes up his mind, I'll be gone and so will the artworks."

Sally was on her feet and taking a couple of steps toward Glenn. "If you're not going to shoot these two, I will. It'd be better that way. I'm the one who should fire the gun. They'll test it, won't they?"

"Yes, they will." Without taking his eyes off the cousins, Glenn moved through the tall grass toward Sally's outstretched hand. He was about to hand over the Luger when he suddenly stumbled, let out a yelp, and fell to the ground. The gun flew from his hand, settling only two feet away from Judith.

Glenn was writhing around in the overgrowth, batting at his legs. Something small but fierce clung to his calf. Judith snatched up the gun and backed away. "Quick!" she called to Renie. "Get my cell phone in the car! Call 911!"

Renie ran toward the alley. Judith kept the gun on Glenn's thrashing form, but also watched Sally, who seemed paralyzed. A hissing noise and several growls emanated from the vicinity of Glenn's shredded pants. At last, the vicious creature desisted and leaped onto Glenn's face, where it sat in triumphant splendor.

"Sweetums!" Judith cried.

Yellow eyes glowing in the dark, Sweetums merely looked smug.

Sally toppled over in a dead faint.

Glenn used his scratched and bleeding hands to try to dislodge the cat. But Sweetums seemed intent on smothering his prey. Indeed, the animal was preening a bit, licking his paws and scratching behind one ear.

Renie had rejoined Judith. "They're on their way." A wicked glint shone in her eyes. "I told them, 'Officer down.' "

Judith couldn't help but smile. "Get his gun. It's probably in a shoulder holster."

Renie walked over to the still-struggling Glenn Morris. "Hi, Sweetums," she said. "Nice work." For good measure, she put a foot on Glenn's midsection. "Stop wiggling and stay put or I'll jump up and down on you until you look like a busted balloon."

"By the way," Judith called to Glenn Morris, "I *will* fire this gun if I have to. And I won't hit my cousin."

A strangled cry emerged from Glenn's throat as he finally heaved Sweetums off of his head. The cat landed on his feet, arched his back, hissed, and went right for Glenn's throat. Renie, meanwhile, had managed to dislodge Glenn's 9mm Glock from its holster.

"Check his legs," Judith said. "He may have another one."

"He doesn't," Renie replied. "Frankly, he doesn't have much left in the way of legs—or pants, for that matter. They're all chewed up from Sweetums's fangs."

The sweet sound of sirens was drawing closer. Glenn, whose face was bleeding, tried to subdue Sweetums. But the cat was persistent, his big plume of a tail swinging like a pendulum as he raked the man's throat with his sharp claws. Sally still lay on the ground, motionless. Judith began to wonder if the woman was alive.

Renie looked down at the pistol in her hand. "Should we disarm ourselves? Don't you think the patrol officers might get the wrong idea?"

"Let them," Judith said grimly. "We need to see them in the flesh before we make ourselves vulnerable." Then, as she heard car doors slamming nearby, she raised her voice as loud as she could: "Backyard! By the back door!"

The officers—a man and a woman—approached cautiously from around the side of the house, their weapons drawn.

Judith set the Luger down behind her. "*Now* drop the gun," she said to Renie under her breath.

Sweetums seemed to understand the cease-fire. With one last swipe at Glenn, he jumped off of his victim and padded over to stand by Judith.

The officers held flashlights along with their weapons. The light blinded Judith. She couldn't see anything but an outline of the two figures. "The perps are on the ground," she shouted. "Don't be fooled, you may know one of them as Detective Glenn Morris."

"Who are *you*?" the male officer demanded. "Identify yourselves, please. Don't move. Put your hands over your heads."

The cousins obeyed, although Renie winced a bit. She'd never quite regained full motion after her shoulder surgery.

"Wait!" The word seemed torn out of Glenn's wounded throat. "These women are burglars! Look at them!" He started to get to his knees, crawling painfully toward Sally.

The male officer swung his light onto Glenn. "I can see that," the officer said. "Did they attack you?"

Not only was the patrolman's voice familiar, but now that Judith could see more clearly, she recognized Darnell Hicks and Mercedes Berger. Their former beat had been Heraldsgate Hill.

"It's me!" she screamed as Glenn neared the unconscious woman. "Darnell, Mercedes—it's Judith Flynn!"

Darnell kept his high beam on Glenn, but Mercedes focused on the cousins. "Mrs. Flynn! Mrs. Jones! What's happening?"

"Come on, people," Glenn urged, trying to sound nonchalant, but hampered by the cut on his lower lip. "Don't let these two fool you . . ."

"We know them," Mercedes shot back.

"You know me, too, don't you?" Glenn said. "I work homicide, I've been on the force for almost a year."

"We've known Mrs. Flynn and her husband much longer," Mercedes declared. "Stay where you are," she ordered Glenn. "I'm calling for backup."

"What's with the woman on the ground?" Darnell asked, catching Sally's inert form in the circle of his flashlight.

Sweetums had wandered over to Sally. He sniffed several times, then wrinkled his nose and went back to Judith.

"She passed out," Judith said. "Maybe you should send for an ambulance, too."

"She's drunk," Renie declared. "When I was wrestling with her, I smelled alcohol."

"We have an ambulance and other emergency personnel on the way," Mercedes said.

"We could use a regiment," Renie asserted. "I don't trust this so-called cop an inch."

But Glenn Morris no longer looked intimidating. His bleeding legs, face, and neck were taking their toll. So were the guns that were aimed at him. But most of all, he seemed defeated. Renie hadn't had to jump on him to make the man deflate.

Glenn's bleary gaze turned to Sally. "For God's sake, at least let me see if she's alive."

"I'll check," Judith said, moving cautiously in the direction of Sally's prone form. "Yes, she has a pulse, though it's quite slow." Her glance at Glenn was curious. "Why are you suddenly so concerned about anybody but yourself?"

"Because," Glenn said in a faint voice, "she's my mother."

TWENTY

AFTER A HALF century of inertia, the house on Moonfleet Street was suddenly transformed into a frenzy
of activity by police, firefighters, medics, and other
emergency personnel. No official arrests had been
made, but both suspects had been taken to the hospital, with squad cars providing escort. Sally had
come to just before the medics arrived, and had
babbled like a spring torrent. Judith had been able
to catch some of her words, but wasn't sure how to
sort fact from fairy tale.

The homicide detectives requested that the
cousins come into the house and answer questions.
Judith and Renie were exhausted, but glad to com-
ply. To their great relief, they knew the team: Edwina
Jefferson and Danny Wong had investigated a murder in the gated community of Sunset Cliffs where
the cousins had been asked to watch over a wealthy
old woman whose life had been threatened.

Edwina, a plump black woman of fifty, beamed at
Judith and shook her head. "I can't believe we're
meeting up again, girlfriend. Though I've heard

about some of your escapades since Junior here and I transferred to the city force after they incorporated the area around Sunset Hills."

Judith sighed. "If only I'd known you two were at headquarters, I would've called to find out what was really going on with this case. Did you have any idea?"

Edwina shook her head. "Junior and I had our own problems with a nasty triple murder in the south end of town." She patted Danny on the arm. He was close to thirty now, a slim, good-looking man of Chinese descent, but to Edwina, he'd always be "Junior." "I didn't know Morris very well," Edwina continued, "but I didn't much like him. Standoffish, cold—and of course, a fairly recent hire. The only good thing was that he took Trash on. Or so I thought at the time. Nobody else wanted to work with Trash after his longtime partner retired. Now I understand why Morris chose him. Trash was too dumb or too indifferent to figure out that Morris was a wrong'un."

Judith frowned. She knew that Glenn Morris would give the police department a black eye. "Wasn't it considered suspicious when the body of Frank—I mean, Fred Pettibone—was secretly released and the story was hushed up?"

"Oh, no," Edwina replied. "That part was legit. The feds stepped in to cover the death of one of their own. Glenn wouldn't have been allowed to talk about it."

"The Pettibones were notified right away," Danny put in. "As far as the government is concerned, Fred died a hero. But any official acknowledgment of his death in the line of duty can't go public."

"It's a shame, really," Edwina said with a shake of

her head. "Fred Pettibone doesn't get recognized for what he did, and the police are going to have to suffer some ugly headlines." She leaned back on the worn leather sofa. "Okay, hit the high spots on your part in all this. We'll take a formal, detailed statement at headquarters tomorrow or the next day."

It was nearing midnight when Judith finished. "Remember," she concluded, petting Sweetums, who was asleep on her lap, "some of my conclusions are speculation, especially the part about Glenn trying to scare Anna in the parking garage. I'm guessing that it was an attempt to make sure her husband gave the *Moonfleet* away. You'll want to ask Phil about that part."

Danny, who had been characteristically silent during Judith's recital, finally asked a question. "I don't quite get it. Just after we arrived—before Mrs. Steiner was put in the ambulance—she mentioned that her other son, Luke, was the one who actually sold the artworks. Did the rest of the family share in the profits, too?"

"Early on, when the children were young, I imagine Sally had someone else as the middleman," Judith replied. "I suspect Sally was sending art objects to them while she was still in Austria and the Blands were given living expenses. Dick Bland apparently didn't ever hold down a job—a neighbor told us he'd come back from the war a shattered man. That would explain why the house seemed so moribund. Jane may have been stuck inside, taking care of Dick and ensuring that he lived in a quiet atmosphere. Luke became involved in investments, which might have included money laundering for Sally's art sales. I figure she couldn't have left Anna out of the loop. Maybe Sally set Phil up in the tugboat business. But in later years, Dick and Jane may have gotten greedy—or scared. Perhaps they were ill and in misery. I'd like to think that, because then it would be more like a mercy killing. Luke and Anna didn't dare go to the police if Sally was their source of big income. And, of course, Sally was Luke's mother."

"Not to mention Glenn's," Renie put in. "That shocked me."

"I heard Sally rambling on about that while they were getting her ready to put in the ambulance," Judith said. "She hadn't been raped—she'd been promiscuous. In fact, she bragged about her escapades after she moved in with the Blands. She'd sneak out at night and meet some man for a romp. In Austria, she'd borne two children out of wedlock before she married Franz. Glenn was the elder, and she let an American couple from California adopt him. Apparently, it took years for him to track down his birth mother, but when he did, he came up here to meet her. She couldn't resist seeing him, which meant he realized right away that something odd was going on and wanted in on it. That's why he transferred from L.A."

"How," Edwina inquired, "did you figure out that no one but Sally lived here?"

"It was the groceries," Judith said. "One box, once a week. There wasn't enough to feed three people. And while wine was included, I'll bet somebody in the family made frequent trips to the liquor store. Maybe somewhere, down deep, Sally felt guilty. Or maybe she was just a souse. She'd once left a delivery from Franz on the porch for a couple of days. What else could account for that but a drunken binge?"

"She was a silly souse," Edwina said in disapproval. "What good did the money do her? Did she enjoy the art?"

"I think she was a miser," Judith said, "but she must have loved the paintings or she would've sold more of them. Only about eight were in the parlor. There were other art treasures, too. I assume Franz sent one annual delivery because of the risk factor—not only possible discovery, but damage. Still Sally must have made millions. But as her sight deteriorated, she couldn't enjoy the remaining paintings, which is why I think she agreed to let Glenn sell them abroad."

"While she settled in with Franz and the goats," Renie put in. "Maybe she thought she'd be safe from the cops in a remote place like Kopfstein. Or she was fantasizing. Alcohol does strange things to people's brains."

"It'd be nice to think those paintings may be returned to their rightful owners," Edwina said. "Assuming they're still alive and could be tracked down. Thank goodness that's not a job for us."

Danny was looking somewhat embarrassed. "Let me get this straight—the paintings and the other art stuff was stolen from thieves after World War Two?"

Edwina offered her partner an amused, if slightly patronizing, look. "Ah, yes, Junior, I keep forgetting you don't even remember the Vietnam War, let alone Korea or the two world wars. You children are woefully ignorant when it comes to history. By the way, did you ever hear of slavery and the Civil War? Does the name Abe Lincoln ring any gongs?"

Danny made a face. "At least I don't think he's a rock band."

"Admittedly," Edwina said, her pleasant face growing serious, "I was born after the war. But my daddy served in it—even though the military wasn't desegregated until after the war was over."

"Gosh!" Danny exclaimed in amazement.

"Anyway," Edwina went on, "a bunch of those Nazi leaders stole all kinds of things including artworks from museums and galleries and individuals. They didn't just kill the poor Jews, they robbed them of everything they owned. Some were rich, and had fabulous possessions." She turned to Judith. "Weren't a lot of those art treasures in Berchtesgaden, where Hitler and his cronies had their vacation hideaways?"

Judith nodded. "Berchtesgaden was in Germany but right on the Austrian border, near Kopfstein. According to my Uncle Corky, who served in that area, some of the allied soldiers ran amok after the war. Not only were they chasing Nazi holdouts and sympathizers, they were enjoying a victor's spoils. Of course there were the pro-Nazi Germans and Austrians who were never arrested and managed to end up with plenty of loot. I assume Sally's husband, Franz, was one of that ilk. His peers may have had some loot, too. Franz may have bartered with them or even outlived them."

Danny was looking thoughtful. "You know, they don't make history very interesting in school."

"That," Renie asserted, "is because texts and teachers don't realize that history is really old gossip. They don't give it any personality. History is about people, as far as I'm concerned, which is far more interesting than politics and ideas."

"I never thought of that," Danny admitted.

"You're not alone," Renie remarked before turning to Edwina. "What will happen to the rest of the family?"

Edwina shrugged. "I leave that stuff up to the prosecutors. Luke and Anna and the others may plea-bargain their way out of it. For all we know, Sally threatened them, told them they'd end up buried in the backyard, too. We'll start excavating tomorrow. Say," she said, pointing to the sleeping Sweetums, "is that your cat?"

Judith grinned. "Yes. I'm not sure how he ended up here, but I figure he was trying to get home from my uncle's and came this way. The poor little guy was probably hungry. He found a feast of mice and maybe even rats, and settled right in. This house may be a den of iniquity, but it's also a feline paradise. I assume that Sweetums was the one who kept tripping the alarm while he was prowling around in and out of the house. There must be at least one or two places where raccoons or squirrels have chewed their way inside."

Edwina stood up, straightening the navy blue linen skirt that wrapped around her ample hips. "It's Junior's bedtime. We've got personnel watching the house. And you two must be worn out." She enfolded Judith and Renie in a big hug. "We'll be in touch. You take care, you hear?"

Judith gave Edwina a baleful look. "We usually try."

"But not tonight," Edwina said. "And by the way, try to avoid the breaking-and-entering act. Next time, we might actually have to arrest you."

Judith smiled fondly at the other woman. "There *is* one more thing."

Edwina looked curious. "Oh? What's that?"

"I want my shoes back."

Judith didn't hear the alarm go off the next morning. When she finally woke up, it was almost ten o'clock. With a shriek, she sat up and took several deep breaths. Her guests must be furious. Gertrude would be wild. In a whirl of activity, she showered, dressed, and scurried downstairs.

But as she was halfway down the second flight that led into the kitchen, she smelled coffee, bacon, and other breakfast aromas. Going along the narrow hallway, she saw Joe hanging up the phone.

"Hi, sleepyhead," he said in greeting. "Feeling rested?"

"Joe!" She flew into his arms, covering his face with kisses. "When did you get home?"

"Just before six," he replied, squeezing her waist. "I took the red-eye."

Judith glanced at the phone on the counter. "Was that for me?"

"Nothing that can't wait," Joe said, ruffling her salt-and-pepper hair.

Slipping out of his grasp, Judith peeked into the dining room. Only two guests remained, enjoying coffee and chatting amiably.

"You got everyone fed? Even Mother?"

Joe nodded. "Not to mention Sweetums. I understand he's been missing."

"Um . . . yes, he has." Judith watched as her husband poured her a mug of coffee. She didn't know where to start. Joe would have to know. The arrest of two murderers and the discovery of a smuggling operation might not have made the morning paper, but he was bound to find out. Judith sat down at the kitchen table with her coffee while Joe finished loading the dishwasher.

As the remaining guests left the dining room and went upstairs, Joe sat down across the table from his wife. Gold flecks danced in his green eyes—magic eyes, Judith called them. "Did you get the trunk lid fixed on the Subaru?"

"Ah . . . not yet," Judith replied, avoiding those magic eyes. "I've been really busy. We had some problems with a guest who ended up in the hospital. Sweetums took a dislike to him. There was something of a fracas."

Joe nodded once. "So that's why he looks so scruffy. Your mother seems pleased to have him home."

"Yes," Judith said, still not meeting her husband's gaze. "I had to take him to the vet, and the wife of the man who was . . . um . . . scratched didn't want him at the B&B while she was still here. After I picked Sweetums up from the vet, I took him to Uncle Al's. But after Mike and the boys went home, Sweetums ran off. Luckily, I found him."

"Very lucky." The gold flecks gleamed again. "Maybe it's a good thing that despite being old, the beast is so tough and ornery."

"Sweetums is fairly typical of his species."

"I wasn't talking about Sweetums."

"Oh." Judith scowled at Joe. "Don't be mean about Mother."

Joe's expression was ingenuous. "I only meant that

she and Sweetums have some sort of bond. It's natural between pets and their humans, I'm told."

Judith heard footsteps on the front stairs. "Departing guests," she said as the phone rang. "Can you get that? I have to play innkeeper."

"Four of them already left," Joe called after her as he picked up the receiver.

Judith put on her gracious face to send off the couple from Sydney, Australia. They were fairly young, enthusiastic, and ready to head for Canada on their North American tour. "G'day!" they called in unison as they left Hillside Manor.

"G'day," she called back. "And come again!" In Judith's opinion, Australians always made good guests.

Unlike the Greenwalts, Judith thought as she closed the door. She was certain she hadn't heard the end of that sorry episode. In fact, it was back to grim reality—worrying about repercussions from the Greenwalts, agonizing over Mike and Kristin, anxiety building over Joe's reaction when he learned what had really happened in his absence.

Judith was frowning as she cleared off the last items from the dining room table and returned to the kitchen, where Joe was hanging up the phone.

"A reservation request for the Labor Day weekend," he explained. "I told them you'd check to see if there was a vacancy and call back."

"There isn't," Judith said, "but I can put them on standby. Oh!" she exclaimed. "What about that other call?"

"Later," Joe said enigmatically. "You need some downtime."

Judith said nothing, but felt a seed of suspicion being sowed in her brain. She was distracted when Phyliss appeared, carrying a load of laundry from upstairs.

"Say, Mr. Flynn," she called from the bottom of the stairs, "how about a hand? I'm having one of my bad days. My back's gone out."

"Sure, Mrs. R, my pleasure." He met Phyliss halfway down the narrow hall. "How's the Lord these days? You seen Him lately?"

"Not for a couple of weeks," Phyliss replied. "He was in the produce section at the grocery store, picking out avocados."

"No kidding," Joe responded. "I would have thought He'd be at the hardware store, being a carpenter and all . . ."

Their voices trailed off as they headed down the back stairs. The last of the guests came down the front stairs. A taxi was just pulling into the cul-de-sac. Judith performed her duties, waving them good-bye from the front porch.

Maybe, she thought, Joe wouldn't come back upstairs right away. There might be time to call Renie and tell her about the morning's events. She was reaching for the phone when it rang.

"Hi, Mom," Mike said, sounding cheerful. "I meant to call you yesterday, but I was real busy catching up on work. How are you?"

"Fine," Judith answered tersely. "More importantly, how are *you*?"

"Good," he replied. "The clouds are lifting up here. It's going to be a beautiful day. What's it like in town?"

Judith hadn't really noticed. She glanced out the

kitchen window. "The sun's out. But I don't want a weather report, I want—"

"Hang on," Mike interrupted, and apparently turned away from the receiver. "Hey, Kris, see if you can find Joe-Joe's farm animals. He can't find them and he's about to shred one of Mac's books."

"*Kris?*" Judith echoed. "As in *Kristin?*"

"What?" Mike was speaking into the receiver again. "Oh—right. That's what I was going to call you about. We made up. She just needed a break. And to make some kind of change in her life."

"Which is what?" Judith asked, flabbergasted.

"She's getting her hair highlighted," Mike replied as a child's angry screams could be heard in the background. "You know, one of those foil jobs. Hey, got to run. Joe-Joe's having a tantrum. I think maybe Mac hid the farm animals. By the way, if you want to send Mac some more books, that'd be great. He's reading up a storm these days. Talk to you soon."

Feeling limp, Judith held the dead phone in her hand for almost a full minute. Joe reappeared just as she was setting the receiver on the counter.

"You look pale," Joe said, frowning. "What's wrong?"

"Nothing," Judith said in a hollow voice. "I mean— something's right for a change."

Joe put a hand on Judith's shoulder. "Like what?"

"Mike and Kristin made up."

"Well, hooray!" Joe embraced Judith and kissed her soundly on the lips. But she still looked shaken. "So what's the problem?"

Judith shook her head. "Young people these days

seem to do the right things for all the wrong reasons. Or do the wrong things for . . ." A faint smile brightened her face. "I don't know. It's just that they're . . . different. Maybe they like drama. Maybe they're too self-centered. Maybe they're . . . just not us."

Releasing Judith, Joe took her hand. "Come on, let's have another cup of coffee. Frankly, you look beat. Didn't that sleep-in help?"

"It should have," Judith allowed as they sat down. "Maybe I . . . oh, never mind. What about your trip?"

Joe shrugged. "No big deal, just a lot of sitting around and waiting for other people to make up their minds. Insurance companies take their time."

"Was it fraud?" Judith asked, beginning to gather her composure.

"No," Joe replied. "It was more complicated than that. The company's branch office hired me to check out a local bigwig who'd bought a painting a while back. He wanted it insured but was suspicious about where it came from. It was a real Van Dyck that had been missing for years. He didn't want to go to the cops for fear of getting in trouble and inviting some bad publicity, so he asked the insurance outfit to look into it. I was hired to make sure the bigwig was on the up-and-up, which he was. Anyway, it turned out the painting had been stolen by the Nazis and somehow ended up in this country. A New York art expert was brought in, but the original owners haven't been traced. No insurance until a search is completed."

Judith had made an enormous effort to retain an interested, rather than stunned, expression. It was the perfect opening for her confession. But somehow she couldn't bring herself to unload on Joe. Not yet, anyway.

"Fascinating," she said in a voice that wasn't quite her own, and promptly changed the subject. "By the way, Mike wants us to get more books for Mac. He's very advanced in his reading, you know."

"That's your field," Joe said. "You know what books to send him."

"I've been out of the library business for a long time," Judith noted. "Except for Harry Potter, I don't know what's new. Of course, there are the classics. I should make a list."

Joe didn't respond right away. He sipped his coffee and rubbed his chin. "I remember one book I really liked when I was a kid. Mac might not be ready for it yet. But jot it down."

Judith had gotten up to get a pen and a notepad. "Which one?" she inquired, sitting down again.

"It was about a little boy in England who gets involved with smugglers. I'm sure it's still around. The name of the book is *Moonfleet*." Joe's smile was ironic.

Judith looked her husband right in the magic eyes. "Yes, I remember that. In fact, I could never forget."

"I didn't think you could," said Joe.

The magic eyes danced on.

For more of Mary Daheim's Bed-and-Breakfast mystery series, perfectly capturing her signature tone of screwball comedy and off-kilter menace, join the cousins on a high-seas adventure . . .

Judith and Renie's dreams of R&R on a deluxe cruise ship are dry-docked when murder occurs at a pre-launch party. But the stabbing death of the cruise line owner is only the first in a trio of homicides. They're in good—and bad— company, however. Fellow travelers Rick and Rhoda St. George may be pleasantly plastered, but their eyes aren't blurred to motive, method and mayhem. Along with the ships' Art Deco decor, the St. Georges' breezy 1930s presence (accompanied by their wheezing dog, Asthma) makes Judith and Renie feel as if they're living in a time warp.

Of course the cousins will be lucky to be living at all by the time they sort through the suspects . . .

DEAD MAN DOCKING

Available Summer 2005
in hardcover
from William Morrow

ART DECO RULED the ship's design, from furniture to paneling to floors. Teak and mahogany flowed in clean curves and sleek symmetry. Glass was everywhere—tabletops, doors, wall inserts, and around the saloon where the party was being held.

"Remember," Renie said as they hesitated in the doorway, "we should get into a thirties mood. Snappy patter, wisecracks, screwball antics."

"For us, that sounds contemporary," Judith murmured as an elegant woman in a Grecian gown of flowing white pleats and three-inch gold sandals approached the cousins. Consuela Cruz definitely evoked the gilded edge of the Depression era. She was as lean as her husband, with jet-black hair combed away from a heart-shaped face.

"We're so glad you're here," she said to Renie. "There must have been a misunderstanding regarding your consulting fees. Mags would never dream of cutting you loose so abruptly." Consuela pointed at a young man at the bar. "You know Paul Tanaka, of course?"

Renie nodded. "He often sat in for Mags at our design meetings." She nudged Judith's arm. "My cousin hasn't met him, though."

"We'll attend to that at once," Consuela said. "He's standing by the bar with Mrs. Giddon and Mr. Brooks. And do call me Connie."

Connie Cruz made a graceful gesture with her right hand. "I'll take you both around the room. Almost everyone is here, I think, except the St. Georges and Émile. Of course, Émile is the ship's purser, and may have business to take care of."

The tall, stout woman with the steel-gray hair swept up on top of her head was indeed imposing, Judith thought. It wasn't just her Amazonian size, but her piercing blue eyes and tight, red lips.

"Serena Jones, Judith Flynn," Connie said, "meet Mrs. George Elwood Giddon."

Mrs. Giddon studied the cousins through a jewel-studded lorgnette. She was wearing a long, straight gown of black lace over white taffeta. A parure of diamonds and emeralds adorned her ears, neck, and wrists. The grande dame's imposing presence practically overwhelmed Judith. "A pleasure, I'm sure," Mrs. Giddon proclaimed in a lofty voice. "Who are you?"

"Who—or what?" Renie shot back with a deceptive smile. "The way you're looking through that lorgnette makes me feel like a microbe."

"I said *who*—not *what*," Erma Giddon snapped. "Are you anybody I should know?"

Renie gave a languid shrug. "My forebears came over on the *Mayflower*—first class. They were fleeing their bridge debts. Judith's ancestors were the first white settlers in our city, arriving circa 1850. Before that, they founded Philadelphia."

Mrs. Giddon didn't seem amused. Connie swiftly intervened. "For many years, Serena has been doing the graphic-design work for Mags. Mrs. Flynn is her cousin. Unfortunately, Mr. Jones couldn't get away from his work."

If Mrs. Giddon gave a damn, she didn't say so. Instead, she turned her back on the cousins and asked a server to fetch her evening wrap.

"It's chilly in here," Erma declared. "The captain must adjust the temperature before we sail. You know I'm inclined to chest colds, Consuela."

"Those cold germs must be really tough to get around her chest," Renie said, lowering her voice a mere notch.

"*Coz,*" Judith said in a warning tone.

But Erma had moved her chest and the rest of her away, commanding the youthful blond bartender to mix her a Manhattan.

"Make that Bud in a bottle for me," Renie called out from behind Mrs. Giddon. "Or mead, if you've got it. My family *really* goes way back."

Judith winced. She had a feeling that Renie was going to be difficult, at least as far as Mrs. Giddon was concerned.

"Please don't mind Erma," Connie begged from behind her hand. "She adheres to a very strict social code. Her own family dates back to one of the original San Francisco railroad magnates."

"Which one?" Renie shot back. "The guy who threw the fusies from the back of the crummy?"

Connie looked pained. "No, a Stanford or a Crocker or a Hopkins or a Huntington. You know—the Big Four."

"I thought they met at Yalta, not Nob Hill," Renie muttered. "Or was that just the Big Three?"

Connie's smile was feeble. "Here's Paul Tanaka. I must find Dixie Beales. She's providing a brief entertainment later on."

Paul greeted Renie with a hug. He was a squarely built young man, part Japanese and part African-American. The handshake he offered Judith was firm and the big smile seemed genuine.

"You're Bill's stand-in, I hear," he said. Like the other men, except for the captain, he was wearing a tuxedo with thirties styling. And like several of the other guests, he was smoking. "What happened to him?"

Renie explained, stopping when the other young man who'd been at the bar came forward with a bottle of Budweiser. "I'm Jim Brooks," he said by way of introduction. "I'm attending medical school at Stanford."

"Congratulations," Judith said, releasing Jim's clammy hand. "I gather it's difficult to get accepted there."

Jim flushed slightly. "Yes . . . but sometimes knowing the right people helps." He gave Judith a sheepish look and nodded at a lithe blonde who was talking to Captain Swafford. "I'm engaged to Anemone Giddon. Isn't she beautiful?"

Even from a distance, Judith could see that Mrs. Giddon's daughter was a winsome, lovely creature. In a lavender floral gown made of organza, she looked like a breath of spring.

"Is her father still living?" Judith inquired.

Jim shook his head. "He passed away from a heart attack almost ten years ago."

"Then," Judith asked, "who's the older bald man that just joined Mrs. Giddon?"

Jim Brooks snickered, a reaction befitting his boyish manner. "The great Horace Pankhurst," he replied. "Like Mrs. Giddon, he owns shares in the cruise line. He's also Erma's financial and legal adviser. Excuse me, I must see how Anemone's doing. The bartender asked me to deliver the beer to you, Mrs. Jones."

"Thanks," Renie said without enthusiasm.

Another member of the party had entered, surveying the gathering over a tall vase filled with calla lilies. He was small and spare, with a goatee and a slight limp.

"Émile Grenier," Paul informed the cousins as he followed their gaze to the newcomer. "He's the purser, and he's French. Ergo, he's the biggest snob of all."

"Quite a mixed background for these people," Judith remarked as Renie drifted toward the buffet, with its ice sculpture of a pheasant with a gold ring around its neck and a spray of frozen tail feathers. "Was Mr. Cruz born in Mexico?"

Paul nodded. "But his parents moved—or should I say swam—to the United States when he was a baby."

"A self-made man," Judith observed. "I have the greatest admiration for that type of person. Bloodlines don't impress me."

Paul smirked. "It also helps to marry the grand-daughter of a wealthy ranchero from Argentina."

Judith's gaze shifted to the direction that Connie Cruz

had taken upon leaving the little group. But their hostess was nowhere in sight. At that moment, the double doors opened to frame a striking couple with a large white dog. The trio stood very still for just a moment or two, giving the impression that they were striking a pose.

Judith gaped. "The St. Georges?"

Paul nodded. He, too, was looking at the handsome pair. Indeed, everyone was staring with the exception of Erma Giddon, who was fidgeting with an earring. Richard St. George wore a double-breasted midnight-blue tuxedo with silk piping and a gardenia in the left lapel. Slowly, deliberately, he removed his homburg hat, which matched his suit. His manner was casual, his mustache impeccable, and his expression was one of perpetual amusement.

By contrast, Rhoda St. George seemed indifferent to the stares. She was the epitome of thirties chic in a theater suit featuring a black velvet jacket lavishly embroidered with gold thread and the occasional small ruby, topaz, and seed pearl. The long skirt was dark green, gathered around the hips. But it was the hat that drew all eyes: black satin fitted to the head like a skullcap with two long, wide matching streamers, black veiling from hairline to neckline, and a golden rose nestled on top. Rhoda looked wonderfully self-confident. Judith couldn't blame her—any woman who could carry off such an ensemble deserved a medal that matched the gold and jewels on her jacket.

Yet in the end, it was the dog that evoked Renie's comment. "Sugliesmutievasa," she declared, returning from the buffet with her mouth full of shrimp.

Judith had grown accustomed to translating Renie's

food-marred speech. "He's certainly an unusual dog, though not necessarily ugly. I don't think I've seen that breed before."

"It's not a breed," Renie asserted after swallowing the shrimp, "it's a conglomeration. It's got dreadlocks and no feet. It's a dog on wheels."

"The feet must be under all that curling fur," Judith said as the dog glided across the floor.

The St. Georges proceeded into the saloon, where they were effusively greeted by Émile Grenier, Paul Tanaka, Horace Pankhurst, and a platinum-haired beauty in a silver satin evening gown that clung to her curvaceous body like melted cheese on hot toast.

Renie leaned closer to Judith. "Where'd *she* come from?"

Judith shrugged. "The powder room, maybe. She's certainly a Jean Harlow look-alike. I'm beginning to feel like somebody's dowdy maid in Mother's old wedding dress."

"You look fine," Renie assured her. "Come on, get something to eat. You need to put on some pounds."

The cousins made their way to the buffet. Judith paused to admire the pheasant ice sculpture, which was holding up remarkably well.

"The caviar's great," Renie said, swiftly refilling her plate. "So are the wontons with crab and the oysters and the gravlax and—"

"I get the picture," Judith broke in. "It's a good thing you're wearing black. Your spillage doesn't show up very much."

"Huh?" Renie stared down at her bosom. "Oh. Right—it blends."

Connie Cruz had returned, looking a trifle worried. "Everyone, please enjoy the food and make sure you visit the bar in the next few minutes. Our cruise director, Dixie Beales, is going to play some of the great old songs from the thirties in the next room at seven o'-clock."

"I never did get a cocktail," Judith noted, carefully choosing a selection of vegetables cut into exotic shapes. "Where's your beer?"

"In that potted palm by the model of the ship," Renie replied. "You know I hate beer. I just wanted to be annoying. Oh, for heaven's sake!" she cried, looking at her cousin's plate. "You're grazing, not eating. Here, have some smoked sockeye salmon *en croûte* and crab dumplings and anything else that might be considered real food. Get the servers to slice off a piece of rare Kobe beef from Japan. I intend to fatten you up."

"Well . . ." Watching a bearded young man wield a gleaming carving knife through a juicy roast tempted Judith. Somehow, she resisted. The cousins had, after all, eaten a late lunch. "Okay, I'll try a couple of dumplings," she said, allowing a waiter with a shaved head and a graying goatee to serve her. "Then we'd better get our drinks before the piano recital starts."

"I'm drinking Pepsi," Renie declared. "I can't bear the thought of alcohol after this morning."

"I don't blame you," Judith said dryly. "Uh-oh," she whispered, "here come the St. Georges with Fido."

Richard St. George nodded at the cousins; Rhoda had lifted her veil and was smoking a cigarette through a silver holder. He ordered two double martinis; so did she. The big white dog with the long curls of fur stopped by the cousins and wheezed at Renie's hem.

"Nice doggie," Renie murmured, trying to disguise her antipathy for canines.

But the large animal moved closer, shedding white fur on Renie's black gown. "Beat it," Renie muttered, holding her hors d'oeuvres plate out of reach.

Wheezing and panting, the dog sat down on Renie's feet. "Excuse me," she said to Rhoda St. George, "would you please make your dog move? I'm immobilized by his very large—yet unusual—body."

Rhoda had just accepted two martini glasses. "Oh, don't mind Asthma," she said with a little laugh. "He's absolutely harmless. In fact, he has respiratory problems. I think he likes you. Or else he's collapsed." His mistress didn't seem particularly distressed by the idea.

Richard St. George, who also had both hands full of martinis, nudged Rhoda with his elbow. "Who's the blond dame with Pankhurst?"

"His latest trollop, darling," his wife replied. "Carole or Cecile or maybe both. I believe she's called CeeCee. Judging from her bust, DeeDee would be more . . . fitting." Rhoda turned back to the cousins. "I'm sorry, we haven't met. I'm Rhoda St. George and this is my slightly inebriated husband, Rick."

Rick had almost finished his first martini. "Swell," he said sarcastically. "You're giving me a poor send-off."

"Don't worry, darling," Rhoda replied. "These ladies have eyes."

"And feet," Renie put in. "I'm Serena Jones and I'd like to move mine. Feet, that is."

"Oh." Rhoda looked down at Asthma, who appeared to have fallen asleep, though it was hard to tell with all the long curls covering not only his body but his face. "Do move him, Ricky," she implored. "Otherwise, Ms. Jones is going to charge him rent."

Setting his now-empty glass on the bar, Rick searched through the fur around the dog's neck, presumably for a collar. "He's a Komondor," Rick said, "a guardian breed, and sometimes considered a working dog. Except I'm afraid he doesn't work very well anymore, poor fellow. Come on, Asthma, strut what's left of your stuff."

"He's . . . big," Renie said. "He must weigh over a hundred pounds."

Rick St. George finally managed to get the dog to move off of Renie's feet. "Yes," he agreed. "Asthma weighs in at a hundred and twenty, or, according to my darling wife, ten pounds more than she does. Good boy!" he said, patting the animal.

Feeling left out, Judith introduced herself. "I'm Serena's cousin."

Both St. Georges expressed their delight, and sounded almost sincere. They were immediately pounced upon by Captain Swafford.

Finally able to put in her drink request, Judith ordered a scotch rocks from Ray the bartender, whose smile was that of a young man eager to please. "Will Glenfiddich do?"

"Definitely," Judith responded.

But there was no Pepsi for Renie, Ray informed her in an apologetic tone. Would a Coke be acceptable? It would, Renie said, between mouthfuls of marinated chicken.

A gong sounded and a sliding door opened at the far end of the room. A golden-haired middle-aged woman wearing a black and red gown that evoked the Orient, held out both arms.

Renie spoke softly in Judith's ear. "May Belle Beales, cruise director—better known as Dixie," Renie said to Judith. "I recognize her from the brochure photos."

"Good evenin', honored guests," Dixie said in a soft Southern drawl. "It's mah pleasure to welcome y'all to an interlude of piano music from that long-ago era of the 1930s. Durin' the cruise itself, we'll have a big band—a verra big band—to play for your listenin' and dancin' enjoyment. Tonight is just a li'l ol' sample, courtesy of mah meager talents. Please join me in the other half of the saloon." With a gracious gesture, Dixie signaled for everyone to join her.

The cousins fell in behind Jim Brooks and Anemone Giddon. The ethereal-looking young woman glanced over her shoulder. "Hi," she said in a breathy voice. "I'm Anemone. Jim says you're the Cousins."

Renie grimaced. "You make us sound like a rock band."

Anemone giggled. "It's how I remember people. I can't ever recall anybody's name, so I give them a description." She pointed up ahead to the St. Georges. "They're the Dipsos, the captain is the Captain, Émile Whoozits is the Purser, my mother's lawyer is—"

"We get it," Renie broke in. "The Cousins get it."

The other half of the saloon was lighted only by mica-shaded wall sconces. Comfortable armchairs had been placed at small round tables. As her eyes adjusted to the demilight, Judith could make out a black grand piano on a cabaret-type stage.

"Sorry about this," Renie whispered in apology. "I didn't know there'd be entertainment that we'll have to pretend to enjoy even if we'd rather be hung from the yardarm."

"That's okay," Judith said, scanning the short program that had been left at each table. "She's going to play just six pieces. Piano arrangements inspired by Duke Ellington, Tommy Dorsey, Glenn Miller, Benny Goodman, and Artie Shaw."

Dixie Beales had arranged herself on the bench. She gazed at the sheet music, flexed her fingers, and scowled. Getting up, she moved to the edge of the stage and spoke to Émile Grenier. He stood up and limped to the rear of the piano.

"A moment only," Dixie announced. "The piano lid hasn't been fully raised."

Anemone and Jim were sitting at the table next to Judith and Renie. "The Fun Lady," Anemone remarked from behind her hand. "I bet she's wearing a wig."

Judith smiled politely. Renie remained immobile.

Dixie had moved to assist Émile. Their efforts were obscured from the audience by the piano itself.

"The lid must be stuck," Jim Brooks said. "Maybe I should help. Émile doesn't look like the strongest guy in the world."

"The purser's small but wiry," Anemone asserted, looking pleased with herself for making the observation. "Though he has a bad leg."

"I'd like to hear some Cole Porter," said Horace Pankhurst at the table adjoining the engaged couple. The big man used a cocktail napkin to pat at perspiration on his thick neck.

"Cold what?" his blond companion asked. "You mean Coldplay? They're a great band. They're Brits, you know."

Horace looked as if he didn't know. "Oh? Well, whatever the music, it's taking long enough to get that piano open. Somebody ought to take a crowbar to it."

"You wouldn't want to use a crowbar on an expensive piano," Renie noted. "My good friend Melissa Bargroom, who just happens to be our newspaper's music critic, says that an instrument like that costs—"

A loud, piercing shriek from Dixie Beales cut through Renie's words. Both cousins stared at the stage. Dixie had disappeared, apparently having fallen to the floor. Émile suddenly went out of sight, too, presumably coming to the cruise director's aid.

Captain Swafford was on his feet. So was Rick St. George. A sense of apprehension engulfed the saloon.

"Stay put, everybody," Rick said in a loud if somewhat slurred voice. "I'll see what's going on."

The other guests seemed to defer to Rick, who bounded onstage, martini glass still in hand. Rick also disappeared behind the piano, but almost immediately resurfaced along with Émile Grenier.

"Is there a doctor in the house?" Rick asked, his speech no longer slurred.

Rhoda St. George burst into derisive laughter. "Oh, Ricky, can't you find a better line than that old cliché?"

But her husband looked serious and ignored the remark, casting his eyes around the room.

Jim stiffened in his chair before looking every which way. "Ah . . ." he began, awkwardly shifting his lanky frame into a standing position. "Um . . . I'm a medical student at Stanford."

"Then you'd better get up here, kiddo," Rick said. "Dixie Beales has passed out." He paused while Jim came forward. "Unfortunately, there's nothing you can do for the corpse in the piano."

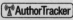